Praise for *The Waking Land*

The WAKING LAND

CALLIE BATES

HODDER

First published in Great Britain in 2018 by Hodder & Stoughton
An Hachette UK company

First published in paperback in 2017

1

A CIP catalogue record for this title
is available from the British Library

Paperback ISBN 978 1 473 638754

Printed and bound in Great Britain by
Clays Ltd, St Ives plc

Hodder & Stoughton policy is to use papers that are natural,
renewable and recyclable products and made from wood grown in
sustainable forests. The logging and manufacturing processes are
expected to conform to the environmental regulations of the
country of origin.

Hodder & Stoughton Ltd
Carmelite House
50 Victoria Embankment
London EC4Y 0DZ

www.hodder.co.uk

For Grandpa Del.
I wish I could put this book in your hands.

Western
Isles

THE TAIL RIDGE
(Bal an-Dracan)

Dalriada

Alfan

Taich-na
Ivaugh

CAERIS

Barrody

Dearbann

Threve

Lake
Harbor

Cerid Aven

TINAN

The Ard River

Portmason

EREN

Ganz

Oise

Laon
Roquelle

Gulf
of
Eren

Great Ocean

EMPIRE of
PALADIS

Tarican
Strait

Middle
Sea

BAEDON

Illustrated map by Laura Hartman Maestro ©2016

The
WAKING
LAND

The Waking Land

PROLOGUE

I felt safe that night in Laon, safer than I had any night before in the city. My nurse and I were eating dessert in the nursery. I never knew her name; I called her Nursie. Downstairs my parents were hosting a dinner party. It was the first time I had ever been in Laon, in the townhouse my family kept for state occasions, aired out only once every year or two. On the newly crowned king's invitation, we'd come south for the Harvest Feast from our country house in the north, and every noise of the city still seemed foreign. So that must have been why we didn't hear them at first: the screams, the clicks as the muskets caught.

I remember cradling my wooden doll, a Harvest Feast gift from my parents, made by a wood-carver in the city. I was feeding her pretend bites of the caramel pudding the servants had brought up earlier, baked in a dish until the sugar on top was crackling hot. Nursie drew the chintz curtains over the wide, sashed windows. My doll and I sat snug and certain in the glow of candlelight. Safe. We were supposed to go home the next day.

Nursie sank down into the armchair across from us and began to tell my bedtime story—our nightly routine with its well-worn words—and I chimed in on my favorite parts. *"Wildegarde came, bearing a flame in her heart and her hair crowned with the pale light of stars. Where she placed her foot, the earth trembled; when she raised her hand, mountains moved."*

A burst of voices echoed from downstairs. Nursie stopped mid-word, her hands braced on the arms of the chair. Her lips were parted. I giggled, then stopped. Her fear breathed out like a living thing. Beneath us, the house shook down to its foundation. Floorboards squeaked outside the nursery door.

Nursie was on her feet before I was aware of her moving, a gilt-handled butter knife in her hand. Her cheeks went scarlet, but her lips were pressed together into a grim line. Her eyes were fixed on the door.

More footsteps squeaked in the corridor. "El," Nursie said in a tight, contained voice, "do you remember Brigit?"

Brigit: my ancestor, who hid beneath her bed when the Ereni soldiers came to kill her. I slid out of my chair, trying to find my slippers with my bare feet. I was wearing a nightdress, a new one Mother had made for me, white, with ruffles cascading down the front.

The door flew open. Men tramped in: big men in blue coats with bayonets strapped around their backs. The royal guard.

Nursie lashed out, catching a man in the face. He staggered back. "Brigit!" Nursie shouted. I finally understood. I leapt for my bed, scrabbling at the frame so I could crawl under the embroidered cream skirt, but a hand tore into my hair from behind me until the roots screamed, and then I was flying up, my feet kicked out from under me, the breath knocked out of my body as I landed on a man's high shoulder. My doll fell; his boots crushed it. I tried to scream but no sound came out.

Nursie was screaming—terrible, bone-shaking screams. I couldn't lift my head around high enough to see her. My heartbeat pounded between my chest and the man's shoulder. I had to be like Brigit, I had to do something, but I could think of nothing.

"Caerisian bitch," another man shouted, and an enormous noise exploded through the room, leaving shards of sound ringing in my ears. The acrid smell of gunpowder tainted the air.

Nursie was no longer screaming.

I glimpsed her as the man holding me began to walk out of the room. She sagged on the flowered carpet, her face remade in blood that looked black in the dark shadows near the floor. The man with the pistol—still smoking—stepped over her legs to throw open the wardrobe door.

Then we were out of the room, in the corridor. The scream that had been building in my chest burst out as a shrieking gasp. The soldier shook me as if to knock me quiet and we jolted down the stairs, my head jostling. Though I knew I was supposed to fight, I didn't dare move. What if he killed me, too?

We reached level ground, and I reared up enough to see the side tables in the lower hall swinging by. The carpet changed to neat, checkered parquet, covered in a snowfall of crushed glass.

"Elanna!"

My mother. The soldier swung me down, gripping me by the neck, and I saw her on the other side of the long polished table. In the tableau of dinner guests, frozen behind their chairs with their hands raised, she was the only person who moved. Then the guard squeezed my neck and I saw my mother stop. I saw her lower her hands, but her eyes did not leave me.

The soldier then twisted me the other way, to face the two men who stood to my left: my father, and the new king of Eren, Antoine Eyrlai. We'd come here for his coronation before the Harvest Feast—a solid month of parties I was too young to attend and ceremonies I found bewildering. And now the king, his wig askew, was pointing a pistol at my father.

I gasped again, too horrified to scream. My whole body was trembling. The day before, when the king made our carriage go last during the Harvest Feast procession even though my father was the Duke of Caeris and should have been second after the king, I knew I hated him for embarrassing my family. Now he'd sent the men who killed Nursie. And he was pointing a gun at my father.

Papa didn't look afraid, though. He looked angry. And it gave me courage.

"Don't you hurt my papa!" I shouted at the king.

Everyone seemed to turn at once. They were all staring at me—including the king. His rage stood out around him, an inhuman thing. In one powerful step, he crossed the room, seized me in his arms—I inhaled the sweaty, perfumed odor of him—and jammed the cold hard end of the pistol against my temple.

I gasped. A hot trickle ran down the inside of my thigh. I smelled the gunpowder from my nursery. I saw Nursie fallen on the floor, the blood black on her face.

"Well?" the king said to my father.

Papa stood there with his hands open. The anger was gone. He looked defeated. Broken. "Don't kill my daughter." He stammered the words. I thought he was going to fall to his knees. I thought he was going to beg.

The trickle of urine reached my toes and dripped to the carpet. A crushing shame welled up in me—for myself, for my father and mother, for my dead nurse. Into the silence, as all the adults were waiting for the king to speak, I began to cry.

The pistol jabbed into my temple. "Stop that," the king commanded. His wig swung against me as he looked at my father. "You're lucky, Ruadan. Your pretender king hasn't yet landed on Eren's shore, so I don't have the evidence to condemn you. I could still have you executed without trial—it would be nothing more than you deserve—but I'm going to be merciful."

He pressed the gun harder into my skin, the lace on his cuff tickling my cheek. I squirmed against him. I didn't want to die like Nursie, crumpled like my doll on the floor.

"Get out of this house," the king ordered. "Get out of Laon. Go back to Cerid Aven and your Caerisian backwater. And if I ever hear you've set foot outside its property, I'll have the child eliminated, and you *will* be put on trial." He paused, then added, "And you won't be acquitted."

He shoved me off into the soldier's arms. "In the meantime, she'll be well treated, provided you don't make any further attempts to ruin my country. Take her outside." As I was marched off, I looked back for my mother, but the soldier's head blocked my view.

The courtyard was wet and blustery and dark. Horses stamped and snorted. The soldier set me on the ground while he talked to another man holding the horses—"The girl's to be a hostage"—and I looked back at the light spilling from the house, waiting for my mother to come after me, to crush me in her arms and sing our song into my ear, to tell me Nursie wasn't dead and we were going home tomorrow.

She didn't come. Nor did my father. Instead the king came, with the rest of his guards. I was made to walk across the streets to the palace, a barefoot girl in a soiled nightdress, the cold cobblestones burning my feet.

CHAPTER ONE

It's been fourteen years, last night. Fourteen years since King Antoine took me hostage; fourteen years since I've seen or heard from my parents. It's the only night I allow myself to remember them, and the only night I dare to look my fear in the eyes and remember why I'm here. And as usual on this night, I haven't slept at all.

I dress in the dark, dragging breeches over last night's silk stockings. Beyond the wooden paneling separating my bedroom from the alcove, Hensey snores. I wish she'd sleep in the servants' quarters, but she protests that I still need her, even though it's been fourteen years and, most nights, I sleep without fear.

I pull my weathered greatcoat over a shirt and waistcoat, tugging its wool collar up high. I look nothing like a boy, but this early no one will look past the bulk of my clothes to see my face. Through the mullioned windows, a gray light penetrates the gloom, revealing the strip of garden beyond the palace. I can't see the drive well from here, but most of the coaches seem to have gone. Eren's courtiers have finished their celebration—not that I stayed to toast Princess Loyce and her favorites, especially after she mocked the trailing silk vines and embroidered flowers wound into my hair. "Lady Elanna, you seem to have a plant growing out of your head," she crowed. "Have you potting soil there as well? Caerisians! You can never get them out of the dirt. Like hogs." I didn't answer her, even though she made me flush with anger; it never does any good to respond to her jabs.

Denis Falconier, her favorite, answered instead. "Why, don't you know that the earth is *alive,* according to the Caerisians? That's why they're always dirty. Rolling about in the dirt. *Making love* in it." He smirked and Loyce laughed and, because she laughed, so did almost everyone else.

Sometimes I think Loyce would be less cruel without Denis goading her on. But maybe he just says what she's already thinking.

We had a gathering in the Diamond Salon instead, my best friend, Victoire, and I—leading the celebration with the latest gossip from Ida, drinking sweet mead, and laughing. Even the king joined us for a brief time, our disagreement the other day forgotten as we talked about my latest botanical work. I don't think he's actually angry; he wants to protect me. I'm almost as much a daughter to him as the princess is—more, maybe. Antoine takes an interest in my work and life, and he's always generous, though I ask for little. Maybe that's why he's so kind to me. Loyce is always demanding more things: new gowns, a better chef, a larger allowance, a new jewel she'll wear once and forget.

Strange to think of him holding a pistol to my head when I was five years old.

I carry my boots out into the corridor before putting them on. Hensey doesn't wake.

I take the side door that slips out below my rooms and head down the maids' stair, out into the vegetable garden. A dim racket echoes from the kitchen. I make my way, unseen, along the hedge to the gate, and out onto Laon's cobblestone streets. The city lies quiet around me—the whole kingdom of Eren lingers under the spell of good food and wine. The people who have food, anyway. Not those who clamor at the palace gates—and are set upon by the palace guard—claiming that King Antoine Eyrlai has stolen their grain for his own bread.

But even the poor aren't out scavenging after last night's celebration. The brisk autumn air is sharp in my lungs as I approach the Hill of the Imperishable. The ground steepens and the elms and oaks cluster together, dense with undergrowth. A trickle of birdsong fills the air.

The great old circle of stones sits silent on the hilltop, overlooking the river and the Tower on its distant hill, lit by a burning autumn sun. No one else ever comes up here. They're afraid someone will accuse them of practicing magic, that they'll be seized and interrogated by witch hunters. When they invaded our lands centuries ago, the emperors of Paladis called our stones nests of witchcraft. They couldn't drag the stones out of the earth, so they set up guards to kill anyone who came up here, sorcerer or no. The imperial army's two hundred years gone, the empire's shrunk due to corruption within, and Eren is the empire's ally now, not her subject. But the fear still lingers. After all, though the inquisitions have ended, some people still practice magic, and witch hunters still capture and imprison them.

I ought to be afraid, too. But no one's watching me—not this morning, nor any morning. I haven't been under guard since I was five years old, once I proved myself a tame hostage.

So there is no one to see me taunt myself with the magic I cannot have.

I stride to the center of the circle, where a flat stone lies buried halfway into the earth. I drop down onto its cold surface. The chill seeps up through my greatcoat and breeches. There was a stone circle in Caeris, I think, that I visited as a child. I seem to remember my father taking my hand in his. People singing while he cut a gentle drop of blood from my palm and let it fall to the stone at my feet.

But maybe I'm imagining it. Maybe I'm inventing what happened when the stone drank my blood. I was just a child; what do I truly remember?

I slip the dagger out of my pocket, balance it in one hand, and throw it into the circle instead. It clatters off the closest stone, loud in the empty morning. Would my mother scold me for doing this? Would she call it disrespectful, sacrilegious? The savage gods they still worship in Caeris, the gods Denis Falconier mocked—the old gods of earth and wood and mountain, not the civilized deities we've adopted from Paladis—would not approve.

I don't remember what my mother looks like. But when I throw the dagger, I remember the warmth of her hand on my wrist, stopping me.

Or maybe it's just my imagination.

I snatch up the dagger and hurl it at another stone. What's the use in thinking of my mother or father? I'm glad they never tried to rescue me; I'm glad I didn't grow up a scrawny, backwoods Caerisian rebel, speaking in a wretched accent and hating the crown. The Caerisians are shepherds, cattle-raiders, fishermen, poor farmers tilling rocky soil; they've scarcely heard of Paladis and the philosophers of Ida. Caeris itself has hardly changed since the conquest two centuries ago, still a land of drunk, querulous half-savages. They're so disorganized that it took the Ereni *one day* to overtake their capital during the conquest. Think how easily Antoine put down my father's foolhardy rebellion! By capturing me, he stopped the rebellion and destroyed my father's hopes for a new king in a single stroke. Imagine what it would have been like if the Caerisians had succeeded! Would we be speaking their barbaric language now, expected to practice their backward customs, bowing to the Old Pretender instead of Antoine? The entire world, and not just Denis Falconier, would deride us as earth-worshipping pigs.

Thank all the gods I live at the court in Laon, where I have friends and my work in the greenhouse, salons and theater and dancing—the sophistication that the north can't even conceive. Thank all the gods Antoine put a stop to a rebellion that wouldn't have benefited anybody except my father, the man who fancies himself a kingmaker. King-mocker, more like.

I start toward the dagger—my throw went wide, landing between two of the toothy stones—and feel a warm trickle between my fingers. I must have cut myself picking up the dagger that first time, because jewel-red blood shines on my finger-pads. It doesn't hurt, but still a shiver runs through me and I look at the stones. With the light burning behind them, and their shapes throwing shadows on the ground, they seem almost as if they could shift shape—or move.

"Don't you dare," I say to them. I start toward the dagger but instead pause by the nearest stone. It is squat, with a small bulge on top, like a head over a square body.

I only come up here once a year, on this day. When I was twelve, Hensey caught me sneaking back in. She saw the cuts on my hands. "What have you been doing?" she demanded. I stuttered something about the Hill of the Imperishable, about what happened when my blood touched the stones—even though I knew I shouldn't tell any-one, not even her. I knew it must be kept, a terrible secret.

"That's *witchcraft*, El." Hensey buried my face in her bosom as if she could smother the magic out of me. "Anyone sees you doing that, you know what will happen? The *witch hunters* will come for you. First they'll use their witch stones to send you mad. Then they'll strip everything you know from your mind. When they kill you after that, it'll be a mercy."

For months after, I had nightmares about the witch hunters com-ing to haul me away to a prison in Ida. Then the nightmares faded; my tutors taught me that, while magic is considered anathema, in truth it simply has no place in the rational, modern world. They said that the Paladisan emperors have made the empire and its former subject states a safer place with their inquisitions and their witch hunts, which not only cleansed our lands but purified the heart of the empire itself. For a while, even I thought we should celebrate the inquisitions that made our world a safer place.

But then the Harvest Feast came around again and I sneaked back up here. I dropped my blood on the stones. Just one morning, I promised myself, just one morning, once a year.

Hensey's never caught me again, and I've grown better at sneak-ing out.

I stretch my hand out toward the stone, my breath stilled in my throat. No, I shouldn't do this. The risk is too great. The taint of sorcery mustn't touch me if I want to go to Ida.

But I want to see it happen again. Just one more time before I turn twenty and Antoine either allows me to study botany in Ida or forces me to marry some safe and dependable man. One last time, before I have to forget for the rest of my life.

I squeeze my palm.

A single drop falls, crimson, winking.

Nothing happens. I stare at the circle of my blood on the stone, willing it, daring it . . .

I'm about to turn away when it happens. A phosphorescent gleam out of the corner of my eye.

The stone blooms into a woman—pale as frost, more insubstan-tial than wind. She moves restlessly, as if she sees me and yet does not. There's a knife in her hand, a twin to the one I just dropped. I stare at her—at the high lace collar that hugs her neck, at the folds of her clothing sweeping over and around and *through* the stone. Her gaze lifts above me, uneasy, intent.

"Mo cri, mo tire, mo fiel," she says.

Her voice cuts through me. Fine as ice, softer than snow, so cold I feel myself freezing into place as I watch her. Every year, I think perhaps she will not appear. But she always does.

"Mo cri, mo tire, mo fiel."

I grind my teeth together against the words. "I don't know that language, you horrid thing."

This is a lie. I do know the language.

But I don't speak it anymore. I've forgotten everything I knew of it.

"Mo cri, mo tire, mo fiel!"

"Speak *Ereni.*" The horrible Caerisian echoes in my head. She'll go on all day, until the blood fades or I wipe it away.

Her gaze lifts. She goes alert, tense, drawing her arm back so that the knife winks in the morning light. The muscles of her wrist tighten. The knife dips backward.

She's going to throw it.

I duck, but she's not looking at me. She's looking at—

I swivel just in time to see him: a man stepping between the stones on the other side of the circle.

The dagger sails through the air. Not spectral. *Real.*

"Look out!" I scream.

The man starts, his gaze jerking to me. He doesn't see the dagger until it *thunks* into the ground at his feet.

The man and I stare at each other.

I look back at the stone. She's still there, a fresh dagger in her hand. She lifts her arm, poises *again* to throw . . .

I scrub the side of my hand over the stone. The blood vanishes, and so does she.

I breathe out a breath I didn't realize I was holding. I brace my palm against the stone. My thoughts scramble, frantic. Why has this man come into the circle? No one comes here. I'm supposed to be safe here, safe to taunt myself with a magic I am not supposed to possess. A magic I still don't understand.

Did he see her? Or does he think *I* threw the dagger at him?

"Are you all right?"

At the sound of his voice, warm and deep and slightly accented, I remember who I am. I hitch myself upright, facing him. He's standing on the other side of the altar stone now, the dagger held between both hands. A flush mounts in my cheeks, burning up into my ears, but there's nothing I can do about that. Like me, he wears a bulky gray coat, with a hat pulled low over his face, so that all I see is the firm line of a jaw above a blue silk neckcloth, a mouth, and the curl of his nostrils.

The dagger gleams in his gloved hands, solid and real. Just like the one that I've forgotten, fallen between the stones. If he looks at it, he'll see it's old-fashioned, a needle-bladed rondel, its bone handle carved with running deer.

I lunge forward to snatch the dagger from his hands. He jumps back, startled, and the weapon falls onto the trampled leaves and dirt. I pick it up, stuffing it under my coat. When I get to my feet, he's standing farther away from me, his hands shoved into his pockets.

"An unusual place for target practice," he says.

I decide to pretend I threw the dagger. Maybe he didn't see the specter after all.

It's possible.

"I didn't see you," I say stiffly. "No one ever comes up here."

Maybe this is a stupid thing to say. I've never seen this man before in my life, and now I've as good as told him we're alone. Who is he? Could Princess Loyce have sent him to spy on me? It would be like her; Denis Falconier and her people are always watching me for the least sign of "Caerisian savagery"—an imperfectly spoken sentence, a poor hairstyle, a breach of etiquette. They have reported back to Loyce, and she to the king, when I've arranged harmless parties with friends and attended lectures at the university. Once, when I was sixteen, I tried to sneak five minutes alone in a deserted salon with a boy I liked. We had hardly even taken each other's hands when Loyce and Denis burst in with a full retinue—no doubt hoping to find me in a compromising position. I've learned to be more discreet, but I don't always hide my tracks.

And if Loyce has sent this man, it's the end of me. She'll finally have the leverage to ruin me, as she's always wanted to. I have no power but the king's mercurial affection, which would vanish as soon as anyone named me a witch.

"I don't see why," the man is saying. He's young, not much older than me. The accent is strong in his voice. Idaean? Why would someone from Paladis be up on the Hill of the Imperishable? "The sunrise is beautiful."

"Is it?" I haven't noticed. I think of the Paladisan guards killing anyone who came up the hill and I shiver, though it was more than two hundred years ago.

We stare at each other beneath the brims of our hats. Can he see I'm a girl? Can he hear it in my voice? Does he know who I am?

"While this has been pleasant," I begin.

At the same time, he says, "Do you know who they are, the people in the stones?"

My voice shrinks in my throat. The man pushes back his hat. His eyes are light, uncanny against his olive skin, and his short, disheveled black hair escapes from the brim of his hat. A flush burns through me. This man, with his bright, intense gaze, makes Martin Bonnaire, whom I've been swanning over for months, look like a sorry sack. And he is staring right back at me, as if I'm worth looking at.

I open my mouth. My heart is leaping. But he saw me—he *must* have—waking the specter in the stones. Why is he here? What does he want?

No man has ever looked at me like this, his gaze skimming the length of my body and coming back to my eyes. As if he's earned the right to look so intimately at me. As if he's searching for something beyond the surface of my skin.

I can't let him look at me this way.

I dart out of the circle, running the long way down the hill, back toward the palace.

It's only when I reach the bottom of the hill that I remember I left the other dagger behind, between the stones.

THE LONG ROUTE takes me to the palace gardens. I hurry down the promenade, past a fountain where a statue of the sea god Ensidione wrestles with a water nymph, toward the glass walls of the green-house. I'm still wearing trousers, my hands scraped and dirty, but it's not as if Guerin will care. His hands are always dirty.

I keep glancing over my shoulder, afraid the man's followed me from the stones. He saw my magic; he could report me. The witch hunters could come for me. But of course he's not there.

Who *was* he? If only I understood the magic in the stones, maybe I could have done something to make the specter vanish or obey my bidding.

Ahead, the yew trees curl against the side of the greenhouse. I need to check on the *Amanita virosa*—hopefully it hasn't withered. I've been waiting for a couple of days, ever since I saw the mush-room growing in the duff beneath the yews. Purest white, slender and perfect, it is as deadly as it is beautiful. It will be one of the last things I study under Guerin's tutelage, the culmination of our course on fungi. Now I'm going to cut it from the ground and make a spore sample from its fleshy cap to observe and record. When I leave Laon, I can't take Guerin with me, or our greenhouse, but at least I'll be able to take the memory of this final examination, as well as the drawings I've made in my book.

I lower myself to my knees and peer into the dark recesses behind the yew's trunk.

The mushroom isn't there. It's not rotting; the damp ground is empty. It can't have disappeared. No creature would eat the whole thing, and no human being would be stupid enough—or observant enough—to pick it.

I scrabble through the dirt. The base, the volva, should be here—somewhere. Maybe a creature, a squirrel, knocked the mushroom over. I tuck myself deeper behind the trunk, patting the soil. My fingernail catches in a fleshy, damp substance.

The mycelium—the root—is there, and the mushroom has been sliced cleanly off.

I surge to my feet and burst through the glass doors into the greenhouse. "Guerin, did you cut the amanita?"

No answer. I come to a stop. The plants sit about me in their pots, a collision of greens; if I listen hard I can hear them breathing, hear the sturdy effort of drinking sunlight. Surely Guerin does not hear this sound. Most days, when he's here, I can ignore it, drown it out in the noise of conversation. But now that I'm alone, my treacherous ears are aware of a gritty murmur just beyond ordinary hearing. It lulls me. My breathing slows, and my hands fall loose at my sides. For a moment, I forget to be afraid. I just want to listen. I want to understand what the plants are saying.

No. I jerk myself from my reverie and march toward the worktables. This is why magic is dangerous. It lures you in. It makes you curious.

Maybe what I hear isn't magical at all. Maybe I just have particularly keen hearing. Maybe anyone can hear plants growing, if they listen hard enough.

On Guerin's worktable, an orchid sits with its roots exposed, stripped from the mossy log where it usually grows. A scattering of dirt lingers on the wooden surface. Someone must have called him away; he'd never abandon an orchid unless it was urgent. He loves orchids, though few grow in Eren, and it's an expense to bring them from other countries; in order to pay for them, he grafts apple trees to produce more fruit. King Antoine likes to remind him that he only keeps a royal botanist to signify Eren's sophistication. Antoine is keen to be seen as a sophisticate; he still grumbles about his visit to Paladis as a boy, and how the courtiers ridiculed his manners and how he made the incorrect number of bows to the then-emperor. This is, I suppose, why he longs for Paladis's approval while at the same time trying the emperor's patience by demanding higher tariffs on the grain, timber, and lead we export. "And for all that," he likes to say, "we are no more than flies stinging an elephant's back." Perhaps this is why he takes my side when his daughter derides me as a backwoods savage. Just a few weeks ago, when Loyce mocked the indexing Guerin and I had finished of southern Ereni plants, Antoine said, "You should be wary of scorning another's work, Loyce, when you set aside your own studies at the age of fourteen." She stormed out. We all know she can hardly add two plus two, and her handwriting is no better than a child's. I could read better than she could when I was nine and she fourteen.

I hesitate—where is Guerin?—but I can't leave the orchid to wither. I lift the plant in my hands. It moves when I touch it, its petals lifting like a face toward me, the exposed roots twisting over my fingers. Their touch is gingerly and ticklish. When I was a child, this sort of thing made me giggle. Now I glance over my shoulder in case anyone has burst into the room—in case anyone sees me performing illegal magic with a plant and turns me over to the authorities for imprisonment and interrogation.

I settle the orchid on its log. It rustles and sighs, its roots twisting around the wood and moss. As soon as I set it down and step back, it stops growing and sits there like an ordinary plant.

It *is* an ordinary plant. All plants are ordinary, until I touch them.

All my life, I've had to hide what happens when I touch anything that comes from the earth—plants, stones, trees, soil, orchids. No one here, in Laon, knows. Even Guerin simply says I have a green thumb.

In Caeris, though, my parents knew what I am. I remember that much.

Surely this is what Denis Falconier meant when he mocked the Caerisians for believing the earth is alive. If he knew what I could do . . .

I push this thought to the back of my mind, as well as the accompanying, ever-present desire to understand my magic better. Because if my touch can make an orchid move and grow of its own accord, if my blood can wake specters in the ancient stones, what else can I do?

Nothing, I tell myself. I can do nothing. I am a botanist, not a sorcerer. Botanists have a place in this world—a respectable place. As the emperor of Paladis likes to remind us, sorcerers are worse than nothing—their impious actions are a mockery of the gods, and their historical conviction that they could rule kingdoms presented a threat to civilization itself, a danger that had to be exterminated. Too many sorcerers schemed against the empire and so, more than two hundred years ago, the empire began its hunts and inquisitions, ruthlessly exterminating magic from its territories. They claim the scourge was necessary, that the practice of sorcery leads to a delusion of godlike power. Yet a few magicians still exist, in secret, and you still hear of one or two every year brought to the prison in Ida— and never heard from again, the poor wretches. I've survived my father's failed revolution to put a different king on the throne of Caeris and Eren. I don't want to die now.

All the same, I can't resist brushing my fingers over the orchid again. Its stalk shivers.

I CAN'T SEEM to focus on my work in the greenhouse, not even reading *The Journal of Botanical Studies*. Eventually I give up and return to my room to change for my meeting with Victoire; today is Lunedia and we have to plan the salon for tomorrow. Maybe Victoire will know where Guerin has gone, though I don't know why she would. Or maybe he'll be back at the greenhouse when I'm done.

The skin between my shoulder blades twitches. The gilt-trimmed corridor is almost deserted—not an odd occurrence given the celebration last night, but still I'm not used to so much silence between these pale walls. My footsteps sound unnaturally loud on the crimson Agran carpet.

Even upstairs, where the maidservants are usually bustling about, it's quiet. When I open the door to my rooms, Hensey launches herself at me.

"Elanna, where in all the gods' names have you been?"

I take a step back. Even though her flounced cap is squished and her hair wisping out beneath it, her sharpness shrinks me down to the size of a five-year-old. "I went for a walk—"

"A walk?" She pronounces the word as if it's a disgusting activity. Her nostrils flare. "You haven't heard the news, then."

"I—"

She plants her hands on her hips. "The king's taken ill."

So that's why the corridors are so quiet. "Probably too much spiced wine. He was singing 'Eren the Undying' at full voice at two o'clock yesterday *afternoon.*"

"They're saying it's poison." She stares at me, dipping her chin to emphasize her words. "They found something. Evidence."

A rush of cold burns up my arms. The empty greenhouse, the silent corridors. Guerin missing.

The amanita, gone.

No. It can't be anything to do with the amanita. No one else knew it was there. No one.

But Guerin was gone, the orchid dropped on the table, abandoned.

"You need to go down there right now," Hensey is saying, somewhere beyond the rushing in my ears. "Stay in the public view."

"Hensey—" My voice hitches upward. "You don't think Guerin—he wasn't in the greenhouse . . ."

She looks at me and points wordlessly at the door.

CHAPTER TWO

A knot tightening in my stomach, I hurry back through the chilly corridors, into the vaulted halls whose ceilings are painted with images of cold-eyed Paladisan gods. My heartbeat has begun to pulse in the tips of my fingers. Where is Guerin?

Closer to the king's grand apartments, I find the crowd that's missing from the other rooms and corridors. Half of Laon seems to be waiting outside the gilt-paneled doors of the grand salon, shop-keepers shoulder-to-shoulder with silk-clad courtiers. Nobody takes much notice of me; I realize I've forgotten to change out of my plain breeches and greatcoat. I look like a boy. It's disrespectful. I should have put on a gown.

Word has gotten out fast. But does it mean he's deathly ill, or just that everyone wants some more entertainment the day after the celebration?

I shove my way to the doors. I step on toes and someone swears in my ear, but then I'm there, pushing past the bewigged footmen in their blue-and-gold livery. They don't stop me; they've seen my face. They know who I am. I grab the cold gilt doorknob myself and then I'm inside, the door clapping shut on the noise in the hallway.

The grand salon sits almost empty, except for a knot of state ministers clustered together by the far door—the one that goes into the king's bedroom. I don't need to hear their whispers to guess what they're saying. They fall silent as I approach, and then, with a sort of collective sigh, Master Madoc separates himself from the others and comes to grasp my forearm. The muscles of my arm tense, but I don't throw him off. He's the minister of finance, and the father of my best friend, Victoire. Sometimes I let myself imagine he's my father, too. Right now he's trying to look paternal, but I see the worry in the lines on either side of his mouth. They've been there often of late—especially since he released that report on the country's revenue. It was intended to pacify the laborers who clamor in the city squares—to show everyone, from the merchants to the poor, that the king has taken no more from them than is necessary to run the country. Most were quelled, but I've still seen pamphlets in the city complaining that the king should pay taxes, too, and that the nobles grow fat off the labor of the commoners—all things that, though patently untrue, lie heavily on the court. Ordinarily Master Madoc looks impeccable, but his neckcloth is carelessly tied, and his waistcoat is coming unbuttoned.

"King Antoine won't wake," he says. "He went to bed with stomach cramps, and now the doctors say he hardly has a pulse. Poison, they think."

"It's not the drink?" I ask, because it is the logical question, the logical solution. I'm proud of how my voice doesn't rise, despite the anger pulsing in my temples.

He shakes his head once. "We've already taken several possible conspirators into custody. The servants, naturally." He pauses, watching me. "And the royal botanist, Master Jacquard. They're saying he would know how to administer a poison, since he works with the plants."

That *damned* amanita. The king's symptoms match its effects. My jaw tightens. I can't tell Master Madoc—not yet. It would only be further evidence against Guerin. "Guerin Jacquard did not try to poison the king."

Master Madoc spreads his hands.

I march to the bedchamber doors and let myself through. The ministers stare but don't stop me.

I pause inside to let my eyes adjust to the dimness. At first glance, the cavernous room seems deserted. It takes me a moment to make out the crumpled figure of the king in the vast maw of his curtained bed, and on a stool beside him, hunched over the bedside, a woman in a voluminous gown. Loyce, the princess. His daughter. The future queen of Eren.

The woman who won't care if I die in a ditch once I turn twenty and am no longer under Antoine's protection.

She's risen to take a step toward me. Despite myself, I stop short, my whole body tensing.

"Get out of here." Her voice grates. She takes another step forward, the paniers beneath the gown swaying so that her skirts ripple. It's the court gown she was wearing last night for the celebration, strewn with pearls and sapphires and worked with gold thread. Only now the pale-blue silk is rumpled, and her hair has begun to fall out of its towering coiffure. The walnut powder bronzing her skin has smeared.

Finger by finger, I close my hands into fists and then release them. "I've come to see him."

"You've come to *gloat*. You Caerisians have always wanted him dead."

"Not me." I barely restrain myself from saying, *Then you would be queen.* "I'm no more Caerisian than you are."

Loyce's lip curls. "You can wash your hands all you want, but the stink of the gutter remains."

I flinch at the paraphrase of Bonneviste's satirical quote, for its accuracy stings. Most Caerisians, after all, are poor shepherds who keep dingy, windowless huts and stink of peat fires. By all rights this should ignite Loyce's charitable instincts, but of course she doesn't care about the poor in Caeris any more than the poor in Eren. She has her servants throw bread at the crowds on holy days, while she sits holding a handkerchief to her nose. Victoire and I are the ones who hand out food on the temple steps. I've looked the poor folk in the eyes.

They terrify me, because I see myself in them. Myself, if Antoine dies.

I have to calm my mind. I have to remember why I came here—for Guerin's sake. While Loyce and I are fencing with words, anything could be happening to him. I say, "I understand you've taken Guerin Jacquard into custody. He's not a murderer. He wouldn't conspire to kill the king. What could he possibly gain from it?"

But Loyce isn't listening—of course. She never listens to me or to anyone. She swings back, her skirts dipping, to study Antoine's shrunken body. I take a few steps after her until we're both close enough to hear his breath. It shakes out of his body and stops with a gasp. In the silence, all the muscles across my shoulders tense. "Don't die," I whisper. If he dies now, it will be Loyce who arranges my future. Loyce who chooses the man I will marry, the place I will live. You can be sure she won't let me go to Ida to study botany. She'll see I end up with some horror of a husband in some dead end of the world—or worse, she won't even arrange a marriage, just send me "into the country" and no one will ever hear from me again.

Antoine draws in a shaking breath and I release the grip I had on my coat cuffs. My fingers are slick with sweat. I can look away from his hollowed cheeks and gaunt skin, but I can't stop hearing the rattle in his throat. This is the man who sat with me at the breakfast table, talking of everything from politics to the latest Idaean play. He took me hunting at his country estate—without Loyce—and we laughed together over how poor my aim is. He's read my botanical notes and studied my illustrations.

Even as he wheezes, I half expect him to open his eyes and say, *A king must not rest. Fetch me my coat! My tea! What's the news?*

His fingers twitch on the coverlet. But he doesn't wake up.

"I always thought it would have been more of a kindness if he had imprisoned you straight off," Loyce says. She doesn't look at me; her gaze is fixed on her father. "Rather than make you think you have a life worth living."

"I—" I clench my jaw against the other words that want to pour out. I want to scream at her, I want to grab and shake her until she looks at me, until she really *sees* me. Until some small compassion enters her heart.

But she'll only call the royal guards. I will be escorted out, and forgotten.

I curtsy instead, reflexively, though it must look absurd in breeches and a coat. Ordinarily Loyce would seize on any chance to ridicule me, especially for wearing men's clothes. She said on my twelfth birthday, in front of the entire court, that I looked like a scrawny Caerisian peasant who's spent too much time in the sun. Even though everyone knows she envies my brown complexion, for it means I don't have to wear walnut powder to fashionably bronze my appearance. But now she doesn't even seem to notice what I'm wearing.

Hensey would want me to say something like *I hope you remember that I came here in your hour of need. When you plan my future for me, I hope you remember that I cared about your father.*

But I can't say the words. They're pathetic.

And my life *is* worth living.

I LET MYSELF out of the bedchamber. The ministers have left the grand salon, and for a moment I'm alone in the dusty light scattered over empty chairs and the neat lines of a pianoforte. I allow myself to close my eyes. Let two tears catch in my lashes. I have no power, no station: This court is the only home I have known for fourteen years, and yet I can't truly call it *home,* because I could be thrown from it at any moment.

The squeak of hinges alerts me to an opening door. I scrub the tears off my cheeks. In walks Denis Falconier, Loyce's favorite, in purple velvet down to his shoes. The man Loyce wanted to marry, though Antoine forced her to wed Conrad of Tinan. Denis is short and blond and genial, and everyone calls him *charming.* A great irony.

He breaks into a smile at the sight of me, though by all accounts he should be overwhelmed with grief and worry. "Lady Elanna! To what do we owe the . . . pleasure?"

I try to compose myself, but the skin between my shoulders has tightened at the sight of him. "I was paying my respects." I wet my lips. Denis has more influence than anyone ought to. If I can convince him of Guerin's innocence, he might persuade Loyce to free him. "Did you know they've accused Guerin Jacquard of conspiring to kill King Antoine? The idea is absurd. We all know he would never—"

"Do we?" Denis says dubiously.

"I'll speak for him. I know him better than anyone else at court."

Denis looks me up and down. "You?" The corners of his eyes crinkle as he laughs, and I am fifteen again, standing before the court in my new gown, feeling beautiful and grown up until Denis says,

Look, the Caerisian has breasts. It must be a girl after all. How Loyce laughed. "Lady Elanna, it's touching that you wish to take such good care of your friends, but I'm afraid this matter must be left up to those in charge. Those," he adds, "who have a bit more knowledge and experience than the daughter of a backwoods traitor."

My hands curl. Once, when I was ten, I actually threw a book at his head. He had a bruise at his temple for a week; my tutor switched my hands with a birch rod, but it was worth it. But I can't throw something at him now. I need his help. "Guerin has no *reason* to conspire against the king. He has everything to thank the king for—employment, supplies, plants."

Denis studies me. He actually seems to be thinking; quite extraordinary. "And how much," he says softly, "do *you* love the king, Lady Elanna?"

Coldness tightens the back of my neck. I remember the weight of the pistol against my temple, the chill of the cobblestones against my feet. I swallow hard.

"I love the king dearly," I say. "Like a father."

Denis raises an eyebrow. "So that argument you had with him last week—that was a bit of paternal affection?"

My mouth goes dry. Of course Denis has twisted things. It wasn't an argument. I had insisted that, upon turning twenty, I would go to Paladis to study botany; Antoine had argued that he had a better plan for my future, including a husband to care for me and a home to dwell in. "You can't live in a garden," he said. "Not even the *Kepeios Basiliskos.*" I said I'd sleep on the ground if it meant I was in Ida. He told me I was being a fool, and then he said, "Get out of here." He said it kindly—but he spoke the words, and now Denis can cast whatever meaning he wants on them.

"All fathers and daughters sometimes disagree," I say.

Denis raises an eyebrow. "And your real father? What does he think of all this?"

I go cold. "You know as well as I do that I haven't spoken to Ruadan Valtai in fourteen years." It's hard to imagine that I was fathered by a traitor who schemed to put a crown on the Old Pretender's head.

"Actually," Denis murmurs, "I *don't* know that."

We stare at each other. He's smiling a little. My throat is tight.

"Well, it's true," I say.

"Hmm." He shrugs. "Maybe."

My breath is coming faster; he can't hold my barbaric father's failed rebellion against me. He can't claim I would kill the king who has fed, clothed, and educated me for fourteen years. He can't.

But he's Denis, and he has power that I don't. He has Loyce's ear as well as her bed. This is the man who has ruined the prospects of young ladies-in-waiting by telling Loyce they looked at her sideways. The man who claimed the Count of Aeroux wrote a seditious pamphlet against the king; the count, an innocent, was locked up and Denis got his lands and revenue. And the man who started the "game" of having me followed, of hunting for anything suspicious in my behavior, trying to undermine my position with the king—and so Loyce gives him more and more gifts, more and more attention.

"It's too bad," he says, "that we found a piece of white mushroom in the king's dish last night. What's it called? Destroying Angel?"

No. No, no, no. I can't breathe.

"I don't know what you're talking about," I stammer.

"Don't you? Some botanist you are." He watches me, smiling. "I don't know the Idaean word for it. Amazita? Emaranta?"

I want to stare him down, but I can't seem to look him in the eyes. The amanita keeps reappearing in my mind, its broken stalk fleshy under my fingers. I swallow. A pale, tingling cold washes up my legs. He's twisting things—twisting *me*. "What are you saying, Lord Denis? Are you accusing me of plotting against the king?"

"Not at all!" He laughs. "We all know your interest in those hideous fungi; the king fawns over your skill in drawing them often enough. How amusing to think you didn't know some of them are deadly."

I suck in my breath. I did show King Antoine my drawings, before many members of the court. But this is ridiculous. I didn't murder the king.

"Arrest me," I say. "I'll prove my innocence in a court of law."

I see myself standing before the judge, in the old law court near the river, presenting my case. *I retired to my chambers shortly before two o'clock in the morning. I rose around half past six and went for a walk.*

And woke a specter on the Hill of the Imperishable.

If they don't arrest me for regicide, they can arrest me for practicing magic—because that Idaean man saw me. What if he tells them? A sweat breaks out over my palms, beneath my arms. I have to find the man and stop him from speaking. I have to talk to Guerin.

"It's so much fun to watch you squirm," Denis says with a lazy smile. He hasn't made a move to alert the guards. Instead he moves past me, his velvet shoes clicking on the parquet, and lets himself into the king's bedchamber.

As if he didn't just accuse me of murder.

I HAVE TO free Guerin—or if I can't, I at least have to speak to him before Denis accuses me to Loyce.

It's easy enough to find out where the prisoners are being held, though I'm afraid my tense countenance makes me look guilty. The conspirators haven't been transferred to the Tower yet. Instead, they've been locked in an old stateroom that Antoine hasn't yet renovated. A full complement of guards stands outside the doors. My legs seem to be made of water. Denis could have sent word. They could arrest me at any moment. I lift my chin as I approach the captain.

"I must speak with one of the prisoners," I say to him. "Guerin Jacquard."

He looks over my shoulder, unimpressed. "No one is allowed in. Unless you'd like to name yourself a co-conspirator?"

My heart leaps in my chest, but he's not actually accusing me. Word hasn't arrived to place me under suspicion.

Yet.

The captain's eyes fix on something behind me. Some*one*.

I turn, slowly.

A man is coming toward us down the corridor, urbane in a cream silk coat and knee-breeches against the old, naked walls. "Lady

Elanna," he calls out, his voice hoarse from years of shouting at soldiers on battlefields. "To what do we owe the pleasure?"

My hands curl into fists. Deep in my stomach, my heartbeat flutters wildly.

Maybe Denis has let out word.

"Lord Gilbert." I'm damned if I'm going to bow to the Butcher of Novarre. "As I am sure you're aware, Master Jacquard, the king's botanist, has been taken into custody—"

He lifts a hand. "We will take the utmost care of Master Jacquard. I intend to listen to each deposition personally."

I doubt the Butcher's ideas of "utmost care" agree with mine.

"Walk with me," he says. "I'm just on my way back to the princess—the queen, I should say."

"She isn't queen yet. The king's not dead. You should pray he lives."

He looks closely at me, breathing through his thin lips. "Indeed. You are quite right. The *princess*." He holds out an arm for me to take.

I hesitate, but touching the Butcher's arm isn't going to get me imprisoned. I put my fingertips as lightly as possible on top of his wrist, instead of sliding my arm around his, aware I'm touching the man who burned the lands of Novarre and sowed their fields with salt during the Border Wars with Tinan that began ten years ago. When he took Tinani men and women prisoner, he had them lined up and shot instead of ransoming them. He's killed fallen soldiers on battlefields, butchered livestock, and flogged men to death. King Antoine always says, "I ask Lord Gilbert to show no humanity, and by all the gods, he never has."

The Butcher's left eyebrow twitches upward, as if he's puzzled by my reticence.

My skin crawls. Was it like this for the Fayette family, when he came to their house after they sold information to the king of Tinan? Did they know, when they fed and housed the Butcher, that in the morning their home would be ashes and so would they?

No one else gave intelligence to the Tinani after that. I was just twelve, and Antoine said to me, "War is an unpleasant business. But you mustn't be afraid of Lord Gilbert. He's always followed my orders. He's a good soldier—and a great general."

I wonder, as I've wondered so often before, if it was the Butcher who turned in some of my father's followers after that failed rebellion, and then oversaw their execution. If it was he who barred the gates on the village of Marose and let the townspeople burn to death for chanting the Old Pretender's name. I know these stories because Loyce has told them to me with glee for years. "Just think of those Caerisians dead like cattle in their highland village. Think of what it must have been like, to receive the justice they deserved."

Antoine did what he had to do, of course. A monarch must protect his people. But the stories have always made me a little sick. How easily, Loyce likes to remind me, it could have been me.

We begin to pace back toward the main building. The Butcher says nothing, only glances occasionally at me, as if waiting for me to speak. I plaster my face into the most neutral expression I can muster while my hovering hand starts to shake and sweat. He's trying to force me through silence into babbling, into making conversation that he can exploit. Into confessing to attempted murder? Has he seen Denis or Loyce? What does he know?

My throat is far too tight to babble the way he wants me to. Finally, he's the one who speaks.

"Fine weather," he says. "For sailing."

What? "Is it?"

"Indeed. Very fine. Fine for bringing a prince from across the sea."

I almost stop short. I force myself to walk. "I don't know what you mean, Lord Gilbert."

My voice trembles.

"I think you do, Lady Elanna," he counters in the most polite manner. "I think you know very well of what—and whom—I speak."

I wet my lips. I do. The rumors have been gathering, whispered conversations the courtiers think no one else can hear. "I haven't spoken to my father since I was a child. I don't know him, and I don't hold with his views. I don't want to bring the Old Pretender's son from Ida and launch a rebellion against the crown."

The Butcher's mouth tucks in, but I can't tell whether that means he's satisfied. "Did you not know the so-called prince?"

"No," I say, more violently than I meant to. "He didn't come to Caeris when the Old Pretender tried to claim the throne. He was only a child."

Like me.

"But surely they spoke to you of him. Fionnlach Dromahair. Your father would have wished you to marry him. He fancies himself the kingmaker; he would have made his daughter queen."

"I don't know that," I say flatly. "We were children. They didn't speak to us of marriage."

A memory flies upon me: my father saying, *How would you like to marry a prince, Elly?*

"Now Fionnlach Dromahair is a man," the Butcher murmurs. "Eager to prove his worth. And you are . . . of marriageable age. Useful."

We have reached the atrium leading back into the newer part of the palace, with its bright windows and pastel-blue ceilings. The Butcher slows us in the arched doorway. I press my lips together. I turn to face him.

"You know as well as I do that my father doesn't want me back, Lord Gilbert. You were there the night they took me."

He studies me for a long moment, and I see him the way I saw him as a child, in the garden behind my parents' townhouse in Laon, in his black coat and low hat. He did not appear frightening then.

I was a child. I knew nothing.

"You know," I continue, my throat dry, "that some things cannot be forgiven."

He tilts his head. Then he nods and pats my hand in an almost paternal fashion; it's strange to think of it, but he does have daughters of his own. "Very well, Lady Elanna. I will inform the queen of your statements. Undoubtedly she will be interested. But I do not know if she will believe it. The mark of Caeris is all over this affair."

With a short bow, he turns to go. Then he pauses. "The king demanded a great deal from you, I know—from all of us. But allegiance is paramount. We must all sacrifice things we would rather not, sometimes."

* * *

THERE'S ONLY ONE thing I can do, while I wait for Denis Falconier and the Butcher to frame me for murder. I make my way to the greenhouse. I'll destroy all the evidence that Guerin and I ever studied that amanita.

My mind is tight with fear, but I walk brisk and stiff-backed across the sunny garden. No one approaches to stop me.

I don't know what scares me more: my predicament or Lord Gilbert's words. The Butcher of Novarre said allegiance is paramount, that we must make sacrifices. We have never before spoken of the secret we share, not once in all the years I've known him, and yet he speaks as if he understands what I gave up. And now he thinks I must make another sacrifice—he thinks I'm still in contact with my father. How? I wouldn't know how to contact Ruadan Valtai even if I wanted to!

It doesn't matter. The Butcher thinks I'm guilty of something. And if he believes I'm a traitor, then I will be branded one, whether it's the truth or not. I suppose he thinks he's being generous, giving me the opportunity to make my own confession instead of having it tortured out of me.

The old minister of finance, the one who held the post before Master Madoc, was accused of embezzling hundreds of pounds from the royal coffers. Victoire told me that he refused to confess; it was the Butcher who made him speak, not only torturing the man but threatening his wife and children. Eventually the minister confessed, though many people still believed he was innocent. But the Butcher had decided he was guilty, and that was the end of the matter.

The greenhouse still sits empty. There's no sign that anyone has rifled through our drawings—yet—but I pull down the big sketchbook and flip through it until I find the drawings I made of the *Amanita virosa*. I stare at the precise lines of the gills, the fringed collar around the stalk, the white crayon shaded with gray and pale purple.

I clench my teeth together. Then I crumple the parchment in my hand and stuff it into the brazier.

If they question me, I'll say I don't even know what *Amanita virosa* is, though I was only studying the plant. I can't let the Butcher have a scrap of evidence against me.

But the brazier, which we keep to heat tea, wasn't lit this morning and the parchment doesn't catch. I crouch, fumbling with the flint and tinderbox until flames flare over the parchment and it begins to curl and blacken, just the way a fungus does at the end of its life. My heart seems to be curling and tightening along with it.

"What are you doing?"

I drop the tinderbox. It clatters on the flagstones. There's a man in the greenhouse behind me. He's wearing a blue silk coat, cut back to show off his figure, and matching tailored knee-breeches with silver trim on the cuffs. Short black hair, in what they call the workman's fashion. Olive skin. Light eyes. It's the man from the stone circle. My heart begins to pound, and at the same time a treacherous flush burns up from the pit of my stomach. In his fashionable clothes, with his thick soft hair, he looks so dashing. I have to remind myself that he is also dangerous.

"I've never seen anyone garden with a fire." He picks out the words carefully, his accent thickening. He gestures toward the smoldering wreckage of my drawing, but he doesn't take his gaze from my face. The way he looks at me makes my blood pump hot, then cold. Here he is in his beautiful clothes, and I'm still dressed like a boy. What does he see in me to possibly intrigue him so?

I stand. My knees creak. I have nothing to defend myself with. If he attacks me, if he threatens me, I'll have to run.

"You forgot this." He reaches into a pocket and produces the dagger I left lying between the stones this morning.

I look from it to his face. "Who are you? What are you doing here?"

"Don't you want it?" He means the dagger, which he holds out again.

His bright curiosity, his foreignness, infuriates me. It's as if nothing matters to him—my life, the fear choking my chest. I snatch the dagger from his hand. It slips from my grasp and ricochets off the side of the brazier, flying away under the potting table. At least it's hidden there.

"Leave me alone," I say, my voice cracking on the last word. Though if he knows about my magic, I mustn't antagonize him. I should placate him. But this only makes me angrier. "I don't know about Ida, but in Eren it's rude to startle someone when they're—when they're—"

"Destroying evidence?" A dimple appears beside the left corner of his mouth when he grins. As if it's a great joke: my life at risk. But despite my own better judgment and the accusations he's just made, I almost trust the knowingness in his eyes. "It will seem more suspicious if they find you."

Cold twinges through me. He knows who I am. Did he see the drawing? Has he been in here that long? He must know what *Amanita virosa* is. The talk will be all over the palace.

Is he trying to help? Or hinder?

Did the Butcher send him?

The humiliating sting of tears threatens my eyes. I will *not* cry in front of this stranger with his daring grin and his too-curious gaze. "Guerin didn't do it. He has no *reason* to assassinate the king. And all the reason in the world *not* to—his family, his position, his career."

The young man's gaze doesn't waver. "And you?"

I stare at him, my mouth open. My heartbeat jumps in an uneasy rhythm. "Me?"

"What have you to gain from killing the king?"

All the warmth drains out of me. "Nothing," I whisper. I have everything to lose. Antoine wants a decent life for me, and he's shown me true generosity: given me a royal education, allowed me to study botany and hold salons. Loyce, on the other hand, has always accused Antoine of being too kind to me—kinder than he ever was to her. She'd delight in seeing me miserable.

I have nothing to gain from killing Antoine Eyrlai.

Unless I wanted revenge. Because Denis and the Butcher think I've been writing secret letters to my parents—plotting another revolution to bring back "the king from across the sea," like the revolt my father failed to win for the Old Pretender fourteen years ago.

"Nothing," I say fiercely. I'm not sure why it's important for this man to believe me, but I want him to—desperately. I want *someone* to hear me. "He may have held a pistol to my head, but I know it was a political maneuver. I'm not angry."

Now the young man seems surprised. "A pistol?"

"I haven't spoken to my parents since I was a child." It strikes me that this is no barrier—that my fool of a father could take it into his head, at last, that I need rescuing. Maybe he *did* arrange for the poison. Maybe he's decided it's time to make another bid for Caeris's independence and bring the Old Pretender back from across the sea in a revolt that will only make the poor of Caeris poorer and let the Butcher slaughter more deluded fools. I say hastily, "But I have no interest in Caeris. I want to go to Ida and study at the *Kepeios Basiliskos*."

He blinks, again surprised. "Ida? I could arrange that for you." He raises an eyebrow. "It's certainly not safe for you to stay here, in any case."

It's my turn to be surprised. "What do you mean?"

"Studying at the gardens—I could arrange this for you."

I'm suspicious. "With Markarades? The imperial botanist?"

"Yes." His voice is firm, unhesitating.

I stare. "Who *are* you? And why should I believe you?"

He shrugs and his lips twitch into another grin. It's a joke to him, all of this. He's playing me, and the pathetic thing is how desperately I want to believe him. "I know Markarades. I could write you a letter. Get you an interview."

I suppose it stands to reason that someone who recognizes *Amanita virosa* might know the royal botanist in Ida.

Maybe.

"But," he says, and I realize I've tensed in anticipation of this, "I must ask you some questions first. In exchange for the help, yes? I want to know about those stones."

No. Not a bargain. Not at all.

"I know nothing about them."

He frowns. "But I saw you—"

A tramping outside the door cuts him off; we both freeze. I'm holding my breath. The young man watches the door, his frown erasing into a half smile, as if we have amused him once again. "They were searching the palace when I arrived. Demanded my papers."

"The royal guard?"

He shrugs. Again. "I thought we'd have more time, but you must go. The king is dead."

I'm going to be sick. "Antoine *died*? He's *dead*? How do *you* know?"

"Everyone was talking about it." He makes a soft noise between a laugh and a snort: a warm, generous sound. "They had opened the doors for the viewing. I didn't look. I've seen enough corpses."

A white light seems to explode in my head. I bolt across the green-house to the back door by the yew trees. My heartbeat pounds through my whole body. I can't go out: I'll be too obvious. The sun is bright overhead; I will be seen, if anyone's looking. But I have to run. I grab the latch just as the first guard comes in.

I can't breathe. Guilty, guilty, guilty. I look so guilty.

But the man's eyes pass right over me and come to rest on the young man. "Have you seen Lady Elanna?"

My new friend blinks, polite but suddenly quite bored. "Who?"

"Lady Elanna Valtai, of Caeris. She frequents this place."

Another guard comes in behind the first, his eyes scanning the room. Again, he doesn't see me.

I am not doing this. I don't have this sort of power. It's his, not mine. My heart leaps with a terrible hope, though I should be afraid. A sorcerer—a sorcerer fearless enough to hide himself in Ida—is a dangerous thing. I don't know what he might do.

"I don't know her," says the Idaean man. "I only got in yester-day."

The guards are remarkably polite. "If you don't mind, Lord Jahan, we'll take a look around."

As they put their backs to him, he looks right at me and points at the glass wall. Motions me to go through it.

Does he mean to go straight through the glass?

Goose pimples prick my skin. Do I trust this magic? Do I trust him? I shouldn't trust him. I shouldn't trust his smile. I shouldn't trust his *name*—Jahan is not an Idaean name, yet he presents himself as Idaean. But I take a step. Another. I stretch out my hand: My fingers slide through the glass as if it's no more substantial than air. The hairs stand up all over my body as I step through into the gar-den. I glance back: The glass looks solid. A guard stands on the other side, squinting straight at me.

I break into a run. Despite the glaring sunlight, he doesn't see me; he'd be out here if he did. All the same I race like mad for the stairs that go up to my rooms, my back twitching in anticipation of a shot.

I should have known, if Denis and Loyce would put the blame on anyone, they would choose me.

CHAPTER THREE

The invisibility—or whatever it is—must have worn off by the time I reach my bedroom door, because Hensey is there, pulling me inside. I'm shaking, but my old nurse looks as steady as any warrior going into battle. She propels me into the bedroom and shuts the inner door. We have the Paladisans to thank for these rooms situated within rooms, and right now I'm grateful for it—grateful for any space between Loyce's guards and me.

He did it. Denis accused me of murder.

I have to get out of here.

Hensey thrusts a pistol and a powder flask into my hands. Where did she get a *pistol*? It's unexpectedly heavy, the stock stamped with intricate knot work: a nobleman's weapon. "You'll need this. Go to the Hill of the Imperishable. A man's waiting for you there. He'll take you to Ganz, and Ganz will see you back to your father."

"My *father*?" I say stupidly as a leather coin purse follows the pistol into my grasp. "The Count of *Ganz*?"

My father is a suspected traitor, and everyone has heard about the Count of Ganz. He's an eccentric, a monster whom they say takes village girls and boys into his employ and makes them do unspeakable things. The children never return to their families. Then there are the experiments he's supposed to conduct on animals in windowless rooms beneath his house . . .

The last time he came to court, though, he seemed more absurd than monstrous. He had an Agran monkey on a jeweled leash. It got away from him, jumped on Loyce, snatched all the outsized silk flowers from her hair and ate them. The muscles in my throat ached with the effort not to laugh.

How on earth will *he* help me? Legions of monkeys?

"Yes," Hensey says with impatience, "and if the man isn't at the circle, get yourself directly to Ganz. That's what the money's for. Here's a butter pastry and cheese. I've filled your flask with good water. You need to put on a different hat."

The food and the flask have been shoved into an embroidered floral satchel, which Hensey now puts in my hands. She marches to the wardrobe, spilling out a pile of hats, all impractical, most festooned with ribbons and artificial flowers.

My mind is reeling. Hensey—solid, dependable Hensey—has been working for my father all these years?

She throws a floppy knit hat at me. "Wear that." Grunting, she gets to her feet, reaching into her pocket. "Oh, and this. You'll need it to identify yourself should any trouble befall you."

It's a ring, large and silver, inset with a plain stone that twists over. The reverse shows a tree wrapped in a circle, its exposed roots twisting into the knot work around it.

The knotted golden pine. The symbol of the Valtais, the stewards of the land. The kingmakers. The symbol of my father.

I hastily turn the ring so that only the plain side shows. It's big, so I shove it onto my middle finger.

Hensey allows a slight smile. "I've been carrying that around for a good long while."

"You mean—you work for my father? But you're Ereni. You're from Jardin de la Mer."

She looks at me. "It wasn't only Caerisians who fought for Euan Dromahair, who wanted to see him crowned king instead of Antoine Eyrlai. I followed your father's cause. I believed his claims that a greater unity with Paladis would bring us more prosperity, and that the people have the right to choose their own kings."

My father's cause? My father's stupidity, to bring a king from across the sea and think the Eyrlais would lie down and let him do it. To think his family has the right to choose and crown a king.

I gasp out loud as the implication strikes me. "So he *did* have Antoine killed! He's done this." And I am the one taking the blame.

Hensey frowns, begins to say, "No, El—That is, I don't know," but at that moment, knocking sounds from the outer chamber. The guards are at the outer door. We both go still, holding our breath. My heartbeat leaps and stutters.

Hensey paces to the inner door, cracks it open.

"Open," a guard hollers, "in the name of the ki—queen!"

The queen. Lord Jahan told me the truth, then; part of me prayed that he was wrong. But Antoine is dead.

Hensey marches back and presses her fingers along the smooth plaster wall beside my bed. "What are you doing—?" I begin, but as I speak, I hear the *click* as the wall springs open.

A narrow staircase plunges down into darkness. I stare at my nurse. I've always known the passage was there. But I didn't think she did.

"Go." Hensey motions at me. "I'll keep them off."

"No, Hensey! They'll—"

"Elanna." She says my full name, and I straighten, swallowing hard. "The stairs. Let me do this for you."

There are tears on my cheeks. "No."

Hensey points at the doorway and hands me the candle she left beside my bed. She's thought of everything. I swallow, taking the candle between both hands, and step toward the hidden passage.

Hensey's already in the other room, the inner door shut tight. I hear her saying, "Lady El will be but a moment—"

My hands are shaking. I close the secret door behind me. The candle flame flickers. There's air coming in somewhere. This passage leads outside, I remember.

Something crashes in my rooms. I flinch and start to turn, Hensey's name on my idiot tongue. Then I hear her voice, strident over the confused racket of the guards. She's alive; they haven't harmed her yet. Not like my nurse when I was a child.

Not yet. And I have to take the opportunity she's risking her life to give me.

I run down the stairs, which twist around in the dimness. Hot wax drips onto my hands.

I'm not going to the Hill of the Imperishable. I'm not going to the unspeakable Ganz. And I'm certainly not going north to the parents who abandoned me. I won't be part of another foolhardy revolution, doomed to failure before it begins. I'm taking Hensey's escape, but not her plan.

No. I'm going to Paladis.

WHAT WILL THEY do with Hensey?

I make my way through the sun-bright city, toward the Paladisan embassy. The streets have exploded with activity, and under the cold, brilliant blue sky everyone seems ebullient, even though they've drawn up hats and hoods against the autumn wind. I pull my collar up; I can't muster a smile. At least the press of the crowd makes me anonymous. As I hurry over King Street, a coach hurtles past me, the horses' hooves ringing on the cobblestones. The sunlight glares off the windows, and I have to hope whoever's inside doesn't see me. I grip the pistol in the sleeve of my greatcoat, though it's almost too bulky to fit alongside my arm. It occurs to me that I'm as likely to shoot off my hand as shoot an assailant, though I'm a decent markswoman under ordinary circumstances—which would be hunting pheasants at the king's country estate. I start to laugh hysterically and force myself to shut up.

I dart up the stairs of the pale stone townhouse and rap the brass knocker. At least the columned portico protects me somewhat from prying eyes. I wait, but no one comes, so I rap the knocker again, harder this time.

They have to let me in. Ambassador Nikerites likes me; I'll drop to my knees and beg that he offer me asylum. I am no traitor, no murderer. I'll tell him I don't feel safe in Laon or even in Eren, because Loyce's men could break into his house and force me out. I'll have to go to Ida. There, I'll make my case before the emperor: While Denis Falconier frames me for regicide, the real murderer is running free. It could be my father or one of his cohorts, set upon instigating another pointless rebellion against the Eyrlais, pitting Caerisians against Ereni. I don't want a civil war, and I don't want to be named a traitor or a pawn again. The emperor will have to grant me sanctuary in Ida.

In Ida, I will be safe. I can go to the royal botanical gardens and prove my worth to Markarades. I'll meet the crown prince, who's said to have an interest in plants, and perhaps I can even match wits with the Korakos, who saved the prince's life in battle and whom they say is both charming and enigmatic. I can spend my life studying plants, far from Loyce and Denis, far from the treasonous father who's let me suffer for his mistakes.

I blow on my hands to warm them from the chill. Where are the servants, always so prompt? If they take much longer, I'm going to have to go. I can't take the risk. I'll have to make my own way to Roquelle, find a ship at the harbor to take me to Ida. Maybe it would be safer than taking shelter here—even if Ambassador Nikerites grants me asylum, Loyce's guards could still catch me before I can get out of the city. I'll have to—

The door opens. It's not a servant whose hand is on the knob. It's a young man in a silver-trimmed blue coat and breeches, his light eyes surprised. Lord Jahan, the guards called him.

We stare at each other. For a moment, I think he's as astonished as I am. Then he begins to smile, deepening the dimple in his cheek. It's hilarious to him that I've arrived on the doorstep of the embassy. My heart is pounding, and at the same time I want to smile back. Who *is* he?

All I know is that he's a sorcerer, and that he saved my life. And no one saves someone else's life for nothing.

An Idaean sorcerer. How does someone from Ida even learn sorcery? The witch hunters burned all the books. But of course there are still people who practice magic; everyone knows the witch hunters still haul renegade magicians off to prison. He must have learned from one of them.

He leans out past me and glances back and forth. Then he grasps my arm. "Come in."

I'm pulled into the familiar foyer, with its marble and hangings and beautiful painted ceiling. There are no servants anywhere. What's going on? Above us, in one of the receiving rooms, I hear floorboards squeak, and the sound of raised voices.

The young man is still gripping my arm. Ordinarily I would protest at being touched like this by a stranger, but his hands are strong and warm and I'm slow to pull away. "I suppose it's good you came here," he says, almost to himself, in Idaean. He switches to Ereni with a facility that surprises me. "They're upstairs. Come with me."

But my feet seem to have become rooted to the carpet. He swings around to face me. A frown disrupts his easy grin; he says gently, "It's all right. You're safe here."

"Am I?" My voice is shaking.

A floorboard squeaks directly above us. We both look up. Nikerites himself stands at the top of the stairs, wearing a shapeless old banyan robe though it's midday. He looks old, haggard, his face carved with lines. He barely acknowledges my existence, but simply nods at Jahan and walks away, in the opposite direction from the raised voices.

Strange.

Jahan bounds up the stairs. I follow, my feet heavy. The filigreed doors of the receiving room stand open, and as I come to the landing I make out the voices. Male voices, raised. "If Benson doesn't return from the stones, then—"

I stop. The stones. Where Hensey wanted me to go.

"But I don't see why we cannot go ourselves," a younger voice responds. "Then make our way north, to the duke's lands."

What is this?

Jahan has turned back, almost exasperated. "It's all right, really. They're your friends."

They are?

A shadow passes over the doorway and an older man steps through it, his riding boots tramping the elegant carpet. "We need to take several horses tonight, north. We—" He stops, looking at me. He wears a dark-gray greatcoat over plain, dark clothes, and his dark hair bristles with silver.

His voice. His accent.

He's Caerisian.

Caerisian. In the Paladisan embassy.

No. Not my father's people, not here.

The man says in an astonished voice, "Elanna? I thought—"

The way he speaks my name, it sounds as if he knows me. As if he *remembers* me. For a breathless moment, we stare at each other. The timbre of his voice, made for singing. The silver in his hair; the lines fanning out from his eyes. The years have not been easy on him.

No. I don't know this man. I *can't* know him.

I whirl, running down the stairs, throwing open the door, back into the crowded streets. If they come after me, I don't know it. I pelt through the alley beside the house and run as if my life depends on it.

THE STREETS ARE quieter now that I've veered away from the thoroughfare near the palace. My feet pound over the cobblestones. A passing woman stares at me with suspicion, knowing that my running means I'm in some kind of trouble. I force myself to slow to a walk, even though my heart's leaping.

I glance back. There's someone—a man; two men—well behind, but following me down the street.

The man in the house. His name is on my tongue. What is he *doing* here? He must know the risk. I've seen his face on the wanted posters. Loyce's taunts echo in my memory. *Did you know him? Was he dear to you, the traitorous, spying Caerisian pig?*

But it's been fourteen years, and I was a child. It's been a long time since they bothered to put his face on the posters. A long time since I squinted my eyes and refused to see the reward for bringing him in. Maybe it's not him. Maybe they're not my father's men. Why would my father's men follow me onto the street, anyway? How badly can he want me back after all these years?

These rationalizations don't convince my heart or my sweating palms. Or the prickling in my back. Now they've found me, they're not going to leave me alone.

And really, would it be so bad to go back to Caeris? I'd be looked after. I wouldn't be tried for murder. I wouldn't be executed.

But it's my father who murdered the king. It's he who left me, who abandoned me here, for all these years. If he wants me now, there has to be a reason for it. Simple, human compassion is not enough in his world.

And what if he knows? What if he knows what I did fourteen years ago?

No. I can't go back to Caeris.

I have to think. I've just run in blind panic, no rhyme or reason to my movement. I'm on a cold white avenue, the blue slate roofs of the houses high above the chilly marble columns of porticos, and the river isn't far away.

The river. Victoire lives near the river.

So I haven't been aimless after all. My body knew—my feet knew. I redouble my speed, feet rushing over the cobblestones, and quickly turn to the right down one street, then swing onto another.

No one behind me now when I glance back. Good.

Two more blocks. I'm so near I can smell the lavender Victoire's mother uses to perfume the house. I mustn't go in the front. I slip into the alley, where the houses cluster around a shared garden courtyard. An ash tree grows by the wrought-iron gate. I duck into its meager shelter and, hoisting myself up into its branches, clamber over the gate.

The garden is a wild tangle of elm trees and dry autumn shrubs, the bulk of a hedgerow beyond it. At least no one is likely to look out a window and see me in all this foliage. I thrash along the over-grown path until I reach a cleared space surrounded by hedges and a wooden swing hanging from an elm. I study the tidy line of sur-rounding houses, trying to get my bearings. The river rushes nearby. I've been in this garden many times, but I always reach it through Victoire's back door. Finally I recognize the sloping lawn running up to the back portico of the Madoc family residence, and in an upper window, the ruffled silhouette of a young woman's morning-robe.

Victoire. I recognize the baize curtains of her room. She hasn't dressed yet. She must be reading a novel—or writing one. Victoire has great ambitions to wield a pen as incisively as a sword.

She's writing a novel, and I'm running for my life.

I clamber up the lawn, digging out a few loose pebbles from the dirt. I toss one at the window. It goes wide, clattering on the stones instead. I try another. This one hits and the silhouette in the window goes still. I throw another.

A round, pale blob of a face presses against the windowpane. Cautiously, I emerge from the bulk of the hedge so she can see me. I pray no one else does.

The window squeaks as it opens. "El?"

"Let me in." I can't seem to catch my breath; I just point at the garden door.

The window claps shut and she disappears from view. I imagine her running down the stairs, sneaking out through the servants' doors, darting through the rose-and-white salon to the door.

It opens. I'm halfway there before my limping mind takes in the heavy shoulders and stern countenance of Master Madoc, Victoire's father, the minister of finance, home too early from the palace. Of course. The king has died. Does Master Madoc know Denis Falconier accused me of murder?

I halt at the base of the steps. His waistcoat is still unbuttoned; he looks even more disheveled than he did when I saw him earlier. A frown pouches his face. Behind him in the house, Victoire is crying out, "But Papa—"

"Lady Elanna," Master Madoc says, and there is no mistaking the sternness in his words. "Come in."

WE MAKE AN awkward circle in the pastel sitting room: Victoire, Master Madoc, and I. Victoire's mother, Madame Suzette, came in a few minutes ago, took one look at me, and walked right out, saying she would fetch a pot of tea. As if tea is going to help this situation. So far Victoire hasn't said a word, just twisted her hands together, looked at me, to her father, and away.

I can barely sit still: I have to stop my legs from moving, trying to push me back up. I study a painted porcelain trinket box on the table. They don't want me here. Master Madoc already knows everything.

"Lady Elanna." Master Madoc is doing his best to shrink me down to size. "You must return to the palace at once and give yourself up. Running away only gives further credence to this claim that you conspired in the king's death."

How can he possibly imagine this is a good plan? "If Loyce Eyrlai is willing to accuse me of regicide, she's willing to have me executed without trial. I can't go back—I have to seek sanctuary somewhere else. Tinan, or Paladis."

"Lady Elanna," he says on a sigh. "You always believe the queen to be malicious. She's reacting as any daughter would to her father's death. Go back and beg her mercy."

"*You* don't understand. Loyce hates me. She's glad to blame me for murdering Antoine."

He simply stares at me, his gaze flat and disapproving. I don't understand how he can be so distant, so formal, so cruel. I've practically grown up in this house. Victoire and I held pretend tea parties in this room. I decided I wanted to be a botanist in their garden. We used to collect plant specimens and store them in the potting shed, much to the irritation of the gardener.

Now he wants to send me back to the palace, to my death. As if I deserve it for running away.

Madame Suzette returns with the tea tray and I lurch to my feet. I need to get out of here. "I'll leave you—"

"*Sit down,*" Madoc snaps.

I stare at him. How dare he order me to sit? Madoc's a good man, on the whole, but I won't be bullied—not even by him.

"Please, Papa," Victoire says. Her lips are tight and her nose red, as if she's close to tears. "Can't we just help El to the border? To Tinan?"

He rounds on her. "I will not aid a criminal! We're risking enough keeping her in our home right now. I'm sticking my neck out for you, Victoire, just by letting her in the door. We'll already have to swear the servants to secrecy. How much more would you have me risk for her? Our home? Our position in society? My position at court? My life? Our lives?"

Victoire is crying in earnest now, rocking forward over her knees. "No, Papa, but—"

I should never have come here. I've brought danger on their house; I knew it, but I thought of myself first.

An exasperated sigh escapes Madame Suzette, whose pot of tea is going cold. "You're not making matters any better, Hubert. Lady Elanna is here. Now let's help her."

He looks at her, unmoved. "When the crown changes hands, no one is safe—especially us. We don't have a long lineage to protect us, Suzette. Loyce Eyrlai can be volatile. There's no telling what she'll do if we're caught harboring a criminal."

A criminal? I am not a *criminal*.

"The people are uneasy enough, with the poor harvest and the broadsheets claiming the king's 'growing fat off the labor of their backs,'" he's saying. "We can't take the risk."

I feel sick. These people, whom I thought considered me like another daughter, are too afraid to risk themselves for me.

"You mean because you lied?" Victoire blurts out. I stare at her. Her cheeks are flushed and her eyes are still bright with threatening tears, but she's looking defiantly at her father. "Because you're demanding more money in taxes to improve the palace grounds instead of helping the poor?"

"What?" I say. Madame Suzette looks sharply at me, then rises without a word and murmurs something about getting fresh water for the tea that none of us have drunk.

Master Madoc has lurched forward in his seat. "Victoire!"

Victoire's chin wobbles, but she stares him down. "I saw the *real* statistics. You left them lying in your study. I read them."

I don't understand. Master Madoc released the report on the nation's revenue, showing the crown's annual expenses for the last five years. There was nothing false about it. Antoine never took more than he needed; he *gave* to the poor.

"*Five percent,*" Victoire spits at her father. "Five percent of the budget went to public works—roads, public bathhouses, bridges. How much went to putting that hideous fountain behind the palace? To renovating Princess—I mean *Queen*—Loyce's chambers so she had a proper Idaean-style solarium?"

Master Madoc rubs his fist over his forehead. He says nothing.

"His Majesty never . . ." I begin.

Victoire turns on me. "Oh, you're so *blind,* El! Antoine Eyrlai gives you nice dresses and lets you study plants—and you eat out of his hands. Did you even know that he defunded a public hospital so that he could rebuild his hunting lodge at Oise? When he's brought those precious orchids to Eren so you and Guerin can study them, that money comes from somewhere. It comes from the people, who can scarcely afford it."

I realize I'm leaning backward. I've known Victoire almost my entire life, and I've never seen her like this. So angry. So fierce. So righteous.

Her fury sparks an answering anger in me. Master Madoc is willing to give me up because of *his* wrong?

"Is this true?" I say to him. "Did you lie to the people?"

He stares at me, his eyes moving back and forth. "The 'lie' is the king's, not mine."

How can this be true? The Antoine Eyrlai I know, the one who sat at the breakfast table with me and chatted about the latest scientific discoveries in Ida and Agra, called himself the father of the people. I saw how the burden of kingship could sometimes exhaust him; how, some mornings after reading his memorandums, he rubbed his temples and said to me, "Elanna, sometimes even a king must make sacrifices." I saw how those sacrifices ate at him.

Or I thought I did. It's true I never sat in on his cabinet meetings; I never looked with anything more than passing curiosity at the memorandums his ministers gave him, though they lay right there on the breakfast table.

No, I didn't look. Instead I saw how he drowned himself in port wine to numb his guilt; how he closed the gates of his palace, shutting out his people, and went to the country to avoid his responsibility.

Maybe those mornings with me, talking of scientific discoveries, were just another form of evasion.

The pieces fall together in my mind. "But Antoine is dead. You're the one who falsified those reports. You're the one who will lose everything if the people discover what you did." Loyce would dismiss him, of course, and he would take the blame. "You could be the one running for your life."

Victoire looks at me, and sudden understanding passes between us. I say slowly, "If you force me to return to the palace, to beg Loyce's mercy, to go to my death, I will spread the word myself. I'll make sure everyone knows what you did."

The words taste bitter in my mouth. I don't like using this against him, the man I used to pretend was my own father. Yet how abundantly he has just proven we are not family.

He steeples his fingers. "You are aware, Lady Elanna, that to threaten me is to threaten my family." A nod toward Victoire.

"*I* did not lie," Victoire exclaims. "And I shall be the first to tell anyone who asks!"

Madoc's nostrils flare. The pouches beneath his eyes speak more than ever of exhaustion. But he does not reprimand his daughter.

"I'm glad you understand," I say to him. His eyes narrow; he does not answer.

I stand and walk out. Victoire leaps to her feet and rushes after me, past the spindly-legged tables and out of the refuge I thought surely would be safe. We make our way through the series of delicate, carven doors to the one that leads to the portico.

She grabs my elbow. "Where are you going to go?"

I can't meet her eyes. She must think me a very great fool, and a raw, raging part of me still wants to insist that all is well, that Antoine would never allow so great a deception, that everything is as well as it has ever been in Eren. I look past her shoulder and force myself to sound confident, though I'm anything but. "I shouldn't tell you. Then you can't be made to tell what you don't know."

The truth is, I have no earthly idea.

"I'm going to come with you. Sod Papa and his—"

"No!" I'm taken aback by my own vehemence, and so is she. She frowns. "If they capture me, they'd capture you, too. It would destroy your parents." It wouldn't be much easier for me, knowing I'd ruined my best friend's life. I bite my lip against the sharpness of tears.

And to be truthful, I don't know if I can bear to be with her right now. Her revelation about the king has upset me too deeply; what if there is more she hasn't told me? I don't know if I can bear more discoveries of my own ignorance.

Her mouth tightens. Then she reaches out to embrace me. "There's a blanket in the potting shed," she whispers in my ear. "I'll bring food out once it's dark. And clothes, in case they're looking for you by a description of what you're wearing."

I pull back. "Victoire, you can't—"

"Don't you dare leave because it's the noble thing to do," she adds ferociously. "I've read enough adventure novels. I know what you need."

I doubt Madoc will fail to notice our conspiring, but I can't say it to Victoire's face. Without another word, I hug her tight and turn to go.

She shuts the door behind me.

I start crying even before I cross the threshold, stumbling down the steps to the garden. I can't go to the potting shed, but where else is there to go? I could hire a horse and make my way, alone, into Tinan. But even on the main roads, there can be thieves and all sorts, not to mention the royal guard. And Hensey gave me a few coins, but not enough to get all the way there, though I suspect King Alfred would take me in.

Still, Tinan seems to be my only choice. King Alfred is known for his generosity, and—like Eren—Tinan is a former subject state and current ally of the empire of Paladis. Unlike Eren, Tinan conducts relations with the emperor so well that Alfred has managed to assemble a standing army without a word of rebuke. Perhaps he will give me safe passage on a ship to Ida. I have to try, even if the royal guard hunts me down. Even if there is no way Loyce will let me escape this sentence.

I wipe my eyes on my sleeve. I should never have come here; it was a cruel thing to do, putting the Madocs in danger, and the price was the realization of my own blindness. I've been a fool, and I won't be again. From now on I'm moving forward on my own.

A branch snaps. Another.

I look up. Men are coming toward me through the garden's overgrown path, past the swing—men—two—three—four—

"It's all right, Lady Elanna," says one of them in his burring Caerisian accent. "We're here to help you."

My breath aches in my chest. How did they find me? How did they know to come here?

"Your father has sent us to help you." It's him. The man from the Paladisan embassy. The man whose name burns in the back of my mouth.

How dare they! How dare they come after me, how dare they assume that I want their help? I don't want to go back to my father. I refuse to have anything to do with Caeris or her people.

"Get away from me," I snarl. I'm so angry I can't even run. My hands rise of their own accord and curl into claws. If any of them come near me, I'll tear their faces off.

A pounding starts under my feet. It surges up into my body, swells through my head. I taste earth in my mouth. A woman's voice screams. *I'm* screaming. But I'm not a woman. My throat is wood and water and sap. I am green and bruised and rocky, and I am angry. So *angry*.

The garden bursts alive.

A man screams as a rhododendron flings him to the earth. Another gasps as tree roots trip him up, and another as the very ground begins to shift and quake under our feet. I'm gasping, fighting down another scream, tremors racing up and down my arms. I've got to run, but the green power still pulses through my body, a counterpoint to the shaking in my limbs.

A hand on my arm. I wrench around to see gray eyes in an Idaean face, before he speaks a word and everything crumbles.

CHAPTER FOUR

Darkness. Movement. Warmth under me, behind me. Fists of trees. An ache between my eyebrows. Hand on my elbow. Stars. So many stars.

The horse slows, bracing itself through a patch of mud. The man behind me tightens his arm around my waist, then pulls me toward him to compensate for the horse's shifting. My head tips against his shoulder. I smell cloves and cinnamon. It feels good to be held.

To be *held*? I force my drooping eyes open. Where am I? We're pounding down an open road in the dark, with no light but the stars. I make out a company of five, six others in front of us. In their dark clothes, moving without words, they seem an extension of the forest and fields we're passing. Not even a lantern to light our way.

My father's men have caught me at last.

My companion, feeling me stir, has loosened his grip. "How do you feel?" The words have an Idaean accent.

It's him, then. Jahan.

He did something to me. Some magic.

Because *I* used magic in the garden—I tasted the earth in my mouth. In broad daylight, for anyone to see, I used magic. The magic I'm not supposed to have, the magic that until now I've kept hidden, made an entire garden come to life. A shiver burns through my stomach. I didn't know I had such power. I didn't remember.

Now I've put us all in danger. Not just myself, but the Madocs.

But I wouldn't have done it if my father's men hadn't come after me. They threatened me; I was trying to defend myself.

And he asks me *how I feel?*

A muzzy taste lingers in my mouth. I can't seem to think of an appropriate insult—it must be the effect of whatever he did to me—so I find myself saying, "I'm at a disadvantage. I don't even know who you are."

His chest contracts against my back. I think he's trying not to laugh.

"My name is Jahan."

"Jahan what?" I demand. "And I'll thank you to state your intentions, as well!"

A snort escapes him: He's definitely trying not to laugh. "Jahan Korakides, at your service, demoiselle. And I swear to you, my intentions are nothing but honorable."

"Indeed?" I say. "A man takes a woman—by *magic*—and knocks her senseless, and she comes to on a horse in the middle of the night, and she's supposed to assume his intentions are *honorable?*"

"If he is a gentleman, yes," he says. "No gentleman would harm a lady."

"Am I supposed to believe you're a *gentleman?* Gentlemen don't abduct women!"

"Do you feel yourself abducted? I was under the impression we were saving your life."

The audacity of this claim shocks all the words out of me. It's a good thing he's got me wedged in front of him—one hand lingering on my waist—or I'd punch him in the face.

"Or perhaps saving you from yourself," he adds, as if he's just thought of it. "From your own intransigence."

"My *intransigence!*" It's his accent that irritates me more than anything, the way it twists the familiar words so that it seems I'm hearing them for the first time, the sound burring in my ears. "I'd like to see what you'd do if you were accused of regicide and taken by a—a—an Idaean *sorcerer!*"

He's grinning behind me, I can just tell. The rogue.

"It seems to me I've saved your life twice now. So you might be reassured that I mean you no harm."

"Indeed! Well!" I can't seem to stop sputtering. "Good! Otherwise I would have to shoot your leg—or something else—off and steal this horse."

"Ah. Alas. I've taken your pistol." Damn him, he's trying not to laugh again.

"You took it? You *searched* me?"

"You dropped it," he says, his voice heavy with diplomacy, but I know he's lying. The gun was tucked into a pocket of my overcoat. He shifts behind me, lifting his hand away from my waist and returning a moment later with a slosh. "Water? You must be thirsty. It was a long spell to be under; I do apologize for that."

I'm still vexed about my pistol; I ignore the waterskin. "Did you think I'd shoot my father's people?"

"Yes," he says frankly. I stiffen in indignation, but I suppose I did attack them in the garden. They probably think me capable of anything. "You'd think we were the ones who want to put you in prison, the way you treated Hugh."

"I don't even know who 'Hugh' *is*."

My voice shakes on the last word, because it's Hugh whose name I've been pushing just out of reach. In my mind's eye, I see him from a child's perspective, a tall, rangy man in a gray coat that smells of autumn, picking me up from the base of the tree in the garden at the house we kept for state occasions in Laon. *Who were you talking to, little El?* he asks me.

Nobody, I say.

He swings me around, making the world spin, and then we go inside together, my cold hand tucked into his big warm one. He tells me the story, the poem I like so well. Even now, the words haunt me. I haven't been able to forget them, no matter how hard I've tried. I whispered them to myself in the dark after I was taken hostage, a small, useless comfort.

"Wildegarde came, bearing a flame in her heart and her hair crowned with the pale light of stars," I mutter under my breath. *"Where she placed her foot, the earth trembled; when she raised her hand, mountains moved."*

I snatch the waterskin from Jahan's hand and take a long drink.

Once I finish and pass it back to him, Jahan reins in the horse, his arm coming around my ribs so that I don't rock forward. Even through the thickness of my greatcoat, I feel his warmth. Ahead of us, the other riders are slowing. The starlight glints off hats and hair, the tip of a musket. A man brings his mount next to ours. I can't make out anything of him but the battered shape of the hat on his head, the forward cant of his body.

"Lady El." It's still a shock, how familiar his rugged Caerisian voice is, as if my childhood sat up and spoke. "I heard you talking. You're all right there with Lord Jahan? We have a few more hours to go."

Hours. My bottom is starting to feel numb, but I say, "I'm fine."

"Good. Have a touch of this." He hands over a flask.

I unscrew the lid and sniff it. "Whiskey? Or are you planning to drug me?"

Jahan snorts.

"It's the water of life, Lady Elanna, nothing more." The other man pauses. "I'm Hugh Rathsay. I don't know if you remember me, but—"

"I remember you. Do you still manage my father's spies?"

There's a pause. I take a swallow of the whiskey. First it tastes of the peat bogs of Caeris, and then it burns. I grimace and pass the flask over my shoulder to Jahan.

Hugh is laughing a little. "I don't know that I would call myself Ruadan's *spymaster*. But very well, if that's what you like."

I think of his face on the wanted poster, Loyce's taunting voice. More fiercely than I meant to, I say, "Isn't there a price on your head? Why didn't you stay in Caeris?"

"One cannot live one's life in hiding." The cadence of his voice makes the words more poetic than they should be. "There'll be a price on your head, too, by now."

"I expect so," I say stiffly.

Jahan hands the flask back to Hugh. He's coughing. I allow myself a smirk.

"Is our Caerisian brew too strong for you?" one of the other riders asks, nudging his horse closer as he laughs. The faint light shines off his pale hair.

"I've drunk worse," Jahan says with dignity, between fits of coughing.

The other rider leans close to us. "Lady Elanna, I'm Finn."

"Finn." I can't make out anything of his face but the tip of his nose, though I hear a smile in his voice. "Pleased to meet you."

"I assure you, the pleasure is entirely mine."

His tone is courtly, and the whole thing seems surreal. Next thing I know, a string quartet is going to start up and he'll ask me to dance.

But Finn is, in fact, asking Hugh a question, which I missed.

Hugh gathers his reins, starting to move ahead, then glances at me. "It's good to have you back, Lady El." He nudges his mount away, to ride beside Finn.

"You *do* know him," Jahan murmurs in my ear.

I ignore this. "Were you following me this morning, up to the stones?"

"Following you? It was coincidence. I wanted to see the circle."

But his arm tenses around me, so I suspect he's lying. The hairs prickle on my back despite the warmth of his body close behind mine. I say, "Do you know where we are?" It comes out sharper than I intended.

"North of the city."

I could have guessed that—and I can also guess that our destination is Ganz, the place Hensey told me to run to.

Hensey. She knew these people. I call after Hugh, "You've suborned my nursemaid. Do you know what's become of her?"

"Alis Hensey?" He's quiet so long that I begin to shiver in fear of what he'll tell me. One of the other men says something, too low for me to hear, and Hugh sighs audibly. "They'll have imprisoned her, along with everyone else suspected of conspiring in the king's death."

"She helped you," I say. "And you're going to leave her there?"

He's quiet again. Then: "She understood the risk."

I cannot speak. Will Hensey be flogged? Executed? Left to rot in prison? And what of Guerin? What of Victoire and her family?

I have left them all at Loyce's mercy, and now I'm headed north with these Caerisian savages, who don't even have the heart to save their own. And the Idaean sorcerer whose arm remains around my ribs, hugging me against him. His body is warm and I feel the imprint of his hand beneath my armpit and left breast, even through the layers of my clothes.

He leans forward so that his breath stirs my hair and pitches his voice just for me to hear. "I know it's hard for you."

Hard? In the space of a day, I've lost Guerin and Hensey to a false conspiracy; the king who treated me better than his daughter has died and I've been framed for his murder; I've abandoned Victoire and learned that Antoine's goodness may have been a lie. And now I'm being dragged north by my father's men.

Taken together, it's all so unbearable that my anger is swallowed by grief. A lump swells in my throat. This man, with his dashing looks and irrepressible grin, does not care about my troubles. And yet he's not laughing now. I can *feel* him at attention behind me, waiting for my answer.

I find myself whispering. "It seems as if I've lost everything, in the space of one day."

"I know." His lips touch my ear as he says it—by accident, I think, but my skin burns with awareness despite the distress aching through me.

"*How* do you know?" I ask to distract myself.

My fingers are digging into the wool fabric of his sleeve, and I feel the strength in his arm beneath it. The horse's back twitches under us. Jahan's breath is moist on my neck. He says, "I am not sure it gets easier, but the pain gets less. I know that."

His hands close over mine, stilling their frantic tugging, and his chin brushes my shoulder. He smells of cinnamon and cloves, horse and sweat. His touch is gentle, and his hands are large enough to cover mine. I realize I'm holding my breath.

"Elanna Valtai," he murmurs. "You're not what I expected." A soft laugh: a warmer puff of air against the back of my neck.

"Jahan . . ." I've forgotten his surname. "That's not an Idaean name."

"No." He sounds amused; his voice has gone low and deep, burring against my spine. "I'm from the Britemnos Isles. My ancestors came from many places."

The Britemnos Isles lie in the sea separating Eren and Tinan from Paladis, right on the trade route. Though they are a subject state of Paladis, they are known for their mix of dialects and customs, blending Idaean language and traditions with their indigenous ones and others brought by sailors and tradesmen. Why would a Britemnosi lord support a Caerisian rebellion? Especially a Britemnosi sorcerer?

Finn comes up beside us before I can formulate a question. "Jahan. Do you hear that?"

We both straighten, though one of his hands remains tight around mine.

"Quiet!" Finn breathes. Everyone else stops their whispered conversation. There is nothing to hear but the faint wind in the trees, the patter of an animal in the undergrowth. I strain my ears.

And I hear it. The sound of hoofbeats, coming nearer.

The horse rounds the curve. A lantern sways from the rider's outstretched hand, a mad arc of light bobbing in the hedgerows. There's a metallic *snap* as one of my father's men cocks his musket. Jahan's drawn a pistol—*my* pistol—from a pocket, and Finn is reaching for a weapon strapped to the saddlebags behind him.

"It could be anyone," I whisper at Jahan. "It could be nothing to do with us."

There's a *clink* and the smell of gunpowder as Jahan pulls out a powder flask and loads it into the pan. "On a dark night? Do you believe that?"

I shake my head.

The newcomer draws closer, and in the wild arc of the lantern's light, I make out something strange about his neck—a profusion of cloth, like ruffled lace. Jahan shifts behind me. He must be shoving the ramrod down the pistol. I feel his arm flex next to mine as he cocks it back.

A voice rings out, high and clear. A young woman's voice.

"Elanna?"

"Don't shoot!" I don't know if I'm shouting at the Caerisians or at Victoire—though the only thing in her hand is the lantern. "She's a friend. A *friend*."

Hugh calls to Victoire, "State your name and business, demoiselle!"

I'm trying to pull myself off the horse, but Jahan grips me hard.

"My name is Victoire Amelie Odette Madoc," my friend cries out, "and I am here to demand that you unhand Lady Elanna!"

Silence.

"Or take me with you," she adds.

I give up trying to dismount and just shout at her. "I told you not to come! Your parents—"

"My father is a liar and a thief," Victoire retorts angrily.

"But Suzette—"

"Mother saddled this horse for me, El."

We're close enough now that I can see the lines on either side of her mouth, the righteous look in her eyes, through the jogging lantern-light. She's not going to go back to Laon, at least not willingly.

"It's too late for me to turn around," she says, reading my mind. "The queen's sent out riders, the royal guard. They'll catch me if I go back now."

Our eyes lock, and something cracks in me. I can't speak. Instead, I dig my fingers into my sleeve—no, not my sleeve, Jahan's. He doesn't flinch.

Hugh says, "Well, it seems you're coming with us, Demoiselle Madoc. We've a few more hours to go. Are you up for it?"

"Are you?" Victoire says.

Hugh actually chuckles. "Well, then. Put out that lantern, young lady, and let's ride."

WE POUND ALONG without speaking for a long while. Victoire has pressed her horse up beside us, nudging Finn out of the way. I'm so relieved that she hasn't written me off as an utter fool for believing her father's—and Antoine's—lies. It still doesn't sit right with me, the idea that I never questioned the king's honesty or the uses to which he put his funds. What else have I been blind to?

The fields turn to forest and back to fields, the hills endlessly rolling. Clouds cover the stars; a light mist dampens the air. We're riding northeast—toward Ganz, presumably, which lies perhaps forty miles outside Laon, in Eren's heartland. Jahan's presence is sure and silent behind me. An Idaean sorcerer—a *Britemnosi* sorcerer. Why is he here?

And why does every movement of the horse rock me back against him, so that I can't forget his presence?

At last, partly to distract myself from his silent warmth, I turn to Victoire. "How did you get out?" I whisper-shout to her.

"We heard what happened in the garden. I went back out and saw you'd collapsed, and this *oaf* hauling you away."

A choking noise from Jahan. "Oaf?"

"He claims he's a gentleman," I say to Victoire. "But his actions so far disprove that."

There's a gust of warm breath on my neck as he laughs. "What? Still no gratitude for saving your life?"

"You haven't saved my life. You prevented me going to *prison*."

"Where you would have been sentenced to death."

"Oh! Really!" I'm spluttering again, and even through the dark I see Victoire staring at me. Us, rather. I clear my throat. "I suppose I am grateful. Even if you did abduct me."

Jahan's fingers brush my waist, and I sense him grinning again. Infuriating man.

"Go on, Victoire," I say. "How did you get here?"

"Well," she says, "I had to do something after we saw them take you away! But Papa was watching me like a hawk, as if he knew just what I was thinking. I had to wait till nightfall. Of course, by then I thought I'd never catch you, but I still had to try. I went up to my room as if I were going to bed, but I put on my coat and boots, and as I was trying to decide whether to crawl out the window, Mama came in. She said she'd had your captors followed—think of it, my mama, contriving to send a maid after them!—and word had just come that they'd left the Paladisan embassy, with you still *unconscious*." Her voice sharpens with indignation. "So Mama saddled a horse. She said I must hurry or I'd lose you. I *would* have lost you, if it weren't for her."

"Why did she do it?" I marvel. Madame Madoc is a delight in the drawing room, but I've never imagined her as much of an adventuress—or willing to sabotage her husband's plans. Except that she, too, must have known the truth about the revenue reports. She must have witnessed her husband's—and Antoine's—dishonesty firsthand.

"I think she was ashamed of how Papa treated you," Victoire says. "And she said I had nothing to fear from these people."

"Maybe she sympathizes with your common people and their desire for a rightly elected king," Jahan says. "Maybe she supports our cause."

"Your cause?" I say narrowly.

"Our cause," Finn calls from behind us, "to free the people of Eren and Caeris from the tyranny of the Eyrlais—"

From the front of the line, Hugh shouts, "That is enough, all of you! No more talk. Do you want to put us all in danger?"

We fall silent. The fields turn to forest again, stone walls falling away to the silent undergrowth of ferns and fallen leaves, as the horses carry us through into morning.

BY DAWN, MY eyes are gritty from exhaustion. Neither Jahan nor I have spoken for hours. Part of me still wants to be cross with him, but I'm too aware of his arm holding me close, the touch of his breath heating the back of my neck. As the horses slow, his hand grasping the reins brushes mine. I'm too warm, despite the chill wind.

"Water?" His voice is rusty with tiredness.

I take the slack waterskin from him, aware of our hands touching again. "Thank you."

We've come into a narrow lane, bordered on either side by high hawthorn hedges. Between the beech trees that lift over the top, I glimpse the blue slate roofs of a bucolic country manor, puffing soft curls of smoke into the sky. It looks almost unbearably inviting. The idea of being safe inside four walls, beside a fire . . .

But surely this is the Count of Ganz's land and home. The man with the monkey. I suddenly wonder if he didn't sow the rumors of his eccentricity himself, to keep people away from the revolutionaries he's sheltering.

But no matter how unthreatening the Count of Ganz may turn out to be, I'm here with my father's men. *They* surely don't have my best interests at heart.

No. My father can want me for only one thing.

I suppose this has been his plan all along—to wait until I'm of age and then drag me back to Caeris, willing or no. Poison the king and let me take the blame, so I'm *grateful* when he comes to rescue me. So that I'll do anything he asks. So that I'll *be* what he wants me to be.

How I wish I'd learned to wield my magic better when I was a child in Caeris! Then I could use it now, in the exact opposite way he wants. So that I can get away from him and his plans.

The line of riders ahead of us turns onto a slightly wider track leading to the side of the manor. We pass a henhouse loud with the irritable clucking of chickens and come to a stop under a large elm. A kitchen girl, walking up from the stable yard with a full pail of milk, emits a small shriek, and milk splatters everywhere.

My stomach rumbles.

"I'm starving," Jahan says, swinging off our horse with a groan. In the morning light, his usual grin is absent. There's a line between his brows. He holds up a hand to help me dismount, but I wave him away; I don't want to be distracted by his touch. When I hit the ground, my legs almost buckle. I stagger in the mud, trying to work the feeling back into them.

Victoire dismounts beside me, grimacing. I wait for Jahan to move away, toward the house, and then I grab her elbow. "We'll get out of here," I whisper to her.

Her eyes widen. Why is she surprised? Does she think I want to be a traitor to the crown, on the run for my life, a pawn in my father's king-making schemes? She whispers back, "I thought you'd want this."

I feel my face contort. "No."

Knowing Victoire, she thinks the whole idea of a revolution is wildly romantic—not to mention a way to put her father in his place. She doesn't know revolutions are messy disasters where people die so that someone who hardly deserves it can come to power.

I stalk toward the house, after Jahan. Victoire follows me.

THERE'S A SWARM of stable hands, kitchen servants, and a woman in blue who seems to be in charge of them all. We are swept into the house, tramping through the kitchen and up the stairs to a morning room upholstered in pastel yellow. A man in an embroidered silk dressing gown jumps up from the table with an exclamation: "Hugh!"

"Hilarion!" Hugh replies.

They embrace with much back-pounding. Victoire and I exchange a glance. So this is what the notorious Count of Ganz looks like at home. It's nothing like the rumors—except perhaps for that dressing gown. It's so ugly it's fashionable.

Two maids bring in silver trays filled with tea and scones and toast and cheese. Despite my resolve to remain stern and aloof, my mouth waters. Hugh has switched into speaking Caerisian, which the Count of Ganz evidently understands, and my ears are too tired to deny they know the words, as well.

Victoire nudges me. "I like the look of *him*," she whispers, pointing her chin at Finn.

I stare up from the food to Finn. He's greeting the Count of Ganz. I suppose he does draw the eye, tall and narrow as he is, with his ruddy-gold hair and the eager pink of his lips.

"Don't bother," I whisper to Victoire. We won't be here long enough for her to make a pass at him.

She pouts at me.

Hugh moves on to introduce Jahan—in Ereni, now. "This is Jahan Korakides, the new ambassador for the emperor of Paladis, come to us all the way from Ida."

"The Korakos?" says the count, with a raised eyebrow. "Our cause must be dear to the emperor indeed, if he sent his beloved son's savior. How does Prince Leontius spare you?"

The Korakos? I stare at the young man who's been riding behind me all night, feeling a flush build from the pit of my stomach to my cheeks. The count must have made a mistake—in translation, no doubt. *Korakides* is similar to *Korakos*. The dashing Korakos, the crown prince of Paladis's best friend, wouldn't come to a backwater country like Eren. He wouldn't grasp my hand and tell me he knows what it's like to lose everything you know. He wouldn't save my life, and he wouldn't look at me the way he does.

Even more than that, the crown prince wouldn't have a best friend who practices magic.

"Quite begrudgingly," Jahan is saying. "But when the fate of a nation is at stake, we must all make concessions." He smiles, making his dimple flash, and it's the quicksilver twist of his mouth, the smoothness with which he answers the count, that makes me realize it's the truth. One can only learn that sort of behavior at court. And his eternal amusement makes a certain sense; it must be the way he has survived the Idaean court, where they prize wit above all else.

But of course he hides behind a mask. He's a sorcerer. He's had to hide that secret, in public, in the largest court in the world, where it's easier to keep gold and palaces secret than to hide magic.

As if sensing my gaze, he gives me a sudden, genuine grin. And everything in me seems to tighten and somehow expand. Korakides: "son of the raven." That's where he got his nickname. But he's not a raven, he's a hawk, with his golden-olive skin and his ruffled dark hair and his sure, easy stance. He's the sort of person anyone would fall in love with: maidens, ladies of the court, storytellers, princes.

". . . Lady Elanna Valtai," Hugh is saying, and I startle away from Jahan's gray eyes.

The Count of Ganz actually gasps. Without any of the formality he showed Finn or Jahan, he crosses straight over the carpet and enfolds me in his arms. This is a rather more candid acquaintance with the dressing robe than I'd expected, but when Hilarion pulls back, there are tears in his eyes. "Dear girl . . . I was there the night they took you. I saw it happen—the king; the pistol—and I thought, *We shall never see that poor child again.* But Antoine kept you alive. And now here you are. You have escaped, and are back with us."

I force a smile. If I had my way, they wouldn't be seeing me again.

The maid brings in a new tray of food. The smell of fresh bread is torture. My stomach growls loudly.

Everyone laughs.

"How rude of me!" the count exclaims. "Of course you must be starving. Seat yourselves and eat." Everyone makes for the table. He squeezes my arm and says to me in an undertone, "Your parents will be so glad to have you back. The suffering your poor mother has endured . . ." He draws in a breath. "It broke her, losing you."

A fist seems to be squeezing my heart. But I wet my lips and look at the food on the table. It broke her?

Well, it broke me more.

Unbidden, I hear the music. The song. Her song. *Just for you, Elly. I wrote it just for you.*

I refuse to hear it.

"Thank you, Count Hilarion," I say roughly. I move past him toward the table, pretending not to see the sympathy in his eyes.

CHAPTER FIVE

After stuffing myself at the breakfast table, I'm so full I think I might not be able to sleep. We're given access to the bathhouse— "Ladies first," says Hugh—and fresh robes and chemises. Now that I'm finally alone, I should make a plan for getting Victoire and myself out of this place, but instead I fall asleep in an enormous canopied bed, with my face plastered into my wet hair.

It's dark when I wake up—not even a candle burning in the cavernous room—and though I can hear the ticking of a clock nearby, I have no way to see the time. My bladder, however, reminds me that I drank a rather large quantity of tea before going to bed around noon. With a sigh, I get up. It's so dark I have to search for the chamber pot by touch, but finally I locate it.

The clock is sitting on the fireplace mantel—the banked coals still giving off some sluggish heat, but no light. The clock heavy in my hands, I pad over to the window to look at the time. It's a cloudy night, but I can just make out the position of the hands—shortly past eight. I'm shocked at how soundly I slept. It feels like the middle of the night, and the warmth of the bed tempts me.

But I need to make a plan. I don't like how quickly I've become comfortable here, and this isn't the time for complacency. I need to escape before it's too late, before we're back in Caeris and I'm facing my father and the truth of what I am. I hunt down my discarded riding clothes. They're hung over a chair by the fireplace, and when I pick them up, the odor of sweat and horse is almost overpowering. But at least I have a clean chemise to tuck into the trousers.

Dressed, I make for the door. The corridor stretches away on either side, long and empty. I pad across to Victoire's door and knock gently.

No answer. I try the knob—it opens without a hitch—and lean my head in. It sounds like she's asleep, breathing long, slow breaths. I start to edge inside, but think better of it. Maybe I should get the lay of the house first, before waking Victoire and trying to persuade her to ride with me to Tinan.

I am *not* going home. I refuse to be embroiled in another revolution, sacrificed again for the good of Cacris. I will not make a humiliating return to Caerisian customs and poverty and earth-worshipping magic, not after Antoine Eyrlai taught me better. I am going to make my way out of here, and live my life the way I want.

Even if Victoire is right that Antoine was a liar and a thief. Even if the life I've lived makes me complicit in his lies.

I creep down the grand staircase, hanging on to the railing. There's a faint glow of light from the back of the house, down a turn of the hallway from the foyer, and through the high-ceilinged library. The murmur of conversation sounds beyond the just-open door. I listen: Hugh, Finn, the count. Jahan.

". . . if she won't come?" Finn is asking.

I hover there, drawing in my breath, my fingertips just touching the door.

"The people won't rise," Hugh says. I hear him sigh. "Or not as willingly. They need something to believe in, something beyond crowns and kingdoms. They need to believe in the old stories. In the power of the land."

The power of the land—the stories he used to tell me about Wildegarde. I stiffen.

The count speaks, his voice muffled. He must have his back to the door. "How do you know she has that gift?"

My hand falls and hits my thigh. So they all know.

I knew all along there's only one reason why my father would want me back after fourteen years. It's not affection or guilt or even a sense of responsibility for my life. No. He wants to use me.

Hugh answers. "She had it as a child. Ruadan kept it quiet—his secret weapon, he called her. I remember once he took her out to the stones, let fall a drop of her blood, and the stones—" An intake of breath. "The stones *danced.*"

I was a girl, barefoot in a blue dress, and the stones pulsed a rhythm through the earth, faster and faster until they seemed to move. To dance. And I danced, too, whirling at their center, the sun hot on my head and the smell of grass in my nostrils, until I fell down, dizzy and panting. The earth murmured in my ears. I tasted the soil and plants growing in it. I was alive and the earth was alive, and my body and the earth were one living thing.

It was all I ever wanted as a child: to play in the land that lived in me.

When we came south for the coronation and Harvest Feast a few months later—to the city where magic was forbidden—my father swore me to silence. He gripped the collar of my dress. *You mustn't tell anyone you can bring the land alive, Elly, do you understand?*

And after the king took me hostage, I buried the secret deep in the pit of my stomach, so deep it was hidden even from myself. But I couldn't hide all of it. Pieces of my gift lingered whether I wanted them or not: the stones that woke to my blood, the plants that grew to my touch.

I can only imagine how it must have galled my father to lose me— the daughter who instinctively wielded the power our family had in legends, in the time when the earth was alive.

Perhaps I still have it. In the Madocs' garden, I woke the earth in a way I haven't since I was a little girl. I can still taste it, the earth on my tongue. But I can't bring the earth alive again as I did in the Madocs' garden. I won't. They'll brand me a witch; they'll take me away to prison and send me mad before they kill me.

And even if the witch hunters don't come for me, I'll never help my father.

Jahan's voice, on the other side of the door, startles me back to the present. "But the duke does not have this power?"

"No." Hugh pauses. "Not particularly. The Valtais have passed the knowledge down, but in the two hundred years since the Ereni conquered us, few have had the ability."

Finn and the count make noises of wonderment, but Jahan talks over them: "This will make gaining the emperor's support more difficult. You understand? We wish to help, but the emperor will never condone the use of magic. Euan Dromahair has made many promises of what he will give Paladis when he takes the crown, but the emperor is more likely to swallow his irritation and pay the Eyrlais' high tariffs on wheat and lead than to support magic. Most likely he'll arrest Lady Elanna and try to erase her very existence. How will you tell all of Caeris about her but not let word slip to Paladis?"

His tone is blunt, pragmatic. He must be used to making this kind of consideration. I suppose if you're a sorcerer-in-secret, the crown prince's closest friend, the most public of public figures, secrecy becomes second nature.

But I will not be my father's figurehead—no matter how much my magic whispers to me.

I back away. The lining of my stomach is quivering. I need to go, now. Horses. We need horses. Except the servants will be sleeping over the stables. They'll hear me if I try to sneak one horse out, much less two.

Hensey gave me some coin. Maybe Victoire and I could walk to the village and buy horses to carry us to Tinan. We'll have to move fast, though; it's getting late and I don't want to arouse too much suspicion by purchasing a horse in the middle of the night.

Victoire first. Two brains are better than one. I hurry from the door, in my panic bumping into a table behind me so that the vases on it rattle. In the other room, there's a cessation of sound.

I flee.

The hallways are dark. All the servants must be in bed, or sent to separate quarters. The foyer remains shadowed as I tiptoe across its marble floor. I should have waited to put on my boots. Just as I turn to go up the stairs, a gleam catches my eye.

I turn back. Through the wide, sashed windows, I see lights spilling into the front drive. Swinging lanterns—many of them—illuminate the bulky shapes of horses and men. I'm at the window now, the glass cold against my forehead. The lanterns sway and bob. The men are dismounting, and the light catches on the polished gleam of their bayonets.

And something else. Chips of gold on one man's coat.

No, not gold. Epaulets. Which means—

I turn to run, and collide with Jahan, my fingernails snagging the buttons on his coat. He catches my arms, steadying me. "Your father's men?"

"No," I gasp.

Boots tramp on the other side of the wall. A fist rattles the door.

"The royal guard," I whisper.

Jahan and I stare at each other. The knocking booms again.

I hope the door is latched.

The same thought must occur to him. We both start to bolt, me for the stairs and he for the back rooms. But he grabs my arm and pulls me with him.

"Let me go," I whisper. "I have to save Victoire!"

The knocking comes again.

"No time." Jahan pulls me back into the shadows, into the long corridor, just as the front door opens.

We both freeze.

A hoarse voice calls toward us, into the darkness—surely he cannot see us here, hidden behind the stairs—"Is anyone at home?"

That voice.

The Butcher.

He came to the Fayette house in the middle of the night, because they had been accused of selling information, and in the morning their home was ashes. They invited him in because they had no choice. They gave him hospitality, and he obliterated them.

Jahan's pulling me down the length of the hallway. I jerk my arm away and begin to run—outpacing him, racing for safety. I don't care what my father's men want of me now, I just want to live. We burst through into the study where the count, Finn, and Hugh are sharing a dram of whiskey amid the tranquil odors of leather and wood fire.

"The Butcher!" I cry out.

"The queen's men," Jahan is saying. "The royal guard—"

"It's the Butcher," I say to Count Hilarion, to Hugh, knowing they must understand; they must know the stories of what he's done over the last fifteen years. Both of them are on their feet. The count, I notice irrelevantly, is wearing a peacock dressing robe. "The Butcher of Novarre. He's here—he's *in the foyer.*"

The count's face goes white. He pushes past us to the door, checking the corridor, the vastness of the library. It must be empty. He looks back and barks, "Get out. I'll take care of the men."

"Victoire . . ." I begin.

"And Demoiselle Madoc." The count disappears into the library, shutting the door tightly behind him.

"I see you're prepared for escape, Lady Elanna," Hugh says, nodding at my satchel and boots. "That's good." He walks past us to the bank of windows, where there's a fragile glass door opening onto the back portico. "Blow out that candle, Finn."

Finn and Jahan exchange a glance, then Finn blows out the candles and, in the sudden darkness, the light of the fire isn't enough for me to see anyone's expression.

Hugh comes back to grab me by the shoulders and I'm steered toward the garden door.

"We can't leave Victoire," I whisper, bracing my feet into the carpet.

"We must. You and Finn are far more important. I won't risk you for her. Hilarion will keep her safe."

"She's my *friend*. I have to get her out. The Butcher—You don't understand!"

"I do, Lady El." Hugh wrestles me to the door and stops, grabbing me by the chin. "But if you make a sound, you'll get us all killed. Now silence, or I'll have Jahan make you quiet. Understand?"

I fight off the threatening tears and nod. How dare he hold me like this?

Hugh lets me go. One by one, we plunge out into the night.

A MIST IS falling. It's black outside, except by the stables, where lanterns blaze as the stable hands are woken to take care of the royal guard's horses. We stop in the shelter of an arbor, its vines still thick with leaves.

"No mounts for us," Hugh says grimly.

I shiver. The damp cold cuts through my jacket; I left my greatcoat in my room. "We could go to town. Buy horses there."

"It'll be under watch."

"So we walk," Jahan says. "To another town. Find horses there."

Finn is also shivering; he's only in a shirt and waistcoat. No hat. The mist shines in his pale hair. "Good plan. Walking."

It isn't a good plan, but we don't have much choice. We break from the arbor, hurrying for the safety of the woods. Finn asks if we have wolves to fear.

"No wolf has ever eaten a human being," I snarl. "You'd do better to fear tripping over your own stupid feet and snapping your neck."

"Lady Elanna," Hugh admonishes me.

"I don't suffer fools. Especially not fools hoping to bring back the Old Pretender and send Eren into civil war."

There's a silence, save for our clumsy feet breaking branches and rustling in leaves. The trees loom blackly around us. Beeches, some elms. A branch nearly pokes me in the eye, but when I touch it, it lowers of its own accord, like a bow. The others are sluggish behind me, struggling against the forest. I stomp ahead, letting my body adjust to the woods, or trying to. I can't seem to find the rhythm that usually comes to me. The trees seem awkward and out of place, as if the forest is disjointed.

There's some rustling. I look over my shoulder, hoping for Jahan, but it's Finn who comes up beside me. He walks with his head down, his shoulders tight. Neither of us says anything for a while. I almost feel sorry for what I said, but then I remind myself that I only spoke the truth. Someone has to dissuade them from their revolutionary madness.

"I wish you wouldn't call him the Old Pretender," he says abruptly.

"Why?" I say. "He's a pathetic man living off the emperor's goodwill, dreaming that someday he might have a kingdom to rule. Letting other people fight and die for his ambitions, while he himself has never even touched foot to the soil of Caeris *or* Eren. He's a pretend king—a king of nothing but air."

Finn's throat clicks as he swallows, but he doesn't answer. I suppose this should make me triumphant, but I'm just tired now. The forest is black and wet. I think of Victoire abandoned in a strange mansion, at the mercy of the most merciless man in Eren. It seems, in the course of the last two days, too many people have been sacrificed for my sake. Guerin. Hensey. Now Victoire.

Tears spill over my cheeks, cold mingling with the rain.

I slow. The rhythm of the forest is coming to me now, the way I've always felt it when I'm alone in the woods, in silence. I feel the stream nearby as a shifting coolness in my body. It's a relief to know this ability I've had all my life has some practical use. "We're coming to water. There's a town nearby."

"How do you know?" Finn sounds cross.

I dodge the question. I may be willing to help, but I'm not about to let these people know all my secrets. "There's a mill holding back the water."

"Good." Jahan comes up behind us. "I'm freezing."

He pushes between Finn and me, his elbow knocking mine, and Finn is forced to drop back. I glance at Jahan, but it's too dark to see his expression. I have the feeling he came up now just to stop Finn from questioning me. As if he's letting me protect my secret.

And even though I don't like what they've done, bringing me here, this simple act makes me want to trust him.

I stride ahead, guiding us toward the river.

AROUND DAWN, WE turn north, onto a muddy, narrow track that barely passes for a road. Hugh procured horses from a farrier in the mill town—I was impressed until he told us the farrier was "a sympathizer"—but my mare's warmth helps to heat me somewhat. On our way out of the town, we had to stop for Hugh to pass out coin to the poor who were sitting on the temple steps. "Their farms have been taken from them," he said to Finn as we rode away. "Their lords wouldn't keep them on after the poor harvest. They own nothing but the clothes on their backs—and even those, a lawyer might argue, belong to their masters. But under *Caerisian* law, anyone may buy his own land. They would not be homeless beneath King Euan."

He also handed out pamphlets. I snatched one and skimmed the long treatise—*by an Anonymous Author*—describing the rights of the people under the traditional laws of Eren and Caeris, as opposed to those we have adopted from Paladis.

I wonder what printer dared to put this treason to press. Even several hours later, I'm still twisting the paper into a tight roll, as if I can rub the ink off the pages.

We must be near the border, and as the sun clears the sky, I see it—the wide river Ard flowing south. On the other side spread the bedraggled fields of Tinan.

But the idea of finding a way across the river only sounds exhausting. And the worn pamphlet in my hand implores me not to go.

Are they in the right? Would changing the king—changing the laws—make our kingdom better, stronger, safer?

Jahan rides beside me when the difficult road permits. He seems to have one eye behind us, though he doesn't turn to look back. His shoulders are taut and alert. I tell myself I shouldn't be watching him—that he'll think me a silly, moonstruck girl—but I keep thinking of the stories they tell about him. How he went on campaign to Chozat and saved the crown prince of Paladis's life, catapulting to fame by single-handedly taking on the two dozen tribesmen who had attacked them. How he stood in front of the crown prince, his rapier flashing . . . they've written songs about it. A miracle, they call it; the gods blessed him with superhuman strength that day.

But I suddenly wonder whether it was a miracle, or his magic. And what does he hear now? Why is he so alert?

I finally ask. "Are we being followed?"

He looks unhappy, but he shakes his head. "I don't think so."

"But something's wrong."

He doesn't answer right away, but he doesn't deny it, either. We curve along above the river. The tracks are rutted; the road must be used by farmers taking their goods to market. I twist the pamphlet so hard it finally tears. Jahan stares straight ahead, his mouth tight. Our horses jostle together on the curve, and he looks at me as if he's just remembered that I'm there.

"Someone spoke my name," he says.

I have no idea why this would upset him. "Probably Finn." The others have drawn ahead, though still within earshot.

Jahan winces, shakes his head again. "No, not like that. I heard it . . . miles away."

It's my turn to stare straight ahead at the churned muck and grass on the road. I don't know why it should be so easy to forget he's a sorcerer—and not only that, but the Korakos. I feel clumsy and ignorant in so many ways. He seems to know so much more about magic than I do. I've spent my life trying to forget the little I know, and now that I need it, I have to confront the fact that my knowledge is a child's.

"I shouldn't have come," he says, half to himself. "Nikerites didn't like it. Didn't like *me*. They don't, you know, most people. They pretend to. Or they make it clear they don't. Nikerites was one of the latter. I had to pull rank, use Leontius's name. He called me an arrogant *puppy*."

I digest this. It is difficult to imagine having so much power, being able to wield the crown prince of Paladis's name like a weapon. "Is it . . . Nikerites . . . you heard?"

"No." He tilts his head, as if listening again. "It was a woman."

"Do you always hear it when people say your name?" I can't help but think there must be many women and men, from Paladis to Eren, speaking his name. His friends must speak it—the crown prince must speak it. They say that after Jahan saved Leontius's life, the prince never lets him out of his sight. Some claim they're lovers. What does the prince call him when they're alone together, if the rumors are true? My ears burn at the thought. Of course most people say the crown prince is just too dull and stupid to make decisions on his own, that he needs someone stronger to rule through him. And why not Jahan Korakides, who's quick-witted and brilliant and dashing?

And to think Victoire and I spoke of the Korakos, too, reading the news from Ida and laughing over the idea of meeting him!

"I only hear it if they're strong about it," he's saying. "Upset, or angry. Or if they're magicians themselves. And they have to use my real name, not my nickname."

I breathe out in relief. We never spoke with *intent,* and I never knew his given name until yesterday. The broadsheets and songs only ever spoke of him as the Korakos.

"Is it . . . dangerous?" I ask. "When someone speaks your name?"

He doesn't answer immediately. I peer over my shoulder and glimpse a strange expression on his face—anger? Frustration? He forces a smile. "Only a sorcerer could use it for harm. Even then, as a spell, it's merely a summons. One would have to be a very great sorcerer— very powerful indeed—to compel me to appear against my will."

The way he says it, he must know someone with such power. "Was it a sorcerer, just now?"

"No—or they would have tried to summon me. This is more . . . awareness. She had a whining sort of voice, a little harsh. No one I know. She didn't say my name right, either."

I venture a theory. "If she pronounced the *J,* she can't be Idaean."

He looks at me, his expression lighting up. "That's right! I am always Yahan in Ida. An Ereni woman, then, perhaps—"

"Loyce," I blurt out. "Whining. Harsh. It fits."

There's a hateful edge to my voice, and I flush. I suppose I want Jahan to think well of me, not to think me the type of person who hates. But don't I have the right to hate Loyce? She's willing to accuse me of regicide without a shred of proof, willing to have me hunted like a dog for someone else's crime.

Jahan doesn't seem to notice. He rubs a finger beneath his ear, where there is the faintest of scars. "I need to go back."

My chest contracts. He can't leave us like this, still so far from my father's house—though of course if he's not in Laon, that will raise suspicion, too. "You won't come to Caeris with us?"

Hugh and Finn heard us. They've slowed ahead, and Finn drags his horse around to face Jahan. I'm surprised to see the panic on his face, mirroring my own. "No," Finn says. "Not yet!"

Hugh says nothing, and Finn seems embarrassed at his outburst. He straightens, but one fist curls on his thigh, and the horse sidles under him. "I'm sorry. You must do as you think best."

Jahan looks between us. "I didn't mean *now.* I'm not abandoning you on the roadside." He lifts himself from the saddle to jostle Finn's arm, and Finn breaks into a brilliant smile. "Come on, let's go."

With a wicked grin, he presses his horse past the others, into a trot and then a canter, down the narrow road. Finn shoots after him.

Hugh raises his brows at me, as if I'm going to race after the boys. "Well?"

I tense in the saddle. It is tempting to rush after them. Tempting not to let them out of my sight.

Tempting to escape Hugh.

Instead, we ride together, not speaking, the only noise the jingle of the harness and squeak of leather, a far-ahead *whoop* from Finn and Jahan, quickly cut off. But I seem only to be half on the road. Part of me gnaws on the words in the pamphlet, surely written by Hugh. And the other part of me is five years old, swept up by the man in the gray coat, feeling the certainty of his arms around me, the high pitch of my laughter. Not my father. I never felt certain with my father. I always felt certain with Hugh.

Who were you talking to, little El?

Nobody.

Nobody, who sat beside me beneath the tree, who asked me what I was doing with the green fern in my hand. *Growing it,* I said, as the fern got bigger and bigger, and the roots sagged into my lap.

Nobody, who asked me other questions. *Do you make things grow often?*

Did your father teach you?

Will you grow things for the king? Not King Antoine. King Euan. Will you grow a new kingdom for him?

What else can you do?

I asked just one question for his many. His name. He ran a thoughtful hand along his chin, and he said, *Nobody.*

Nobody! I thought that was marvelous. I laughed and laughed, and when I looked over, he was leaving, slipping through the gate that bound our garden.

Nobody—who didn't have a name until I met the Butcher of Novarre. Until I began to understand what real fear is. Until it became clear that it was I who had, with a child's ignorance, betrayed my father and his rebellion. I, who gave the Butcher and Antoine Eyrlai the proof they needed to break into our townhouse, to take me hostage, to destroy villages and lives and exile my father to his home.

Hugh sighs, startling me out of my thoughts. "I know you blame Ruadan and Teofila for what happened to you. The gods know, you're right. But your parents didn't abandon you willingly. They had no choice."

The memory of music crowds my ears—my mother's song. *Just for you, Elly. I wrote it just for you.*

And maybe she put some magic in it, because after all these years, I still hear the melody.

I clear my throat. My hand has clenched around the reins, and Hugh is watching me.

"That's not why," I say, my voice tight in my throat. "If that was the only reason—"

But I cut myself off. Even if my father forgave me for betraying them into the Butcher's hands, I know I was born for only one thing. There's only one reason he wants me back.

Hugh frowns. "Then what *is* the reason?"

I swallow the other words to the back of my throat—deep inside me, where they will never be spoken, never be seen. Quietly, I say, "My father is a fool. An ambitious fool who thinks he has the right to play kingmaker. I despise men who want only power."

There are so many reasons not to go home.

"You dispense judgment quickly, for not having met him since you were a child. Do you understand why Ruadan tried to crown Euan Dromahair king in Antoine Eyrlai's place? Or have they filled your head with lies?"

It's hard not to glare at him. "The Dromahairs have been lusting after a throne ever since it was taken away from them during the conquest. The Old Pretender—and my father—took advantage when the old king died suddenly and Antoine inherited the crown."

"And why do you think they did it?" Hugh's voice is patient.

I throw up a hand, dismissive. "They wanted power, of course."

"You're right," he says, and I'm so surprised he agrees that I stare at him. He nods at me. "We did want power. We wanted the power to speak our own language and worship our own gods. To live according to our own laws and govern our country according to the traditions passed down by our ancestors, not imposed by the Ereni. To *dress* in the clothes of our clans."

"But you still wanted the throne of Eren."

"No," says Hugh, "we wanted *Caeris* to be free. And if the Ereni chose to join us—and many of them did—so much the better." He adds under his breath, "I should have guessed they would fill your head with lies."

"Then tell me the truth," I snap. "Tell me what really happened."

He looks at me. "Your father and King Euan began to plan their rebellion long before Antoine's father died. It began when they met as young men in Ida—your father and I went there, as youths do, to see the famous city and make our bows before the emperor. The Dromahairs were living then, as they do now, as a court-in-exile under imperial auspices, and naturally Euan knew the current emperor, then crown prince—and knew him well. We all met, raced horses and so forth. The prince liked us. But he didn't like Antoine Eyrlai, whom he thought was an arrogant, insufferable brat, considering he came from a backwater like Eren. He thought it would be good fun to put Euan on the throne instead."

I think of Antoine's stories about the imperial court; how they mocked him and he soldiered on. I swallow. "It's all a game to Paladis, isn't it?"

"The then-emperor didn't think so. He liked the idea of having a stronger, personal tie to Eren and Caeris—an easier way to get our resources and make us do his bidding. The Eyrlais, he said, were too headstrong, but the Dromahairs were more biddable. I think he meant more desperate." Hugh sighs. "But Euan's father was obsessed with the idea of reclaiming what was his, and Euan, I suppose, inherited that desire. It's difficult to call yourself king when your territories are held by someone else."

"And you wanted your freedom," I say. I don't mean to say it; it just comes out.

"Yes." Hugh gives a faint smile. "And so we returned home with the promise of imperial aid. And when Antoine's father died, a decade later, we tried to act. We had spent years undermining the Eyrlais, spreading the truth about everything from their misuse of tax revenue to their compulsive lies."

I clench the half-destroyed pamphlet in my hand. It figures that Hugh also knows about the recent financial deceit—and more.

"Your parents were summoned to Laon for Antoine's coronation—we couldn't act quickly enough to depose him before it—and then 'invited' to remain until the Harvest Feast. It was not an invitation; Antoine and his advisers suspected us. I told your father to give up, to retreat and try again. But he was determined. Euan Dromahair had already set sail from Ida. People were rioting around the country, following the coronation. Your father insisted that we could still win, even from Laon; he thought we could bring in Euan under

Antoine's nose. We had begun to infiltrate our people into the palace—like your nursemaid, Hensey. It was going to be a coup, as bloodless as we could manage." Hugh pauses. In a quiet, hard voice, he says, "And then someone betrayed us. We still don't know who."

I hardly hear his next words—"And you were taken captive"—for the ringing in my ears. Someone betrayed them. Yes, someone did, didn't they?

"So my father wanted to kill Antoine all along," I burst out, but the ringing in my ears doesn't subside. "And now he's murdered him and let me take the blame. Tell me how that's noble. Tell me how that's the act of a good man, a just man."

"Killing the king?" Hugh says. "Elanna, he didn't—not this time . . ." But then he shakes his head. "What do I know? You'll have to ask Ruadan about that. I'm not privy to all his secrets."

"Yes," I say. My mouth is dry as dust. "Yes, I will."

When I see my father, in three days' time.

I'm going back to Caeris. Fourteen years after my father attempted his coup; after he was betrayed.

And I'm not angry, or sad, or even happy. I'm none of those things.

I'm terrified.

CHAPTER SIX

"We need to angle back west," Hugh says. We've stopped on a hill overlooking the Ard, where the twilight lingers on the slate roofs of a sleepy town beneath us, and the line of a westerly road cuts off to our left. He points two fingers along the road. "Another eight miles or so along that, then north. We've another two days, at least, till we reach Caeris; more, if the roads are mud and we have to slow our pace."

And here I thought we might get to rest.

"Is it safe, on a main road?" Finn asks.

Hugh looks at Jahan, who runs a finger behind his ear again, his lips pressed together, thoughtful. "Yes," he begins. Then he grimaces. "I'm not the most skilled at listening beyond my body, through the earth and air."

They all carefully do not look at me. I stiffen nonetheless. They say nothing, but we all know these are skills I possess.

But I won't use my magic to help them. It's too dangerous, and it gives the others ideas. It makes them think I might be what they want me to be.

I can't be pulled into some absurd and hopeless bid for Caerisian freedom. I won't be made to use my magic—the magic that puts me in mortal danger—to further my father's ambitions, Finn's ambitions, even Jahan's ambitions.

I won't.

For Hensey, for Guerin, for Victoire, I have to get away from Eren. I can make a bid for their safety from Tinan.

"I don't sense anyone," Jahan offers, though he's already said it means little.

"Maybe they didn't send anyone north," Finn says. "How would they know, after all?"

"Oh," says Hugh, "the queen will have sent someone north. It's four days, riding hard, from Laon to the southern border of Caeris. The crown keeps a garrison at Portmason. The queen's men may well reach it before we find our crossing place. From the garrison, it's a simple matter to alert the watchtowers along the border. They'll be looking for us."

The way he says it carries weight, like a prison sentence. We are all quiet. Jahan seems to be concentrating, listening, but I don't know whether he hears anything at all. I hear the ford whispering over rocks, and sparrows singing, and the liveliness of the trees.

Once, when I was a little girl, I heard more. When I listened to the world, I heard the earth's heartbeat.

It's both a relief and a torture, finally letting myself remember. A tear catches in my eye. I dash it away. I can't regret losing this connection to the land. I can't afford to be a sorceress. So I heard the earth's heartbeat in the Madocs' garden. I'm putting myself in danger even by thinking of it.

But my throat is still tight. When I was a child, I felt so *alive*.

No, if I'm going to Tinan, I have to go now. I have to get away from this treacherous longing—this pointless yearning for a child's memories, this nagging guilt that I am somehow complicit in worsening the people's lives. I need to go before we move away from the river, cutting west and then north. On the other side of the water, the hills of Tinan form a drowsy silhouette. Loyce won't have sent anyone to Tinan. Not yet. I will be safe there. King Alfred, being Eren's traditional rival, would love to thwart Loyce by keeping me out of her hands. I won't practice my magic. I'll bury it again where no one will ever see it—not even me.

Gathering the reins, I nudge my mare forward. The others swivel after me. I smile at them, showing my teeth.

"I'll scout the hill," I say. "Check the path to town."

Jahan begins collecting his reins to follow, but Hugh holds out a hand. "It's all right. Let her go." He gives an approving nod; he's been trying to show me more trust after he told me the story of my father's failed rebellion. "Five minutes, Lady El. And if you're not back by then, we come after you. Whistle if you're in trouble."

"Like this?" I make the sound of a hawk coming in for the kill.

He flashes a smile. A real one. And I almost hesitate. I almost say, *Please, Hugh, help me. I can't go to Caeris. I can't face my father. I can't do what you want me to do.*

But I don't say it. Because Hugh would never betray my father.

Pulling my hat lower, I urge my mare over the lip of the hill. We sidle down the path toward the village.

Hugh's voice drifts after me, speaking to the others just loud enough for me to hear. Maybe he means me to. ". . . good to see her like this."

I loosen my breath. Five minutes.

I check behind me. They're no longer visible. Pushing the mare to a fast walk, I emerge onto a narrow lane between houses, and then onto the village's main street, lined with simple half-timber buildings. The town is quiet, its main street a morass of mud, the buildings in disrepair. A girl walks ahead of me, leading a donkey whose ribs show beneath the pack carrying dirt-encrusted vegetables. Each time the girl takes a step, the sole of her left shoe flops down to expose a dirty sock. Her pale hair falls in a thin tail between her shoulder blades. She's probably not much older than me. As we pass a tavern, a couple of rough-looking men leer at her and frown at me, then shrug and look away. Bundled in my coat and hat, I must look enough like a boy from a distance. The tension in my neck eases a fraction. Surely I have more to fear from Hugh's anger—from Finn's and Jahan's—than I do from these villagers.

The mare twitches, sensing my worry, and I pat her neck. We're on our way toward the ford.

As we approach the town square, the girl with the donkey turns off and my mare slows. There's a sorry collection of booths lining one side of the unpaved, mucky square. The girl makes her way to a booth and starts unloading the donkey's bags, passing them over to a woman running a vegetable booth. A few other people are perusing the goods for sale. I stare as one woman commences haggling with a man over the price of a single carrot.

They *are* poor. I think of the revenue report that Master Madoc falsified, of the poor who press into Laon and must be cleared away by the royal guard. Of the claims that Antoine Eyrlai has abused and mistreated his people in order to build a bigger fountain behind the palace. Of Hugh's pamphlet, with its claims of a better future under traditional Caerisian laws.

The girl with the donkey exclaims; the sole of her shoe has come right off.

I am a heartbeat away from riding over and giving her my own boots when a hammering begins. I glance to my left. A man is nailing a paper to a door—a paper with my face on it.

My body goes numb.

The mare sidles. I've stiffened so much she's protesting against me. I tug my collar up, pull my hat down. The man's just about done. He steps back to survey his handiwork and nods with satisfaction. He doesn't wear livery, so he must be a town official. The mayor, perhaps.

I have to read that paper. I know the desire is perverse, idiotic. But I must know.

I urge the mare across the square. Still no one takes much notice, though my heart is beating harder. They must often have travelers passing through, to and from Tinan. I am just another traveler. I hitch the collar still higher toward my face.

The likeness of me is taken from a portrait Antoine commissioned in the summer, saying it was a worthwhile expense to have me painted if it found me a decent husband. It's flattering, even in bare black lines—the hard angle of my chin is softened, my curling hair looks artful rather than wild, my chest is delicate in a low-necked gown. As for my face, though the artist has shaded it to hint at my tawny-brown skin, I look like a child—nothing like myself. Certainly not like myself in mud-splattered trousers, a dirty coat, and a hat.

The mare clomps closer, and my eyes are drawn to the words written below the image of my face.

Elanna Valtai:
Dangerous Caerisian Witch
She has already murdered our King
Stop her before she endangers all of Eren

I can't breathe.

I am not a witch.

I am not a murderer.

I am—

The man who nailed the paper up is standing next to me. Was he there all along? He looks at the poster and back at me. His eyes are a worn brown, widening with surprise. I don't look like the girl in the portrait; he can't recognize me. He's only a country man, not too clever.

"Elanna Valtai?" he says.

My heart leaps. It's my skin. My tawny-brown skin that doesn't need walnut powder; in the city, no one takes any notice, but here, among these pale country folk, I stand out.

My body's shaking—no, it's the ground. The earth is trembling. I can feel it, shivering up into my legs, and my horse shifts with it, rolling her eyes. No, not my magic, not now, not here—

The man, who'd taken a step forward, now scrambles back toward the door, grasping its handle to hold himself steady. "Witch!"

The horse's skin twitches all over. She sidles. I cling to the pommel. Behind us, a tree grows in a circle of cobblestones at the center of the square. I'm aware of it with sudden violence, like another limb lurching out of the ground at my back. It seems to be moving, to be waking. No. I can't use my magic. I have to get out of here.

"Witch!" The man's cupped his hands to his mouth, bellowing. He launches himself past me, toward the gong that hangs from the tree's limbs, snatching up a fallen branch to strike the alarm. But the tree sways and the gong swings out of his reach.

Others have heard him, though—men and women run out of a nearby tavern. I'm frozen on my horse, my hair moving, electrified, into an aureole around me. I swell and swell. I am in the earth. I am shifting.

The earth rumbles.

And my mare bolts. I'm flung up out of the saddle, but somehow I stay on. The mare charges through the town, toward the slow-moving river that separates us from Tinan. I slip, fling my arms around her neck. Even the saddle is twisting. I'm going to fall, going to get trampled, then killed by the villagers—

"Elanna!"

Hugh shouts somewhere behind me. But the horse and I have already plunged into the black water. Her hooves slide on the gray rocks. I slip—and I'm falling.

Cold water drenches me. It seeps through my trousers, into my shoes, up the back of my coat. I try to crawl upright but slip on the rocks. My head goes under. I shove my hand down into the silt, then push myself upright, gasp in air.

I'm kneeling in the middle of the ford. The water that tried to suck me down can't be more than three feet deep. The mare stands up to her fetlocks in the water beside the Tinani shore, her sides heaving, nostrils flared.

I have to move, but I'm shaking. I scrub a hand through my hair, my fingers snagging in its wet, chestnut-brown snarls.

How did that *happen*? Why does my magic keep bursting out of me, whether I will it or not? I used to have more control than this. All the years I lived at court, I never revealed myself.

Except I never allowed myself to think enough of my magic for anything to happen. And now that I'm aware of it, I can't control it.

The horse snorts. I glance over my shoulder, toward the Ereni bank, which I see now is grown up with thickets of hazel and alder. Hugh hasn't yet appeared. I still have time to get to Tinan.

If Loyce has branded me a witch and a murderer, King Alfred won't offer me sanctuary, no matter how much he likes to thwart Loyce. He won't risk himself or his country for my sake. The witch hunters will be the only ones waiting for me. They'll clap me in irons and ring me with witch stones and drag me off to Ida. To madness and death.

Still. I have to try. I won't go back to Caeris. And sitting in the middle of the Ard isn't doing me a damned bit of good.

I flounder to my feet—just in time to hear rocks and water splash behind me. I startle, slip-sliding on the slippery stones, down into a hollow in the river bottom, so I'm up to my thighs in water.

Hugh's edging toward me through the ford. I'd almost prefer it was the villagers.

"She's here," he shouts over his shoulder. Jahan and Finn gallop to the bank. Finn's got a sword in his hand, and Jahan's face is strained. He tumbles to the ground, his hands cupped before him. He kneels there.

Hugh gestures for Finn to follow him. "Get across the river."

Finn obeys, urging his horse forward, upstream of me. He doesn't look me in the eyes.

Hugh reins in his horse. He's listening. I hear it then, too: voices raised, coming from the village.

Oh, no.

I flounder back toward Jahan, who jerks his chin at Hugh. "Get across. Quickly."

It's no quick thing to ford a river, but Hugh listens. The horse moves toward me.

I break into a run, spraying up water and slipping on rocks. Hugh makes a grab for me, but there's too much space and rushing water between us. I launch myself at Jahan, grabbing his elbows, his horse's lead. "Come on."

He looks up, startled. "I can't. The queen will know I'm helping you. I'll be under suspicion. You go. You stay safe."

"He's protecting us, you fool," Hugh calls at me. "Come across before those villagers put your head on a pike—or worse!"

I am not leaving Jahan, even if it means Loyce discovers he's working against her. I refuse to sacrifice another person for my safety. "You must come."

Our eyes lock. For a dizzying moment I see what he sees, or feel what he feels—the effort of cupping a whole ford in a swathe of nothingness, of invisibility. *There is nothing here but water and rocks.*

Then his concentration breaks. "I have to go back before your queen or her people realize where I've been," he says. "I'll misdirect the pursuers."

"You can do that *with* us."

The shouting villagers are drawing closer. Jahan shakes his head, and suddenly I'm angry—angry that he must leave, that this is my fault, that *his* magic is protecting *me*. There must be a way I can stop the villagers from crossing the ford, a way I can protect Jahan so he can escape to return south.

And . . . maybe there is. If I have some control over plants and stones, then perhaps I have control over water. For Jahan's sake, I have to try.

I rush back through the river, the heaviness of it weighing down my legs. My soaked clothes drag at my body. The fish murmur beneath the river's surface, and the water itself is alive and shining . . .

Such a simple thing, in the end, to lift my hands. To summon more of it.

"Go!" I shout to Jahan.

He gets to his feet, staring at me. Then he glances over his shoulder, back toward the village, and in one swift movement launches himself onto his horse's back. They plunge deep into the alder thicket just as a crowd of villagers spills around the curve toward the ford, armed with pitchforks and decrepit muskets.

The river swells. It gathers itself. It crests into a wave, crashing around me. But I don't break. I don't fall.

Jahan got away. Downriver, the shrubs bob as his horse moves through them, unseen by the villagers, toward the south.

The water pours around me. The villagers are shouting, some in wonder, some in horror, some in both. I am water and I am a woman. I am the land. I'm everything. Just as I was as a child—though I tried to bury the knowledge so deep I couldn't find it. But I didn't put it deep enough.

I collapse backward so the water supports my head, so that I am floating just over the surface of the earth, a hair's breadth from unity. I want it, this total awareness of the land. *Come. Consume me.*

But fingers twist in the back of my jacket, dragging me toward the Tinani shore.

FINN WON'T LOOK at me.

But Hugh does. We've moved up the bank; he caught my horse. I'm so wet my bones seem sodden, and I've begun to shiver. But I did it. I helped Jahan escape. I protected us from the villagers.

Of course, I also blew our cover and tried to abandon my would-be friends for King Alfred's dubious sanctuary.

"Well," says Hugh, in a tight, hard voice. "Now we are in Tinan.

We'll ride up the Tinani bank to Caeris." He nods at Finn. "After you." A glance at me. "And you."

I sit my horse. I am still not going to Caeris.

"Elanna!" Hugh's temper finally bursts. He jabs a finger at Finn's back, though Finn has turned to stare at us. "Follow a simple order."

He speaks to me in Caerisian, the language I've given up. The language I don't speak, do not know.

But it comes bursting out of me all the same.

"I *won't* go home!" I shout in childish Caerisian, a little girl's Caerisian. "You can't make me."

Now that I've made this stellar showing, I begin to cry. Small, useless tears.

Finn and Hugh both sit there, watching me.

I refuse to wipe my eyes—too much like a child—so I stare at the trees through my blurring vision.

"I have one question," Hugh says. "Where did you think you were going?"

Though I shake my head, my eyes jerk to the road ahead of us.

"Tinan? Damn it!" Hugh glances at Finn. "Go ahead. We'll catch you up."

He swings off his horse and walks to me, grasping my mare's bridle. I look down into his worn face. His eyes are both stern and kind. He closes one hand over mine.

"El," he says, and the deliberate gentleness of his tone makes me feel even worse. He is trying so hard to hold down his anger. "It isn't a matter of *want*. You need to come with us. There's no other place for you. You know this."

I nod, wordless. The tears start up again, leaking from my eyes even though I will them to stop.

In a soft voice, Hugh asks, "What are you afraid of?"

The breath catches in my throat. I can't answer that. I can't tell him about Nobody, and how I betrayed them all.

Hugh's hand comes up to cover mine in silent sympathy. Then he begins to speak. The words are old and raw with memory. "*Wildegarde came, bearing a flame in her heart, her hair crowned with the pale light of stars.*"

My head jerks up. It's the poem—the words I've hidden within me for years. I stare at him. He taught me the words, didn't he? He and my old nurse? I have a sudden memory—or is it just my imagination?—of my child's voice galloping after his deep, grown-up one.

"You're not my father's spymaster," I whisper.

He smiles faintly. "No. I am his *Ollam*." His poet. The Chief Poet of Caeris. That's what Hugh is: the keeper of legends and singer of songs.

He squeezes my hand and recites the lines. "*Where she placed her foot, the earth trembled; when she raised her hand, mountains moved. The trees moved with her, the golden pine, the white ash, the ever-living cedar. Down she walked into the soft valleys of Caer-Ys, and the people came out from their dwellings to see what manner of creature moved among them, to see what threat or marvel awaited their eyes . . .*"

He looks at me, almost a challenge, and I find myself answering, the ancient, practiced words rolling supple over my tongue. I used to repeat them to myself when I lay in bed as a child, all the meaning stripped out of them and only the comfortable rhythm remaining. And maybe . . . maybe Hensey spoke them with me. Hensey, who infiltrated the palace as my father's spy. Maybe it was she who saw to it that I never forgot. "*They saw but a woman, white as snow, all grown over with leaves as a tree is.*"

Hugh takes the villagers' part: "*They said, 'What art thou?' *"

I whisper, "*She said, 'I am the wildness.' *"

"*They said, 'Why hast thou come?' *"

My horse shifts, impatient. And my words are so soft that her hooves trample them into the ground, into nothing at all.

" '*For thee.' *"

CHAPTER SEVEN

We ride along the Ard—on the Tinani side—and I twist my fingers into my horse's mane while Finn asks Hugh questions about everything from Caerisian customs to Caerisian sheep to Caerisian weather. My ears ache with talk of Caeris this and Caeris that. Finally, about midday, two days after we crossed into Tinan, Finn eagerly says to Hugh, "Is that Caeris across the river?"

"Yes. That is Caer-Ys."

Hugh pronounces it the proper way, like a caress, instead of the careless way we say the name in the south of Eren. Finn reins in his horse to stare beneath the overhanging boughs of the firs. I watch him. There is something golden about him—maybe it's his hair, but maybe it's his hope. I want to shudder away from it, and at the same time I can't stop looking.

A frown is falling over his face, chasing away the boyish enthusiasm. Hugh's gone on ahead, and for the moment, the two of us are alone. My heart kicks and I tell it to be quiet. I don't know what Finn expects of me. Maybe he doesn't expect anything.

"I thought it would look different, somehow," Finn says. He doesn't look back at me, but the words seem to be offered in my direction. "But it looks the same as all the land we've been passing through."

I say nothing. What is there to say? It does look the same.

Now he swivels around on his horse with a creak of the saddle leather. His forehead is still wrinkled. "It seems as if we've been waiting to see Caeris so long. All our lives."

I press my lips together. I don't see why he wants to include me in this statement. We are not the same.

"I grew up in Ida," Finn says. "Sometimes I feel I don't belong here."

He waits, still twisted around in his saddle, as if he expects me to chirp an agreement. Or maybe he's fishing for sympathy.

"That's because you don't belong here," I say. "Neither of us does."

He looks at me. I look back at him. I don't want to be his friend. No. That's a lie.

I'm afraid to be his friend. I'm afraid of what he will expect of me if I offer him even a grin.

But he's the one who muscles his mouth into a smile, and my jaw tightens. That's my smile—the one I wore when I faced Loyce and the Butcher, the expression that allowed me to pass through the royal court.

Finn turns and urges his horse ahead. But it's too late—too late to pretend that our conversation didn't happen. Too late to pretend I didn't see myself in him.

AFTER THREE MORE days of slow going, we glimpse the mountains. The hills have turned high, tumbling into one another, and through the gaps between them I see the distant peaks of the Tail Ridge, snow crusting the horizon. Hugh doesn't call it the Tail Ridge, vaguely sneering, like everyone in Laon. He says it's the *Bal an-Dracan*—the Dragon's Mouth.

Which makes me shiver.

As we ride on, Hugh tells us stories, legends of dragons sleeping beneath the snow in the highest mountain peaks, taking in an orphan child whom they called Wildegarde. Wildegarde, who came down into Caeris and woke the land, who could look through the eyes of a tree or a bird, a brook or a stone. "She lived in the time before Eren and Caeris were divided into two nations, centuries before the Paladisans conquered us. In the time when the Children of Anu were new to our lands, having followed our gods here."

It should not surprise me that Hugh still believes in the old gods—

after all, he told me himself that's one of the reasons the Caerisians want their own king—and that even Finn is nodding eagerly. I think of Loyce saying with scorn, *Those stinking shepherds and their legends of Father Dagod. As if any god would think* Caeris *a heaven on earth!*

Hugh must sense my skepticism. "When the Paladisans conquered Eren and Caeris, they tried to drive all memory of our gods out. But we clung to them in the deep valleys of Caeris; the mountain people held on to them. In any case, the Paladisans weren't here long enough to eradicate our beliefs." He laughs. "Their empire had grown too large for them to control. One too many rebellions in Ida, too much corruption at the court, and they had to pull out."

"And so Eren conquered you instead," I say crossly. "Because Caeris was weak and disorganized, and easy prey to attack. They took your capital in a single day, and you should be glad. Otherwise Caeris would just be an impoverished backwater. What sort of economy would you have? What sort of life would you live? Oh, I know, you'd have your gods and your language and your customs, but what's that worth if you can't even govern yourselves?"

Hugh turns in his saddle to study me. "I didn't think it was possible for them to have fed you so many lies."

"This is the truth," I snap. "I've had the best tutors in the kingdom."

Finn stares between us, his eyebrows rising.

"The truth," Hugh says, "used to give you nightmares. You used to run downstairs from your bed, begging your mother to hide you from the Ereni monsters come to murder you in your sleep."

A pulse of rage surges through me. I am no longer five years old; all the nightmares I've ever had come from *him* and what they did to me by letting Antoine Eyrlai claim me as a hostage. "Tell me your version of the truth, then, Hugh. And I'll compare it with what *I've* been *taught.*"

Hugh reins in his horse, causing Finn's to skitter off into the shrubs. Reaching out, he grabs my horse's bridle. I start to protest, but the look on his face silences me.

"Let's start at the beginning," he says. "You know that Caeris and Eren used to be one nation?"

I roll my eyes. "Until the rival queens, Rionach and Tierne, four hundred years ago. Yes. Rionach was elder and might have ruled both, but Tierne claimed Eren for herself, because she knew her sister was greedy and shortsighted." My Ereni tutor had a dramatic account in which Tierne cried out, *Let my sister be queen over a nation of cowherds and thieves if that is what she desires!*

Hugh says under his breath, "Of course she was." He sighs. "Queen Rionach kept the traditions—the tripartite division of rule, most notably—while Tierne scorned those customs and claimed the crown belonged to herself alone. That is why Eren has devolved into a kingdom ruled by absolutist monarchs who have no responsibility to their own people."

"Well, Rionach was a fool," I shoot back, "because that tripartite division is what got her nation conquered."

Hugh looks at me. "Do you know what the tripartite division *is*?"

"Of course—it's the monarch of Caeris and the—the—"

"The steward of the land and the warden of the mountains," Finn supplies. "By keeping the sacred number of three, they maintained a balance against any one of them gaining too much power."

I glare at him.

Hugh resumes his history lesson. "So, a little less than two centuries after Eren and Caeris divided into two nations, the Paladisans conquered us. That is, except for the *Bal an-Dracan,* because the mountain folk possess a magic even Paladis's legions could not overcome. Under Paladisan rule, though it lasted barely a generation, the tripartite division was officially abolished and the role of *Caveadear,* steward of the land, nearly forgotten. Thus Ossian, the last king of Caeris, was both monarch and steward of the land."

"But the Paladisans withdrew because their empire had grown too large and too many insurgents clamored for power in Ida," I say impatiently. "And their gods had already declared magic an abomination, saying the earth must be cleaned of sorcery. So Caeris and Eren were scourged with the witch hunts and the inquisition, like all former Paladisan subject states."

Hugh nods; at least there's one piece of history we seem to agree on. "And in the wake of the Paladisan withdrawal, the Ereni conquered Caeris."

"In one day," I gloat.

"No, El," he snaps. "The Ereni wrote the history, you know. They've cast it the way they want to see themselves, as the victors, instead of a miserable force who clawed their way through Caeris—over many *months* of fighting against the land itself—to murder the royal family, the Dromahairs, on the footsteps of Barrody Castle."

My blood runs cold, despite myself. So this is why I used to have nightmares.

He's looking at me. "The king's heir, a little girl named Brigit, hid beneath her bed when the invading army came. But the Eyrlais dragged her out and slaughtered her."

The hair stands up on my arms. This is the way I tried to hide from Antoine's men when they came for me as a child. My nurse must have known it was doomed, but she urged me to it anyway.

"King Ossian escaped the bloodbath," Hugh says, "but he died in the mountains. There have been no stewards of the land since, and no kings. Only the warden of the mountain remains, and he rarely appears in the lowlands."

I find it difficult to speak or meet his eyes. In my history lessons, there was nothing about a massacre on the footsteps of Barrody Castle. There was nothing about how the entire ruling family died out; they simply did.

"The Ereni butchered whole villages," Hugh goes on. "They forbid us to practice our magic and worship our gods and speak our language—though those things are now merely frowned upon. They killed our chiefs and gave away our lands to their own people—most of whom never even set foot in Caeris. They let in the witch hunters, who tortured and killed our sorcerers. But," he adds with grim satisfaction, "the Valtais have hung on."

"And they still want to make kings," I say sourly.

"Ever since Ossian's death, the Valtais have kept the title of steward of the land. Kept it alive, until a new steward could wake the land." Hugh gives me a searching look. "By tradition, one of the steward's duties was to acclaim the new king or queen of Caeris. Now that right belongs to your father."

Finn shifts in his saddle. I ignore him.

"It's a sacred duty," Hugh adds. "Naming the king."

I allow myself a thin smile. "Then no wonder my father is so eager to do it." I nudge my horse into a trot, leaving them behind on the trail.

As if I can so easily escape the net my father has cast.

THE NEXT MORNING, Hugh calls a halt on the riverbank. From the narrow, rambling track we've been riding, he plunges off the trail, apparently into a hazel thicket. Finn follows, and after a moment, whether I will or not, my horse plods after. Hazels jab at my arms, at the mare's belly. I almost rein her in and force her around.

But there's nothing for me to run back to now. She plods ahead into scrubby pine.

The trail, such as it is, plunges down to the river—a rocky, unused ford. Looking across to the other side, I don't see anything but trees, a collage of russet oaks and dark evergreens. No trails lead into Caeris.

Caeris.

My mare, sensing my nerves, prances, though I try to hold her back. Hugh looks over his shoulder: Finn has already churned into the water.

I bare my teeth in a sort of grin. "Coming."

Hugh nods. I nudge the mare after him. The water splashes up, cold, toward my face. My hands are shaking.

I clench the reins hard as the mare steps onto the rocky Caerisian soil. My body seems to swell; my heart is too full. I gasp. The others are well past me, so I let myself sag low enough to hug the mare's neck, the only comfort I have. A sweat has broken out all over my skin. I want to fall to the ground.

Am I so afraid of going home?

Grinding my teeth, I push myself upright and urge the horse forward. I can endure my father; I can endure Caeris. I have no choice.

Ahead of me, in a clearing surrounded by oaks, Hugh turns to Finn, drawing a dagger from his boot. Finn's eyes have widened, whether in anticipation or fear I can't tell. He wets his lips. Forces a smile.

I fold my arms tight over my chest and let my face form a scowl. Given my shaking, perspiring limbs, it's not hard.

Hugh pauses and glances at me. "Lady Elanna, would you care to go first?"

I purse my lips. "I am appalled that a man of your intelligence enslaves himself to such superstition."

Hugh merely raises an eyebrow and turns back to Finn, who swallows. "The story goes," he says, "that the land knows who walks on it. When we cross into Caeris, we make a sacrifice. One drop of blood. To make ourselves one with the land."

Or, I think nastily, *to promote a fanatic devotion to a country that no longer exists.*

Hugh pricks the tip of one finger with the dagger's blade, then squeezes his fingertip until a single drop of blood wells and falls at his feet.

Into the earth of Caeris.

A contraction presses through the ground beneath my feet, a single pulse rocking up into my body. My heart jerks. Fresh sweat breaks out on my forehead.

I study the men. They don't seem to feel anything. Finn takes the dagger, pricking his finger now, just as Hugh did, his lip caught in his teeth. He shakes his finger, unpracticed, and the blood smears before he gets a drop to fall to the earth.

This time, the tremor echoes up into my knees. A bird flies away from a nearby tree, crying out. I fold my arms tighter. The strange, swollen feeling floods back into my chest, and I can't tell if it's fear or something worse than fear.

Hugh has tears in his eyes. But he only says, "The earth of Caer-Ys receives your blood."

Finn seems overcome. He drops to his knees and actually kisses the ground, the crown of his red-gold hair gleaming. My heart starts pounding under my breastbone. I cough and look away.

Finn rises. Hugh blinks the tears from his eyes. He offers me the dagger again. "Lady Elanna." Not in question, but in expectation.

Finn bares his teeth in a grin. "It's not so bad, El."

The earth trembles underneath my feet, a strange steady humming, a beat. I think about the stones coming alive on the Hill of the Imperishable, and I know I do not want to drop blood onto this land, the land that seems to recognize my very body. I don't know how the earth will respond if I do—I don't know how my body will respond—but I know what Hugh and Finn will say. I know what they'll expect.

I wave Hugh away. "No, thank you. I don't indulge in such barbaric customs."

THE LAND ON this side of the river looks much the same as Tinan—steep hills, verdant moss, and great stands of trees—but every part of my body beats with the knowledge that we are in Caer-Ys now.

I don't remember this place at all.

We ride through a dense oak wood—the Valtai Oaks, Hugh tells us, as if we should have some idea what this means. We've crossed onto my father's lands. He lives in exile in his own country, in the house where (Hugh tells me) I was born. But I do not remember the oak wood or the parkland that we pass into. Night is falling as we come in sight of a sprawling house—all gables and colliding roofs and the stumpy shape of a defensive tower, lit against the dark-blue sky. Lights glow in the windows, though no one emerges to greet us. We pass a bank of empty windows—a salon or ballroom—and come around into the paved courtyard.

A man emerges from a doorway. He wears green-and-white livery—my father's colors. *"Ollam?"*

"I'm here," says Hugh, swinging down from his horse and clapping the other man on the back, while the other exclaims with delight.

My heart is rattling in my chest, but somehow I get off the horse. Finn stands next to me, unusually quiet. "Do you remember this place?" he asks me in an undertone.

"No," I say shortly.

He swallows so loudly that I hear the click of his throat. "Elanna—" But though it sounds like a question, he can't seem to pull out any other words. I have an urge to reach for his hand and hold tight, as if we're two children about to be in trouble with our parents.

Then Hugh says, "This way, please," and the moment passes. Stableboys have taken the horses, and we follow Hugh into the orange warmth of the house. A woman hurries to us through the foyer whose ceiling towers three stories up to an open oculus. I glimpse tapestries, several marble statues of gods and heroes, a gilded bronze chandelier strung with rock crystals.

Of course, my father is rich. The richest man in Caeris.

The kingmaker.

We follow the woman—Neave Thiebault, the housekeeper—up an impressive staircase to the upper floor, where even the hallway is richly carpeted, the rugs woven in traditional Caerisian designs, knot work with stylized herons and dogs chasing stags. You hear all the time how Caeris is a poor nation of shepherds and cowherds and fishermen, but so far you wouldn't know it in my father's house.

Neave Thiebault opens the door on a room full of conversation, men's and women's voices, which stop as she walks in, followed by Hugh.

Finn is in front of me, but he hesitates. His shoulders shift forward; he seems to be bracing himself. On the other side of him, I hear Hugh speaking Caerisian in the room beyond, and a man's deep, ringing voice answering him. There was music, but it's stopped.

I touch Finn's shoulder blade. He startles, looking back at me, and I give him the most confident nod that I can. I know how terrifying it is to walk into a room full of strangers.

The flicker of a smile touches his mouth. He swallows again. "Thank you," he whispers.

Then he lifts his head. He puts back his shoulders, and even out here, the glow of the lamps burnish him and shine him into gold. He looks simple and brave, like a prince out of a storybook, his shoulders just broad enough to carry the burden of his people.

He steps through the door.

My palms are wet and cold. A tremor runs up the bottom of my arms. But I, too, have to move forward. I have to step into the room.

I do—but I may as well have stayed outside. All the pounding terror leads to nothing.

Because no one sees me. They're all looking at Finn. He seems haloed, his ruddy-gold hair aglow, even in his rough traveling clothes. All conversation has ceased.

A man stands across from Finn. There are others in the room, but at the moment I see only him: He seems to occupy all the available space, to press out into all the corners, as if he has orchestrated everything—this room, these people, Finn's arrival. He's a tall, lanky man, with a thick curling thatch of chestnut hair touched by gray, and brown eyes the color of my own. He wears a somber velvet coat to the knee, unbuttoned to reveal the red silk waistcoat underneath.

Everyone in the room is looking at Finn, but I can't take my eyes off my father.

He doesn't even see me.

"The prince is come," he says at last, his resonant voice filling the room. "The prince is come from across the sea."

I close my eyes. I can no longer stop my ears and pretend I don't understand, that I don't know who Finn is. I knew the moment I heard his voice in the darkness that night outside the city.

My father drops to one knee. Everyone else in the room does the same, even Hugh. Even Neave Thiebault.

Finn says something, but I don't hear what it is. A buzzing fills my ears. I'm backing out of the room, back into the blessed dimness of the hallway, and then I'm walking away from that room and the boy they want to make their king.

MY FEET SEEM to remember this place even if my mind doesn't. I come to a stop where the corridor jogs to the right, into what must be private apartments—my parents' rooms?—while to the left another stair curls away upstairs. My body lurches toward the stairs, and I actually have to stop myself with a hand on the wall. What am I doing?

There's a sound coming from one of the rooms. I freeze. All of my muscles tense. I want to clamp my hands over my ears. I want to scream.

It's music. The tender sound of a pianoforte, with all the heart-ache being wrenched out of it.

I don't want to hear this.

The hallway is silent; the twist in the walls blocks me from sight of the room holding Finn and my father. Slowly, as if the strains of the melody pull me down, I sink to the floor. She must be on the other side of the wall, and it seems I can feel the vibrations of the piano, just as I did when I was a little girl, when I would lie down underneath it and feel the humming press up through the floorboards into my spine. I can imagine it, even: the plain pine underneath, the outside of the instrument painted teal blue, with bunches of flowers.

I bring my knees to my chest, close my eyes. The music hums through me.

"Excuse me?"

There's a maid standing in front of me, a blanket folded over her arm and astonishment on her face. "Who are you? Can I help you?"

"I—" I pull myself to my feet, wiping my face. "I'm—I came with Hugh—"

The door to my left opens. The music has stopped. She's standing in the doorway, more fragile than I remember—but what do I remember? I remember nothing. She wears a shapeless velvet gown, her hair is loose, like a dark animal. "Jenny, I thought I heard you out here. Will you bring me a cup of—" She stops, seeing me. I am so stricken, I know I'm staring, but I can't look away from her. Her eyes are large, black, widening at me. Her skin is a shade darker than mine, a deep sepia brown. She grasps the collar of her gown in some alarm. "Who's this?"

She doesn't know me. My mother doesn't know me.

Of course she doesn't. Why would she? She abandoned me to Antoine Eyrlai fourteen years ago.

"This . . . person . . . came with Hugh Rathsay, my lady."

My mother leans out, excited. "Hugh's back?"

"Yes, he—"

"Brought your prince," I say, the words exploding from my mouth with shocking bitterness. "The prince from across the sea. The one you've been waiting for."

My mother blanches. Then her lips tighten. I expected her to burst with joy like all the others, but instead she seems almost angry. Almost as angry as I am. "He wasn't supposed to come until spring."

"Well," I say, "he couldn't wait any longer. He was so eager to prove his worth to Caeris that he persuaded a Paladisan lord to smuggle him into the country."

My mother looks at me for the first time—really sees me. "You're a girl."

"I know." The maid laughs. "I thought she was a boy at first, too."

I look between them. The anger tastes bitter in my mouth, as if it's turned to grief instead. "You really don't know who I am, do you, Mother?"

She turns as white as paper.

"I'm Elanna," I say. "Your daughter."

A LOW SOUND pours out of my mother's throat—like she's been kicked, like she's in pain. Then she's in front of me, her hands lifting my face, touching my hair. She commands the maid to bring a light. I stand, unable to move, while she looks at me, while her eyes fill with tears and her lips move soundlessly over a prayer. She speaks in Baedoni, in the language of her home country, and the sound of it falls on my ears with a painful gentleness. It must be the language she spoke to me when I was a child. I flinch at the rhythm of it.

Then she reaches down and takes my cold hands in hers, folding them against her stomach. Slowly she pulls me against her. I'm crying again, too, now—stupid, heavy tears, my nose running, my mouth open. She releases me, stares into my face, and embraces me again. And again. Her body is strong and slender and she smells of roses and spice.

"Every day," she's saying. "I prayed—every day."

Even the maid is crying.

"But you never came for me," I say. "You left me there. You left me—"

"No," she says fiercely. "I was always with you. Every day. Every moment. I am your mother, and I was with you."

CHAPTER EIGHT

I wake to sunlight dappling the rosebuds embroidered onto the coverlet on my bed, and a strange feeling warming my chest. I can't place it, and I lie there for a while until I finally realize that it is happiness.

Then I remember my father and the idiotic smile I'm wearing fades. My father, and the prince from across the sea.

I kick my way out of the blankets twisted around me. The ormolu clock on the mantel reads eleven. I've slept late from exhaustion and no doubt missed breakfast. A platter loaded with pastries and fruit and boiled eggs sits on a side table, along with a swaddled pot of tea—still hot. It occurs to me that we got in too late for supper last night, and though my mother fed me shortbread, it wasn't enough to last fourteen hours of sleep. I gorge on the food until I think I'm going to be sick, then cautiously open the bedroom door. The hall stands empty, lit by daylight from the distant atrium, brushing over the gilded frames of paintings on the walls. A woman is talking in a nearby room, and somewhere down the hall I hear my mother's touch on the piano. Does she play *all* the time?

There's a sudden rumble of male voices, and my father emerges from a room down the way, Finn and Hugh behind him.

I close the door. My palms flash hot and damp.

Some helpful maid left a gown draped over a chair for me, with a flounced underskirt to go over one of those hideous old-fashioned stays that squeeze your whole middle and breasts together in a rigid cylinder. I much prefer—and only ever wear—the Paladisan style, shorter and softer, so that I can breathe and bend over all the way. I dig through the cedar chests and armoire, but I can't find the clothes I wore here. They must have taken them to be cleaned. Not even a decent pair of trousers or a reasonable coat—I've been supplied with a lady's wardrobe, all frills and fluffs and pastel pinks. Don't they realize I'm a scholar as well as a lady of fashion?

My own stays have disappeared with the rest of my clothes. I give up and put on the flounced underskirt beneath a morning-robe; no stays. I can't lace these bulky stays up myself anyway, even if I wanted to. At least they supplied me with a decent pair of shoes— brown leather and sturdy around my ankles. Instead of a proper coat, there's only a sort of capelet, but nothing can be done about that. I thrust a cap over my messy hair and peek once more into the corridor. No one.

I edge into the hall. Mother is still playing her piano. There are other voices, but no one around. I decide to go outside. I make my way down the grand stairs, not looking behind me, even though the high oculus in the foyer begs to be stared at.

I let myself out into the autumn day. It is light and bright and glorious.

The front drive makes a neat sweep before me—a party of horse-men rides toward the house through the distant elms—while off to my left, among the oaks, only the wind reigns. I run to the trees, my feet kicking through the leaf litter.

A tremor runs through the ground, like the memory of the earth's heartbeat. I stop short, the breath catching in my throat. Tears spring to my eyes. I want to hear the sound of the earth so badly. I want to feel it in my bones. In my heart.

Yet if I do, it means I choose Caeris; I choose my father and his revolution.

And I can't be a figurehead for the father who forfeited me like a pawn in his play for a Caerisian king.

I'm standing beneath the wide arms of the oaks. A hush has set-tled around me. Looking up into the interlacing tree branches, I seem to shrink. I'm a child again, holding my breath in wonder at the enormity of the forest around me. A line of mushrooms scrabble up a nearby ash tree and, high above, songbirds make curious calls. The air smells moss-sweet and autumn-dry.

A wild exuberance builds in my chest.

I glance behind me to be sure no one's watching—none of my father's lackeys, eager to report that I do, in fact, like this place. That part of me still loves it with a child's uninhibited joy. Then I run. I gallop through the woods until even the outline of my father's roof has disappeared, until the ground pitches upward toward a hill.

I almost step on it. White, delicate, fringed: *Amanita virosa,* pressing up through the leaves.

Rage burns through me. I lift my foot to step on it—deliberately.

A single mushroom has ruined my life.

Branches snap behind me. I drop my foot in surprise and see a young woman staring at me from the other side of a pine tree. She's tall and blond, with eyelids so pale they're almost pink, and her neat, square-necked gown is woven in a pattern of the same color. She holds a basket stuffed with pinecones and neatly clipped boughs.

"You must be Elanna," she exclaims. "You came with the prince. Is he as admirable as they—" Her gaze is open and eager, but now she flushes and presses her lips together as if embarrassed.

Maybe my stare has turned into a glare. I try to put the proper amount of civility into my "Yes?" but I'm not sure I succeed.

"I'm Sophy," she says, still flushed. "Sophy . . . Dunbarron. I heard you'd come home."

Home. I *am* glaring. I look at the contents of her basket, willing myself to breathe.

Sophy's gaze follows mine. "Oh! I was collecting things. We're making wreaths today, so they'll last all winter."

Wreaths. What a useful occupation, with my father about to start a war.

"Are you lost?" she asks. "I'll show you back."

"I'm not lost," I begin, but stop. I can't really say that I came out to remember my magic, to see what I could manage to do with my power. What's the use? My father killed the king with an amanita and is letting me suffer the blame. I kick the mushroom with my foot, scattering it into fleshy white shards on the forest floor. And then I follow Sophy Dunbarron back toward the house.

* * *

WE HEAR THE shouting before we see them. A boy's high clear voice: "Take your own horse, you shit-faced southerner!"

Sophy drops her basket. We exchange a glance, then we're both running toward the front drive, where the shouting came from. Just before we burst through the encircling elms onto the gravel, I grab Sophy's arm and drag her to safety behind a tree trunk. Our shoulders press together. We peer around opposite sides of the tree, to where a fight is breaking out on the front steps of my father's mansion.

For a long moment—too long—my mind struggles to make sense of the confusion of bodies. Brown, green, blue, gold. A thrown punch. A stableboy spitting at a man a head taller than him. The sharp *ring* as a man in blue-and-gold livery draws a sword.

Blue-and-gold livery. The queen's men.

The royal guard is here.

"Ow," Sophy whispers, and I realize my fingers have tightened into her arm. I let go, digging my fingernails into the tree instead.

The boy who spat is now getting his head bashed in. The royal guardsman strikes him, hard, across the chin, and again, and again. More guardsmen hit more stableboys; more stableboys hit guardsmen. Maids have run out from the kitchen door, three of them, swinging heavy black objects. Frying pans, a kettle. Men run behind them in a flash of green-and-white livery, their swords and bayonets shining—my father's guards.

The spitting boy falls to the ground and lies very still. Too still.

Sophy draws her breath in with a hiss. Before I can stop her, she's running out into the melee, unarmed, shouting. "Stop this! Stop this at once!"

A guardsman throws a punch into her stomach. It brings her up short. She staggers around, gasping, heaving.

This is not my fight. It is not.

But I'm running anyway.

On the periphery of my vision, I realize the ash trees Sophy and I ran through have begun to move, to dip and sway, as if a great wind buffets them. A flight of birds swoops up over the mansion, dives down toward us. I smell earth in my nostrils.

I grasp Sophy by the waist and pull her toward safety. "You need to get Hugh. Somebody with my father's authority." I push her toward the house so hard she stumbles. But then she picks up her feet and goes.

Most people just need orders. Then they'll do the sensible thing.

The ground trembles under my feet.

The fallen stableboy is still lying there, amid the fighting. I dart between the fighters, past a maid cracking a pan into a guardsman's ribs. The boy lies with his head twisted to the side, blood smearing his mouth and nose. Gods, no. He can't be dead. I fall to my knees, feel his neck for a pulse. Sluggish, but there. Another stableboy trips over the fallen one's legs.

The ground is shaking and the trees are billowing. I hook my hands under the boy's armpits and drag him, one step at a time, toward the doors. A stray punch glances off my cheek. I move backward, full-bodied, into someone else. I grind my teeth together and keep moving. A guardsman flings a punch into my eye, then trips over the boy's knees.

Stone beneath us. The doorway, finally. The boy makes a gurgling sound. The blood bubbles in his nostrils. "Damn you, Belenus," I hiss, and then I curse myself for using the name of the Caerisian healing god, not the familiar Idaean one. Hugh's stories must be getting in my head. The boy needs a doctor, not a botanist. I yank off my morning-robe and stuff it under his head, not even caring that it leaves me in a chemise and underskirt, practically naked. My skin burns and splits into cold shards.

It's begun to rain. And they're all still fighting. For what?

I surge to my feet. "Stop this!" But my shouting just sinks in with the other voices, buried beneath the roar of the wind. The day has turned black.

Not my doing. It can't be—but of course it is.

I widen my stance. The wind doesn't buffet my clothes alone: I feel it in my body, a howl spreading through my lungs. As it sweeps through me, I know what to do. I clap my hands together, and thunder rumbles. It rumbles from the sky down into the earth, burrowing, ferocious, shaking and tumbling up through my bones—through everyone's bones. The fighters have fallen back from one another, except for two locked in a kind of embrace.

Some of them are staring at me. Others turn to look. A guardsman swears. Thunder trembles in my legs. My hair rises up, wild, an aureole around my head, just as it did when I saw the poster in the village. I am electric, ablaze.

Lightning flares.

I feel its heat through my body, jolting me back to common sense. What have I done? I've just shown the Ereni I'm here. I've just proven, before the queen's own guards, that those charges of witchcraft are true.

A hand grasps my shoulder—Sophy. I'm almost grateful to see her.

Until I realize her face is white, and the hand on my shoulder cold and clammy. "You need to come inside. Now."

A HUSH LIES over the house, despite the storm booming outside. Sophy's hand tightens on my wrist. From the rooms behind the grand staircase, a voice echoes, a man's, sonorous and rising.

My father's.

Sophy releases a breath, and I realize I'm holding mine, too.

"Come on." She tugs me toward the staircase, but I dig my heels in.

"We've got to smuggle you out of here," Sophy says fiercely. "We can't let them take you."

Smuggle me out?

There's a flurry at the top of the stairs and the housekeeper comes running down, breathless in her flounced cap, the keys on her belt jangling. She slows, seeing us, and whispers loudly, "Lady El! Come up at once. We'll get you and the prince out of danger."

So they're getting Finn out of here, too.

I almost let Sophy drag me up the stairs. I almost let them take me to sanctuary elsewhere. It would be almost a relief to go into hiding—from my father if no one else. I don't need to meet him; I don't want him to look me in the eyes and say it's me he's been waiting for.

The door bursts open behind us: one of the stableboys. "Domnall's almost *dead*. He needs a doctor."

But I am so tired of running away.

Sophy's grip had loosened at the boy's words, and I wrench my wrist free. Before she can stop me, I'm marching beneath the high oculus to the receiving room beyond. It is a white-and-gold salon, delicate and regal. My father stands at the center, seeming to occupy the whole room.

But another man challenges him for that position. A man in gold-and-blue livery, a bowlegged man who carries a cane, whose hoarse voice cuts beneath my father's.

"Your *beliefs* do not amount to *evidence,* Your Grace, and the evidence is against your daughter."

I go cold. I should turn back. I should run.

It's the Butcher.

"And what makes you think my daughter is here?" Like last night, my father hasn't even seen me yet. I might as well be a shadow in the doorway. "This would be too obvious a place to run, for a regicide cunning enough to poison the king with a mushroom."

The way he says it makes it obvious he thinks it's funny. And maybe it is, if you don't value your life.

"Lady Elanna is here," the Butcher says. "Where else can she go? No one else will welcome her now the world knows her as a witch *and* a regicide."

"She did not kill the king."

My father speaks in a matter-of-fact voice, firm and certain. I catch my breath, waiting for him to say what I know he must. What he will, because he has no shame. He considers it another strike for Caeris. The king's death, the confusion, the blame, the prince from across the sea. His daughter, a sorceress.

I wait for my father to name himself the murderer, to proudly own the blame.

But he doesn't.

"I am afraid that decision must be left to a judge and jury," says the Butcher, "although running away does rather diminish her chances of getting off. She will be well treated until her execution, I assure you. I dislike cruelty."

This is so absurd—and so patently untrue—that it shakes me from my shock. Antoine used to boast that the Butcher has never showed a scrap of humanity. I take a step forward.

"Perhaps we might come to an agreement," the Butcher adds. "Lady Elanna has helped us before."

I freeze. I think my father does, too, just for a moment, though his face remains a stern, polite mask. But I see how his whole body goes still.

"Oh, yes." The Butcher is enjoying this, damn him. He links his hands behind his back. "What put a stop to your last attempted insurrection? Who told us the Pretender Euan Dromahair was about to land on Caerisian soil? It was a child who gave away your revolution, Lord Ruadan." He pauses. "One should never entrust children with great power."

To my father's credit, his voice remains level. Close to calm. "I never plotted against the king. I was exonerated."

"Indeed, you are too clever to let any direct evidence condemn you. But willing enough to let us keep the daughter who betrayed your cause."

My father's lips tighten. He says nothing.

It's true, then. He's known all along, all these years. That is why he did nothing. That is why they never came to rescue me, why he won't even look at me now that I am here.

What am I even doing in this place?

I seem to be outside my body, at once present and separate. I watch myself move forward. I observe as I open my mouth.

"Then, Lord Gilbert, I give myself up."

THE BUTCHER SWINGS around and I fall into my body, my heart flaring white. It pounds in my throat, but my hands clench each other, cold.

My father sees me now.

Everyone sees me now: my mother, Hugh, the others gathered behind them.

I clench my hands in my skirt. I force myself to meet the Butcher's eyes.

He gives a courtier's smile. "Lady Elanna." A nod at my face. "That's going to turn purple."

I had forgotten that one of the guardsmen struck me. I bare my teeth in a smile. "You ought to train your guardsmen better, then, sir. They're brawling with my father's stableboys."

The Butcher clucks his tongue, but at the same time he's reaching into his pockets. One hand emerges holding a pistol. He cocks it at my face.

The other object he holds is far more dangerous: a small, clear quartz stone.

I swallow hard. Already I can hear the small stone humming— a high-pitched whine, just beneath the level of my hearing. Witch stones, they're called. The witch hunters used them during the witch hunts, to track down witches and drive them mad. I prayed I'd never see one in person.

The world knows I'm a witch, now. I've given the game up myself.

Stretching out his arm, the Butcher walks toward me, the pistol pointed at my head and the witch stone held against his chest. It is just like what happened when I was a little girl. Just like every terror I've had since, imagining it would happen again.

I close my eyes.

Boot heels ring on the parquet floor, and a warmth moves in front of me. I look up at my father's back.

He's standing between me and the Butcher.

Between me and the pistol.

Between me and the witch stone.

"You will have to kill me first, if you want to take her from here," he says.

I think I'm going to collapse.

"Lord Ruadan." The Butcher explodes a sigh. "You are obstructing the queen's justice. I could very well have you arrested, too—"

My father swings around to face me. We are a breath apart. I want to shrink back.

"Elanna," he says, "did you murder the king?"

The word sticks in my throat. I force it out. "No."

"Do you know who did?"

"No."

He turns back to the Butcher, snapping his fingers. "There you have it. She didn't do it. She doesn't know who did. You will leave her here and return to the queen, saying you received her testimony and deemed her innocent."

The Butcher raises his brows. "Will I?"

"Oh, yes," says my father, "or Elanna will see to it that you don't return to Laon at all."

My heart leaps. He means my magic. I knew it. Already, he's using it—and me.

The Butcher's mouth twitches down. They stare at each other for a long minute, then the Butcher lowers his pistol. He thrusts the witch stone back into a pocket.

He walks past us toward the door. But at the threshold, he pauses and looks back.

"You realize how I must treat you now, Lord Ruadan," he says. "There are many ways to betray the crown."

"Then," my father says, "I am a traitor."

THE SOUND OF the front door closing behind the Butcher echoes through the house. My father turns to me. He puts a warm, solid hand on my shoulder. Our eyes meet. His are a deep brown, flecked with gold, just like mine.

The line of his mouth deepens. I almost speak, but what is there to say? This time, he saved my life. This time, he stepped between me and the gun.

I don't know my father. Not at all.

Still, he's ready to use me for his purposes, willing to manipulate the power I have. I swallow.

He turns back to the room, still clasping my shoulder. I see a press of unfamiliar Caerisian faces, along with my mother and Hugh. Hugh's face is set, stern. My mother looks troubled. She's holding her elbows, the fingers of one hand playing a rapid melody on her upper arm.

Father speaks to Hugh, but the words are for us all.

"Light the fires on the hills. We're going to war against the queen."

A thrumming shock runs through me. Just like that, we're at war with Eren, with Loyce.

Did I think *we*?

Scattered applause shakes through the assembly. Hugh doesn't clap, but he does say in his dependable voice, "It will be done."

But my mother has put her back to us. Her shoulders hunch; she seems shrunken. Without a backward glance, she walks out of the salon.

FINN TAKES THE news less well than I would have expected. He looks from my father to me, his nostrils flared. A muscle works in his jaw. He seems to be struggling too hard against some emotion to speak.

My father and I came up here together, by mutual, unspoken consent. It turns out Neave Thiebault hid Finn in the old nursery— a dusty, lifeless room where I must have spent my forgotten childhood. Finn shifts, and his foot knocks against a rocking horse, its bridle painted bright red. Another object I don't recognize.

"I thought you'd be brandishing the Dragon," I say to Finn, referring to Caeris's flag, long since forbidden by the Eyrlais, but not forgotten. It shows a dragon rampant, encircled by a knot-work tree. "Running up on the high hills, summoning all of Caeris under your banner, for king and country."

He folds his arms tight across his chest. "After you confront the Butcher of Novarre? Maybe you should take it up into the hills yourself, El."

I want to step back, but my father's right behind me. Finn's not upset. He's angry.

Of course he's angry. They made him hide up here in the nursery while I tried to give myself up. We're going to war, and he wasn't there to see the moment it became inevitable.

He looks at my father. "I thought we'd have more time."

"We all thought we would have more time." My father glances at me, and in a breathless instant, shame sweeps over me. They would have had more time. We would have had more time, if not for me. If I had let Sophy and Neave smuggle us out of here, the Butcher would not have pointed a pistol at me, I would not have tried to give myself up, my father wouldn't have defended me and, by doing so, declared himself a traitor to the nation. My father, who even in his first attempted revolution was so careful that they could not condemn him by direct evidence but merely confined him to his country estate and took his daughter away.

I worry at the ring on my finger, twisting over the middle to expose the Valtai knot.

"It may not come to battle before the winter," my father is saying, "but we must be prepared. The queen has superior manpower and artillery."

"That's why Jahan came to Eren," Finn says, still with that edge to his voice. "To bring us the emperor's support. We can't go to war without the black ships from Paladis. We have to wait."

Father spreads his hands. "Loyce Eyrlai won't wait. Jahan had better send for the ships today."

The muscle jumps again in Finn's jaw. "We have to delay. He's been gathering information—writing up a report to outline the reasons why the emperor should offer us his support. He meant to put it together in one docket as soon as he got back to Laon, but I . . ."

He trails off. I look around to see the expression on my father's face. It would silence me, too.

"Your Highness." Somehow my father's deliberate politeness is worse than Finn's barely suppressed anger. "I was under the impression that the emperor had already committed to our cause—that he had already agreed to send the black ships."

For a long moment, Finn says nothing. I bite the inside of my lip. How could he lie to my father about the emperor's support?

"It's not so simple," Finn says at last, and his tone is almost belligerent. "Prince Leontius stands by us, but the emperor . . . His Imperial Majesty feels that Caerisians do not always keep their promises. He wants assurances that we will lower the tariff on goods and encourage enrollment in the imperial army—not only from my father, but from you." He swallows. "Any revolution in Caeris must take place under imperial auspices."

Imperial auspices? A shiver runs down my back. The last time the Paladisan empire involved itself in Caeris and Eren, it conquered us and ravaged our lands with witch hunts. That may have been two centuries ago, and the empire's borders have shrunk, but we all know what the emperors are like. If they believe they should have something, they take it.

My father seems to be thinking the same thing. "Do you mean that the empire means to annex us? Will we be vassals to Emperor Alakaseus?"

"No," Finn says hastily. "We will remain an allied state, as we are now. Well." He has the courage to meet my father's eyes, at least. He does not look at me. "Unless we renege on our bargain. If we use magic."

Me. He means me. "That's what Jahan's doing," I say with a gasp. The irony shocks me. "He's gathering evidence that we're not using magic."

Finn nods. He still doesn't look at me.

There is a silence. "Well," says my father, bringing his hands together. "Perhaps we shall not concern ourselves so much with the emperor just now. There is much to be done, and many in Caeris who will rise to the Dragon." An ironic glance at me. "The fires on the hills will rally supporters to come here. It's an old code. We'll send word to the mountain lords, as well; they have their own ways."

Even to me, this doesn't sound like much against Loyce's army— against the Butcher of Novarre, who has slaughtered his way to the highest command.

Finn presses his fist against the window. "We don't stand a chance without the black ships."

"We do." My father seems to be addressing me, rather than Finn. He smiles. "We have something—someone—Loyce Eyrlai does not have. Someone she'll never have."

I stare back at him, willing him not to say it, even as a strange, desperate hope tightens my throat, even as I know it will make us enemies of the emperor of Paladis himself. Part of me *wants* him to say the words, as if they can cure all the years between us, even though this is the whole reason I didn't want to come home in the first place. Even though he's already proven his willingness to use me for the power I command.

This is what I was born for. It's the whole reason I exist, the reason my father wants me back now. Because of what I am, even though I have spent years silencing the knowledge of it.

He says, "We have the steward of the land."

CHAPTER NINE

I drop onto a cushioned stool in my bedchamber and stare at the mirror over the vanity. The bruise on my eye is turning a queasy yellow, and dried blood from the fallen stableboy splatters my chemise. (The boy himself is concussed, but he'll live.) I'll look a sight at supper—not that the Caerisians will mind. They've already decided that my moment of insanity, when I tried to give myself up to the Butcher, was pure heroism.

They've also already decided I'm the true steward of the land. My father has carried the title all these years, but not the magic. And I have the magic. I've already heard the Caerisians whispering that the storm was my doing. It won't be long before rumor becomes reality for them.

A sigh unravels from within me. I wish I could talk to Jahan. I liked the way he listened to me, as if he really heard me—more than that, as if he *understood* what it's like to hold secrets buried so deep you don't even let yourself see them. As if he understands what it's like to be born for a purpose you never chose.

And I liked the way he looked at me—as if I were someone worth seeing.

I rub my eyes and blink. I seem to be seeing his reflection in the mirror. That's it; I've lost my mind.

His finger taps, and I hear it. A hard sound, fingernail against glass. I freeze.

"El?" He's talking on the other side of the mirror, though I can't hear his voice the way I hear the tap of the fingernail. Instead, I hear it in my head—oddly, without an accent. His lips move, but I hear his words in my mind. "I've been trying to reach you, but you haven't been near a mirror or anything I could speak through! Your magic must be different from mine. You didn't hear me calling your name, did you?" He grins at me, but then his gaze drops to my chest and his eyebrows lift. "Are you hurt? Where are you?"

I remember my bloody chemise and feel a dull flush spread over my face, even though I stood in front of my father, the Butcher, and a room full of strangers without embarrassment. But I'm in the intimacy of my bedroom, wearing only a chemise. In front of him, the fabric feels very thin indeed. I'm almost *naked*. What if I had started to undress, thinking myself alone? I tell myself I'm being absurd. He needs to know what's happened. My modesty is unimportant.

I explain that we're at my father's house, that we're going to war, that the blood isn't mine. That he needs to persuade the emperor to send the black ships while covering up any use we might make of magic. "And," I say, "my father's given me a new title." I clear my throat. Just preparing to say the words makes the pulse pound in my temples. "I'm the steward of the land now."

Jahan's eyes widen a fraction. He knows what this means, I realize. Finn—or someone else in the Dromahair court-in-exile—must have told him about the tripartite division of rulership, must have educated him on Caeris's history and legends.

He gives a sudden laugh, and I seem to feel the vibration of it even through the mirror. "This is more than I ever expected!"

I find I'm smiling back at him. "What do you mean?"

He just shakes his head and leans forward so his nose is almost touching the glass. It magnifies his face: I see the mole tucked alongside his nose, the tracing of lines across his forehead as his brows lift. "So, steward of the land. I suppose you won't even speak to me, now that you've been named to such a lofty position! Will I have to beg?"

"Only if you say things like that." I'm laughing. But then I think how dangerous my position is: I'm the first steward of the land in two hundred years. The first since the great witch hunts, the first since Caeris was conquered by Eren. I am a threat to everything Paladis has built.

If the emperor finds out, he'll destroy me. More than that: obliterate me.

"You'll hide this from Paladis," I say. "Won't you? You've hidden yourself all this time. You can . . ." He can hide me. I can't make myself say the words, though, ashamed of myself for hoping for his protection.

I dare to look at him, and the sympathy in his eyes makes my heart beat faster.

"It's so much power in one person," he says softly. "So much for you to bear."

As if his acknowledgment breaks a dam in me, tears start in my eyes. I've been running from this for so long. "That's why my father wants me back. Not for me. For my power."

The tears blur my vision. I can't see Jahan. I don't want to cry in front of him, or in front of a mirrored image of him. I don't cry in front of anyone. I breathe hard.

"El." Jahan's hand comes back up to the mirror, his fingertips pressing against the glass so that their tips pale.

I blink away the tears—two fall, cold tracks on my cheeks—and look at him. Our gazes touch. A heat burns up from the pit of my stomach. Catching my breath, I bring up my hand and fit my fingertips to his, one by one. It seems as great an act of courage as revealing myself before the Butcher; my very blood is singing. It's the way he's looking at me, his mouth quirked so the dimple shows, the black beat of his eyelashes as he blinks.

"But you *can* bear it," he says. "This is what you were born for, you said so yourself."

It takes me a moment to readjust to our conversation. I pull my hand from the mirror and fuss with my hair. "I don't think I can be what my father wants me to be."

"What do *you* want to be?" Jahan has dropped his hand, too, but his gaze is still intent.

I don't know that, either. For years, I've been telling myself I want to be a botanist.

But then I touched my magic again.

As if he hears my thoughts, Jahan says, "Your power is part of you. You can't run from it forever." He makes an odd expression, between a wince and a laugh. "I should know that better than anyone."

He looks away, then, as if he hears something. Behind him, I recognize the white plaster walls and elaborate moldings of the Paladisan embassy in Laon. Jahan's dressed for a formal supper in a blue brocade coat with gleaming brass buttons, fitted smoothly to his figure. Lace smothers his neck, although, in keeping with current fashion, he hasn't bothered to tie the cravat properly. It exposes the olive skin of his throat. Then I remember that he's not keeping up with current fashions—he *sets* the fashions. I wonder why he chooses to look so careless—or if carelessness is his way of showing the social conventions for what they are.

His short, mussed black hair looks so soft and thick. My fingers twitch. I want to touch his hair; I want to touch *him*.

"I have to go." He turns back with a smile and then, to my utter shock, blows me a kiss. I reach up reflexively, as if I'm going to snatch it out of the air like a child. But before I am crushed by embarrassment, the image in the mirror jostles and settles back on me, alone in my unfamiliar room, with the skin darkening around my eye.

WORD HAS SPREAD about what happened in the audience room—the Butcher's accusations, my father sacrificing himself for me. The maid who comes to help me dress for supper seems torn between shy silence and wanting to question me while she does my hair. The tight stays put me in an uneasy mood, made worse by my effort to quell the strange mix of embarrassment and longing stirred up by my conversation with Jahan. I'm not some silly chit, swooning over a man's fine looks, yet I can't stop reviewing our conversation in my head. If the glass hadn't separated us, our hands would have touched. He blew me a *kiss*. I barely hear the maid's attempts at conversation, only making the polite, appropriate noises.

The maid finishes. A weight seems to settle on my chest, and I forget Jahan. At supper, I will face the people of Caeris. I will face their expectations of me. More than that, I will face the truth of what I am, what I've spent my life trying to forget.

The maid curtsies and goes out. I'm so preoccupied I almost forget to thank her.

It's time.

I trip out of my room—literally. This underskirt and petticoats are a few inches too long; I'm told Sophy has loaned them to me. Dratted things.

Raised voices echo behind a door to my left. My parents' quarters.

Finn is talking from the other side of the hall. I hear doors thump and floors squeak as others emerge for supper, but the twist in the hall hides me from them.

My thin slippers are good for tiptoeing closer, even if the paniers make my tucked-up skirts unwieldily wide. I patter over to their door and listen.

". . . you wouldn't," my mother is saying.

Father's response is lost, a rumble. He must have his back to me.

"The risk!" Mother cries out. "Another war—and we've only just gotten her back! I don't think I can bear it—"

Another rumble from Father.

A silence.

"If it is her choice," Mother says at last. "But you can be sure it isn't mine."

A maid swings around the twist in the corridor, carrying a stack of linen. I jump and sidle away from my parents' door, pretending I was fixing a ribbon in my bunched-up skirts. A rumor that I'm a spy as well as the steward of the land and betrayer of the cause is the last thing I need.

THANKS TO MY eavesdropping, I arrive late in the drawing room. I see Hugh standing with a cluster of men and women—the people from the audience chamber today. All of them are drinking whiskey from little cut-crystal glasses. As I enter, Finn walks over to the fire, cradling a lone glass against his chest. The people in the crowd glance toward him, and, as I enter, toward me.

I choose Finn. But then, beyond him, I see Sophy sitting on a window seat between some swagged curtains, almost hidden. She's been watching Finn; her glance toward me is guilty. So I swing past Finn and go to her.

She rises to greet me. In a cream gown embroidered with pale-blue flowers, lace softening her collarbone, she looks almost regal, like the goddess Astarea, born out of sea foam. We curtsy and make the usual pleasantries, but I see her glance cut again to Finn.

"Have you met the prince?" I inquire.

As I might have expected, a flush stains her milky cheeks. If you grew up on all those tales of King Euan Dromahair and a free Caer-Ys, Finn cuts a romantic figure. He's wearing an old-fashioned knee-length scarlet justacorps with an enormous quantity of lace pooling out the sleeves. It does look rather dashing on him, since he's so tall and lean.

"I couldn't possibly." Sophy stares down at her clasped hands.

"You're here, aren't you?" I point out. If she's here, she's worthy of meeting him.

"Yes, but—" Her flush deepens. "Only as your parents' ward."

She keeps talking, but my ears have stopped, repeating the words. My parents' ward? My parents have a *ward*?

"I don't remember you from when we were children." Too late, I realize I've interrupted her.

She doesn't seem to mind. Maybe she really doesn't want to meet Finn. "You wouldn't," she says. "I only came to live here after you'd gone, when my mother died. Lord Ruadan and Lady Teofila raised me with the utmost kindness," she adds, a warmth in her voice. "As if I were one of their own."

The words strike me as hard as a blow. My parents raised Sophy. They replaced me with her.

Humiliating tears sting my eyes. Of course they'd replace the daughter who betrayed them with one who would obey. Who would owe them everything.

After all, I replaced them with Antoine Eyrlai. A man whom I seem to know less well every day.

Sophy's noticed the tears. "Oh! I didn't mean—" She digs in her sleeve to produce a handkerchief, large and sensible, like herself. "Here."

I mop under my eyes.

"That's going to be a horrid bruise," she observes. "You poor thing. You looked so brave up there."

I don't feel brave now; I feel like a fool. I press the handkerchief back into Sophy's broad, damp hand. She pats my arm. We both start to smile at each other.

"El." Finn bangs his glass into my elbow. I jump. How many times have they refilled his glass since he went over to the fire? His usually perfect hair is rumpled, and his mouth has that vague look people get when they're drinking. What's the matter with him? My father took him to task about the black ships, so he's drowning his sorrows?

He whacks me with the glass again. "Who's your friend?" With the whiskey loosening his tongue, his faint Idaean accent is turning loud, drawing out the words, thickening them. It makes it hard to forget he was born in Ida, that he doesn't know Caeris's people or her customs, despite his father's pretense of kingship.

"Sophy Dunbarron." She stares into his face as she says it, then drops into a curtsy when he only shrugs and turns to me.

"El," he says, "I've got to tell you, you look *lovely* tonight."

"Finn . . ." I'm not sure how to even start. I lower my voice. "What are you *doing*?"

He blinks. "I gave you a compliment."

"Yes, and I'm so grateful. You look very nice, too. But—"

He pats the glass against the brass buttons on his coat, letting out a tinkling sound. "The color of kings, this."

"How is King Euan, Your Highness?" Sophy asks in a loud voice, evidently trying to change the course of our conversation. Thank the gods. "Does he do well in Ida?"

"Hates it," Finn declares. A slow, deliberate wink. "But, mind you, he hates everything. Food. Sun. Books. Wars. He mostly hates that he's not actually king of anything. What'd you call him, El? King of air? Ha, ha!"

Sophy and I stare at each other and away. This is awful.

"He must be proud of you," Sophy says, her voice tight with diplomacy.

"Hmph." Finn runs the glass over the buttons again. The sound makes me wince. "Well, I'm here, running his revolution for him. Just the way he wanted."

I can't look at Sophy. My ears are burning—I'm embarrassed for Finn's sake. How many times did I want to numb myself with drink in Laon at Loyce's parties, at which I was always an unwelcome guest? But unlike Finn, I never dared for fear I would say something that could be used against me. I flounder for something to say, something to calm Finn, to steer him back to safe territory.

Too late. "It's the gout, I reckon," Finn says. "That makes my father hate everything."

Out the corner of my eye, I see Sophy catch her breath.

"Finn." I try to hold his wandering, bloodshot gaze. "You're drunk."

"That's right!" He examines his glass. "Get me another." He thrusts the glass at Sophy.

For a moment, as her lips compress and her shoulders bunch, I think she's going to hit him. I raise my arm. Sophy catches the movement and breathes through her flared nostrils. If I ever thought she considered herself of low class, I know better now.

"Of course, Your Highness," she says, her voice sharp with politeness. "Let me take that for you."

"Where does she get off so high and mighty?" Finn says crossly to me while Sophy walks away, the glass pinched between her thumb and forefinger. "Dunbarron isn't a noble name."

"She's my parents' ward, you fool." Exasperation wins out over sympathy. "You shouldn't treat her like a servant."

But he doesn't seem to hear. His gaze has gone distant, and his fingers twitch. "We went on campaign last year. Chozat. I know what it's like. I know, and I still agreed to lead this revolution. That's all I was born for. Reclaiming Caeris for my father."

The bitterness in his voice shocks me—perhaps the more so because it sounds so much like my own. I reach out to touch the brocade of his sleeve. Beneath the cloth, his arm trembles with nerves or anger, I don't know which.

He looks at me, the skin pinching between his eyebrows. "I wish Jahan was here. We survived Chozat together. I figured we could survive this." He drops his gaze. Then his hands fumble out, capturing mine in his warm, slightly damp grip. I jerk back instinctively, but Finn doesn't let go. After a moment, I let him hold me there. He meets my eyes. "You. You're the steward of the land. We can win this together."

There's a catch in his voice. I hear the desperate hope beneath all his fear.

I give him hope.

Me, Elanna Valtai. The hostage from the backwoods, the girl who trusts plants more than people. I look up into Finn's blue eyes, and I can't find my voice.

A bell rings.

"That's supper," I say, and draw my hands out of Finn's.

WE ARE PLACED next to each other at the dining table. Everyone stands behind their chairs while my father smiles around, lifting a two-handled cup in his hands. "This is a *cuach,* a sharing cup," he explains for the benefit of Finn and me. "An old Caerisian custom. All of us shall drink from it, to show there exists no animosity among us. And also in honor of Prince Fionnlach and my daughter Elanna, the steward of the land."

Everyone claps. Around the cup goes, touching lips, passing from hand to hand. Finn drinks—not that he needs another drop—and passes the cup to me. It's heavier than I thought, wide and silver. I see the flash of my reflected eyes in the liquor a moment before I drink.

The whiskey sears my stomach.

I hand it to the lord on my left, someone I don't know but who remembers me as a child. As he drinks, I look around the table. These unfamiliar faces, these unremembered people, have welcomed me back to Caeris as if they believe I can save them.

My father is watching me. I see the pride in his eyes.

Mother watches me, too. Her lips tighten, but she smiles.

I want them to look at me this way forever.

Supper unfolds the way I might have expected, with talk of the harvest and the war. Just before dessert, Hugh stands up to recite a poem in Caerisian. The words travel, fleeting and cold, down to the small of my back.

"Beautiful," Finn says, more to my breasts than to my face. He's switched to wine. It's certainly not helping to sober him up.

"Finn." I point at my eyes. "Look *here* when you're speaking to me."

He sags his chin onto one fist and stares into my face. "I could look there forever."

The lady on his other side titters.

"Get control of yourself," I hiss at him. "You're the king's son—"

"That's the problem," he retorts.

"What's wrong with you? They're going to think you don't want to lead this revolution. They're going to think you're not cut out to be king."

Finn smiles—a real smile. Mocking. "Maybe I'm not," he whispers back.

"Well, you're here, so you don't have much choice."

He points at me, and his voice drops even lower. "And you don't want to be steward of the land, do you?"

I open my mouth to say *No,* but then I stop. My father's face flashes in my mind's eye, so proud, and I think of the way Finn himself looked at me before supper, as if I were the best thing in the world. As if all his hope rested on me.

Finn leans back, looking pleased with himself.

Maybe he's not as drunk as I thought.

After supper, we retire to the drawing room, where my mother sits at the clavichord. She plays a few opening notes, and a warmth spreads through my chest. It's the song she wrote for me. Her gaze lifts, finding mine.

"I wrote this song for Elanna," she says, but though she's addressing everyone, she's speaking to me. Her fingers continue to move, stroking out chords. "When she was a child, the stones sang to her. I fashioned a melody from the sound they made. This is the land's song."

A knot has tightened my throat. I grip my hands together.

My mother nods at Sophy, who stands to sing. I didn't remember there were lyrics. I just remember the melody.

It begins softly, the keys of the clavichord almost whispering in that troubling fall of notes that seems to encompass, somehow, all the grief and desperate hope I have ever held. My eyes drop shut, then fly open as Sophy's voice alights above the soft melody of the clavichord, scraping the song I've known so long from the depths of raw emotion to a bright, angelic height.

When dawn overtakes the lone stars
And the heights of the misted mountains
The land still dreams in the light of day
And sorrow sleeps ever within her.
Yet even asleep to our blood she sings
And to our hearts she calls
Awake, awake, my people awake,
In dreams and silence we hear her.

I might have known the whole damned thing is about revolution—and the steward of the land. But a tear is drying on my cheek and I've lurched forward over my knees, as if to draw closer to Sophy and my mother, as if I can crawl into the music.

Finn stands beside me, a hand pressed to his heart. His face, when I look up at him, seems vulnerable, almost naked. His eyes shine. I think how overwhelming it must be, to bear the fate of an entire kingdom, and I have to look away.

Then my father drops down beside me. I see him follow my gaze to Finn. Watch him smile.

"It's good to see you have a friendship with the prince."

I think of what the Butcher said to me, back in Laon, when he asked whether or not Fionnlach Dromahair and I were betrothed. I remember my father asking me, when I was five years old, *How would you like to marry a prince, Elly?*

I sense Finn's tension. Did he hear? Does he know what my father just said? I don't know how to answer. I don't want to marry Finn. I like him, but I hardly know him, and I certainly don't love him. I hardly know my father, come to that.

So I give my father the smile I learned at Antoine's court—a smile that could mean almost anything. And I turn back to listen to the song my mother wrote for me.

CHAPTER TEN

Finn isn't at the breakfast table this morning; he's probably hung over. My parents do a marvelous job of not really talking to each other about anything. Mother and Sophy discuss obscure musicians from the Ismae, while Father and Hugh pass letters back and forth. I study my porridge, wishing for *The Journal of Botanical Studies*, Guerin's undemanding company, and a pot of steaming tea amid the earthy smell of the greenhouse.

Guerin. If Loyce has executed him, if she's dared to believe he could be responsible for Antoine's death . . . And Hensey is imprisoned as well. And what of Victoire?

Cold pinches my nose. I blink rapidly. I am not going to cry in front of these people.

"Father," I say, when there's a pause in his conversation with Hugh, "there are some people who helped me escape. My old nurse and the royal botanist. They're in prison now. Is there any way you can—" I falter, but I do not weep. "—get word if they're still alive?"

My father passes me a smile, but it's Hugh who answers, as dependable as ever. "I'll send for word with the post."

"Can you get them out?"

The men exchange a glance. This time, my father answers. "If they are not in danger of execution, it may be safer for both them and our people to leave them where they are. The danger of an attempted escape is far greater." A pause. Quietly, he says, "They understood the risk."

"Guerin didn't." I'm growing angry. Is this what they tell themselves, when they lose someone, that it was *inevitable*? "You may have suborned Hensey, but Guerin is innocent."

My father looks at Hugh, eyebrows raised. "Is that true?"

Hugh does not quite meet my eyes when he says, "I've sent men to speak with the royal botanist over the years, but I don't believe he ever committed to our cause."

Such anger clenches my throat that, for a moment, I can't speak. At last, I manage, "You did *what*?"

Hugh leans across the table. "I sent men to speak with him because I wanted him to look out for you." A glance at my father. "We wanted to be certain you had people to care for you."

Tears and anger form a hard lump in my chest. Does this mean Guerin only taught me because he was *pressured* to do it? What of Hensey? Did she genuinely care for me, or only for my father's cause?

And why, in the names of all the gods, did they send people to talk to Hensey and Guerin but not *me*?

The table has fallen silent. With sudden vigor, Sophy and Mother return to a discussion of overtones and fermatas. I sense my father watching me, but I can't look at him. A sheaf of fresh paper, an inkpot, and a pen sit in the middle of the table. I tug the pen and paper over to me and begin to sketch a series of violent black lines.

Quietly, my father and Hugh resume their talk.

The sketching calms me; the black lines turn into the impression of trees. Since we crossed the Ard, I've noticed the forest composition has changed, the soft, spreading elms and poplars of the south giving way to pine and cedar. Though most flowers are past, even the mushrooms seem different. The Butcher once called Caeris's forests dens of darkness, good for nothing but to be cut as timber. But I hold with Markarades, who talks of the knowingness in the deep silence of the forest and how trees, understory plants, flowers, mushrooms, and the creatures who inhabit these places form communities as much as human cities do. Markarades, though, has never visited Caeris. He's never seen the golden pines, the legendary trees that now grow only in the Tail Ridge—or the *Bal an-Dracan*—having been cut from the lowlands of Caeris, where they once also flourished. Their sap supposedly sings. The trees are ancient, and

legends claim that they hold great wisdom, for those who can understand their song.

I sketch a general view of the forest, making notes as to composition, the estimated height and girth of the trees, the cedars growing
with twisting roots along the banks of the Ard. I note several trees
that I have never seen except in books. Then I find myself drawing
the Ard as it looked in flood, and birds that flew in the branches
above us when we rode.

What did I do to make the Ard surge so? I made myself one with
the water, somehow. I floated over the earth, and I felt both the land
and the water within me. I frown at the marks of my pen. I don't
know how to put my magic into words—and even if I did, I don't
dare write it down. Though the whole world knows I'm a "witch"
now.

In the old poems and stories Hugh told us on the way north, my
oldest ancestors—the earliest stewards of the land—had the power
to make water rise and mountains move. There's a story in which
Wildegarde makes an entire forest grow overnight; the next morning, the trees rip their roots from the ground and walk.

A shiver passes up my spine. That much power sounds terrifying—
and thrilling at the same time.

A gentle cough pulls me from my absorption with pen and paper.
Everyone else has gone, unnoticed, and I'm alone with my father,
who leans an elbow on the table.

"May I see?" he asks.

I hesitate, my hand spreading protectively over the top sheet. But
it's not as if I have anything to hide. Any natural philosopher could
make these notes.

I pass the paper to him and watch as he studies each page, raising
his eyebrows and murmuring to himself.

"It's a wonder you didn't dig up the soil and draw that while you
were at it," he says at last.

"I didn't have time."

He looks up, his eyes crinkling. "I meant that as a joke, Elanna."

His ignorance irks me. "Soil is incredibly important. The type
determines what kind of plants will be able to grow in it, and in turn
what animals will live there. One should always look at the soil."

He folds his hands on top of my notes, looking at me thought-fully. "Hugh says you wish to be a botanist."

I nod.

He smiles. "It is only fitting that the steward of the land should be well apprised of modern science." He flips through my notes again. "These are quite extraordinary."

"They're just notes. Nothing special." But still, this pleases me. I feel myself wanting to grow toward him, as if I am a flower and his approval is the sun. It's hard to focus on the fact that I have been angry with him all my life, but it's also impossible to forget. No matter how I feel drawn to this land, I don't belong here—and I don't belong at the forefront of his revolution. I stare at the way his mouth quirks as he studies my notes. The old anger pulses through me. At last I say, "Why didn't you ever come for me, until now?"

My voice doesn't shake. I'm proud of that.

He lowers the notes, lifting his brows. His lips part. He sighs and runs a hand through his hair.

I wait. I've been waiting a long time to ask this question.

"It was not easy to lose you," he begins. "Your mother—we all suffered with you."

I fold my arms. I don't believe it. It's hard to suffer with someone you scarcely know, still less to do so for fourteen years.

He must see the skepticism in my face. He says, "If we had tried earlier, we could not have guaranteed your survival, much less our own. Antoine Eyrlai left me with no choice. In order to save many more lives, I had to give up my daughter. And to keep the peace, I had to abide by his terms."

"So why now?" I sound as collected as a lawyer.

He meets my eyes. "King Euan declared himself ready to make a bid for our freedom, and his son was old enough to lead the revolt. The time had come."

"It's lucky it came when it did." I was wrong. I don't sound like a lawyer. My voice is hard and angry. "Otherwise Loyce Eyrlai would have executed me for regicide."

My father's hand reaches out, almost instinctively, for mine. But he stops short of touching me. I stare at his fingertips; then I bring my hand back, beneath the table, away from his.

He leans forward. "We are lucky, yes, that it happened as it did—that Hugh was there with Finn and Jahan to smuggle you out. But we would never have let Queen Loyce—" His voice roughens. He shakes his head. "We would never have let any harm come to you. We would have brought you out, no matter the risk."

I can't speak. I don't know whether I believe him, or whether he believes what he's telling himself.

At least he didn't kill the king. Did he?

After all this, I need to know. "Did you arrange for the murder of Antoine Eyrlai?"

He looks into my eyes. "Why would I do that?"

"Don't answer my question with a question!" I flare.

He holds up his hands as if to pacify me. "I can't pretend that Antoine Eyrlai's departure from this earth has caused me any great grief. But no. I had no involvement in his death."

A long breath exits my lungs.

"And," he adds, "I would never have let you suffer on that false accusation. We were always going to come for you; it was only a question of time. You're my daughter, as well as the steward of the land. All sentiment aside, our revolution depends on you. We would never have let you go."

We look at each other. The years lie between us, and no matter what he says, he can't erase them. They will always be there. I was sacrificed for the good of the people, and now I'm back to save the people again, as steward of the land, a destiny he's had in mind for me since I was born. In my father's world, there is no distinction between private lives and politics, between daughters and sacrifices.

"Elanna," he says. "Thank you. No child should have to bear the burden you bore."

Tears start in my eyes, even though I want to say I didn't have to bear it. When Antoine Eyrlai put the pistol to my head, Father could have stepped forward. He could have offered himself.

But he didn't. It was better to lose me, a child, even though I had the land's power, than for Caeris to lose him, the kingmaker, the bringer of hope. As always, the good of the people came before any love he had for his daughter.

In someone else, it would be admirable. But I am that daughter, and I've had to live with the consequences of his actions.

He clears his throat and stands up. "Come out to the garden with me."

I hesitate. My father does nothing idly, not even going for a stroll in the garden. Yet we are both here, and he's told me that he always intended to come for me. I see the emotion still in his eyes. Like me, he doesn't often show his deepest feelings. Perhaps I ought to give him the chance, give us both the chance to understand each other better. He did not willingly give me over to Antoine Eyrlai, after all.

"Very well," I say, and get up from the table.

I FOLLOW HIM outside, into the gardens that border the house. The plants are drab with autumn, and they don't seem to have a particularly skilled gardener, as far as I can tell. Several hedges grow untamed.

For a moment, I am overwhelmed by the desire to be a humble gardener—an ordinary person who only loves the earth—and not the steward of the land. I have to put a hand to my chest.

Father turns to me. "Do you remember this place?"

He's mistaken my desperate fear for sentiment—but maybe they're the same thing. I look at the rows of flowers, the brown-tinged hedges. A part of me still knows this place, deep in my bones. Some distance away sits a round stone building, its arched entrance open to the elements on two sides, so I see a gleam of light coming through it. I had opened my mouth to say *No,* but something about the building makes me pause.

"You were the most curious child," Father says. "We could barely persuade you to come indoors, no matter what the weather." He chuckles. "Once I had state visitors—from Tinan—and you ran inside all covered in mud and slathered your hands over one lady's silk gown."

This startles a laugh out of me.

"Your mother was furious," Father says. "So was the lady. But you had a handful of seeds and, when you saw everyone so angry, you made the seeds grow into a bouquet of wildflowers. Asters, I think, and bergamot."

My laughter fades. I suddenly remember trying to do this in Laon as a little girl—making things grow in my hands. I knew I wasn't supposed to, but I tried anyway because I loved to do it. I remember thinking it should be easy. But it wasn't; I couldn't make a whole flower sprout from a seed. Not in Laon.

"We knew you were meant to be the steward of the land, even then," my father says.

I study the fading colors of the garden, my throat tight. Another memory surfaces; I don't know whether it's from Caeris or Eren. I remember being outside, barefoot in the mud, about this time of year—making a fort, persuading the wildflowers and hazel bushes into a neat circle to hide me. Did I want to be the steward of the land as a child? I suppose I did. But I didn't understand what it meant. I only understood how proud the words made my parents.

Yet even now, the land calls to me. I want to strip off my shoes and walk barefoot in the grass, feel each damp blade between my toes.

I wish I could be free to be one with the land, without having to hold the title and the expectations that come with it.

"Come along," Father says. He strides off across the lawn toward the stone building. I hesitate. There is something about the building, some significance, but I can't remember what. I remind myself that I'm supposed to be giving my father a chance.

Besides, even from here, the place feels *warm*. Warmth emanates from its old, mossy bricks, through the ground, up into my feet. I can't stop myself from following him.

It's dim inside, and I have to pause for my eyes to adjust. The building appears to be empty, except for a raised fount at its center. No, not a fount—a stone balanced on a circular platform.

"This is the Valtai Stone," my father says, reaching out as if he'll pat its seamed surface, but he drops his hand. "When a new steward of the land is named, they come here to drop their blood to the stone, so that they bind themselves to the land here at Cerid Aven and the land knows them. It's said the stone speaks to the steward, if they have the ears to hear it."

I stare at the stone. It seems to look back. Out of nowhere, a memory wings down: trying to persuade my mother to let me sleep out here. I loved this stone. I remember climbing over it, feeling its cool scratchy surface against my bare legs, leaning my ear to it so I could hear the faintest whisper coming from within. I tried to understand the whisper. I thought the stone was speaking to me—a language only I heard, a language only I could understand.

"The ritual wasn't always blood." Father hasn't noticed that I'm struck still. "Before the Ereni invaded Caeris, it was an acclamation. The steward would shout their name to the stone, and the stone would shout back."

"But it changed," I say. A shiver is running up the backs of my legs. Part of me wants to run. The other, larger, part wants to draw closer to the stone—to touch its seamed surface. My fingers twitch. "Why?"

"Two centuries ago, when the Ereni conquered our kingdom, the last king of Caeris bound himself to the land by blood. You know the invasion story?"

A coldness seems to clench my chest. "In the south, they taught me that it was easy. Done in a day. But Hugh said it took months. That the royal family . . ." It sickens me too much to say it.

My father is nodding. "The Dromahairs were slaughtered. Many Caerisians were. The last king, Ossian, was also the *Caveadear*—the steward of the land—and he brought the land alive. The Ereni had to fight their way through shifting forests and hills; they drowned in streams that appeared out of nowhere and valleys that seemed never to end. So by the time they reached Barrody, they wanted more than conquest. They were half mad. They wanted blood."

I shiver. "But our family survived."

"We did." He pauses. "We survived by cunning and treachery—by giving up the secret of how to reach Barrody through the shifting land, so that the Ereni army could make its way there."

I stare at him. *We* betrayed Caeris?

But it was two centuries ago. The responsibility is not *ours*. Yet I see by my father's tightened shoulders that it weighs on him, this ancestral guilt.

He clears his throat. "King Ossian escaped the slaughter, but he was gravely injured. Near death. He knew the stewards were weakening—that his power was not as great as those who had come before him—and he knew that he did not have time to induct a new

Caveadear into the mysteries. He believed that, without a steward, the borders would disappear and the magic that lingered in the earth of Caeris would vanish. So to protect his land for future generations, he began the blood rituals. Blood has power, you see, even if customs and knowledge are forgotten. So we offer our blood to the Valtai Stone in the hope it might waken the earth once more."

He turns and holds out his hand for mine. "It won't hurt. When my father brought me out here, nothing at all happened." He gives a rueful smile. "I hoped it would shriek and break apart—something dramatic."

I seem to be standing on a precipice—between the future I imagined for myself now, and the destiny I knew to be mine as a child. I have tried to hide my magic for so many years. But even so, deep within, I am hungry for it.

Maybe, for me, the stone will shriek.

Maybe I want it to. To prove the years of exile were worth something. To prove the magic that's claimed as my birthright really does belong to me.

I hold out my hand to Father. He cradles it in his and smiles at me. My heart's beating too hard for me to quite manage a smile back. What if nothing happens?

What if something does?

Father pulls a dagger from his pocket. With the most delicate movement, he scores the blade across my palm.

Blood drops to the stone.

Father curls my fingers over my palm to squeeze the flow of blood to a stop.

I'm holding my breath, but nothing has happened. Not even the faintest whisper. Father shrugs. I am shocked to find myself disappointed—almost angry. After all this, the stone doesn't even make a sound? I should be relieved: I don't want to be the steward of the land. But instead I feel almost betrayed.

I reclaim my hand and start to move away when an unholy noise shakes through the stones. I flinch backward. Father swings around to face the Valtai Stone, his lips parted.

The stone is *crying*.

All common sense tells me to get out of the building—to preserve my hearing, if nothing else. Instead I find myself crawling toward the stone, as if the cry is pulling me to it. The noise is almost unbearable, an endless throb. My ears seem to be bleeding as much as my palm. But all the same, I press my hands against the stone. I lean in to embrace it, just as I must have when I was a child. I rest my cheek against its surface, rough here and smooth there. I close my eyes.

The sound fades so slowly I almost don't realize it's gone. My father stands beside me, one hand on my shoulder. I look up at him. He's wearing the expression I feared he would: astonishment, mingled with awe.

"*Caveadear,*" he whispers.

Steward of the land. The title that belongs to me, no matter how far I try to run from it.

The stone pulses under my fingers. I have a feeling that if I lean against it again, I will hear it whispering. I should be glad. After all, I wanted it to cry out. But my stomach clenches. I can't look at my father. Now there's no question of what I am, and no question of what he'll ask me to do. I suppose it's always been inevitable.

I study the stone. I stroke its seams and bulges, familiar to my touch as an old friend. I say, softly, "I've returned."

CHAPTER ELEVEN

I'm studying the forest composition of the Valtai Oaks when a branch snaps behind me and I look up to see Finn approaching. We haven't spoken much since his drunken episode; I've spent the last days with my parents and, when I'm alone, haunting mirrors in the event that Jahan is looking for me. Once I even whispered his name. It made me giddy and flushed but nothing else happened. I don't know how Finn has been occupying himself.

At first I'm not sure he means to find me, but when he gets closer, he calls out, "Any objection to some company?"

"No. I am working, though."

"I'll be very quiet."

He props himself against a tree, watching me sketch, and though he does keep quiet, I'm too aware of his presence to concentrate. Finally I turn back to him with a sigh.

He springs upright. "Want to walk?"

The smile he offers is tentative. Real. I tuck my notebook into a pocket. "All right, then."

We stroll in companionable silence beneath the massive oaks, the ground turning steep under our feet.

"I've not been to the top of this hill," I say. "Shall we?"

Finn shrugs and gestures me forward. We thread our way up the hill, hauling ourselves over mossy stones and autumn-dry streambeds. When we pause to catch our breath under a pair of pine trees, he starts to talk.

"Father made me join the Paladisan army when I turned

nineteen—the same military duty all the sons of Idaean nobles have to fill. I wasn't under obligation, not being Idaean—or really anything. But still I did it." I see his jaw clench. "Jahan and I knew each other from the imperial court. We'd become friends because we weren't like the others; neither of us came from generations of blue-blooded Paladisan families. We rebelled together. Cut our hair short. Mocked our fathers and our teachers. Scorned our 'comrades' the same way they scorned us." He stares down at the tree roots braiding the trail. "Then we went on campaign to Chozat."

I say nothing—I don't want to interrupt him—even though I know the story about Jahan single-handedly fighting off the two dozen tribesmen. But all the popular ballads I've heard don't mention Finn, the son of a would-be king, living on the generosity of the Paladisan emperors. It reminds me how small we are. How, in the world of Ida and its court, Caeris seems like nothing.

"Jahan saved the crown prince's life by magic," Finn says. "The Getai ambushed us in the middle of a wood. They surrounded us completely. They had muskets and swords and bayonets, and what did we have? A few pistols. Some rapiers. We were stupid; we thought no one would come so near to the walls of the city. We were supposed to be scouting, but most of us had started making bets and shooting at squirrels instead. Then—*bang*!" His fist pumps into the air. "They were all around us. Shooting. Our comrades were falling, the horses were screaming . . . and I couldn't do anything. I was *frozen.*"

I swallow hard at the look on Finn's face. The memory of his shame.

"Jahan pushed me to the ground. We were at the back of the party, and the Getai were already swarming the crown prince. There was no way Jahan should have been able to get there in time. But I saw him. He . . ." Finn hesitates, as if wary of telling even me this truth. "He moved so quickly I couldn't see it. *Compressing space,* he calls it. Then he was in front of the prince, defending him with his rapier and, when he lost it, his bare hands. With his *magic.* The Getai fell back; he was moving too fast for them to kill. He told me later he sent thoughts at them—reflected back their own terror. And then he broke their guns."

"But no one recognized it for magic?" I'm baffled. It must have been obvious.

"They *should* have. But Leontius had taken a blow to the head. I think . . ." Finn pauses again. In a quiet voice, he says, "I think Jahan did something to his memories. Changed them, so Lees thought it was a sort of miracle—that the Getai had bad guns, wet powder, and Jahan got there just as all of them jammed, and he was able to beat our attackers away. Leontius decided Jahan was like a hero of old, that he'd gone berserk, inspired by the gods. And the others accepted the story, because . . ." Finn purses his lips. "Because it absolved them of the shame of not saving Leontius themselves."

I draw in a breath. I'd guessed that Jahan used his magic in that famous episode. And still, I can't help wondering, did *all* the others accept the story? How secure is Jahan's secret, really?

Maybe that's part of why he came to Eren with Finn. To get away from the secret he'd exposed, then been forced to hide in plain sight.

"I don't know if any of the others still have nightmares about it," Finn says, "but I do."

And who wouldn't? The Getai could have killed them; their comrades could have killed Jahan, if they had realized he was a sorcerer.

He glances at me, as if to gauge my reaction. I look back at him steadily. "King Antoine put a pistol to my head when I was five years old," I say. "I understand nightmares."

Finn's mouth quirks. "I suppose you would."

"I haven't had any since we got here, though," I say, surprised to realize it's true.

"Lucky," he says. Unthinkingly, I reach out and touch his elbow. He manages a smile. "I wish—it's a stupid, useless wish—but I wish our revolution wouldn't come to battle. At least not so fast. I'd do anything to delay it, but I'm not supposed to say that. I'm supposed to be brave. Fearless."

"Sometimes I wish we could just . . . act the way we really feel," I say, fumbling for the words. "Not have to disguise what we really want."

"I know. My father made it clear that coming to Caeris was my responsibility once I came of age. He didn't raise me to do anything else but win his kingdom back for him."

I hesitate to ask, but then I say it anyway. "Is there something else you want?"

His forehead wrinkles. He shakes his head very slightly. "I don't know." He turns and resumes climbing. I follow.

The trees fall away abruptly ahead of us, leaving a bare rock outcropping—and on the height of it, a stone circle open to the gray sky.

Finn slows. "I didn't expect this. Did you?"

I shake my head. The stones are old, tipped against one another, green and crumbling, figments of my childhood come to life. They seem ready to be folded back into the earth at any time.

I clamber up to the height of the outcropping and catch my breath. The rocky hilltop is clear of trees, and from it we can see Caeris spreading out below—the great ribbon of the Ard, the smoke curling from Cerid Aven. Far to the west, the sea shines between fingers of land, and when I look north the tumbled peaks of the Tail Ridge, the *Bal an-Dracan,* smear the horizon.

Finn gasps and points. "There—that's Lake Harbor. And Barrody."

We both stare northwest at the mirrorlike lake, rendered minuscule by distance, and the cobbled impression of buildings clinging to the surrounding hills. Barrody, Caeris's capital, the seat of her kings—and, now, an Ereni garrison.

"Varro-Dé." Finn gives the city her Caerisian name.

It means "the dwelling of the gods on earth." The old gods, not the ones we've borrowed from Paladis. In the legends I've been reading in my father's library, they say Dagod, the Father of the Gods, played his harp on the hill and the city took shape to the strains of the music—palaces and avenues built of rainbows and glass. Then our people, the Children of Anu, followed the gods here. The gods gave up Caeris to us, departing for the islands beyond the veil, and our ancestors, being made too much of clay, could not keep the crystal city from being destroyed by their too-heavy feet.

Finn's longing, his fear, his hope, is palpable in the cold, uncluttered air.

I can't bear it. I move past him, into the shabby stone circle. As my feet cross the invisible perimeter of the stones, the earth begins to hum under me, the way it always did at the Hill of the Imperishable. I should feel comforted, but instead it makes me uneasy. What lies in these stones? What does this land want from me?

I have my dagger from Laon in my pocket. I slide it out now and let it rest on my palm. The blade gleams, dull with promise.

Finn has followed me in. The humming twists in response to him, a higher pitch that sets my teeth on edge. No. I can't try it, not with him here.

But as I start to sweep the dagger back into my pocket, Finn reaches for it. It goes flying off among the tall stones on the north side of the circle.

"Sorry," Finn begins.

I ignore him, hurrying to the stone and dropping to my knees. A patch of gorse pushes up through the rocks here; the dagger must have fallen into it, for I can't see the glint of metal anywhere.

My palm itches. I wipe it impatiently against the nearest stone, but it only starts stinging terribly.

I snatch my hand back. Too late, I realize what happened.

The ground trembles.

"Finn," I say as calmly as I can, "get back. Get out of the circle, if you can."

But he stays there. His gaze is wide, almost awed.

Because of course the dagger made a gash on my palm, and my blood has woken the stone. I thought a specter would emerge from it, as they did in Laon, but no specter has appeared.

Instead, the stone is *weeping*—just as the Valtai Stone did when Father spilled my blood on it. It is a terrible sound—a harsh creaking, a deep cry that seems to be pulled up from the bottom of the earth. Part of me wants to back away, get as far as I can from this thing and its terrible noise.

But, again, I find myself crawling forward on my knees. I put both hands on the stone. The surface, which should be rock-hard, feels tremulous, malleable, like skin. Warmth emanates from it, and there's a trembling beneath as if it has veins carrying blood through it. I lean closer.

Finn's hands grab my shoulders, and he drags me back into the middle of the circle, holding me so tight against him I hear the thump of his heartbeat. Behind me, the stone still weeps.

"I can't stand it," Finn says, his teeth clenched, his set jaw bumping my forehead. "I thought—I thought it was going to *swallow* you."

I pull back from him. He looks at me through squinted eyes, for the weeping has begun to throb through both our bodies, through the air itself.

"Hold on." I flash a crazed grin. "I'm going to try something."

I always wanted to do this at the Hill of the Imperishable, but I never dared.

Fishing the dagger out of the gorse, I score a fresh line over my palm and let the blood fall onto a second stone.

It *shrieks*.

Finn backs out of the circle, his hands clapped over his ears. "Make it stop!"

But I'm not going to. I'm going to see what happens.

I drop my blood on the next stone.

It begins to sing. A wordless voice, cutting beneath the shrieking stone and above the weeping one, until it begins to seem to my demented ears that they are making *music*—a strange and inhuman kind, but music nonetheless. It seems as if it could resolve into a melody, if I just listened carefully enough.

Finn shouts my name again, and the almost-song dissolves into pure noise. This time he's pointing at something in the forest below us.

"Riders," he's saying. "Shots!"

I drag myself by main force from the stone circle and hold myself steady on Finn's shoulder, peering over the ledge into the forest. A flock of birds bursts skyward as a report of gunfire explodes in the trees. It's coming toward us, toward Cerid Aven.

Finn's already running back to the path. I start to follow, then pause to look at the stones, still making their strange music. *Is* it a song? Again, I have the sense that a melody floats within the noise, for ears skilled enough to hear it. Perhaps this is what my mother heard; perhaps, with her training in music, she fashioned her song out of this formless noise.

Finn calls for me. I tear myself away, pocketing the dagger, but allow myself one last backward glance.

The stones seem to have begun to move, to dance their grief in the motionless earth.

* * *

MY FEET SKID on the steep ground, and I fall onto my backside, gathering dirt and pine needles on my trousers and coat. I fish the dagger out of my pocket again. Finn runs ahead of me down the hill, leaping rocks and downed logs.

Shots echo nearby, ricocheting through the forest. I can't tell what direction they're coming from.

I scramble to my feet and pelt after Finn.

Where the ground levels, he turns to look back for me, bracing one hand on a pine tree. His chest flashes as he pants. "Are you all right?"

I look down to jump a log, look up.

Look again.

"Watch out!" I scream. A man comes hurtling through the woods, straight for Finn's back. Finn spins, off kilter. The man wears Loyce's colors. Blue and gold.

No conscious thought passes through my mind. I just lift the dagger and throw.

It goes wide, barely nicking the soldier's shoulder. But it startles him. He reels back, and Finn rams a punch straight into the man's face. Blood spurts from his nose. I don't like the way his head jerks back. Finn punches him again, this time in the stomach, knocking the man backward.

"Finn!" I shout, running closer. "*Leave him.* Let's go—"

But beyond Finn and his attacker, more soldiers burst into the woods. I leap back, not that it does much good to protect me. Then I realize they're not running to attack us. They're running from something.

One stops to reload his pistol. Others simply sprint, bayonets careless at their sides.

Whooping shouts echo through the trees. I stop running for Finn and stare. A man—several men—bound into view, shouting ululating cries. They've got swords, some bayonets, some crossbows, but that's not what makes them terrifying. No. It's the sound coming from their mouths, the brilliant yellow-and-red cloaks strapped around their bodies. I almost run myself, but they're Caerisian. They won't harm me.

I think.

The Ereni soldiers pelt past us, not even seeming to see Finn or me, though Finn's attacker has rebounded. They're locked head-to-head now.

A shouting Caerisian breaks off from the pack and lopes to Finn. He swings out a pistol and brandishes it at the Ereni soldier's head.

Neither Finn nor the soldier notices.

I can't seem to move. Finn is my friend, but the Ereni soldier is my countryman, too. I don't want to wade into the fight and hurt Finn. I don't want to hurt the Ereni.

I am Ereni, not Caerisian. How many times have I told myself that?

The Caerisian clears his throat. He's cut his hair and put pomade in it so it sticks straight up, as if in terror at being on his head. His face is young and fierce.

Finn pulls back. The Ereni soldier lunges after him, but the Caerisian efficiently wrangles an arm around his neck. He places the muzzle of the pistol to the man's temple. The soldier goes still. His face is a mess of blood, and so's his shirt.

The Caerisian shakes him. "That there is the crown prince of Caer-Ys. What do you think you're doing, trying to kill him on my watch? Eh?"

The soldier twists. The Caerisian holds him harder, pushing his head to the side. The man stills.

Finn shakes out his sleeves; he doesn't look much better than his attacker.

"Your Highness." The Caerisian shoves the Ereni soldier to his knees. "Let me dispatch this swine for you. Say a last prayer, southern pig."

He cocks his pistol. The soldier looks into the forest, straight at me. Beneath the blood, his face is pale and young, and I hear him stutter. "Ha . . . have mercy—"

The Caerisian grabs him by the collar. "*What* did you say? What language do you call that? Say it again in Caerisian and I'll think about it."

A low, pathetic sound escapes the young soldier.

"Ugh. Rather than speak our language, he pisses himself." The Caerisian shakes his head, cocks the pistol again. "One, two—"

"Stop!" The word rips from my throat.

The Caerisian looks up, startled.

I'm walking forward, though my legs seem to belong to someone else; I'm shocked at my own audacity even as I march to him. "If you kill him, you're no better than they are."

He stares at me. "Who the hell are you?"

Finn answers, quietly. "She's Elanna Valtai."

"Lower your gun. Let him go." I fight to keep my voice sharp with authority; everything I've been taught tells me to back down before a man with a gun. But everything I know to be right in this world tells me to protect the life of the man on the ground. I can't see an Ereni soldier killed. He could have been on guard at the palace or one of Antoine's country estates; I might have met him on tour at the training yard, and not remember.

To my astonishment, the Caerisian obeys me without hesitation. His jaw clenches, though. "There, *Caveadear Caer-Ys*. Do what you want with his sorry life."

I look down at the wretched Ereni soldier. I'm more like him than I'm like these Caerisian thugs. "Go on. Find your regiment. Run." My Ereni sounds crystalline and aristocratic, completely out of place in these woods.

The soldier crawls forward. "Lady . . ."

This groveling makes me want to squirm, and I can't help seeing the narrow look in the Caerisian's eyes. I gesture in the direction the others ran. "Go."

But still he seems afraid to move.

"Your justice may be short-lived, *Caveadear*," the Caerisian says—almost smugly. I want to hit him. "My Hounds will see to him if he's not careful."

I glare at the Caerisian. "It seems to me your 'hounds' need a good leash!"

"He is a *soldier*. We are at *war*." The Caerisian folds his arms, glaring back at me.

"Take off your colors," I order the soldier, and he does, throwing the sash to the ground. I point south. "Go that way. You're less likely to run into trouble."

"Thank you, lady," he whispers.

I grimace at the blood cracking around his lips and pull my handkerchief from my sleeve. I don't care whether it makes me seem like an Ereni sympathizer to Finn and the self-proclaimed Hound-Master. "Take that. Now off you go."

He crawls to his feet, takes one look at the three of us, and hobbles away toward the south.

Now I don't have a handkerchief for Finn. He's mopping his face on his sleeve. The Hound-Master is watching me, arms still folded. He's a wiry young man of middling height, not much older than Finn.

"What's your name?" I say. I refuse to be cowed, to feel guilt for helping the "enemy."

He sweeps a bow. "Apologies, *Caveadear,* for not presenting myself to you immediately. I am Alistar Connell, leader of the Hounds of Urseach and brother of the Countess of Lanlachlan. Clearly you do not recall our childhood friendship."

"Alas," I say. "No."

"What happened here, Lord Connell?" Finn asks. He's cleaned up his face, for the most part.

Alistar Connell drops to one knee. "Your Highness."

Finn's mouth twitches with impatience. "Please rise."

Alistar springs to his feet in a single bound, the show-off. "We were making our way to Cerid Aven, answering the duke's summons, when we spied a party of Ereni soldiers headed in our direction. We decided to scare them up a bit." He grins widely. "Brought us straight to your side, as requested, sire."

"And saved us, for which I am grateful."

I snort. "If Hound-Master Connell and his men hadn't decided to *scare up* the Ereni soldiers, we wouldn't have been in danger in the first place. You don't know who that man was—if he'd been born on this side of the border, he could as easily be fighting for you. Caeris was conquered two centuries ago. We all live in *Eren* now. You nearly murdered your own countryman."

I'm breathing hard. I didn't mean to say all that. Alistar Connell is watching me, his eyebrows lifted, while Finn stares at the ground. He's flushed. Maybe my words mean something to him. Maybe at least our prince understands the danger of a civil war.

The Hound-Master, however, obviously thinks I'm out of my

mind. "The Ereni took you hostage. Their queen wants you imprisoned, sent mad by witch hunters, and executed. And you defend them?"

"You don't understand," I flare. "I *am* them."

Alistar Connell just looks at me. There isn't a shred of comprehension in his face.

I huff out a breath and stalk past the two of them to fetch my dagger from the grass. Then I swing back to say, in my most irritating court drawl, "It's been diverting, gentlemen, but you'll have to excuse me. I have some unnecessary blood to wash off my hands."

I storm away through a patch of birch trees. The moment their voices fade behind me, my trembling legs betray me and I have to lean against one of the birches. The breath heaves in my chest. My fingers scrabble against the birch's smooth, papery bark. I see again the Ereni soldier's terrified face. Hear his halting voice, speaking the language I know far better than Caerisian.

I am them. It's true; fourteen years in Antoine's court have made me far more Ereni than Caerisian. How can I take up arms against the people who raised me? I speak their language, I know their customs, I call them friends. Loyce may be vile, but she's a single person. And that Ereni soldier isn't her. He's a young man who joined the army—for money, for glory—and was sent to Caeris to do his duty. He doesn't have Alistar Connell's fanatical passion or Finn's sense of responsibility to his father's cause. He's just earning his pay.

I can't witness people dying like that, for me or against me. I owe who I am to those years at Antoine's court. I can't lead a revolution against the people I still consider my friends.

Finn's and Alistar's voices echo through the woods behind me. I push myself upright and put one foot in front of the other, toward home.

CHAPTER TWELVE

Word comes a few days later: Loyce has had her coronation, and she's declared war on us. It was inevitable, but still the breath stops in my throat at the thought of fighting against the Ereni.

Guerin's still in custody, though Loyce has not declared him guilty of regicide, since I am a more appealing villain. Hensey, however, has been pronounced guilty of aiding the murderer—namely, me. My father's people are working on a plan to help her escape prison; they don't need to tell me that she's been sentenced to death. Some of the guards at the Tower, they say, are amenable to the Caerisian cause, and may be willing to help.

It makes me sick to think of Hensey locked up, awaiting death after a sham trial, but there is nothing I can do except ask my father, day after day, whether she's yet been freed. At least it seems the Count of Ganz is keeping Victoire safe.

My father disappears for days on end, taking the Hounds of Urseach and sometimes Finn, but always Hugh. Hugh has begun to look haggard, and the line between Finn's brows seems fixed, but my father strolls about, robust as a fox, as if revolutions only give him life. The Hounds—and Alistar Connell—seem as aquiver as the dogs they name themselves for, eager for a fight.

They're going to gather support, and to someplace where their followers train in secret. Finn always returns smelling of gunpowder and mud.

They don't invite me to come with them, even though I would have thought Father would insist. The first days, I consider that I'm being insulted by being left out; but then I consider that perhaps Alistar and Finn mentioned to Father what happened with the Ereni soldier in the woods. Perhaps my father understands how I'm torn between Eren and Caeris. Perhaps he doesn't want my views to inflame his men, either to anger against me or to sympathy for the Ereni they're supposed to hate.

I tell myself I should be relieved, but I only feel wrenched apart inside. I know I will have to choose between Eren and Caeris, that I will have to decide which one I truly am. It isn't right. The truth is that I'm both.

My mother doesn't join the men, either. "Your father manages to risk his life quite well without my help," she says when I ask why she stays. Quietly, she adds, "All our lives."

Instead she talks to me of our past—all the many incidents I've forgotten from my childhood, the story of how she and Father met when she came to Laon at the age of twenty-two to perform on the pianoforte before the court. Her compositions were widely acclaimed and—even I have heard this part, albeit through gossip— her beauty and graciousness won her many suitors. My father was among them. Being from Baedon, Mother knew nothing of Caeris or the Ereni conquest or Father's hope for revolution—at least not at first. "How did you choose him?" I ask, for though she doesn't boast, it's clear she had several offers.

Her mouth curves in a secretive smile. "He was the one who seemed to really see me. And he talked to me, not at me. He was interested in everything."

Is that the way Jahan looks at me? As if he really sees me?

We tour the house and grounds; she plays music for me. Sometimes Sophy joins us, quick to smile at me and laugh at Mother's stories, and soon I find I've forgotten my brief resentment of her.

One day when he's home, Father presents me with a stack of books on Caerisian history. "Much of the knowledge of the land has been lost, except for the secrets the mountain lords keep. You may be able to glean some understanding of the *Caveadear*'s power from these, though."

So, when I'm not with Mother and Sophy, I read. It's easier to lose myself in the conflicts of history than to decide where my own loyalties lie, though the histories contrast so starkly with what I learned in Laon that I cannot forget the divide. The more I read of Caeris's tripartite government, the more logical it begins to seem, despite the sneers of my childhood tutors. How else is one to keep a single person from holding too much power? Maybe that is what brought Antoine to lie, to value his personal gains before his people. Maybe being answerable to others would make Loyce a more responsible queen. I don't know, but I wonder.

I read more about Caeris's last king, Ossian, and his efforts to wake the land—though, frustratingly, the books tell almost nothing of how he used his magic. Perhaps the writers did not know; my father called the *Caveadear*'s power a mystery. And I cannot help but feel the history is incomplete, especially the explanation of the blood rituals. Dropping my blood to the stone circles does not seem to wake the land; it wakes the stones—or, in some cases, the ancestors within them. There seems no way for me to access the amount of power Ossian possessed, much less guess what he did.

In an effort to find more information about the magic, I give up on the recent histories and wade into the books written before the Ereni invasion. Few survive. Time—and the successive waves of first Paladisan and then Ereni conquest—has destroyed many volumes and censored others. The volumes that remain confirm that most towns in Eren and Caeris were built around stone monuments, which in turn were believed to have been erected by the gods. It seems the stewards of the land used the circles, but in what way, and to what purpose, remains shrouded in vagary. Maybe the historians didn't dare put their knowledge to paper.

Hugh comes upon me one afternoon while I'm in a state of deep frustration. "This book," I exclaim, "has been censored! There are pages missing!"

He takes it from me, shaking his head as he leafs through it. "After the Paladisans conquered us, many libraries were purged. People often censored books themselves, removing the text about magic so the witch hunters couldn't find it. The only complete library is in Dalriada, in the mountains, where the invading armies did not come."

"Then I should go to Dalriada," I say.

Hugh looks at me. "If only it were that easy. I'm afraid you'll have to wait for an invitation; you'll never find your way there yourself. Now, if you want more information on the stewards, look in the books of legends and folktales. The old writers often hid true things in supposedly harmless stories." He winks.

But the legends are obtuse. Several times, I read the story of how Wildegarde wedded the land. The people wanted her to marry, so that by having offspring her blood would continue to bless them forever. But instead she went out on the Day of the Dying Year and laid herself down in the earth, and in the morning she went back to her people and said she *had* married—not a man, but the land itself. "Now I am within the land always," she said. "I am always with you. *Mo cri, mo tire, mo fiel.* This is my heart, my land, my blood."

I start, reading it. It's the phrase the specters spoke on the Hill of the Imperishable. And, in fact, throughout my reading, the words are often echoed in various stories about the *Caveadears*. It makes me wonder whether the stewards also wedded the land, in some ceremony similar to Wildegarde's, for I find references to the *Caveadears* "uniting with the earth." But as ever, the writers seem to be deliberately obtuse.

And they don't tell me *how* Wildegarde did anything; nor are they at all clear on how *Caveadears* after her performed their magic.

Perhaps it's because it isn't possible to wake the land, and wedding her is simply some arcane ritual justified by Wildegarde's supposed existence. These are legends, after all. Are we expected to believe they tell the literal truth? It can't be so, and if this is what the Caerisians expect me to do, they're setting themselves up for disappointment. Oh, I can make a plant grow quickly—but what good does that do to win a war? How can dropping my blood to the stones defeat the Butcher and Loyce's army?

We need the black ships. We need Paladis's might, her resources, her manpower—not my unreliable and forbidden skills.

But I have little else to occupy my time, so I revisit the Valtai Stone, and though it roars for me again, I can discern no meaning from it.

I go alone to the Sentry Rock, the stone circle on top of the ridge. This time, I drop my blood onto each of the stones, finishing at the

one in the center. By now the weeping and shrieking is almost deafening.

Then my ancestors step from the stones.

They are spectral, as if only half remembered, dressed in garments
whose names are long forgotten. The terrible noise comes from them
as well as the stones; I cannot fathom how my mother shaped it into
true music. As I watch, the dagger in my hand, my ancestors begin
to dance. They dance slowly, as if their feet are heavy, as if grief
weighs them down. It is not a dance of joy. Every movement of it
signifies mourning.

I watch them dance for a long time. They do not seem to see me.
Their movement does not tell me what I need to know about my
power, or what I should do about the divide between Eren and
Caeris. They don't tell me what truth, if any, exists in the legends, or
whether I can hope to use it.

At last I wipe my blood from the stones and go back down to the
house.

A FEW EVENINGS later, as we gather before supper, my father an-
nounces that he and Finn will be gone for several days. I look up. He
has not announced his departures before, and certainly not in such
ringing tones.

"Hugh will remain here. He knows what to do should we fail to
return," Father says with an easy smile.

"Fail to return?" I say. "Where are you going?"

He leans forward, putting a finger to his lips conspiratorially.
"Across the border. To Eren. We must make a meeting with an important man." His gaze grows thoughtful. "Perhaps, Elanna, if you
were willing . . ."

My mother's face darkens. "No, Ruadan! It's bad enough that
you're sending yourself into such danger. You won't take my daughter with you." She's glaring now, and when I draw a breath to speak,
she whirls on me. "No arguments."

I don't try to argue. She's been in a black mood for the last week,
shut up in her room composing with single-minded ferocity. Now
she thrusts a sheaf of paper at Sophy, who looks, blinking, down at

a line of scribbled lyrics. Mother marches to the clavichord and, without counting in the beat, launches into the music. Sophy catches up a moment later, faltering on the words.

The song tells of two centuries of Caeris's grief, of a desperate search for a people's forgotten glory, of odds almost insurmountable. It reminds us of how the Dromahair family died on the steps of Barrody Castle; how the last king, Ossian, died too, and how all of Caeris's hope died with him. And it tells us that Eren invaded Caeris in revenge for some slight done to an Ereni princess; it reminds us that, before the conquest, the Caerisians tormented Eren with endless cattle raids and squabbles over the border.

Sophy's voice shakes on the final line: *"For though the land cries for liberty, it demands the cost in blood."*

I swallow. This is why I never liked music. It makes me *feel* too much. I want to sit on the floor and weep.

Finn grimaces at me.

Afterward, Mother comes up to me and strokes an imaginary hair back from my cheek. She leans close and whispers in my ear, "I wish I could spare you this."

This: the impending war, being the figurehead in a revolution I can't believe in. The hope in my father's eyes when he almost asked if I would come with him into Eren.

I climb the stairs and let myself into my bedroom. I clamber into the embrace of the window seat. A candle burning behind me casts a suggestion of my face onto the glass, and on the other side of the window, the lawns of Cerid Aven are lost to darkness.

"El."

It's soft as a whisper, but still it startles me out of my thoughts. I had given up on hearing from Jahan after those first few days of haunting mirrors and tentatively whispering his name. But now, instead of the shape of my face, I see his in the window glass, well lit and intent.

"When we first met," he says, "you told me you wanted to go to Ida. Do you still want to?"

"I—Do I—Ida?" I stutter to a stop. Do I want to go to Ida? It's a solution to my dilemma, a way out of the conflict within myself. In Ida, I would be neither Ereni nor Caerisian; I would just be a foreigner. No one would demand that I do the impossible and wake the earth. No one would accuse me of witchcraft and regicide.

I see again the Ereni soldier in the woods, the stark terror on his face as Alistar pointed the gun at his head. I see my father, standing between me and the Butcher, between me and the gun. I see the shards of glass on the carpet, feel the weight of the pistol against my own head.

Jahan is watching me, his eyes bright. A wave of heat sweeps through me. "Would you go, too?" I ask.

He smiles. "Yes. We would go together. I need to make a case before the emperor—so that he'll provide us with the black ships, munitions, aid. And what better way than to bring you with me?"

"But . . ." My father needs me here. And there is the terror of exposing my magic before the imperial court.

Jahan seems to read the concerns from my mind. "We all know we need the emperor's support to win this rebellion. He's reluctant because he only has Euan Dromahair to speak in Caeris's favor, and, between you and me, Euan is about as dashing as a lamppost. But if a charming Caerisian lady came to plead for her people's freedom? You could stir everyone's hearts to sympathy for Caeris, not just the emperor's." He leans forward with an eager smile. "They would love your accent, and your botanical studies, and your wit, and . . . well, everything about you."

Heat floods into my face. Jahan Korakides thinks *I* could charm the emperor of Paladis?

"Of course you're worried they'll discover your secret," he adds quickly. "But as I know all too well, the best way to hide your gift is in plain sight. And if the court likes you, they won't believe you capable of such a heinous crime as sorcery. You'll be the darling of Ida—everyone will want to be your friend." Somewhat self-consciously, he adds, "How could they not?"

I realize I'm staring at him—at the brightness in his eyes, and the way he ducked his chin a little after he said that.

He glances up and flashes a smile. "And if you're popular with the court, that only increases our chances of succeeding. We might find funding and supporters beyond the emperor himself." He's all business now, but then he adds, softly, as if he's offering me a secret,

"Also, during the great witch hunts, not all works on magic were destroyed. Some still exist, in the university archives in Ida. There are some that pertain to Caeris, and the magic of the *Caveadear.*"

My heart leaps. Ida—the city I have always wanted to visit, and the answers I seek for these preposterous feats of magic. A vision flashes through my mind of myself on Jahan Korakides's arm, being presented to the emperor. But I have to be rational; this journey could be very dangerous. What Jahan proposes is a daring scheme—hoodwinking the imperial court. If it worked, though . . .

"I don't know," I say. "I—I'll have to present the plan to my father."

Even without asking him, I know he'll view it as a betrayal. The *Caveadear* belongs in Caeris, the figurehead of the revolution and our nation. But a figurehead cannot win a war—unless, unimaginably, I managed a magic as great as Wildegarde's. No, it's not possible. To win a war, you need manpower and resources we don't have. And my father has almost as great a daring streak as Jahan. Maybe he'll like the audacity of the plan.

"Think on it," Jahan says with a grin. "You're coming with them tomorrow, yes? I'll be there, of course, for the negotiations. If you and Ruadan agree on the plan, you can join me. We'll make straight for the port after we put the terms in writing."

So that's why my father is courting danger by crossing the border into Eren. He needs to meet with the Paladisan ambassador, to negotiate an agreement between himself and the emperor. Between an independent Caeris and the empire. It's the agreement Finn failed to achieve before coming here, so now my father is forced to do it himself, despite the danger.

They want me to come so that I can add my name to the agreement. And so I can protect them on the way there, with my magic.

And, though earlier I thought Father's intent to go south was pure madness, now I find I want to say yes so badly. It's not just because Jahan's scheme thrills me, or because I want to see Ida and the imperial court. No, I want to look into Jahan's eyes, in person. I'm struck with a sudden, visceral memory of how he smells: of cloves and cinnamon.

Jahan glances over his shoulder. "I have to go. See you tomorrow." His eyes meet mine in the glass with a sudden intensity. He presses one hand against the pane, and I raise mine to mirror it. Our fingertips touch—it almost seems I feel the fleeting warmth of his skin against mine, a bright, electrical pulse. I lean forward, unsure what I'm going to say, but sure I need to say something.

Only he's gone. The silhouette in the glass just shows the outline of my own tangled hair. My shoulders sag. I feel a little foolish; I don't know what I thought he might say.

Do I want to stay here, or do I want to go? Wield my magic or hide it? Fight openly in Caeris, or through deception in Ida?

The questions jumble against each other, and I have no answer. I don't know what's best. I do know that, though the land speaks to me, I can't bear to see Ereni die. I would give anything to delay this war.

And I don't have to come back.

The thought strikes me like a physical blow. I could stay in Ida. I could avoid this war; I could avoid choosing between Caeris and Eren.

My father doesn't need me—he wants a figurehead for his rebellion. And the powers conferred upon *Caveadears* in myth can't be achievable, not for a real person; my own power is so much smaller. It's the emperor's support that will win this rebellion, not a figure out of legends. It's Paladis my father needs, not me. So I will give him Paladis's help.

And once the rebellion is won, I could give myself a life in Ida, studying botany with Markarades. I could live the life I've dreamed of, visiting salons and theaters, discussing science and discoveries with the most brilliant minds in the world.

I run my fingers through my hair. Then I walk down the hall to my parents' chambers and tap on the door. Father answers, raising his brows in surprise to see me.

"I want to come tomorrow." The simple, truthful words feel like a deception, though they shouldn't. This is for the best; I'm trying to help him. "I've just heard from Jahan. He told me his plan. To go to Ida and present our cause before the emperor and the court, in person. He—he's asked me to come with him."

Father's brows rise even higher. "And the advantage of exposing you to the imperial court would be . . . ?"

"It's not enough for Jahan to make our case alone; the emperor needs to see that Caerisians desire his help, too. Not only Euan Dromahair, but someone from Caeris."

"And who better than my daughter, young and charming and well spoken?" He gives me a knowing look.

I hope the dim light conceals the blush darkening my ears.

Father is thinking it through, his eyes moving as if reading the book of his ideas. "It's a bold move, since you stand accused of regicide as well as witchcraft. Jahan—and you—would have to play it just right. But if we sent you with a delegation of Caerisians who made our cause known throughout the court . . ."

"Jahan will make it popular."

"Jahan will make *you* popular," my father counters. He nods. "I can see the advantages. You would pull their heartstrings; play to sentiment as well as politics. It might indeed be more easily accomplished with your presence. I can't imagine King Euan stirring many to action."

"Yes—and we need the empire's support. I don't see how we can win without the black ships."

He folds his arms and looks at me. "I say I see the advantages— and I do. But I also see the danger. You are the steward of the land. If anyone were to discover your power, the witch hunters would seize you. We would lose you, and we'd lose any support we have thus far gained. The emperor will never condone the open use of magic."

"But I've hidden my magic for years in Laon. Jahan says the best way to hide is in the open—and he should know!"

Awareness of the land beats within my bones. If I go to Paladis, I wonder, will my magic be numbed? Or will it still explode out of me, even more dangerous than it is here, because I'm at the imperial court?

It can't. I won't let it. I'm strong enough to hide it; strong enough to claim the aid my father needs and then live the life I want.

I draw in a breath. "At least let me come, and we can talk to Jahan together." He can help persuade my father that it's worth the risk.

"It's dangerous." Father's gaze is assessing. "Not least because the queen's men will be looking for us—you heard your mother's reaction."

For a future in Ida, I can survive the danger of crossing the Caerisian border, though I'm not keen to incur my mother's wrath so soon after we've reunited. But I can't stay here for her sake. "Mother will have to understand, if she wants us to succeed. I could help you—you need my help. I can feel creatures moving through the forest. Maybe I will be able to tell if enemies approach. I could conceal our presence better than you could do alone."

A look comes into his face, and I am astonished to see that it is pride.

I swallow hard.

He puts a finger to his lips. "Dawn. The stables. Dress warmly. And don't tell your mother."

I'M UP AT dawn. I haven't slept half the night for fretting over my decision—over the idea that I might be daring enough to take Jahan's plan and make it my own. I feel buoyed by my own courage. I could live the life I want.

And yet . . . the land's heartbeat pulses in my own body. My father needs me. No one has ever *needed* me before. But I don't want to fight in his war; I don't want to destroy both Eren and Caeris in this conflict. Perhaps, with the emperor's aid, it would be less bloody, less destructive. If I remain in Caeris, I'll be thrust into the role my father has envisioned for me since birth—even though I can't make forests walk, even though my power is too small to make me anything other than a figurehead. A doomed figurehead, if we don't secure the emperor's help. If I go to Ida, if I choose to return to Caeris, at least it will be my own decision. At least we'll all stand a chance of surviving.

I feel flushed, too hot in my riding gear, addled from lack of sleep. The cold air, sharp with frost, restores me somewhat to my senses. By the stables wait a cluster of yawning stableboys and sleepy horses. The Hounds are there. I hear footsteps crunch the icy grass behind me and look around to see Finn.

"You're coming?" he says, registering my presence.

"I'll help to know where the Ereni are. I have some uses, you know."

It's too early in the morning; my attempt at humor falls flat. Finn just blinks at me.

The Hounds greet us with whoops. Alistar Connell performs an exaggerated bow in my direction. "Lady Elanna. What have we poor fools done to deserve the honor of the *Caveadear*'s presence?"

"Someone has to keep you out of trouble," I say tartly, but the tension must come through in my voice. Alistar Connell frowns, dropping the pretense, and comes over to me instead, holding out his hand.

"Here. You look as if you could use it."

It's a cheese bun, still hot from the oven. "That's yours." I try to hand it back to him, even though my stomach rumbles. "I couldn't."

His mouth quirks. "I was saving it for later, but you could use it now. Eat up. The green ones always make that mistake, Lady El, thinking they don't have to eat."

I drop my gaze. "Thank you."

My father arrives. Alistar moves off and we all mount up, Finn pressing up beside me. "I should have given you my extra roll."

I feel suddenly aware of being the only girl in a group of men. My father glances over his shoulder at us, and I don't miss how his lips twitch as if he's holding in laughter.

"That's all right, Finn," I say, and eat the roll.

We ride through the morning. I haven't been so long on horse-back since our journey north, and when I slide off the mare, my legs wobble. About four gentlemen lurch forward to offer me their arms and morsels of food. In spite of myself, I feel rather singular.

I really shouldn't have come.

"The Butcher is moving several regiments north," my father says, while we stretch our legs and eat the cold packed lunch Cook provided for us. "They'll achieve Portmason this afternoon, so our objective is to meet the Paladisan ambassador outside town. Jahan Korakides has come with the Butcher, on the pretext of examining Eren's defenses. He's been telling Loyce Eyrlai that he will recommend the emperor send the black ships to support her cause— though of course he will send them to support *ours*."

"How do we know he's not playing both sides?" Alistar Connell asks.

A wave of outrage sweeps through me, but Finn gets there first. "I have known Jahan better than anyone, and I assure you, he believes in our cause."

"But he's the Korakos," says Alistar, apparently unperturbed by Finn's outburst. "Saved the crown prince's life—and comforted him in more ways than that, if the rumors are true." He smirks. "Shouldn't a nobleman support other noblemen who follow the imperial model, and not us—especially when he knows we have the *Caveadear*'s magic?"

Finn looks guarded. "He has his secrets. Let me tell you, just because one becomes a favorite of royalty does not make imperialism dear to them."

"If Prince Finn believes we can trust Jahan Korakides, we can trust him," my father says.

Alistar Connell looks unconvinced, but shrugs. Somehow I think he almost wishes Jahan is untrustworthy. It would make for a challenge, for more excitement, and prove him right about the imperial model of rulership.

My father comes over to me, putting an arm around my shoulders. "We'll be across the border in an hour or so. Do you know what you'll do?"

I nod. I don't know if it will work, but I'll try. "But I thought you said we'd be gone for days."

"We'll dip south, so Finn can speak with the people in Eren, too."

My mouth drops open, the implication of what he says striking me. "But you said this revolution is for the freedom of *Caeris*. Not to start a war over all of Eren."

He smiles. "If our brethren in Eren wish to rise as well, so much the better."

There's a ringing in my ears. All this time, I've been assuming my father wants to divide Eren and Caeris—that I'll have to choose between being one or the other. Even though Hensey and Hugh told me that some Ereni supported the Old Pretender in the first rebellion, it didn't seem real to me.

"That's what you want?" My voice seems to float, far from my body. "Unity?"

Father raises his brows. "Would it be such a terrible thing, to be unified under a Caerisian king instead of an Ereni one?"

"No." I want to weep, such relief sags through me. "No, it wouldn't. Not at all. The Ereni deserve better than the Eyrlais. They deserve better than *Loyce*. They . . ."

I stop. Another thought has occurred to me, a terrible one. I look at my father who watches me with a frown, as if he's struggling to follow my jumbled thoughts. Do I dare say it?

I have to. After all this, it must be asked.

"But will Euan Dromahair—a man who's never even set foot on Caerisian soil—be any better than the Eyrlais?"

He looks at me, then draws me farther from the group. I glance back to see Finn's eyes on us before he quickly looks away.

"A king doesn't rule alone," Father says softly. "Especially not a Caerisian king. A king of Caeris is first among equals, the head of a council, and his will is subject to others'."

"The stewards of the land," I whisper.

Us. My father, and me.

"It has always been thus in Caeris," he says. "The king needs the stewards of the land and the wardens of the mountains. He needs their power, and their validation." He pauses. "When the mountain lords arrive, you will understand. The wardens have a power even the stewards do not, and they possess knowledge of the laws and customs we have lost. In any case, there is much less to fear from a Caerisian king than from an Ereni queen."

I think of Loyce's pettiness. "How do you know Euan Dromahair will rule as a Caerisian king should, and not in the manner of the empire?"

Father lowers his gaze and sighs. When he speaks, he does not quite answer the question. "I know his son."

We both regard Finn, who sits on a rock looking up at one of the Hounds holding forth on past exploits.

"He's young yet," Father says, "but he can grow into a true king. I see it in him."

And I see, in my father, the strength it takes to rule a kingdom without really ruling it. The strength to hold on to beliefs of a better future, a better home, when the world seems pitched against it. The strength to lose one revolution, to lose freedom, to lose a daughter, and yet stand up and fight again.

Suddenly, I realize why Antoine Eyrlai didn't have my father executed or imprisoned when he had the chance. Why he took me instead.

Because if Caeris had lost my father, her people would have revolted in earnest. They would have fought even harder to get him back, this man who fought all his life for them, than they fought to bring a strange king from across the sea to rule them.

So instead, Antoine tried to disempower Ruadan Valtai, to take me from him so I could not learn to be what Caeris needed me to be. So that I did not even know the truth of my own history. But somehow, we are both here. Together, fighting for Caeris's freedom.

And I want it. I want Caeris to be free. I want Eren to be free. Both countries, together, under a new king, a new regime. The hope that bursts through me is so strong my chest contracts.

A part of me still yearns for Jahan and Ida. And I know we need the emperor's help. But can I leave now?

Father squeezes my hand. "Time to ride on."

NO DISCERNIBLE DIFFERENCE marks the border between Caeris and Eren—and yet I *feel* it, like a current running beneath the earth, trammeled and broken in places, but still there. Before I know what I'm doing, I've flung myself off my horse and am kneeling on the earth, my hands pressed into the damp autumn grass of the moorland. Around me the others rein in their horses. A single pulse echoes from the depths of the land, up through my palms, shaking my arms. I gasp.

"El!" Finn's in front of me, with Alistar Connell on his heels.

Father watches from his horse behind them, his gaze thoughtful.

I am shaken, disoriented—so much that I let Finn take my arm and guide me onto my feet. As I step across the invisible line that demarcates the border, I feel a coldness, a deadening, wash through me. It is as if my hearing is blocked, or my eyesight dimmed. The pull to go back to the north side of the line is magnetic, so strong I have to grasp my horse's saddle and hold myself from crossing back into Caeris.

Finn's asking me what's wrong.

"It's the border," Father says. "The old magic still lingers here, the spell that has protected Caeris for so long. The stewards can feel it."

The sweating and swelling in my chest I felt when we crossed the border with Hugh, though I pretended I didn't feel it—that must have been the magic. I wonder how much stronger yet it would have been if, like Hugh and Finn, I'd spilled my blood to the earth. With shaking hands, I pull myself back into the saddle. When I lived in Laon all those years, I must have been partly deaf, partly blind, and I never even knew it. Perhaps this is why the earth no longer woke to me, why my magic became a small, isolated thing, reduced to growing plants' roots and waking specters in stones; perhaps this is why I didn't understand any of it.

Perhaps this is why it was easy for me to forget.

Father falls back beside me as we ride on.

"You see, El, if we can wake the land, we can wake the border. Make Caeris safe again, shielded from those who would bring her harm."

Protected, but isolated. I stare straight ahead, chewing on my lip. Would there still be trade, knowledge of the expanding, living world, of science and medicine and faraway lands?

Because with such obvious magic in use, Jahan's plan will fail; Paladis will never come in on our side. And the emperor will see to it that we are isolated. Alone. Vulnerable.

There would be only Caeris, her justice, her people, and her magic.

Is freedom—is magic—worth that kind of price? How many people would have to die for it to happen? What is the cost?

Father seems to read my thoughts. "Raising the border does not mean no one will be able to cross into Caeris—or out. After all, the Ereni conquered us despite it. But it will give us more protection."

"So that you may practice your customs," I say.

"And you may practice your magic." He looks at me. "So that we may become a kind of haven, for magicians the world over who are hunted down for their abilities."

Like Jahan, who has to hide his skill in the most public and intolerant court in the world.

Like me.

But it still means a revolution. It still means a cost in lives. How likely is it that we would win? And even if we win, the chances that the emperor of Paladis will let us build this sorcerers' haven would be laughable. After centuries of eradicating magic, Paladis will not look at us benignly. We could win the war with Loyce, only to find ourselves in a far greater war against the empire itself. Or, worse, fighting both at once. How on earth would we win that? When would the fighting ever stop?

My hands tighten on the reins. It's impossible. Choose to fight once, and you will have to fight again and again.

I don't know how to resolve the struggle within me, so I feel instead for the knowledge of the land, undulating, unrolling within my body, steady and certain. It grounds me. I listen, and I fall into it.

"There are riders to the west on the coast road," I say. "But if we keep to the east, to the forest, we should be safe."

Father nods, and looks away before I can quite see his smile, or the gleam of tears in his eyes.

CHAPTER THIRTEEN

We have arranged to meet Jahan at an old watchtower built by the Dukes of Touyron to defend their territory against Caerisian "barbarians," long abandoned since the conquest. Night falls before we arrive, but Father won't permit lanterns. Clouds cover the moon, forcing us out of the forest onto a wider track that leaves my spine feeling alert and exposed. I try to send my senses out into the land, but all I can gather is an uneasy feeling, of no use to anyone. The wood around us comes awake with night, and I am no longer sure I can distinguish humans from animals. My uneasiness prevents me from feeling the land clearly.

"Anything?" Father calls to me.

I can't very well say that my skin is prickling with danger. I must be inventing things. Close ahead, the stone tower weighs down the land. I see blood soaking the ground. A marching army, a man dying in agony, flames burning up the tower roof. More blood. I start to retch, and it brings me back to myself, my hands clamped at my chest. What *was* that? Am I losing my mind now?

I try to focus again on the tower, but I have no idea whether anyone besides Jahan actually occupies it.

"I don't—I don't think so."

Alistar Connell mutters something on my left; he's riding beside me now. "Doesn't feel right."

I shake my head to clear it, but it doesn't do any good. Part of me sees a line of Caerisian soldiers marching along this road, sometime in the past or even future, and a coach dashing toward the great house, Ereni bayonets, the scent of gunpowder—

I have to stop making these things up. Jahan is waiting at the tower. I have to concentrate on him. Maybe I'll feel his presence. Maybe that will make sense out of the jumble of time.

But I don't feel him at all.

Alistar Connell reins his horse in, the silhouette of his hand in the air. Our line jerks to a stop. I hold my breath. Alistar is holding his breath, too. We all listen.

Nothing but the wind in the trees. A small mammal scurrying up a branch.

In the past, someone died here. I feel the echo of their shock, the sudden pain, traveling up through the earth.

I'm losing my mind.

"I thought—" Alistar begins, then breaks off. This time I hear it, too: a snort and stamp ahead of us. We are quite close to the tower. I can taste the limestone it's built of.

"That will be Jahan," Finn says, his voice bright and eager.

And loud. Too loud.

"There are men ahead," I say, but my confidence is cracking. My heartbeat pulses in my ears, distracting me.

Alistar must hear it in my voice. He pulls out his pistol. It *snicks* as he cocks it.

Father knows, too. "El. Alistar. Some of your Hounds—"

"I'll stay with the *Caveadear*," Alistar says. "Nevan. Art. Go ahead with the duke."

"Are we in danger?" Finn's voice is taut.

"Just taking precautions." Father sounds easy. "You stay here, stay safe."

"No. I'm coming with you. I'm the only one who knows Jahan."

Father draws in his breath, then just sighs. "Stay at the back, then. Ready?"

They ride off with a squeak of leather, leaving me alone, in darkness, with Alistar Connell and several others. I start to say, "There can't be anyone else at the tower. How would anyone know—?"

He interrupts me. "Do you have a weapon?"

I swallow. "Just my dagger."

"Can you fire a pistol?"

"Yes, but my aim wouldn't be good from the back of a horse."

This is no time to lie about my skills as a markswoman. I think about pheasant hunting on the king's country estate, with the patient shooting-master cocking the guns for us, the careful, leisurely shots we took. It seems like it happened to someone else.

"All right. If we have trouble . . ." He pauses. "You ride ahead. We'll cover your flank."

"What if they're behind us?" I whisper.

Silence. Then Alistar Connell says, "Do you—"

"Yes, I think it's a trap."

I listen. More silence. Then gunfire bursts through the night. My horse bucks and shudders, and I struggle to hold her down. "Into the wood," Alistar Connell shouts, "into the wood!"

The gunfire flames red and yellow, sparks illuminating the near roof of the tower. More shots report. Men holler. Stampeding hooves trample the earth. The sparks leave bright fragments on my night vision. A rider barrels toward us along the road: "Run!"

It's Finn.

We barely move out of the way in time for him to hurtle between us, thundering north, toward Caeris. Toward more Ereni soldiers, maybe.

Alone.

Gunfire reports at the tower.

My father. Where is my father?

"Go after the prince," Alistar orders. "I'm going to the tower."

"I'm coming with you," I blurt out.

"No. It's too dangerous. You have to protect Prince Finn." And he rides off without another word.

I breathe in. I know what I have to do. I turn to the remaining Hounds. "Follow the prince. I'm going with Alistar."

"But Lady Elanna—"

I pull Alistar's own trick, wheeling my horse off toward the tower before they can argue or stop me. The gunfire seems to have ceased, so quickly after it began. My horse stops dead as we round the curve. I nearly catapult into Alistar.

"I told you to go after Finn," he whisper-shouts.

"You need me." I can't say why, but I am convinced I'm required at the tower.

"Then shut up and do as I say. Get off your horse. Do you hear anything?"

I dismount and listen hard, through the soles of my feet as well as through my ears. My ears hear little, but my feet—

"Riders, going that way." I point before I realize he can't see me. "South."

He curses. "Tether your horse. We'll go on foot."

We leave our horses at the forest's edge, cropping grass as if nothing at all is happening. Alistar grabs me by the wrist, pulling me to the left—off the main approach and into a clump of bracken. We both go still, but our noise is not met with other noise. He paces forward. I follow, trying not to catch my feet in the tangled stalks of grass.

A light appears, guttering on the other side of the tower. A torch. Alistar slips closer, then bends down to grab a branch from the ground. He pitches it across the opening behind the tower.

No one comes running.

And then I hear it. A soft moan.

Alistar swears again, under his breath this time. I pull my dagger out. Someone is in the tower; I feel it in my bones. I also feel that many people have died here, more than once in the past. But I know someone is there now. Are they our friends or our enemies?

We ease our way up the slope to the tower, a few paces at a time. Still nothing. Neither of us dares speak. As we close in on the door, Alistar gestures at me to stay back—this time, I obey—and pulls a second pistol from the holster beneath his coat. He cocks both pistols. He creeps along the wall, one wary step after another. I press myself to the wall as well. I feel a beat, but can't tell if it's only my heart.

He pauses. We stand there, and stand there.

Then Alistar lunges into the doorway.

A shot explodes. Sparks shatter through the night.

He rolls onto his knees, dropping the first pistol, coming up with the second in both hands. It reports, echoing in the chamber. More sparks flare.

I feel the shudder as the body falls to earth.

Alistar clambers to his feet, collecting the weapons. There's none of the arrogance he's shown in the past. His mouth is tight. "That's the only one." All the same, he pauses a moment to reload his pistols, his fingers brisk and efficient as he tips in powder and stuffs the lead shot down the barrel. He holsters them, and walks ahead.

I follow him into the tower.

An Ereni soldier is dying on the floor in front of us, eyes rolling, his chest a mess of blood and his—

I run back outside to vomit in the grass.

Alistar storms out after me. "No one else there. They must have taken the duke and the others."

I straighten and point, wordlessly. He hasn't seen them, but now he does: the two fallen Hounds tumbled to the ground.

But not my father.

Not my father.

"Where is Duke Ruadan?" Alistar says, echoing my thoughts. He seizes the torch off the wall and marches into the woods in search of tracks, swearing under his breath.

"They captured him. Or they killed him, and . . ." The thought is too terrible for me to voice. I've just gotten my father back, and now I've lost him again. Sudden rage pounds through the numbness in my head. If Loyce has ordered him to be murdered, I'll kill her. I'll find some way to wake the land, and I'll use it to destroy her.

"Here," Alistar calls. "Tracks going south." He swings his fist—an empty gesture—and returns, shining the torch in my face. He shakes his head. "I was right. The Idaean's a double agent."

"He is *not*." At least, I don't think so.

But then, how well do I actually know Jahan?

Alistar's jaw clenches. "You and the prince seem very convinced of this matter, but how else do you explain what happened here?" He gestures to his two dead men.

I have no words, only this useless rage tightening around my skull. So I walk to the dead, crouching beside them. Alistar follows me and kneels down across from me, glaring at me over their bodies. I can't look at the terrible things death has done to them, so I stare back at him. We need to bury the Ereni soldier, too. I may be ready to murder Loyce with my bare hands, but her soldiers are simply men following their orders. Will Alistar agree, though? I have to let it pass. We don't have time for an argument. "I don't know the customs," I say.

"The customs." He spits the word. His nostrils flare. Then he leans over the bodies and kisses each man on his bloodstained forehead. I do the same. Their skin is cold and smooth. Alistar folds one man's arms over his chest; I follow suit with the one closest to me, though my hands become sticky with clotted gore.

Loyce has done this, and the Butcher's carried it out. If I had gotten here sooner, if Alistar hadn't killed the Ereni soldier before he could kill us, it could be Alistar or me lying there on the ground.

A tear rolls off Alistar Connell's chin. In halting, archaic Caerisian, he says, "Now I am with the land always. I am always with you. *Mo cri, mo tire, mo fiel.*"

"My heart, my land, my blood," I say. It's the phrase the specters speak at the Hill of the Imperishable—the line taken from one of the books in my father's library.

Alistar nods. "From our old poem about Wildegarde, after she weds the land." He gestures for me to repeat the phrase. I mumble the words over Nevan's body.

There's a silence. Then Alistar stands abruptly, a fist pressed to his lips. "Let's go."

"We need to bury them."

"There's no time."

He turns, but I can't move from the bodies. It's *wrong* to leave them here, exposed, their empty faces naked to the night. My hand curls into a fist on my knee. Beneath me, as if in response to my anger, the earth shifts. I call to it: *Come.*

I scramble backward as the soil reaches up and tumbles the bodies of the Hounds deep into it. Alistar Connell whirls, an outcry stillborn in his throat. More soil is falling over to cover the bodies. It is finished in a matter of moments, but we both remain, staring.

The earth knew what I wanted. It did as I asked.

I look away from Alistar's open tears, for my own eyes are wet, not just with grief but with the shock of triumph. The land answered my bidding. Maybe there is more to these stories than legend, after all. Maybe the *Caveadears* really can wake the land—maybe not as powerfully as Wildegarde did, but wake it all the same. Maybe I can win this fight.

But how? And at what cost?

I look at the freshly turned earth, and my chest flushes with anger.

These men lost their lives for no reason. None. They died so that we could be betrayed, so that my father could be captured. The Ereni soldier died because someone commanded him to remain here: a quirk of fate. Whatever powers I have, whatever powers *Wildegarde* had, can't give these men back their lives.

Just this morning I was ready to depose Loyce, to give Eren and Caeris a new king. Now I want the queen dead. I want her taken captive and locked up behind bars, so she knows what it's like. So she really understands fear. I want revenge, and it burns under my skin, sure and steadying, without logic or reason.

Alistar Connell stands up. "Well," he says. "Shall we go see if the prince has gotten himself killed as well?"

"I'M A COWARD," Finn says. His voice is flat. He's shivering, and not trying to disguise it.

I don't answer. There's nothing to say that won't result in raised voices, and we can't afford to be overheard. We came upon him and the Hounds beside a ditch on the main road. Finn was being sick into a shrub. Not far away, we could all hear a soldier whistling on duty. Our prince, in his panic, took the easiest road: straight to the gates of Portmason.

Alistar insisted on going in, while we got off the road and into the woods. "They'll have brought the duke here."

"We don't know that," I said. "And it's probably just what they want us to do—go in after him. How do you propose to get in, anyway?"

"Have you never scaled a wall before, *Caveadear*?"

Part of me wishes I'd gone over the wall with him, instead of waiting in the woods with Finn and a couple of Hounds. It's getting cold out here, without a fire, and I can't stop thinking about my father. About Jahan. Everything certain seems to be slipping out from under me. Father's captured, and Jahan betrayed us or, at the very least, got caught. I want to ride to Laon and burn down the palace; I want to scream in Loyce's face and demand my father back. Instead we're sitting here, in the dark woods, my trousers growing damp with condensation.

I think about that conversation with Jahan, the one we had after my father declared me the steward of the land. I've run through it in my head so many times it's memorized. He said, *This is more than I ever expected!* And when I asked him what he meant, he avoided the answer.

Not only that, he wanted to take me to Ida with him. It made sense that my presence would make a difference in helping our cause—or I thought it did. Has this all been a ruse? Has he been trying to isolate me all along so that he can hand me over to Loyce? Or—I flinch at the thought—the emperor?

But he's a sorcerer himself. Why would he betray me? Maybe it would make his position more secure; if he's seen handing over another magician, he's less likely to be accused of practicing magic himself. I feel sick to my stomach. Have I misread the way he looked at me, the meaning of his smiles? Was that last, burning look, the fleeting touch of our hands, not about me at all, but about the indemnity he envisioned buying with me? Was he playing me all along?

All I know for certain is that my father's gone, and Jahan may have orchestrated it. And the man who's dedicated his life to Caeris's freedom will soon be paying for that dedication with his life. There's no question what Loyce will do with him.

"I bolted," Finn is saying. The self-loathing in his voice is almost unbearable. "I heard the gunfire and I *ran*—like the most lily-livered coward."

I dig my hands into my sleeves. I wish he would stop telling me this.

"It took me back. To Chozat. The Getai came upon us out of nowhere. They called it a true test 'of whether you were a man or not.'"

"It's a good thing you did run. Imagine if they'd caught you both. It was *intelligent*."

His jaw works. I stare into the night sky, flecked with stars between moving clouds. Heaven knows what the other Hounds are making of this conversation. Caeris's would-be prince shouldn't be admitting to his own terror in the face of battle. Yet here he is, spilling the words as if desperate to confess. He doesn't know that, beside him, I'm struggling with such impotent rage. I want to snatch a pistol and ride into Portmason, brandishing it. I want to wake the land and let its magic vent my fury. Even though I don't know how to fight, even though I know that violence only begets more violence.

Maybe fighting *is* the only way.

A pale slice of blue touches the sky as I watch. Dawn.

I still can't believe Jahan betrayed us. No, someone else must have found out. They must have stopped him. Only . . .

I wish I dared to believe this. But it's so easy, now, in hindsight, to read all our interactions in another way entirely.

There's a creak and stomp; one of the Hounds stands up. I'm on my feet a moment later: I heard it, too. A low hooting, like an owl.

Except no owl actually sounds like Alistar Connell.

Bran hoots in reply.

In another moment Alistar and Declan run into our little grove, throwing hot buns at us. Mine catches me in the chin.

"Mount up," Alistar says grimly. "They're after us."

Good thing we didn't unsaddle the horses—though the fact that their mission did not go well is obvious simply from my father's absence. As we swing onto our horses, a shout rises behind us.

"That'll be them."

In the dense woods, we can't move fast, but neither can our pursuit. At last we achieve the edge of a farm field, and Alistar and the Hounds shoot off, leaving Finn and me to scramble in their wake.

We catch up to them around midmorning, beside a stream. The horses are tired, breathing hard. I rub mine down and give her a good bag of feed, then go straight down to the water, plunging my hands in and flinging the shining, icy-cold droplets onto my face. My eyes ache, my body aches. Everything in me aches.

They've taken my father. My desire for revenge has shrunken to a small, cold thing, a weight in the pit of my stomach. I'm afraid of the way I'm thinking now—of how easily I've begun to think taking up arms against the crown might be a reasonable course of action.

Mostly I'm afraid of how much I want to.

Behind me, Finn is asking Alistar if they found any sign of Father in Portmason.

"No. They took him south, by the looks of things. To the Tower in Laon, most likely."

"You aren't going to pursue him?"

"Well, Your Highness, we have you and the *Caveadear,* don't we? The duke knew the risks he ran. He always did."

Why do they always write off their own people, saying they knew the risk? Hensey has already been so easily dispatched.

But Alistar's tone is heavy, and I wonder how much he believes his own words. I saw his tears last night. My own eyes feel bruised with the effort not to cry. I feel as though I almost understood my father, and now he's been torn from me.

The water clears, revealing my reflection, hovering over the river stones and soil. I start to reach for another scoop to drink—I am so thirsty—but stop just as my fingertips touch the surface.

My face has transformed. Jahan stares at me, his lips parted, wide-eyed.

"Are you safe?"

I wonder if I'm inventing the breathless panic in his voice, if I simply want it to be there. After all, I hear him in my mind, though the words are his.

"The Butcher's caught your father—they knew somehow, I don't know how, and they stopped me from going to the tower. I've had to pretend complete ignorance about the duke. I tried to find you, but—"

I can't believe him. I want to. I want to so badly. But I can't afford to take the risk—to make the mistake of wishing him to be our ally when the truth is that he's a double agent, protecting himself and his own secrets before anyone else.

When he could be trying to hand me over to the witch hunters to disguise the truth of his own nature.

"Don't pretend," I whisper to the water riffling over his face. "Don't lie."

Then I plunge both hands into the stream, destroying his reflection.

CHAPTER FOURTEEN

At noon, when we cross the border, they find us. Shots ring out. A shocking hiss of lead shot passes close to my face, leaving a stinging cut of blood. I reach for a weapon to fire back, but I have only my dagger.

The border magic. Maybe it can save us.

The land is already pulsing with renewed awareness under my skin. Last night, I persuaded the earth to cover the Hounds' corpses. What if making it do my bidding is as simple as asking?

Come, I call. I think of the history books I've been reading. Ossian called mists to confuse the Ereni soldiers; he sent them through valleys that appeared on no maps.

The earth whispers under my skin.

Fog rolls up from the ground, gathering so densely around us we seem to be smothered. Alistar shouts for us to change formation, though we can barely make out one another's shapes in the thick white mist. The shots behind us have stopped. I hear someone shouting, still some distance away.

"Is this your doing, *Caveadear*?" Alistar calls.

"It is." I feel a bit foolish; I've effectively blinded us as well as our pursuers. Even the Hounds' sense of direction won't help us in this impossible fog.

The earth pulses again. And, perhaps because I can see so little, I realize how much I can *feel*. There are layers to the pulsing—lines, I might almost say. "Cerid Aven," I whisper.

The sensation coalesces into a tugging, like a rope pulling me forward. "Alistar. Has anyone rope? Let me lead. I can—" I'm embarrassed at how foolish the words sound, but I say it anyway. "I can *feel* it."

Alistar Connell does not question me. We loop a rope through the horses' stirrups, throwing one to the other. Then I am in the lead, following the tugging in my sternum into the hills of Caeris.

Once I can no longer detect pursuit, I let the fog dissipate. It fades immediately, leaving us in a damp, dark forest. The men send up a cheer. I can't help smiling at what I've done, out of shock as much as anything else. The Hounds recognize this patch of wood, and I fall back to let Alistar lead us home to Cerid Aven.

But when we approach the house, long after nightfall, Alistar calls a halt. Our exhausted horses pull toward their stables, and we have to hold them back. Lights burn in the sashed windows that face toward the garden. I don't see the problem until Alistar points at the drive. The wink of bayonets shines, strapped on shoulders; a swinging lantern glows.

"They could be ours," Finn begins.

But we all hear it. My brain, dumb with lack of sleep, registers the words slowly. The guards on duty are singing—an Ereni song.

No. Ereni guardsmen can't be here. Loyce can't have sent them already.

My mother. Sophy. Hugh. They're all here.

"Someone knew we were leaving," Alistar says, his voice soft and tight. "Someone planned all this."

He looks at me, and my irrational heartbeat spikes into my ears. He can't think it was *me*—can he? Does he think, because I betrayed them as a child and lived as a hostage in Laon, I'd actually give them up when my own life is at stake?

But he says, "Your ambassador."

"Jahan wouldn't," says Finn, but the protest sounds weak even to me.

I say nothing. Alistar is watching me, not Finn, as if despite my fears I am the one he trusts, the one he believes. But all I know is that we can't afford to trust Jahan. Until he's proven innocent, we have to treat him as the enemy. It makes my stomach curdle, even as I suspect Alistar is right.

I wish my father were here. He would know what to do. I don't want the responsibility for this, for people's lives.

Alistar seems to be waiting for me to speak. In fact, they all are. I look around at their faces, smeared with gunpowder and mud, squinting from exhaustion, but still ready to take action at the first order. My order, not Finn's. Perhaps it's because my father was their real leader. Or perhaps it's because Finn himself seems to be waiting for me to make the decision.

Or perhaps it's because I called up the fog to protect us. I led us safely into Caeris. I used the magic of the land to save us.

I swallow. But I was born for this, wasn't I?

"Let's see what we can find out," I say at last. "Alistar, you and I will do reconnaissance. Finn, take the others to make camp."

They all move to obey my orders, and I breathe out in relief that I seem to have said the right thing.

Alistar and I go alone across the lawn, running from oak tree to pine. I wish for some of Jahan's concealing magic, and then I wonder if Jahan has even lied about that. What if he's a witch hunter only pretending to be a sorcerer? It makes no sense, and yet I can't shake the thought. My stomach twists, sick and angry. I seize a broken oak branch from the ground and let it grow in my hands, sprouting leaves and shoots, the way I used to in the greenhouse, but openly now. It makes me feel better, more solid. More real.

We creep up to the low windows fronting the salon. It doesn't seem that the Ereni stationed guards on this side of the house. Evidently they expected our approach to come from the obvious route: the front drive. Or maybe they didn't expect us at all. By now, they must know we planned to be gone several days.

Shielding my face with the leafy bough, I peer into the salon. The darkness helps to hide me. Hopefully anyone glancing out the window will think I'm just a bush, blown by the wind into view.

Strangers occupy the familiar room along with my mother. She sits upright at the clavichord, her back to us. My heart leaps at the sight of her.

Standing to her right, I see Sophy, clearly preparing to sing, and equally clearly unhappy about it. Her face is set and stern; her hands press hard together. Her eyes flicker toward the window. Does she see me here? I sink lower to the ground.

Just in time—the gentleman beside her turns to look as well.

The Butcher. I might have known. I utter a curse worthy of Alistar.

"What's that?" he whispers.

"The Butcher of Novarre. Whoever betrayed us told *him,* and he's in there with my mother and Sophy—"

Alistar grasps my arm while I bite down on my lip to keep from shouting my rage. Then he takes the branch and peers into the salon himself. He's back down in a moment. "I don't see Hugh."

"He's a wanted man. There's a price on his head from the first revolution. He took the blame when my father . . ." Tears choke my nose and eyes; I'm so frustrated I strike the wall with my open hand.

"They'll have him in custody, then." Alistar's tone is pragmatic.

"Probably." First Guerin, then Hensey and Victoire, and now my father and Hugh. I can't bear this. I fight to keep my breath under control. "Unless he escaped."

"He might have, but only if he knew they were coming."

"How did they even get *in*? I thought we'd put up defenses, I thought people were mobilizing—" My voice is rising again. I pull the words back.

Alistar shakes his head. "There's no fortress guarding Cerid Aven. The queen's men can walk in if they want to. The question," he says without humor, "is whether we'll let them back out again."

I strike the wall again as Alistar crawls away into the darkness. I'm about to follow when a shadow splits the light at the window. Someone's looking out. I flatten my back against the wall, my heartbeat jerking an unsteady rhythm. They'll see Alistar. They'll see me. At least Alistar's got the branch. I've got nothing. I could call fog again, but they might still glimpse my silhouette when I stand.

I roll my eyes as far to the left as I can. Still all I can make out is the imprint of a shadow blocking the light.

Across the lawn, Alistar glances back at me. I see the pale shape of his face, and know whoever's standing in the window must see it, too, if they're looking closely.

Pray all the gods it's not the Butcher.

It must not be. Alistar stands up, waving at the window. I crane my neck and glimpse Sophy, her hand raised to the glass, just before she ducks out of sight.

I breathe out in relief. At least it's not Sophy who betrayed us and invited the Ereni in.

I jump to my feet and run.

Alistar's waiting for me beneath the nearest oak. I collapse against the trunk, panting. My father, my mother, Sophy, Hugh, Guerin, Hensey, Victoire—who will they take next? How can we possibly stop them? I dig my fingers into the oak's bark. It's the only thing that seems to control the terrible feeling of impotence mixed with rage.

Alistar watches the house, chewing on his lip. "I hope she saw me. She's probably praying for her life right now. If they know who she is, there's no chance for her. Gods!"

I blink at him, startled out of my anger. "What are you talking about?"

"If they know who her father is, she'd disappear faster than you can say *royal bastard*."

I draw in my breath. "Sophy's father is the Old Pretender?" It shocks me, but it shouldn't—because it all makes sense. Her odd attitude toward Finn, why my father would take on a ward in the first place, her pride despite her non-noble name. "Does Finn know?"

"It doesn't seem like it. I'm glad you didn't know. If you didn't, maybe the Butcher doesn't."

My skin goes cold. "We have to get her out of there."

We have to get her out before the Butcher realizes he's got a prize on his hands: Euan Dromahair's bastard daughter and her royal Caerisian blood.

AROUND MIDNIGHT, THE lights finally go out. The cold is gathering beneath the oaks; I can't stop shivering. Finn and the Hounds have made camp up the hill, as close to the old stone circle as they could manage. Alistar went to look in on them and returned; I refused to leave sight of the house. If Hugh is indeed gone, we can't lose Sophy and my mother as well. Alistar was away so long I began to worry that the Ereni guards had captured him. He returned at last, out of breath and with a sack of food and water. "Finn made a good decision, camping near the stones," he said. "They will protect us if we need protecting."

I looked at him.

"The land conceals those in danger, if you call upon her," he said. "It's more reliable near the old stones. And with you being the *Caveadear,* the power combined should make us as safe as we can hope for."

I haven't asked him what, exactly, he expects me to do. Tiredness has stolen my voice. Tiredness, and fear.

They've taken my father. They've taken our house.

Can we still raise a revolution, without my father or Hugh?

Alistar stands up, shaking me out of my reverie. I sit upright, my blood pounding me alert.

"Wait," he says.

We watch the lights gleam briefly in the upper windows: my mother's room, the stateroom where Finn slept until two nights ago, and two more along the hallway. Soldiers call out in the front drive, their Ereni voices clipped and brisk compared with the Caerisian accents I've already become accustomed to.

"Changing of the guard," Alistar notes. "We'll have to go in through the kitchen."

My stomach is churning. "Or the conservatory."

"Yes. No one would expect that, would they?"

I climb to my feet, trying to shake my tired, cold limbs awake. It doesn't do much good. A significant, and foolish, part of me wants to go in and sleep in my own bed, forgetting this revolution and my fear.

"Where do you think they're holding Hugh?" I ask to distract myself.

"Could be anywhere. We'll find Soph first. She'll know."

Soph? How well do Alistar Connell and Sophy Dunbarron know each other?

The light in my mother's window goes out.

Another remains lit, in the staterooms where Finn slept. It must be the Butcher. He seems like the sort of person who doesn't need to sleep, not being quite like normal humans in habits or humanity.

Alistar starts forward, stops. I follow so closely I nearly run into him. He holds up his arm to keep me back.

A shape moves in the darkened conservatory windows. I hold my breath. As we watch, a door silently opens, and a figure in a dark cloak steps out onto the portico. I glimpse the long white line of her neck, the pale peek of lace on her sleeves.

Sophy gathers her skirts and runs across the lawn.

I stare up at the lighted window, willing the Butcher not to part the curtains and look out.

Unable to hold himself back any longer, Alistar lurches into a run, meeting Sophy halfway across the lawn. She gasps, then grabs his arm, and he pulls her to the safety of our trees. In another moment they're here. Safe. I throw my arms around Sophy's neck. She hugs me back, panting.

"It was so easy," she's saying. She sounds as though she's trying to hold in hysterical laughter. "They don't have guards posted in the house. It's as if they think we're *welcome guests* at someone's country estate! Or as if we women aren't bright enough to think of simply walking out the door."

She's still wearing the gown I glimpsed her in earlier, the cream confection she had on the other night. It is probably the least practical thing I can think of for escaping through the rugged land of Caeris, but I won't say anything. What I took for a cloak is, in fact, a thick brocade curtain stripped from a window.

"I said I was going to bed and then hid in the linen closet. And when everyone else had gone, I walked out! It was so *easy*."

Alistar meets my eyes, as much as he can, in the darkness.

"Sophy," I say, "we'll get you to camp. But what about my mother? What about Hugh?"

Her breath catches just long enough for me to hear it. Then she says, "Don't worry about Lady Teofila. She's being treated like the guest of honor at a rural hunting party. Lord Gilbert loves music."

Alistar is quiet. I cannot speak. Is Sophy suggesting we *leave* my mother at Cerid Aven?

"And Hugh?" Alistar says at length.

"They took him straight to Barrody." Sophy goes silent, then, and I feel a tremor run up her arm.

I'm going to be sick. So they'll lock Hugh up at Barrody and pretend to administer "justice." But it will not be justice. Justice would mean a trial, a hearing, an uncertain outcome. We all know Loyce will have him executed. I run a hand through my hair, trying to calm myself enough to think rationally, but I can't stop trembling.

"Well," Alistar says on a long sigh. "It is a risk to go in for Lady Teofila."

"She's next door to the Butcher. You wouldn't stand a chance. I don't think the man sleeps."

Silence. My breath rattles, too loud, through my open mouth.

"Let's go, then," Alistar says quietly.

"We can't!" I burst out. "I won't leave my mother at the mercy of the Butcher of Novarre. I won't! What's the use of my magic if we can't get her out?"

I turn away, but Sophy grabs my arm, pulling me back between her and Alistar. "El, your mother's all right. Believe me."

"I just don't *understand*—"

"Listen." Sophy holds me by the shoulders. Her voice is low and firm. "I've known your mother for fourteen years. Fourteen years you *haven't* known her. I know her better than you. And I'm saying, she will be fine."

"But when they find you're gone, he'll hold her for ransom. He'll threaten her, to get us to come for her, and then he'll kill her if it doesn't work. I know the Butcher. You know my mother, but I know him."

"He won't harm her," Sophy insists. "Teofila swears he won't. She . . . She *trusts* him, for some reason. And he likes music. He wants her to play études for him."

This is the most idiotic thing I've ever heard. The Butcher is not going to hold back from using my mother as a pawn because he likes listening to her play *études*.

"She's delusional!" I hiss.

"She's *not*. Your mother is the most rational person I know."

Before I can point out that this seems quite unlikely, given the circumstances, Alistar says quietly, "Look."

We both turn. The light has vanished from the stateroom, but appeared in the conservatory. Sophy gasps. It floats closer to the door, the figure of a man just visible holding it. The door opens. He steps outside.

I hear a low buzzing, cold and prickling in my ears.

He's got the witch stone.

"Hello?" he calls out into the night, in an urbane voice, as if it's quite ordinary to invite your enemies to come out of the woods and have tea with you. "Is anyone there?"

I drop to the ground, scrabbling in the dirt. I don't know what I'm looking for, I just know that I have to make contact with the soil of Caeris, or the witch stone's ringing in my ears will drive me to distraction.

Above me, Sophy slowly draws her curtain-cloak over her face. I see Alistar reach for her hand, and how she returns a warm squeeze.

The land pulses, steadying me, driving out the buzzing in my ears. I let myself sigh a little in relief. *We are wind,* I think. *We are still as the trees themselves.* And it seems as though my bones and skin stiffen like bark, as if my feet turn a little woody and my veins start to flow with water instead of blood.

The Butcher turns and goes back into the house. The buzzing stops.

"Come on." Sophy and Alistar begin to run. I let myself stare at the house for half a breath, but it's no use. The Butcher knows we're here. We have to go. I scramble to my feet and hurry after them, leaving my mother behind.

CHAPTER FIFTEEN

I come awake too fast, not knowing what startled me from sleep. The forest is quiet around us; I hear only the even breathing of the others, rolled up in cloaks and coats, the snort and stamp of the horses. Alistar mumbles in his sleep. Off to my left someone hums softly to himself—the Hound who's on guard. A single star winks above me between the boughs of the firs, almost faded to invisibility in the lightening sky.

Beneath me, the land shifts and thrums. It almost seems as if it, too, is dreaming. As I relax, images float to me, a hundred men and women climbing the Sentry Rock in procession. Their faces blur from time, but I feel the pressure of their feet. Then they slide back into forgetfulness and I remember instead the stones being tugged uphill, partly by strength and partly by magic. But I cannot see who built the circle. Memory of them is lost to time.

I sit up, and the present rights itself. The Hound on watch glances over at me. I manage a smile, pushing myself to my feet. The crowd of sleepers burrowed together in the forest appears vulnerable, almost eerie. We all slept here last night, so fragile.

I look down at their sleeping faces and remember how they all looked to me last night for direction, even though Alistar and Finn are more accustomed to being leaders. But I am the steward of the land. These people belong to the land, and, therefore, they're my responsibility.

It's a strange feeling.

I step over Sophy's legs and onto the path to the hilltop. The forest lies so still about me. I seem to feel the delicate weight of each fallen leaf, the twist of tree roots into the soil, the rustle of owls' wings. I am aware of it all when I look sideways in my mind, beyond and behind my thoughts. Then the awareness vanishes when I start to think about Jahan and my parents and the disaster that may be our revolution.

I lost my chance to escape, if I ever really had it. Who knows, Jahan might have simply handed me over to the Butcher—or maybe he's being watched so closely we would never have had a chance.

In any case, I'm here now. I can't leave. There's nowhere left to run to, and no choice that wouldn't mean deserting this land and my people.

My people. Another strange thought. I'm still more Ereni than I am Caerisian, at least in my mind, but maybe the truth is that I've always belonged to Caeris, too.

Does that mean this revolution is my responsibility, too?

I don't know how to answer that question, so I keep walking. The hill grows steeper. My calves and thighs strain. I'm not sure what to do when I reach the top of the hill, but maybe the land itself will tell me. Maybe it will remind me, through its own memories, how to wake it, how to align the border for its protection.

But a small voice in the back of my mind tells me that no matter what I do to align the border, my father and Hugh will still be in prison, and Loyce Eyrlai will still reign as the queen of Eren. The Butcher will still be camped in Cerid Aven, with my mother.

Whatever I do in the stone circle cannot possibly be enough.

I push myself over the final lip of rock, onto the bare outcropping. I lean over my knees, panting. My body's tired from all the activity of the past several days, and my mind isn't much better. Already, I want this to be over.

When I straighten, I discover the circle isn't empty. I startle backward, almost slipping on the stones. I have to windmill my arms to stay upright. The nearest level ground is very far below.

I look again into the circle.

What a fool I am. She's a specter. The woman sitting in the circle came out of the stones—that, or she's such a vivid memory from the land itself I'm seeing her in physical form. *From the cold mountains behind the moon, Wildegarde came* . . . A prickle runs up my spine. Maybe this is Wildegarde, her black hair blown by the wind, cocooned in her dark-blue cloak, waiting to give me the answer I seek. Maybe she will dissolve all these problems, rescue my parents and Hugh, and drive the Ereni from Caeris. Maybe then the knot in my stomach will disappear, along with the burden of responsibility.

I step forward. My foot scatters some loose pebbles, sending them chattering over the bare stones.

The woman looks around, then rises, pushing back her cloak so I glimpse the bulk of a broadsword under it, and see the daggers holstered on either hip.

"*Caveadear,*" she says, inclining her chin a fraction forward.

I slow. This is no specter. This isn't Wildegarde, come to me through the mists of time. This is a young woman about my own age, her face seamed and tough as the rock on which we stand. A woman strong enough to wield a broadsword.

"I hoped you would hear my presence." She studies me as she says it, her gaze openly critical. Her accent thickens the words so much I can hardly understand her. If mountains talked, they'd sound like her. "I am Rhia Knoll. My father sent me to tell you we will not lend our aid."

"Your father," I say in my Ereni-tinged Caerisian, and her lip curls at the sound of my voice. "He must be one of the mountain lords."

"He is Ingram Knoll, the warden of the mountains."

"Oh," I say stupidly. "*Oh.*"

The mountain lords won't lend their help?

But we have been counting on them. I need their secrets to understand my magic. They are true Caerisians, tough and stubborn, clinging to the old customs. If anyone wants to be free from Eren, it should be them.

Except, apparently, it's not.

"Why?" I ask, unable to think of a more intelligent question.

She snorts. "Your revolution has already failed. The Ereni occupy Cerid Aven while you and your supporters sleep out on the ground."

"We were *betrayed,*" I snap. "Someone captured my father. Someone gave us away."

She shakes her head, tossing back her hair. "This is what comes of not electing the king in the proper way. You want to bring back Euan Dromahair from across the sea and expect the land to welcome his son? The land knows when we do not have a just king."

"The land doesn't know anything." I'm spluttering worse than I used to when Denis Falconier goaded me. I have to calm down. I force myself to breathe. "Finn has no bond with the land. It's me and my father who—"

"You are wrong," Rhia Knoll says with stunning arrogance. "The land is older and wiser than you or I. Just because you do not know how to speak to her doesn't mean she doesn't hear. She knows Fionnlach Dromahair has not been selected by the majority, and she refuses to subject herself to him."

Does this woman believe her own words?

"How do *you* know?" I demand.

Rhia Knoll seems almost smug. "I was raised on this land, unlike you. I know her ways."

"Really. That's marvelous." I can't quite keep the sarcasm from my tone. "Why don't you go back to the mountains, then? It's so thoughtful of you to inform us of the error of our ways."

She narrows her eyes. "My father requests your presence at Dalriada. We will go together, now. We must reach the mountains before the Day of the Dying Year."

I will go with this stranger to the Tail Ridge, leaving my friends to fight this war on their own, leaving both my parents captive? I've already lost my parents and Hugh to that ill-conceived notion to go to Ida. Who else would we lose if I leave now? Finn and Sophy need me.

"You must be out of your mind," I say.

She gives me a tolerant look. "There is no other way. The *Caveadear* must come to the mountains. You must be there for the Day of the Dying Year. That is how it is done."

"Well, it's not how *I* do it. I won't abandon my people for yours."

We stare at each other. Rhia Knoll's squinted eyes are light, sky-colored, her mouth a hard line. A tracery of blue marks covers her cheeks and forehead, paint that didn't quite wash off—a recollection of spirals and diamonds.

"El!" Someone below the ridge calls my name. I turn in time to see Alistar Connell leap up onto the outcropping as lightly as the hound he's named for. He grins at me, but then he sees Rhia Knoll. A scowl transforms his face.

"I don't suppose this means a whole army of mountain lords is waiting on the other side of Barrody?" he says, without greeting her.

Rhia Knoll folds her arms. They obviously know each other. "This war has not begun in the proper way. A call went out to the clans, but when did the clans vote? The laws say such a war may only be declared by a meeting of the steward of the land, the warden of the mountains, and the king. But you have declared Euan Dromahair king without an election, and the *Caveadear* declared war without consulting my father—"

Alistar interrupts her. "The laws also state that the *Caveadear* has the right to decide a war if the warden and the king cannot be present or if agreement cannot be met."

"Only in cases of utmost need," she shoots back. "When all of Caer-Ys is in danger. We are not in danger of anything but your greed, Dog of Urseach, and the greed of your 'prince' and followers!"

Alistar's nostrils flare, and he points a finger at her. "You, Rhia Knoll, know nothing up in your mountains but—"

"Stop it. Both of you." I can't tolerate any more of their arguments. "My father may be dead. My mother is captured. Hugh is bound to be executed. It doesn't *matter* what the laws say, because clearly Loyce Eyrlai has already declared war on *us*." I'm startled to realize that I mean the words. We don't have a choice; we have to fight, or be destroyed by the Ereni.

Rhia Knoll purses her lips. She does not seem impressed.

Alistar gives me a gods-help-us look. He says to Rhia, "So what does your father want?"

The young woman nods at me. "I am to bring the *Caveadear* north for the Day of the Dying Year, as is the custom."

"I already declined this generous offer," I say.

"It is not an offer." Rhia Knoll looks at me as if I'm simple. "It is what must happen. You will never learn how to wake the land otherwise. We've guarded Caer-Ys's secrets since the invasion, while you lowlanders were prostrating yourselves to our conquerors. If you don't come to the mountains, you'll never learn the traditions— or the truth."

I bite my lip.

"But the land is already waking, is it not?" Alistar says, challenge sharp in his voice.

She gives a reluctant nod.

"Then your father should come here, and complete the *Caveadear*'s instruction here."

"On a hilltop overlooking a house captured by the Ereni?" Rhia says with scorn.

Alistar groans. "Not *here*. That's not what I mean. We need to move camp." He pauses. "How did you find us, anyway?"

She looks superior. "The land guided me. She does not speak to the *Caveadear* alone."

As much as I want to shake Rhia Knoll, I am beginning to wonder if she understands the magic of the land better than I do. And why do the laws require the warden of the mountains to declare war as well as the king and the steward of the land? The history books at Cerid Aven mentioned the wardens and the mountain lords, but they never said what they do—as if it's either too well known to mention, or a secret.

There's a lot I need to learn from this irascible woman. But I don't see how I can without abandoning everyone again.

"Five days," Rhia Knoll says. "As is the custom. If the *Caveadear* will not return with me, then I go alone."

WE TRAVEL NORTH as soon as we break our modest camp. Rhia Knoll says that only the principal roads are being watched, and if we keep to the back ways, we should be able to avoid the Ereni. We'll make for Dearbann, which means "white oak," the home of the Counts of Lanlachlan and the Hounds of Urseach.

Again, before we set out, Alistar looks to Finn, and Finn looks to me. "Do you approve, *Caveadear*?" Finn asks.

I feel everyone's eyes on me like a physical weight—and none more critical than Rhia Knoll's. I clear my throat. Why must I be the one to choose? I suppose the land is supposed to be guiding me, but, unlike yesterday when we crossed the border, all I feel is a humming heartbeat, not the tugging in my sternum.

"Is it safe?" I ask Alistar.

He gives a fierce grin. "Even the Butcher of Novarre would think twice before attacking my family."

The Hounds growl agreement at his boast. I spread my hand. "Then we must go there."

Around midday, our small band encounters another, also fleeing Cerid Aven, and we join company. "My family has room for us all," Alistar says.

The following day brings us to Dearbann. It's east of Barrody, a comfortable tower house that we do, indeed, all manage to squeeze into, side by side with Alistar's siblings and cousins. Due to the cramped quarters, I am given a room to share with Sophy and Rhia Knoll. There is only one bed. Sophy and I stare at each other across the coverlet woven with entwined dogs and flowers. In the back-woods, it's customary for people to share beds, but this seems a bit excessive.

Not to mention Rhia Knoll seems more likely to stab one of us than sleep.

"I'll take the floor," she says conveniently.

Sophy lets out a breath. I wink at her, and we both try not to giggle.

Sophy's still in her cream gown, now rent and splattered by the elements, but Alistar's sisters arrive with fresh clothing for all of us and the offer of a bath. I eagerly accept a deep-green gown, old-fashioned but pretty enough, made of warm wool. It does not re-quire paniers, and I'm able to stride about freely. Sophy picks a scarlet one, the only thing big enough to fit her tall frame.

"Here," I say to Rhia Knoll, selecting an ice-blue gown from the pile. "It's the exact color of your eyes."

She turns up her nose. "A mountain woman doesn't wear such frippery."

I see Sophy biting her lip to keep from laughing, and have to force myself not to look at her. "Do you plan to wear the same clothes until you go back to the mountains? I hope you intend to bathe, at least."

"El," Sophy says, "that's rude."

Rhia Knoll stares between us, then seizes the gown from my hands and storms off, presumably in the direction of the bath.

"It's very peculiar, wearing trousers all the time," I say to Sophy.

Her eyes crinkle. "Is it? You seem to favor them yourself."

I decide not to correct this misapprehension. Trousers are quite comfortable and practical for botanical work and walking in the woods, as well as for escaping cities in fear of your life. Indeed, if I had to worry about my safety all the time, perhaps I would dress just like Rhia Knoll.

When we gather in the great hall later, Rhia is wearing the blue dress—with the daggers still strapped to her hips, naturally. She looks almost dainty, though the gown reveals the lines of hardened muscle in her arms. I didn't realize how small she was, before.

Finn and Alistar have also bathed and changed, and news has arrived from Barrody. It seems Hugh is being kept in the garrison prison, under watch. He's due to be executed when the new Duke of Caeris comes to Barrody in five days' time.

"New duke?" I say, my chest tight with the effort of suppressing my futile anger.

"Yes," says Alistar's sister Oonagh, who is brisk and competent, running the Connell household with the efficiency of a drill sergeant. "With the war, the queen's named someone new to govern the dukedom. It seems the governor they installed to replace Ruadan didn't work out, since we were revolting against him."

"The Butcher, no doubt." I feel ill. "Is he still at Cerid Aven?"

"So far as we know. They've sent out a search for Demoiselle Dunbarron."

Sophy flinches, and Alistar gives her a steadying look.

"So we have five days," Finn says, "to get Hugh out of prison. And then we need to find Duke Ruadan."

We all look at him.

His brow is rumpled, his nostrils flared. He stares around at us—our golden prince, clinging tight to his principles. In this moment, I could love him.

"You're not thinking we will let Hugh die, surely," he says. "Or Ruadan."

Alistar smacks the table. "Of course not."

Oonagh gives him a quelling look. "That's very well, Your Highness, but Barrody is heavily guarded. To attack it, we'd need the full force of our Caerisian army, including the mountain lords." She does not look at Rhia. "We can't possibly assemble them in five days. We can't negotiate with Eren, either, having nothing to bargain with. And Duke Ruadan has been taken south to Laon, well out of our reach."

The skin at the back of my neck tenses.

"No," Oonagh continues. "Hugh Rathsay understood the risk when he wrote songs inciting the Old Rebellion—when he took over gathering intelligence for Duke Ruadan, and spreading sedition through pamphlets and stories. And Ruadan Valtai also understood the risk when he crossed the border into Eren. He welcomed it. He would not ask to be rescued."

I close my eyes, my hands curling into fists. First they tell me to let Guerin and Hensey and Victoire go. Then my mother. Now my father—because this is his choice, because he, too, knew what might happen to him. And Hugh, too. I can't stand it. I'm going to crumple, or I'm going to grab a musket myself and lead a band to Barrody.

"We would do better to start gathering our army," Oonagh is saying. "The people of Caeris are already rising to your Dragon, Your Highness, and to word of the *Caveadear*. Even the Ereni are muttering about rebellion—there's a girl spreading pamphlets through Eren's towns, telling them how much better life will be under King Euan. We need to bring all our people together."

Finn bows his head. "I understand. But a man's life is at stake. Hugh has done so much for Caeris. It is difficult to sacrifice him, even if he's willing."

Rhia Knoll folds her arms. "If it's too hard, it's not too late to go back to Ida. The people of Caeris never elected your father king. You don't have to claim responsibility for a people you don't even know."

Finn's eyes widen. Even Oonagh gasps.

"The prince is here to fight for Caeris," I say, no longer shocked by anything that comes out of Rhia Knoll's mouth. "And he's going to stay because that is what decent people do. Decent people don't start rebellions and then abandon them. Decent people don't leave their countrymen to die, even if they don't know them. Even if they haven't been elected by them."

As soon as I say it, I realize it could as easily apply to me. I almost ran to Ida. I almost abandoned the people who look to me for their future, for their hope. If I go to the mountains with Rhia, I leave Finn alone leading the rebellion; I leave all our followers without the promise of my power as *Caveadear*. Even if I can't do all Wildegarde did, I can at least do something. And if I go with Rhia, I won't be here when I'm needed. I could return from the mountains to find Finn and Alistar and Sophy in chains as well as my parents and Hugh. I could circle back to the same disaster.

I understand my responsibility, now. I don't have a choice.

Rhia Knoll stares at me. The blue gown does nothing to soften or diminish her. If anything, its color only serves to make her look more uncompromising.

"Thank you, El," says Finn, touching my arm. "And you're right. I will not abandon my people."

The words *my people* ring out. Alistar begins to applaud, and so does Sophy, and soon they all are clapping. I press my hands together. Even Rhia makes a small inclination of her head—more likely in defeat than appreciation.

"I will do everything in my power to see the people of Caeris achieve their freedom," Finn says. "With the steward of the land beside me."

I look at him. A week ago, I would have blushed and shook my head. Now I find myself beginning to smile. I am the steward of the land. If Finn wants me beside him, that's as it should be. It is my rightful place.

They're clapping for me, smiling, whooping. Finn lifts my hand to his lips and kisses it. Then he holds our clasped hands up together, in a fist.

"The prince and the *Caveadear*!" Alistar shouts.

Rhia Knoll watches me. I meet her eyes. Let her look. I was born for this. I'm more than just Ruadan Valtai's daughter, who grew up as a hostage in Laon—a clever girl with a green thumb. Already this war has claimed my father, my mother, Hugh, and my home at Cerid Aven; it has claimed my comfortable life in Laon, my friends and nursemaid. I won't let Loyce Eyrlai take anything more from me.

I find myself smiling at Rhia Knoll. I feel my smile showing the points of my teeth. She raises her eyebrows, but looks away.

FINN FINDS ME in the evening, drinking a tisane in a cushioned window seat. The deep recess, half hidden from view, is as close to being alone as I've been in days. "May I?" He gestures to the cushioned seat beside me. I scoot over, and he sits.

"I've been thinking," he begins.

I nod. "About Hugh. And my father."

He grimaces. "Oh, El. I'm sorry. Truly, truly sorry." He leans over to put his hand on top of mine. "I wish there was something we could do. But he's made his choice. They both have."

I can't look at him. I grip my teacup. "You changed your mind awfully fast."

Finn draws in a breath. "I didn't want to. But if I am to be worthy of leading this revolution, those are the choices I have to make." He pauses. His hand tightens on mine. "I know you're fond of Hugh."

"Fond?" The words pour out of me, thick as tears. "He taught me to read! He taught me the poem about Wildegarde! He was like a father to me! All my memories of Caeris, before I was taken hostage, all my best memories, have Hugh in them. And I—I—" I betrayed him. I can't even say it aloud. "He brought me back here—to you, to my parents. He taught me the *truth*. He's given me so much, and you would give him—You would give my *father*—"

I choke on the words before I start to cry. Finn puts an arm around my shoulders; I shrug him off. The land rumbles under me, seeming to sense my distress.

"I'm sorry," Finn says. "I like Hugh. I like Ruadan. I don't want to see Hugh die like this. I don't want to see your father rot in prison."

"But you won't do anything about it."

"I can't afford to sacrifice more people in a mission that may be futile."

I glare at him through the tears blurring my eyes. "You sound like a pompous pig."

My words hurt him. "What do you want of me?" he snaps, but then he gathers himself. "I am trying to act like a king. I'm probably making a shambles of it. But I have to try."

"Of course you do." I glower into my teacup. Neither of us says anything. I don't know what's right—is Finn being noble and self-sacrificing, or just taking the easy way out? I feel bruised with shame and grief. The steward of the land should put Caeris before herself. Maybe my father had that kind of self-abnegation, but I don't. And I don't want to. I don't want to say, the way they all do, that Hugh or my father or Hensey knew the risk. Because after you've said it enough times, it simply means you're giving up. I can't give up on the people I care about. I won't.

But Finn *is* trying. So I say, "I see you're doing your best."

"It's all right. I understand why you're angry." He pulls in a deep breath, seems to brace himself. "But I've been thinking about something, El, and I need to ask you about it."

I sit upright, wiping a stray tear off my cheek. He doesn't quite look at me.

"With you being the steward of the land, and me being the crown prince," he begins. A pause. "It's good we have a united front. But I wonder—I think it would be stronger if—"

He stops.

Finally I say, "Yes?" in my most encouraging manner.

He turns to me, pulling a smile onto his face. It's meant to be charming, but I see the strain in it. He gathers my hands in his.

"I think we should announce our engagement."

What?

My mouth has fallen open. I've jerked my hands back to safety against my chest. I say, the words seeming to come from someone else, "I didn't know we had agreed to *become* engaged."

His smile becomes fixed. "This isn't quite how I hoped you'd react."

"Yes," I explode, "because you never *asked* if I want to marry you!"

"We've been betrothed since we were children."

"We have *not*."

Finn's voice rises. "My father has a document, signed by your father, agreeing to our engagement and marriage once you turn twenty."

I stare at him. I'm gaping again; I must look a complete fool. I'd forgotten about what my father said to me as a child. *How would you like to marry a prince, Elly?*

It seems he went ahead and agreed that I would. On my behalf. When I was five years old. And then let me be taken hostage. I calm my surge of rage only by remembering that Father is now in an Ereni prison, waiting for Loyce Eyrlai to decide his fate.

Finn huffs a disgusted sigh. "Ruadan didn't tell you."

"No. He didn't."

Finn stands up, pacing the length of the cushioned bench. "Well. I'm not going to force you to marry me. I thought you knew. I thought you were agreed to it. I thought . . ." He pauses. "I thought you might not find it a bad thing."

A bad thing. I look at him. Finn is not a bad man; he wants to be good, and just, and strong. But I can't imagine taking his hands and calling myself his wife. I can't imagine binding myself to him for the rest of our lives.

I get up. "It's not your fault," I tell Finn, "but I have to think about this."

My words seem to calm him. He stops pacing and looks deep into my eyes—so intent that I want to step back.

Because I do not want to marry Finn Dromahair, no matter his golden charm or his hope or his desire to be a truly good king. Even though maybe I should marry him—for the future of my family and the future of Caeris.

With the utmost gentleness, he touches his fingertips to my cheekbone. He says, softly, "I wouldn't mind being married to you, El."

I TAKE THE steps to my shared bedroom two at a time, throwing open the door so hard it rocks on its hinges.

Rhia Knoll looks up from the writing desk, where she appears to be composing a letter. So reassuring to see she is literate; in Laon they're always claiming Caerisians can't read. "What's wrong with you?"

I shake my head. I wish I could talk to someone—Victoire or Hensey, or even my mother. Someone who could explain to me what I'm supposed to do.

Someone who would tell me it's all right that I want to run.

Rhia Knoll is eyeing me askance.

I fling myself onto the bed and glare up into the shadowed canopy, bordered in a knot-work pattern, trying not to mind when I hear the scratch of Rhia returning to her writing. It's not as if she really wanted to know what was the matter.

I need to clear my head. I need to make the right choice about marrying Finn.

It is not a choice I want to make.

I think of Hugh, in his prison cell at Barrody, and rage burns up in me again, because even if *he* made the choice, it is wrong to let him suffer the consequences. I think of my father, locked up in the Tower in Laon. It is so wrong. I am the steward of the land. I have the power to make decisions—without the king or the warden of the mountains, if the situation is dire enough. My father may not want a rescue, and the others may be right that we can't free him, at least not yet. But Hugh's execution is dire.

Then an idea strikes me. A terrible and *possible* idea. An idea that might work. An idea that would, at least, avoid me saying no to Finn's face—or worse, a coward's yes.

I sit up. Rhia is still writing, though to whom, I cannot guess. I watch her until she senses my gaze and looks around.

"Do you think you could free a man from prison?" I ask.

She draws herself up. I watch her consider the daggers tucked around her hips, the broadsword leaning against the near wall, me. "Perhaps," she says.

"If we did it together? If I used the land to cover our escape?"

"Perhaps," she says again, unmoved.

I roll onto my knees. "Rhia Knoll, if you help me free Hugh Rathsay from the garrison prison, I will go with you to Dalriada and treat with your father and the mountain lords. If we free Hugh now, we'll easily make it there before the Day of the Dying Year—and in time to come back before the first snow."

Her lips begin to form a word, but then she hesitates. I know she can see the sincerity in my face. The desperation. She taps the pen against her lips.

Then she says, "How soon do we leave?"

CHAPTER SIXTEEN

This is not a good idea.

Rhia and I lurk outside the gates of Barrody, which loom huge in the twilight, lanterns blazing at the gates and soldiers pacing the wall above, the tips of their bayonets winking. The garrison squats just over the wall, and I recognize the neat square windows high on its tower that open to release cannons.

I seem to be shrinking. The walls are very tall, and I am fragile and human and wanted. The dusky color of my skin alone could give me away; like the Ereni, Caerisians are lighter-skinned than my mother and I.

The words *let's go back* are on my lips, but instead I say to Rhia, "Do you think we can manage it?"

She purses her mouth. I brace myself to hear her say *no*. But she says, "If luck is with us. Yes."

We dismount from our horses and walk through the gates of Barrody, into the capital city of Caeris, the heart of our country. A place I have never been. The walls stretch thirteen feet thick and, for a moment, in the cold dark underneath them, I seem to be suffocating. A guardsman will stick a lantern in my face. He will see past my wrapped scarf and lowered hat. He will recognize me.

We emerge on the other side, onto a cobblestone street. It smells of food and damp.

No one stops us.

Rhia remounts her horse, taking the lead. I follow. The buildings are a jumble of timber, stone, and shadow, and the people we pass wear somber colors. My body is aware of the land beneath it, the gape of Lake Harbor off to our right, but my breath seems stuck in my chest. I have not been in a city since Laon. It should feel comfortable, tame after being in the woods, on the open road, on the run. But instead I feel trapped.

In Green Square, just below the Queen's Way that winds up to the castle, Rhia turns off into an alley. We thread among several tall buildings before emerging into a quiet square. A single bell tower occupies the middle of a greensward. Rhia slows. "The university," she says. "It's not much farther. I took the alley in case we were being watched."

I tighten my grip on the horse's reins.

Up the slope from the green, tucked in among a labyrinth of narrow streets, Rhia urges us through a small passage into a tiny, sheltered courtyard. Even in the damp, cool air, it reeks of food and waste. I tug my scarf over my nose. At least, in the embrace of the close, we seem less exposed.

Tethering the horses to a hitching post, we climb the stairs to an inset doorway. Rhia knocks—an unsteady rhythm. It must be a code.

A code for the underground system of Barrody's rebels.

We wait only a moment before the door opens and a girl ushers us inside. Her glance flicks over our shoulders, furtive, her lips pursed. She takes our overcoats without a word and gestures for us to remove our boots.

I hand mine to her. "Thank you."

Rhia puts a finger to her lips and glares at me. The girl gives a shy smile, pointing us through the cramped, dim foyer toward a sitting room beyond. "I will see to your horses," she says, and vanishes out the front door.

"I wish you wouldn't speak," Rhia hisses at me. "Anyone will know you in an instant if you open your mouth with that awful Ereni accent. You sound as if you belong in the queen's Diamond Salon in Laon."

She says it as if the Diamond Salon is, by nature, a despicable location. I grimace, but she did tell me to let her do the talking. "I only said thank you. I doubt she'll know my whole history from that."

"You'd be surprised."

Rhia marches down the brief corridor to the well-lit room, made comfortable with carpets and paintings and well-used furniture. A young woman looks up from setting a pot of tea on the table, crinkling her eyes in a not-quite smile.

"I must have had a presentiment. I just made tea. Will you have a cup?"

It's a large pot, and the room has the feeling of just being vacated. The ceiling squeaks overhead. There must be an attic above us. Whoever else stays here ran off just as we came in. The Barrody underground, indeed. I'm glad they take precautions, even with their own.

Rhia has plunked herself on a settee, accepting a cup of tea and a chunk of bannock with enthusiasm. I lower myself onto a chair and take the food and drink as well. Our hostess wears her dark hair pinned back in a severe knot, and a sober, high-necked gray gown. Ink stains splatter her hands and, on a desk off to the side of the room, I spot a stack of recently written-upon paper. As she turns to pour herself a cup of tea, I peer more closely at the paper. It's not secret letters, as I half expected. It's drawings. Sketches.

Anatomical sketches.

I am out of my seat, pulled by curiosity straight over to the desk. The sheet on top shows a study of the nervous system, the notes interrupted in midsentence.

"The prince is in Dearbann?" our hostess asks Rhia, then says hastily to my back, "Please disregard my work if it offends you."

I turn to her eagerly. "*Your* work? Are you an anatomist?"

She looks me up and down, her eyes widening. "I'm training to be a surgeon, actually. But they say a woman isn't fit to perform surgery, so I'm left to make the drawings alongside learning everything the boys are expected to."

"The same thing happens all the time in botany. Do you know no woman has ever been allowed to name a plant's genus and species? As if we can't even decline nouns!"

Rhia Knoll is watching our exchange with full attention. But when I glance at her, expecting a scowl, she just rolls her eyes and keeps eating her bannock.

Our hostess extends her hand to me. "I'm Sorcha Kerr."

"I—" I pause. This is probably the moment to use my alias, Islie Valmont, but surely we are among allies.

She gives her not-quite smile again. "I know who you are, *Caveadear*. Though I have to say, I didn't expect you to come yourself, with only one other."

"If any Ereni soldiers try to attack Rhia Knoll, they're greater fools than I think," I say.

Rhia actually blushes, and Sorcha Kerr smiles this time—a real smile. She sits, and I move back to join them around the table. "What brings a Knoll and a Valtai here alone, with all of Caeris in such an uproar? I assume you wish to gather supporters?"

Rhia points her gaze at me. I cough.

"We must free Hugh Rathsay, the *Ollam* of Caeris. He's due to be executed—on Lunedia, I believe."

Sorcha's eyebrows lift. She hides her surprise behind her teacup. When she sets it down, she seems to have composed herself once again. "That may not be easy. The *Ollam* is a very public figure, now that they've captured him. The Ereni are making quite a stir about it. The execution is to be public, of course."

"You must have contacts within the garrison," I say. "Supporters."

She nods. "But it is—I do not quite know how to say it, Lady Elanna—it is quite a risk to those who are there. It would put many people's lives in danger to save one man."

It shouldn't surprise me to hear this philosophy yet again, but I still have to unclench my jaw.

"I don't intend to put anyone but Rhia and myself in danger," I say. "We will go in alone."

Sorcha looks at me. There seems to be pity in her eyes, and suddenly I feel young and rather foolish. "No one in this revolution is ever alone," she says. But she does not try to argue us out of it further.

THE ATTIC IS reached by a trapdoor in the living room's ceiling. We spend most of the next day up there, cramped in the narrow room with a sloping ceiling and single window, the two trundle beds leaving little space to walk around. Sorcha will not permit either of us out in daylight, so I can only guess at what Caeris's capital city looks like by day through the smeared glass window. It shows nothing more than a gray autumn street: gray cobblestones, gray slate roofs, gray stone walls. Occasionally we hear the squeak of floorboards and sound of voices below, and the girl comes up around noon with some lunch. But otherwise, we seem almost invisible—forgotten—though I know we are far from it. Sorcha doesn't need to say more for me to know we are putting others in danger with our rescue attempt, no matter what precautions we take.

I try to put the guilt from my mind. I tell myself it's too late for it.

Rhia teaches me how to play a Caerisian board game with flat wooden pieces and a bowl. It passes the time.

Somewhere in the afternoon, she stands from the game and stretches. I realize I have been contemplating my turn for several minutes too long, but she doesn't seem to mind. She paces to the window.

"I used to think Barrody was the best place in the world," she says, leaning her elbows on the window frame. "My mother brought me here once when I was a girl, after the Old Rebellion failed, when things had quieted down again. I remember she ordered me a new dress, and we went to the draper to take my measurements. I'd never had a dress made by somebody I didn't know, especially somebody in a city. I thought it was the best thing."

I lean back against a trundle bed. "What color was it?"

"The dress? Blue, with pink roses embroidered onto it. And ribbons. When I got home, my brothers stole all the ribbons to make me angry."

Brothers. I wonder what it must be like to have siblings, someone else to turn to, who knows your mind—a true friend for life. Then I think of the blue dress we made her wear at Dearbann, and how angry she was to put it on. She doesn't look angry now, for once; she seems reflective.

"I never wore the dress," she says.

"Why did your mother buy it for you, then?" I smile, trying to picture this stern young woman as an eager little girl.

"I think she felt sorry about what she was going to do. It was her way of atoning."

"Atoning?"

Rhia doesn't look at me. "She left. I got up one morning, while we were here, and she was gone. She left a letter for my father, saying she couldn't bear it anymore—the mountains, our way of life, the hatred and resentment of the south."

I try to contain my shock. No wonder Rhia didn't want to wear the dress. "But where did she go?"

"Back to her family, I think. She came from the south of Eren. The revolution upset her. She didn't like violence." Rhia pushes herself back from the window. "It doesn't matter anymore. It was a long time ago. I think of it when I come to Barrody, that's all."

"I'm sorry," I say, not knowing what else to say. "It's a terrible thing, to be abandoned." And I swallow, because this is not something I want to talk about, either.

Rhia looks at me. She opens her mouth to speak.

Just then the trapdoor lifts up. Sorcha pokes her head into the attic. "We've sorted it out." Reaching back, she shunts two bundles of clothing between the trundle beds. One hits my legs. "Put those on. You're going in an hour."

CHAPTER SEVENTEEN

It takes longer to reach the garrison than I expect—partly because we are on foot, and partly because of the nerves tremoring through me. I keep reviewing the plan in my head, afraid that if I forget a single step, the whole thing will unravel into disaster.

Rhia and I are dressed in Ereni military uniforms, our hair bundled into hats and our figures obscured by the bulk of heavy wool coats. Though it's common enough for women to act as informants, the Ereni have never employed female military officials, and my heart beats an uneasy rhythm. I am to draw a fog around us so that we are less easily recognized. A Caerisian conspirator will be waiting at the gate to let us in. If any other guards get to us first and recognize our voices as feminine, I will have to claim we have special dispensation to work as spies and dress in men's clothes. I will lie through my teeth to get into that garrison and meet our Caerisian contact.

Our contact will bring us into the building and direct us to Hugh's cell, which we will find "accidentally" unlocked. We have to wrangle Hugh into another uniform then, and get him out the back gate; someone else will guide us there. This assumes that whoever watches the back gate won't know two soldiers, not three, came in the main entrance. Once we get out, we head for the woods. I will use the magic of the land to confuse any pursuers while Rhia guides us through the woods. Sorcha has arranged for horses to be left in a hamlet outside the city. Then we ride like mad to Dearbann.

It's simple. So simple it should work. Rhia is ferocious, and I have my magic. Both may help.

And for once, it's Rhia who must remain silent. I am the one who must speak if required, because my perfect Ereni accent will allow us to pass through without question, even though my voice is light and modulated. Hopefully they'll think we're boys.

My palms itch with sweat.

"Pretend it's already done," Rhia advises me. She seems alert but calm, as if she breaks into garrisons every day. She probably does. "They'll sense your nerves. You've got to convince yourself you are exactly what you say. That will make them believe, too."

She's right. I try to focus. I am an intelligence officer employed by the crown. I have new information that requires me to question one of the prisoners immediately—Hugh Rathsay.

"And don't think I've forgotten our bargain," Rhia says. "We drop him at the house, and then we go north."

I nod, distracted. We might not survive the next few hours; I can't wrap my head around what might come after.

The garrison's squat tower appears between rooftops ahead of us, black against the night sky. My heart leaps. Rhia gives me a stern look. I pause beneath a swinging tavern sign. Two beggars eye us from the ground. I try to calm my racing pulse as I reach within me for the feeling of the land. I touch the dampness in the earth; I imagine it slipping into the air, crowding us in fog.

When I open my eyes, a mist is leaking down the rooftops. A sound accompanies it—a strange creaking, like trees buffeted by the wind. The beggars gather up their blankets, muttering about strange weather. I suppress the urge to give them coin.

"Let's go." Rhia has gone tense. She strides away from me into the pooling fog, and I hurry to catch up with her.

The gates loom abruptly out of the misty dark, far taller than I imagined they were. Their iron seems impenetrable. I swallow hard. I am too small, too human, to survive this.

A guard pushes open the covered window above. "Who's there?"

My voice sticks in my throat. I have to clear it. "Officers Valmont and Knoll—" I sound thready and high-pitched. *Girlish.* I struggle to deepen my voice. My Ereni accent punches the words through the air, aristocratic and perfect. "We're here to make a report."

The door to the side of the gate opens on a soldier, the winking epaulets on his uniform just visible through the fog. He calls up to the gatekeeper, "I've got it, Quentin. We're expecting them."

Closer to, I see he's wearing a lieutenant's stripes. He nods at us. No special gesture. No reassurance that he is, in fact, our Caerisian agent.

We just have to trust him.

"Come in," he says.

We walk after him into the garrison.

He leads us through the gatehouse. In the courtyard beyond, the gathering fog obscures a company of soldiers dismounting from their horses. The gleam of lanterns makes their shadows huge. Voices seem to lurch out of nowhere in front of us, sprinkled with laughter. "Damned Caerisian weather!"

"You shouldn't mock it. It's like the old stories. The ones where the land . . ." The speaker is hastily shushed; someone laughs again. The men—two young officers—come into view before we can slip around them. The one who just spoke stares at Rhia, then away. They brush past us and are swallowed by the fog.

I sneak a glance at Rhia. With her hair tucked into her hat, her features are still delicate—but her expression is set with such ferocious gravity that no one would dare to question her even though she still looks feminine. No wonder the young officer looked away.

I hope I appear half as terrifying.

Our contact—he does not name himself—guides us into an old tower that dominates the complex, its stones weathered with age. It must have been built before the Ereni conquest. We pass through an empty hallway to a staircase that winds up into darkness above us.

He stops here and hands me a bundle of neatly folded clothes, lighting a candle from a nearby torch and passing it to Rhia. "The prisoner you want is on the third floor, the last cell on the left. All the prisoners have been fed and no one else should be there. You'll find a door directly across from his cell that will take you down to the back side of the tower. A private is waiting for you there."

"Thank you, Lieutenant," I say in my most official manner.

He salutes, hand out, in the Ereni fashion, copied from the Idae-ans.

I return the gesture.

The lieutenant presses his lips together. He touches his fist to his heart. He mouths, *"Caveadear."* Then he walks out.

We are left in utter silence—but not alone, because the eyes of Barrody's underground watch us. I glance at Rhia. She nods back at me. I take the candle from her.

Then I start up the stairs.

I DIDN'T COUNT on there being so many cells, or the stone hallway being so cold and dirty. I didn't count on there being so many prisoners.

One calls after us through the grille on his door. "Hey, hey, soldier boys, come to get me free? I'll give you a deal. How'd you like a deal? Hey, hey—"

It's well after dinner now—closing on midnight. I thought they'd all be asleep. I am suddenly grateful for the locked door keeping the singing prisoner from us.

We turn a corner, blocking us from his view.

The last cell on the left. I have to stop myself from running. I keep my stride even.

This door has a grille, too, but there's no movement on the other side, only darkness. Rhia faces the corridor, standing guard, while I put back the latch.

The door swings open. The walls are lost to shadows, and I hear the terrible rustle of a rat over the stone floor. Then there's a louder movement, of a man sitting up from his pallet bed.

I rush in, dropping to my knees beside him. He smells, but I pretend not to notice. His face is bruised, crusted with blood around the nose, but he's alive. He begins to gasp my name, catches himself, falls into a fit of coughing.

I embrace him. "We're getting you out of here," I whisper.

"You shouldn't be here," he whispers back.

"Yes. I should." I drop the uniform into his lap, the gold and blue pale in the dim light. "Put that on. Hurry."

I pace back to the door while he changes, giving him what privacy I can.

Rhia is on edge. "I heard something."

"What kind of something?"

"Voices. Below."

We both listen, but I don't hear anything. Trying to listen through the earth does little good; I'm so tense I can sense next to nothing.

Hugh scrapes across the cell behind us. I turn, grabbing his arm as he stumbles. "What mercy," he murmurs.

Rhia marches to the door across the hall. A narrow, dark stairway curves down into apparent oblivion. I pass the candle to her. With Hugh between us, we begin our descent.

Nearly out.

By the final landing, I can see that Hugh is limping, and he has to lean against the wall to catch his breath, hissing in pain. "Broken ribs," he grunts.

Oh, no. What if we need to run?

As if she's thinking the same thing, Rhia shakes her head at me. She strides out into the darkness behind the tower, raising her hand to shine the candle as far as it will go. I wedge my shoulder under Hugh's arm. He winces but says, "That helps."

I hope he's telling the truth.

Rhia returns. "There's no one here," she hisses. "Someone was supposed to meet us. There's no exit. We seem to be in a sort of well between the tower and the city wall. That lieutenant betrayed us."

My heartbeat jumps. We're stuck.

Betrayed.

"Maybe it was too dangerous for someone to come." I try to think if my magic can help us, though I had not intended to use it again until we'd fled the city. Can I speak to the stones and tear down the wall? It would be impossible to do that without attracting notice. A door would be so much easier. "There has to be a way out. Why else does a staircase lead to this place?"

She just looks at me. "Where else do you think they execute people when they don't want it done in public?" She storms off. "I'll look again."

Hugh squeezes my hand. I'm trying to hold down my nausea. Now I see it in my mind's eye, remembered by the land. These walls weep with blood. All the forgotten dead. The unremembered cruelty. The punishments meted out for no good crimes.

"Under Caerisian law," Hugh whispers, "capital punishment is almost never accord—"

"Shh." Something passed through my inner vision. I'm concentrating, trying to see it again. This is a shallow space, between the two walls, and where they meet—

"Stairs," I say aloud. Stairs, not a door.

I drag Hugh toward where Rhia is combing the wall. I point to where the two walls join. "Steps. Onto the outer wall."

We run for them, Hugh hobbling on my arm. Rhia finds them first. "Careful. They're slippery." They are old, covered in moss. I slip and bang my knee once, but keep climbing. Hugh's breath becomes labored ahead of me. I insist on going behind.

On top of the wall, Rhia has turned to look back at the tower. I don't like the way the candlelight plays on her face.

I glance over my shoulder. I see what she sees.

Light. A light glowing in the darkened tower.

Hugh reaches the top. I stumble on the final step. On the other side of the wall, the ground is a long way down, and there aren't any stairs to reach it. These steps must be here for defensive purposes, built back in the days when Barrody was under siege by the Ereni, during the conquest. We're on an open walkway, our view of the city's main gate blocked by the shoulder of the tower. We can't go to the gate. If we go the other way, who knows what we'll find— another gate, also guarded?

The light has vanished from the window behind us. The dull tramp of boots echoes in the stairwell.

How do they know? Who told them?

"Blow out the candle!" I hiss at Rhia.

She looks at me, and I see an expression on her face I never expected to find there.

Fear.

I reach for the candle. I mean to blow it out, but I overreach and knock it from her hand by mistake. It goes flying down into the woods on the other side of the wall, briefly flaring in leaves and branches before being snuffed out.

The woods. I should be able to—

I stretch out my hand. The wind sifts through the forest below me. I try to put out of my mind Rhia grabbing onto Hugh, the boots coming closer down the stairs, even the thump of my heartbeat. All I hear is the woods. The trees. The growing things.

An ash tree grows close below the wall.

Come higher, I invite it. I reach out as if I'll hold it. The ash wakes, stretching up to meet me. I feel its bright green awareness, the sturdiness of its branches.

"Halt there!"

Lights below and behind. *Ignore them.* I hold my awareness of the ash, whose top I can just see over the wall. It's growing fast.

"Jump," I say to Rhia and Hugh. "Go. Go!"

Hugh goes first. He crashes down into the tree branches. The ash dips but holds him.

A shot bursts out behind us as Rhia leaps.

Again, the ash quivers but its branches hold. I feel Hugh drop to the ground.

"Stop in the queen's name!"

I lunge forward.

But there's a hand on my ankle. And I am falling—not into the arms of the ash, but back down onto the hard stones, into the solid form of a soldier on the steps behind me, back into the place between the walls, where too many prisoners have died.

CHAPTER EIGHTEEN

They lock me in Hugh's cell, with the rats.

Time passes.

I lie on the blankets that smell of Hugh's sweat and pain, and the sweat and pain of many before him. The guards stripped my stolen uniform from me, and at some point in the night I sit up and put on Hugh's discarded coat, much too big for me, grimed with filth and blood. But it's wool. It's warm.

Did they escape? They must have escaped.

Was it the lieutenant who betrayed us, or someone else? It could have been the gate guards or those two young officers who passed us in the courtyard. It could have been someone else entirely, who got word of our plan.

I doze somewhere toward dawn, and jerk into alertness as the prison wakes to the arrival of slop, shoved in bowls through the narrow openings on everyone's doors. I stomach three bites and leave the rest for the rats.

Time passes again.

My mind has gone blank. I cannot even form a hope.

More time. Endless time.

Keys jangle in the hallway. Footsteps. The rattle of a lock.

My door opens.

Two men walk in. The first is an officer I have never seen, and the second is a bandy-legged man whom I know too well. He's wearing a silk coat and breeches. The dim light catches the sheen of the fabric.

"This is the prisoner who claims to be Elanna Valtai, sir," says the officer.

The Butcher leans over me, looking into my face. "You've got yourself in quite a pickle this time," he says to me, shaking his head. "King Antoine would have had you executed tomorrow in Hugh Rathsay's place, for all the little stunts you've pulled recently. But our new duke is the kind who likes to play games. You've been granted a reprieve."

The new duke? But I thought Loyce had named the Butcher to that position.

He stands, then glances back down as if puzzled by my lack of response. "Well, come along. Get up."

I ache with bruises. I am not sure if anything is broken. I crawl to my knees and then, by some feat of strength, I'm standing.

"The lady is shaken," says the Butcher. "Give her your arm, Captain Renold."

Captain Renold's head jerks in surprise, but he gives me his arm.

I make it to the door and stop, bracing myself on the jamb. I have something to say to the Butcher. I wait for him to look at me, and when he does, I speak.

"Don't think I'm coming willingly. I don't collude with Caeris's enemies."

Captain Renold's arm stiffens.

The Butcher looks interested. "Would you die for Caeris?"

I blink. My numb mind stutters. "I don't know," I say.

He raises his brows. "You don't know?"

"I'm going to die anyway, so I might as well be honest."

He lifts an eyebrow. "You are not going to die quite yet, Lady Elanna."

But soon I will; that is clear. "And Hugh. Did you—did you recapture him?"

The Butcher looks at me. He sighs. "Ordinarily, under such a circumstance, I would be obliged to tell you whatever I felt might give you the greatest pain. But I have been given no particular instructions. And it is rather a pity to see such a promising young lady reduced to your present state."

"That means you didn't catch him."

"No, Lady Elanna." A faint twist of his lips. "We didn't."

I sag in relief.

Then he adds, as if he can't quite help himself, "Not yet."

THEY LOAD ME into a coach—plain black, unmarked. My hands are not bound. The Butcher and I sit facing each other, quite alone.

He looks me straight in the eyes. "You had a nursemaid. Hensey, was it?"

My heart goes cold. He knows her name perfectly well, and I know what he's going to say. I close my eyes, as if it will block out his next statement.

"She seems to have escaped from prison," he says with irritation.

My eyes fly open; I lurch to the edge of my seat, gripping it with both my hands. He's watching me with both his eyebrows lifted. I shouldn't have betrayed so much feeling, but I can't will away the tears starting to fall down my cheeks. I can't stop myself from whispering, "She's alive?"

"I had expected you to know more." He frowns at me. "Her whereabouts, for instance."

I can't speak. Hensey's *alive*. Free. He could be lying, of course, but what would be the point?

He sighs, drumming his fingers on the windowsill, watching me. I look away so I can wipe the tears from my face.

Unfathomably, he starts to talk about the weather.

"Started off quite *wet* this morning, but about midday the sun began to poke through, a welcome relief, I must say. Do you find Caeris quite as dreary as I do, Lady Elanna? No, perhaps not, considering the rebel attitude. In any case, it promises not to get much better—and of course, there is already snow in the mountains—"

The sheer inanity makes my head ache; perhaps it's one of his torture techniques. "Where are you taking me?"

"To your new quarters." He peers out the window with a sigh. "Ah, more's the pity. It's clouding up over the lake."

I dig my fingers into the stuffing that's coming out through a hole in the cushion. He let me know Hensey is alive and free, and even if part of me worries it's not true, it's still enough for me to hold on to for the moment. The coach moves uphill now, and between the houses I glimpse the ruffled water of Lake Harbor.

We're going uphill. That must mean he's taking me to the castle.

After a few more minutes, the coach slows as it rolls onto level ground—a courtyard of flagged stones. From one window spreads a glorious panorama over Lake Harbor and the rumpled blue hills surrounding Barrody; from the other, the castle's faceless towers block out the sky.

We rattle around to a stable yard and jerk to a stop. The Butcher mutters something deprecating about Caerisian coachmen. He climbs out.

My feet hit the hard cobblestones. I do not feel myself at all; my feet seem very far from my head. A crowd of guardsmen emerges from the stables, apparently waiting for our arrival. Their captain salutes the Butcher. A length of rope hangs from his other hand, ready to be tied around my wrists.

But the Butcher offers me his arm instead.

I don't understand. I'm a prisoner. The Butcher himself has accused me of regicide, of witchcraft, of insurrection. The *Caveadear* is a threat to Eren, to the society the empire of Paladis has worked so hard to create, untouched by magic. He shouldn't be treating me like this.

"You will find yourself much more comfortably accommodated here," he says to me, strolling us toward the nearest door and up a set of recessed stairs. My legs and thighs protest at the movement, but I can still climb. That's good. Maybe I didn't break anything. The Butcher even takes some of my weight: "Lean on my arm, Lady Elanna."

We emerge into a carpeted hallway, its walls hugged with tapestries. Servants and guardsmen move about on business. It's strange to think this is the castle in which Finn should live, the place from which he should rule as king of Caeris.

I've dug my fingers into the Butcher's sleeve. I release him, trying not to grimace at the thought of holding him so close.

"Why here?" I whisper.

"The new duke, as I said, is eager to play games."

I close my eyes. So this isn't mercy at all. Someone has a plan for me. The new duke—whoever he is. But why would Loyce give the title to someone else?

He draws me on, through a series of pleasant rooms, to a study that smells of leather and ink. A man occupies a wide oak desk, his blond head bent over spread-out maps. His fingers drum the desktop. He appears quite unaware of our arrival.

The Butcher utters a delicate cough.

The man looks up. His face is round and genial, and, at the moment, rather cross.

I flinch.

It's Denis Falconier. The man who called me a murderer. The man who had me followed for years in case I betrayed some treason he and Loyce could use against me. The man who has insulted everything from my appearance to my accent to my history. And the man who has taken from others the riches and titles he desires, thanks to Loyce's love of him.

I should have known. I should have known if Loyce ever had the chance to appoint her favorite to a dukedom, she would take the opportunity.

"I'm rather busy," he's saying. "These maps are damned unclear. They tell me the farther north you go, the more the land begins to shift, and things don't stay put where they're meant to be. Not just landmarks—whole mountains! Forests! Lakes! I've had a Caerisian mapmaker in here telling me I have to read the place through *my feet*. I'm telling you, Lord Gilbert, *my feet* don't read maps."

"Indeed," the Butcher says. "Generally speaking, one's manual digits lack sentience." He glances at me. "Perhaps not yours, though."

Denis, oblivious as he stares at the map, thinks the Butcher is talking to him. "I assure you, my feet are quite stupid."

"Hardly a surprise considering the rest of you," I mutter.

The Butcher's arm quivers. I don't look at him, in case he's actually chuckling.

Denis hears me: His head jerks up. He stares at me. Then a slow smile slides across his face. He straightens, coming around the desk, and paces toward me, his hands behind his back. He's wearing a yellow embroidered coat tailored to fit his short frame with fashionable precision, and matching yellow knee-breeches. The ensemble looks ridiculous.

"Why, it is Lady Elanna," he says, drifting closer, right up to me. He picks up a clumped piece of my hair and sniffs it.

His cologne smells worse than me.

"Don't touch me," I snap.

He bursts out laughing—the boyish guffaw that makes him so popular at court and with Loyce. "Watch out, Lord Gilbert! She has claws."

"So you're the Duke of Caeris now." If he's going to kill me anyway, I don't see why I should mince words. "What have you done with my father? Is he still alive? And my mother—what have you done with her?"

Denis rolls his eyes. "So many *questions*. In case you forgot, *I* am the duke and you are, well . . ." A smile. He leans back against the desk, folding his arms. "A regicide. A murderess. A witch."

"I prefer to be called a *revolutionary*. And the steward of the land."

"She thinks she has power," Denis says to a divan beside the fireplace. "She's always been a bit delusional. Too much studying mushrooms."

"Delusional?" I spit the word. "I did not kill the king. But you drove me north. You forced me back to Caeris. So yes, Denis, I am going to fight you and Loyce. You took everything from me. Like Guerin Jacquard. What have you done with him, whom you also wrongly accused of murder?" I almost ask what he's done with Hensey, but then I remember what the Butcher told me. I don't dare say anything; I don't know what games are being played here. And that makes me angrier than before.

I can't believe I ever questioned the rightness of this revolution. It's worth taking up arms against Denis Falconier alone. The cold, angry knot tightens in my stomach.

He groans. "You really are the most tiresome girl." He shakes his head at me, at the Butcher, and turns again to the divan. Inexplicably, he speaks in Idaean: "You see, these rebels are quite mad. I am glad she has given you such an excellent example of her vitriol."

I turn.

A young man is sitting on the divan, reclining so that his short, disheveled hair is burrowed into the cushion. He is half smiling. He has one foot propped on his opposite knee and he looks utterly comfortable. Amused. His glance skims me and returns to Denis.

"I do see," he says. "She seems quite *spirited,* I must say."

My head buzzes. I open my mouth, but I can't speak. Too much rage surges up in me, too much betrayal—and worst of all, too much hope.

Because, of course, it's Jahan.

SOMEWHERE OUTSIDE THE echoing in my head, Denis is speaking, still in Idaean. "This is Ruadan Valtai's daughter, Elanna. She's not at her best now, but she cleans up prettily enough."

Jahan is supposed to be on a ship to Ida. He's supposed to be begging the emperor for aid. Or at least he should be in Laon, fulfilling his role as ambassador. What is he doing *here*?

"Her mind seems quite sharp," he says to Denis. He's watching me, his mouth quirked so his dimple shows. He looks so at *ease*. As if betraying us has cost him so little.

But Denis has introduced us. If Jahan betrayed us, Denis would know we've met.

Yet the way Jahan is regarding me—as if I'm an entertaining diversion—is nowhere as intense as the way he looked at me when we met before. Maybe the whole thing has been an elaborate act. Maybe he's not here to help Denis or me or anybody but himself. But what good would coming here do him?

"Women's minds." Denis waves a hand. "What happens in them usually doesn't amount to much."

The Butcher coughs. "Surprising words from a man who owes his career to our queen."

Jahan glances at him with amusement. Do they know each other, then? Have they talked about Finn and me, about the Caerisian rebellion and the emperor's black ships? I wonder if it was Jahan who told the Butcher that my father and the Hounds would be leaving Cerid Aven—if he was the one who told the Butcher to occupy it and take my mother prisoner.

Heat pulses through me, followed by cold. I'm almost certain I've been used. And yet . . . Jahan isn't looking at me. Is it deliberate? Perhaps I so want him to be on our side that I'm inventing something that isn't there.

Denis is speaking to them in a confidential manner. "All that's required is a little pressure applied in the right places, if you know what I mean. If you pet ladies, and flatter them, and provoke them just enough, why—" He snaps his fingers.

Jahan's upper lip curls, but then his expression flattens into a smile. "That's the secret, is it?"

"You're disgusting," I burst out. Even I'm not quite sure whether I'm saying it to Jahan or Denis.

Jahan's eyes flicker toward me, then away, telling me nothing. He shifts in his chair, but that, too, could mean he simply doesn't like being insulted.

Denis laughs. "Thank you for your honesty, Lady Elanna. I had quite forgotten how much you dislike me."

The Butcher gives me a pointed look that I can't interpret.

My head throbs. "Please, just tell me what you're going to do with me. What you've done with my parents."

I can't keep the tremor from my words. They all hear it.

It pleases Denis. Of course, he loves to watch me squirm. His awful grin stretches wider. "But that would be so dull, telling you about imprisonments and death sentences. Let's play a little game. For every piece of information I give *you,* you will answer one of *my* questions. First on the docket—Fionnlach Dromahair. The 'prince.' He's in the country. Tell me about him."

The floor seems to rock beneath me. My parents—both of them—condemned to death? And Guerin, too? How many people have to die because of me? Our revolution might be the only course of action we can take, but why does it have to come at the cost of all these lives I hold dear?

"She's not well." Jahan's on his feet. He takes a step toward me and stops, frowning. He lowers the hand he has raised. Perhaps he meant to touch me, to put his hand under my elbow.

I don't know.

"Naturally, she's not well," the Butcher says with rare impatience.

"The men had to drag her off a city wall last night. I expect she suffered some injury. And the news that one's father is awaiting trial and execution does not generally promote well-being."

Denis just smiles.

Jahan shakes his head. "If she's injured, we should send for a doctor. I insist!"

"Such humanity," Denis says, rolling his eyes. "But if the ambassador insists . . ." He shrugs.

He's playing a game. I know he wants the information I have.

And what game is Jahan playing? Is he genuinely worried or is he playing on my feelings again? He meets my eyes. He frowns, and I read a question in his look. *Are you all right?*

Or maybe I'm imagining it.

"Rest and food will improve her spirits," the Butcher says. "I will take her away."

He slides his arm around mine, and I am too shaken to shrink from his touch. We start to walk from the room.

"Oh," Denis calls after us. "I almost forgot. Perhaps it would improve Lady Elanna's state if she met our other guest—unless the shock will be too much for her? Do see they're reunited, Lord Gilbert."

I CAN'T BEAR the Butcher's silence.

Neither of us speaks as we pace back out into the hallway, which makes a left-hand turn into another wing, where the ceilings are lower and older, but recently refurbished with fanciful molding. It seems Caeris's general poverty has not affected the Ereni governors who occupy Barrody Castle.

As we walk down the hall, I hear it.

Music.

A pianoforte is being played—a thunder of low notes spiraling up to a high, tender key.

Sophy said the Butcher liked music. She said my mother *trusted* him. How could my mother trust a man who has done the things he has?

I realize I've stopped beside a polished sideboard, my fingers digging into the crimson runner that covers it.

"Come along," the Butcher says mildly, pressing a hand between my shoulder blades.

I look at him. "You have children, Lord Gilbert."

A muscle works in his jaw. "Three daughters. You have met them, I believe."

"Yes." A parade of girls' faces presents itself in my memory— slender, serious children with rigid backs and perfect manners. I am no longer sure why I brought it up. Maybe just because I want to hear him say that he would never harm them. He would never abandon them.

He does not say it, but I know it's true. Maybe this is why my mother trusts him, because she sees the sliver of humanity in him.

King Antoine always told me the Butcher was utterly inhuman. But then, King Antoine made a lot of claims that I now know are false.

I let him lead me down to the open doorway. We enter a pleasant salon, done in soft blues and creams. A gilded harp sits by a window. Several ladies occupy settees by the wide fireplace, their hands busy with needlework, their heads tilted as they listen to the music.

But then I don't see them any longer. I only see my mother, bent over the pianoforte. She plays with her eyes closed, no music before her. She plays by touch. By passion. Her head bobs. I notice she's well dressed, a fringed shawl swathing her back and shoulders, her hair arranged by a skilled maid.

The music changes—into the song she wrote for me when I was a child. The song that the land sang to her; the sound it made waking to my presence.

The Butcher stands by the door. I take one step forward. Another. Mother looks up.

The music rattles to a halt. In the abrupt silence, I hear one of the ladies say, "Don't stop now."

Mother shoves back her bench, scrambles to her feet. Tears stand out in her eyes. She clutches the ends of her shawl over her chest. "Oh, my darling. I thought it had gone the worse for you. I thought—"

Her gaze seeks the Butcher; he nods. She comes toward me. I cannot move. Then her arms are around me, and I smell her scent, feel the strength in her arms.

My mother is alive. My mother is *well*.

"You left," she breathes into my hair. "You went on reconnaissance with Ruadan, didn't you? That's why you weren't there."

A tear slides down my nose. "Yes. I was lucky. Then."

She pulls back, and I realize she's angry. Her nostrils are flared. "He should never have taken you with him. He should never have put you into such danger."

"Better than being captured and sentenced to die for a crime I didn't commit." I pause. "Mother, they seem to be treating you well."

"And you might have been safe, too, and Sophy as well," she hisses at me. "If you had stayed at Cerid Aven."

I blink at her.

She cannot be saying what I think she's saying. But her eyes are bright and fierce. She means it. She believes that if we had stayed at Cerid Aven, we would all be safe now.

"Mother," I say slowly. I've taken one step back. I take another. My voice dies down to a whisper. I can hardly bear to say it. "Who—Do you know who summoned the Ereni?"

Again, she glances at the Butcher.

I do not want to see their eyes meet. I do not want to hear it.

"It might have been anyone," Mother says.

Yes. It might.

But I am certain, now, that it was she. Not Jahan. Whatever games he's playing, this is not one of them.

How could she? *Why* would she? Why put her trust in the Butcher, of all people?

She reaches out to touch me, but then lowers her hands and twists them into her skirt. She looks at me. "We will look after you now. Everything will be all right."

I want to scream at her. *I will be put to death the moment Denis decides he's bored with me!* But I can't say the words. It seems like cruelty, more cruelty, and I can't bear more than this.

I turn to the Butcher. Somehow I manage to say, "I would like to go to my room now."

"Of course." He frowns at my mother but gestures to the door.

I force myself to look at my mother, still standing beside the pianoforte, clutching her skirt. There is a kind of desperate strength in her, something I understand too well. "I am glad to see you're being well treated, Mother," I say quietly. "I expected they would sentence you to death, as Father has been by now."

She flinches.

I walk out, away from her.

CHAPTER NINETEEN

They give me a secluded bedchamber on the upper floor, tucked into one of the towers. Two guards stand duty in the hall outside it, but within the room, I am alone. Massive leaded windows look out over Lake Harbor and the hills, and an alcove holds a writing desk. The room contains little else besides the bed, with its towering canopy, battened by curtains of florid pink. Two chairs sit by the fireplace, and there is a heavy carved trunk in the middle of the floor.

I lower myself onto the bed and stare at my hands. The brief courage I felt when Denis granted me reprieve is gone. He must have known it would devastate me to learn that it was my own mother who betrayed us into their hands.

The music patters around in my head, over and over again, the song she wrote for me. I press my hands over my ears, but that does nothing to stop it. The land's song, indeed! As if she ever cared for Caeris. Yet the rhythm won't leave my head. This is why I hate music. I hate the pianoforte.

A tap sounds on the door. I have no idea how much time has passed. Two maids enter, their arms piled with towels and clothes.

"Lady Elanna, we're to take you to the bath." The first maid, ruddy-cheeked and broad, does not disguise how distasteful she finds me. She says to the other, "Hold your nose, Annis."

Annis, plump and girlish, looks wide-eyed at me.

"I will not bathe," I say. "You may go."

The ruddy-cheeked maid utters an exclamation. "But we're to dress you for supper with the duke!"

Supper with Denis? That would be enough to put me off food for a week. I set my jaw. "That will not be necessary. I will eat no meals with Denis Falconier."

The ruddy maid exclaims at me, but I lie down on the bed and close my eyes. Eventually they leave. But they come back a while later, grunting as they set down basins of wash water and a tray holding celery soup, cold meat cuts, cherry cakes, and tea.

The smell of food makes my mouth water. I roll over and burrow my face into the coverlet. I'm not going to eat Denis's food. I wonder if I can go without eating until I find a way out of here.

Or until Denis or the Butcher take care of that for me.

"Lady Elanna?" Plump Annis bends over me. "Please, please bathe. And we've found the prettiest dress for you."

I shake my head.

"It's not our fault if she won't take the duke's charity." The ruddy maid huffs. "Better than these so-called revolutionaries deserve, if you ask me."

Finally they leave. I drift off to sleep, which promises oblivion. My last thought is a hope that Rhia and Hugh have managed to make a clean escape.

A RATTLE STARTLES me awake into near-darkness. I sit up. A man is lighting a taper from the fire. A flare of light shows the hands on the clock above the mantel. Past midnight.

"What are you doing here?" I demand. My voice is hoarse from sleep.

Jahan paces to the door and rests a hand against the wood. He listens for a moment. Then he says, in an ordinary voice, "That will keep them from hearing anything."

"I asked you a question."

He comes over to the bed. The flames throw shadows into the hollows beneath his cheekbones, around his eyes and mouth. He crouches before me. He's not amused, for once. He looks worried. "You have to eat. And bathe. If you have any wounds, they're going to fester."

"I don't have any wounds." I remind myself that it's my mother who betrayed us. But there can be more than one betrayer and more than one means of betrayal, and the words burst out of me, hard and angry. "I thought you were on a ship to Ida. You're supposed to be gaining the emperor's support for us. What are you *doing* here?"

My voice is rising. It's a good thing he bespelled the room.

Jahan takes a breath; his hand goes to the scar behind his ear. "When we came north to meet you, when your father was taken— I told Denis I wanted to see Caeris. That if I could observe the rebels and their magic, I could report to the emperor and have the witch hunters sent. And the black ships."

"So you're on *tour* with him?"

He looks at me—and even though I'm angry, warmth builds in my stomach when I meet his eyes. Then he reaches out as if to take my hands. I snatch them away.

"El." He leaves his hands open. "I didn't betray you."

"You're still a double agent. You haven't sent for the black ships at all, have you? The emperor's not going to help us." *This is more than I ever expected!* he said when we spoke in the mirror. I press on, suddenly suspicious that I'm right. "So why *are* you here? What do you really want from us?"

"Finn's my friend. I want him to succeed."

He's getting angry, fighting to keep his voice even, and I know he means it. He does want Finn to succeed. And yet . . .

"Where are your other friends, then? Why have you come alone to help him? Why do you *care?*"

He rocks back onto his heels. "Why do you think I would collude with Denis Falconier? There's nothing in it for me."

"Isn't there?" I snap. "You're the one who told me that you hide your magic in the open. It seems to me that the best way to throw witch hunters off your scent would be to throw someone else to them."

He looks up, and I'm not imagining the shock in his face. "You actually think I would give you up?"

"I don't know. I don't really know you at all. But to save yourself? Yes, I do."

He drops onto his knees and reaches for my hand. I tell myself not to be swayed, even as he breathes my name. "Elanna, you don't understand. I came here for you."

Most likely he uses this line on any girl he wants to soften up. I scoff. "No, you didn't. I'll wager you didn't know I existed before you got here."

"I did," he insists. His eyes gleam in the candlelight. "Finn's people told stories about your ancestors, about the magic the stewards of the land possessed. You're right." He leans closer. "I didn't come here just because I wanted to help Finn. I came here looking for your magic."

This is pure flattery. I fight to stay skeptical, even as I want to believe him. "Why?"

Again, he scratches behind his ear. I can't tell whether the gesture betrays a lie, or if it means he's struggling to tell the truth. Sometimes I think the latter may be harder for Jahan than deception.

"As a sorcerer," he begins, and halts. He starts over. "At the imperial court, I am . . . very much alone. When I was fifteen, I ran away from home. I've cut myself off from other magicians, except for those in books, and even then I have to be careful not to let anyone see what I read. The idea of a sorcerer being one of the three rulers of your country—the idea that we might *use* your magic— well, surely you can see what it would mean to me."

"But I thought you said the emperor would never help us if we used magic openly."

He's shaking his head. "Yes, but—El, don't you see? If we make this a nation where we *do* practice magic openly—even if it means fighting off Loyce Eyrlai *and* Emperor Alakaseus—it could change the face of the world." He's growing impassioned now; his hands make sweeping movements. "Magic is only anathema because the Paladisan empire decided it was. Because magic *threatened* Paladis. But I've learned what actually happened: A cabal of sorcerers almost destroyed their court. It wasn't about the Paladisans calling sorcery an abomination and insult to the gods; it was that magic could have ruined them and so they set out to destroy it. And I'm not the only one who thinks sorcery might make our society better. Think what we could do with it—we could communicate more easily, heal people, summon rain and sun . . ."

He stops; his hope seems to have overwhelmed him. He rises, rubbing a hand over his mouth, and swings away. There are so many questions to ask—a cabal of sorcerers nearly destroyed the empire?—

but what shocks me most is his passion. He really does believe in our cause.

And yet . . . he came here looking for my magic. He had a plan for me. That's why he's here now, because he wants me to help him win his own war. He doesn't see *me;* he just sees my power. Just like everyone else.

It shouldn't hurt so much, after I believed he'd betrayed us.

"El?"

I look up at him, but I find I can't quite meet his eyes. I don't know what I was hoping he would say. "Well," I say, "it's a worthy cause."

One corner of his mouth twitches down. "Impossible, probably." He gives a shake of his head. "But it's not why I stayed. I meant to leave for Ida, as I told you. But I . . ." He glances at me, then stares off over the top of my head, as if telling the truth means it's hard for him to look right at me. "I couldn't leave when you still believed I'd betrayed you."

"Me?" Is he saying he stayed in Caeris for my sake?

He finally meets my eyes. His jaw shifts, but he can't seem to say it.

He did. He stayed for me, not my magic.

"Well," he says, as if almost-confessing the truth has returned the glibness to his tongue, "I couldn't abandon you here to ruin my reputation. I had to keep an eye on you."

"Really?" I want to smile and shake him at the same time. Why can't he just *say* things? "How exactly would I have ruined your reputation?"

He shrugs. "Telling people I have a heart, I suppose."

"I'm not sure how I would have known that."

"Wouldn't you?" He's enjoying this far too much now. He flashes a grin. "Besides, I had to tell you I know you didn't kill Antoine Eyrlai."

I fold my arms. "Your excuses are getting worse."

"No, it's the truth." He stops grinning. "And I know who murdered him."

My heart seems to lurch into my mouth. I can't even speak to ask him who.

He tells me anyway. "Denis Falconier."

"What?" I gasp the word. Denis Falconier didn't even know what the amanita was *called,* and he poisoned the king with it?

Jahan shrugs. "Maybe he thinks Loyce will divorce her husband and make him king. Or give him power in other ways, since I understand Antoine disapproved of their relationship."

I press my knuckles into my eyes. "Does Loyce know?"

"That is impossible to say. But I know Denis did it, because . . ." Jahan's lips press together. "Because of the way he spoke about you. He couldn't hide his own self-satisfaction at framing you for murder."

I'm shaken, and yet anger is burning up through my gut. Denis did this to me. He ruined my life, and it made him happy. "But you only suspect him. You don't have proof, do you?" Denis would be more careful than that.

"He's bound to slip up somehow. It's a matter of time." He adds, "I'm not the only one watching him; I don't think the Butcher trusts him, either."

I look at Jahan. So this is why he's stuck close to Denis Falconier— not only to hide his own role in our rebellion, but to seek proof of his complicity in the king's death. So that *I* can be exonerated.

I hold out my hands, and Jahan gives a slow smile. He takes my hands, bringing them up to his lips, and brushes a kiss over both of my middle knuckles. His skin is warm to my cool, and his mouth is moist. It makes me a little breathless. I say, "We'll look for proof together, then. Tomorrow."

"And we'll get you out of here." He doesn't let go of my hands. "I've sent word to the Barrody underground."

I feel myself smiling at him. He's watching me, intent. It's not the way he looked at me when we first met, as if I were some extraordinary object; he looks at me now as if he sees *me*. As if he's trying to glean my thoughts. For a moment, I think he's going to lean closer—or that I am. But then he simply squeezes my hands and says, "Come to breakfast. Let Denis have his entertainment of you."

I look away from his mouth. "I will."

He releases my hands and crosses the room. With a parting smile, he walks through the wall—the fabric of the tapestry and stones swallow him up. I bring my hands to my nose. His smell lingers, cinnamon and cloves.

I go over to the tray of food, all gone cold. It's time to eat, and bathe as best I can with the chilled wash water. I need to prepare myself for tomorrow.

CHAPTER TWENTY

"Look who deigns to grace us with her presence," Denis exclaims at breakfast, lurching up from his boiled egg to gesture at me. "Sit there, Lady Elanna. Why," he says to Jahan, "I hardly recognize her from yesterday, do you?"

Jahan glances up from the preserves. "She was more entertaining in trousers."

I feel my eyes narrow—but Jahan is looking away from me, and I can't let Denis guess that we share a secret. Or that I know the truth about him. I quickly settle myself in the chair Denis indicated I should take. My clean hair is swept up in a loose knot, and Annis left several strands to trail over the shoulders of my gown—a pretty thing woven from dark-blue wool.

I busy myself with my plate. My midnight snack of congealed soup and cold meat did little to blunt my appetite, and my stomach is awake and eager, even though I can't help thinking I'm dining with my enemy. I help myself to toast and tea, and a maid brings me two boiled eggs in cups, along with a rasher of bacon.

Denis watches me, trying to unnerve me. I have to ignore him; otherwise, every time I look in his face I want to scream at him. How could he kill Antoine? I don't understand what would drive anyone to take someone else's life merely for power.

But maybe, if I ignore him, he'll let slip some evidence.

"What a well-behaved prisoner," he says at last, settling back and folding his arms. "I had hoped to give Lord Jahan a better idea of your barbaric Caerisian customs. Speak to us in Caerisian, Lady Elanna."

I look up, my mouth full of egg. Is he serious?

He sweeps his hand through the air. "Go on."

I swallow my food. What are the chances Denis knows a single word of Caerisian?

With deliberation, I say, "It's only a fool who shows his hand before the game's played."

I watch his face for any sign of comprehension. Nothing. He claps and grins, glancing at Jahan to see how this demonstration goes over.

"How do you like their savage lingo?"

In the moment before Denis looked at him, Jahan's eyes widened. *He* understood me—he must have taken Caerisian lessons with Finn as well as learning Ereni. Now he merely yawns. "I must say, Lord Denis, it's a bit early in the morning to listen to such a hideous racket."

Denis produces his laugh. "It's hard on an empty stomach."

"I have the strongest stomach of all," I say in Caerisian. "Eating breakfast with a murderer."

Jahan raises his eyebrows meaningfully at me. I suppose I've said too much, even if Denis doesn't understand.

"That's quite enough Caerisian," Denis says, sensitive to Jahan's reaction even if he doesn't know my actual words. He puts his shoulder to me, and starts talking to Jahan about how the Ereni soldiers brought civilization to Caeris when they conquered it, effectively cutting me out of the conversation.

It's strange to hear the same stories I've heard all my life—stories that I now know are lies—coming out of his mouth.

But at the same time I'm glad. If all Denis wants is to have me speak in Caerisian for his entertainment, I can suffer that—and I will, until I find a way out of here, with Jahan's help or without it. And with or without proof of Denis's complicity in Antoine's death.

An aide brings in a fresh dispatch of letters. Denis skims them, then snorts. "Have you heard, Lord Jahan? There's a girl running all over Eren, telling the people the Eyrlais have been stealing from them. *Five percent of the crown's resources go to the people!*" he parrots. "If I never hear *five percent* of anything again in my life, it'll be too soon."

I catch my breath. But he can't mean Victoire. She's in hiding—and she's no rabble-rouser.

But she kept the secret of her father's deceit, and the *five percent* is burned into my mind. She followed me out of Laon. Maybe I don't know her as well as I thought.

Jahan pours fresh tea into his cup. "These Ereni women are quite warlike."

"Oh, please, this one's not a warrior. She's just a nuisance. But now the people are in a lather, fomenting in village squares and making tirades against the queen. I'm sure such a thing never happens in *Ida*."

"Actually, our rhetoricians can be quite outspoken," Jahan begins.

But Denis isn't really interested. He raises his eyebrows at me over the top of his letter. "I don't suppose this troublesome chit is a friend of yours?"

I stare back at him. "I doubt I've met her. But I certainly wish her the best of luck."

"Oh! Oh!" He pretends to stab himself in the chest. "I'm wounded, really I am." He says to Jahan, "That's all right. We'll find another way to make her talk."

We don't have to wait long.

The servants have hardly cleared the breakfast dishes when Denis is out of his chair, herding us out the door, back down the hall to his study. Yesterday's maps remain spread over the desk. He points at them and looks at me.

"Read this for me."

I stare down at the contoured lines indicating hills and valleys. The town names are written in such a crabbed hand I can scarcely make them out. I lean closer. These can't all be towns. Within a single hillside, five names collide. It makes little sense—unless the mapmaker was trying to deceive. But I don't know why anyone would deceive by making up names . . .

I press my finger to the name written largest. "This is a town. But I don't know what the rest are."

"You don't *know*?" Denis clucks his tongue. "Some Caerisian rebel!" he says to Jahan and the Butcher, who's just come in. "Tell her what all those names mean, Lord Gilbert."

The Butcher comes to stand across the desk from me, cool and professional. "Those place-names belong to hills, streams, trees, and rocks. You see, on this hillside alone, they have named not only a grove but the stream that springs from it, a rock formation, and so forth."

I feel a fool for not recognizing this.

Denis wags a finger at me. "Lady Elanna, you will have to be more useful. If you can't help us even the smallest bit, then . . ." He shakes his head and draws the finger across his neck.

And laughs.

The Butcher does not laugh. He looks at Denis, and a vein stands out in his temple. His arms are taut, his hands clasped behind his back. He glances at me across the table, assessingly.

IN THE AFTERNOON, they question me.

"Tell me, Lady Elanna," Denis says conversationally. "Where is Fionnlach Dromahair? What's he doing?"

Murderer, I think. I turn the ring around on my finger, struggling to put my rage aside; I have to outwit him. In this comfortable study, with its odors of leather and old books, it's hard to believe I am really in danger of my life or of giving away Caeris's secrets. And so I say, "I couldn't be quite sure, but I imagine he's taking tea about now."

Denis lunges down in front of me. "Hilarious! Answer the question."

"I don't know where he is."

"Where did you leave him, then?"

I shake my head. I won't answer that.

Denis puts his hands over mine, trapping them on the arms of the chair, slowly digging his fingers into my knuckles. He's getting angry. The tendons bulge on the back of his hands. "Tell me where Fionnlach Dromahair is."

"No." The pressure on my knuckles hurts in a distant sort of way—a bearable pain. I force myself to think of Finn. Of Sophy, Hugh, Rhia. If only I had tried to convince them to mount a rescue, all of us together—maybe then I would not be here alone.

If I ever see them again, we will fight Denis and the Butcher to-gether. I envision Finn in this room, ruling as king of Caeris, and Jahan and I using magic openly in defiance of Eren and Paladis. The image gives me strength.

Denis looks over his shoulder at the Butcher, who watches us impassively. He probably knows how to extract information better than Denis does, but Denis is too proud to let him take over. At least I can be grateful for Denis's arrogance. They sent Jahan out on a pretext, so that he wouldn't see this.

"I would hit her, but it seems uncouth to hit a woman," Denis says to the Butcher. "Should I hit her?"

"Not yet." The Butcher pauses. "There are more effective ways to get her to answer than physical pain."

But he does not say what they are. I look at him. He regards me evenly, his hands clasped again behind his back. Why is he being obtuse? For my sake? Or simply because he dislikes Denis?

Denis, evidently frustrated, looks back at me. "Let me try this. A bargain. You answer one question a day, and it's another day you get to live. How's that?"

I swallow hard. My resolve is slipping, and the vision of Finn is only a fantasy. The pulse in my head sings *coward, coward, coward.* I do not want to die.

"I won't take that bargain," I say. Even though I want to.

Pain. Sharp pain across my face—he struck me. I didn't even see his hand move. I reel back, my cheek flaming. I cradle my hands over my face.

He stomps away, swings back around. He shouts into my face, "Tell me where you left Fionnlach Dromahair!"

A fleck of his spittle lands on my nose. I shudder. I shake my head. I cling again to the image of Finn in this room. Even if I die, he can still win against Denis. Let him rule Caeris as a just king, a free king.

Denis raises his hand again—apparently he only meant he wouldn't strike me if he wasn't angry enough. But he is now. I al-ways knew this rage lurked under his charming surface. I knew, but I never wanted to see it.

He's screaming at me. "Tell me about Fionnlach Dromahair, you little Caerisian bitch!"

I glare back at him, though my ears are ringing. I won't betray Finn, my friend, my future king.

There's a squeal of hinges. Feet pound across the floor, then slow to a halt. "I heard raised voices. Is everything quite all right, Lord Denis?"

It's Jahan. I slump a little in relief, even though I know he can't stop Denis.

"I am *trying* to get the little bi—" Denis bellows, then cuts himself short, looking at Jahan. In a reduced voice, he says, "Lady Elanna is our prisoner, Lord Jahan. She owes us answers to our questions. When a prisoner refuses to cooperate, it is customary to interrogate them."

Jahan lifts an eyebrow. "An interrogation? How tiresome. Come, Lord Denis, surely you know there are easier ways to get women to talk than that."

I glare at him, even though I know he's saying it to buy me time.

Denis barks a laugh. "If only we had the luxury of persuading her to succumb to our charms, instead! That would be very Idaean. I should like to see you try."

Jahan looks at me speculatively. "Well . . ."

Just before I think I'm going to explode from embarrassment and rage, the Butcher intervenes. "We wouldn't wish to impose upon you, Lord Jahan, to aid in such a distasteful task."

"Always so dull, Lord Gilbert!" Denis exclaims. "No wonder they call you the Butcher, instead of—of—"

"The Philanderer?" I say nastily. "That would certainly be appropriate for you, Lord Denis. Oh, I forgot! That's already what they call you, since everyone knows you share a bed with—"

His palm strikes my jaw, knocking the name *Loyce* off my lips. I reel back.

Denis raises his hand to hit me again, but Jahan grabs his shoulder in a firm but friendly grip. "Look at her, Lord Denis!" he exclaims. "You're only giving her satisfaction by getting angry. Let's try it *my* way—gentle, then fierce . . ."

With a growl, Denis throws him off. He seems to be gathering himself for another blow, but there's a sudden knock on the door.

It's an army officer. "Your Grace," he begins as Denis marches over to him, anger stiff in his gait. They have a swift, murmured exchange.

The Butcher has taken a step toward them; they've made no effort to include him in their conference. Jahan sends me a quick glance, tapping his jaw.

I nod. It hurts, but I'm all right.

Denis comes marching back over to us. I do not like the way he's smiling.

"Lady Elanna." He holds out his hand to me, a courtier's gesture, as if he weren't hitting me two minutes ago. "Please fetch your hat and coat. We're going on an excursion."

THE COACH RATTLES down the hill, and inside it, the silence is thick. Jahan sits next to me, his body tense though his smile is easy, and across from us Denis and the Butcher occupy the bench seat in reluctant companionship. I don't think Denis meant for either of them to come—he wanted this to be a moment of power between me and him. Whatever we're doing, he certainly doesn't want Jahan here.

And maybe he doesn't want the Butcher, either. They obviously dislike each other, and Jahan said Lord Gilbert doesn't trust Denis.

We jerk over a pothole. Denis swears under his breath. Jahan's shoulder bumps mine. I dig my fingers into the fabric of the seat cushion as the coach slows. We've come to the bottom of the hill, down into the heart of the city.

"There's a crowd," the Butcher observes. "Was that your intent?"

He's asking Denis, but Denis pretends not to hear.

Outside the windows, I see a jumble of hats and faces on either side of the coach. We're creeping through the crowd now. I can't see any buildings. We must be in a square—Green Square—the one Rhia and I passed through on our way to the garrison.

Rhia. Is there any chance the rebels are in this crowd, waiting for me? That I am not alone?

Then I look out and see the scaffold.

It's not that tall—a tiered wooden structure dominating the square. A square frame surmounts it, with three ropes hanging from it.

No. No, no.

Denis is smiling at me. "Enjoying our outing, Lady Elanna?"

I try to form words, but my mouth has gone dry. I seem to be shaking. Jahan leans his weight toward me, so I feel the press of his thigh against mine. But it is not enough to give me courage.

"Don't worry," Denis says, still with that terrible smile. "You're not going to be put up there. At least . . . not today."

I shudder. My stomach is rebelling; I think I'm going to throw up. I know who it must be; I know who will hang there. And all at once I break.

"I can't do this! You can't force me to watch this!"

"And we won't," Denis says. "Just answer three questions for me. One question for each life."

I stare at him. Bargaining with my own life seems nothing, compared to this. I own my life. But whoever he's about to have killed—how can he give me the power over them?

Denis murdered the king. It should be he who hangs.

Three ropes. It will be Hugh and Rhia, caught as they tried to escape. It will be my father.

I reach out blindly to clutch at Jahan's arm. He shakes me off—he has to, to protect his cover—and his abrupt movement startles me back to my senses.

"No. I won't make the bargain. I won't watch you kill my people!"

"There is no bargain," Denis says, his teeth clenched. "You answer three questions. If you don't answer, they die. It's quite simple."

I can't seem to catch my breath. "What's the first question?"

Denis smiles grimly. "Tell us where you last saw Fionnlach Dromahair."

Relief rings through me. It's an easy question. An easy lie. Without hesitation, I say, "Cerid Aven. They're camped in the woods." Finn won't have gone back, of course, but they don't know that.

Denis looks at the Butcher—for confirmation, I realize. I'm going to be sick. Do they actually know where Finn is? Have they tricked me?

Is he one of the captives coming here for execution?

The Butcher's gaze flickers toward me. With a soft, irritated sigh, he says to Denis, "It's unlikely. The prince is not that foolish."

Denis shakes his head at me. "Lady Elanna, you shouldn't lie."

"I'm not lying!" My voice is high, pinched.

The Butcher stares Denis down. "This is not the way to conduct an interrogation."

Denis waves him off. "Enough! Lady Elanna, it's time to show you your future, and the future of your countrypeople." He swings out of the coach without a backward glance.

Jahan pushes me gently; I climb out of the coach. My hands are trembling, slick with sweat, as I land among a knot of soldiers.

But at least they don't have Finn.

WE ASSEMBLE ON the cobblestones. Four soldiers flank me, but Jahan manages to stay by my right hand. The Butcher is on the left, arms folded and stiff with anger: "This is not," he says again, "the way to conduct an interrogation." Denis paces in front of the scaffold, ignoring him.

"Why are scaffolds always made of wood?" Jahan wonders. "Lady Elanna, do you know?"

This seems so profoundly irrelevant I can't even reply. My father is surely coming here to die, along with Hugh and Rhia Knoll, because I cannot lie well enough to Denis Falconier. And I cannot give up anyone by telling the truth.

The building material of scaffolds doesn't matter.

We've been standing here for minutes. Are they ever going to begin? The hangman tromps up the scaffold's steps to inspect the nooses.

Then a wagon comes rattling through the crowd, stuffed with soldiers and three boys, with their hands shackled. The wagon stops. The boys are guided through a line of soldiers to the stairs, up onto the scaffold. It takes a moment for my mind to catch up with what I'm seeing. A sickening relief guts me. It's not my father, nor Rhia or Hugh. These are boys I do not know. Boys who, in this skirmish over crowns, do not matter.

I'm sick with myself for thinking it. Of course they matter. They aren't expendable simply because I don't know their names.

"These men have been found guilty of violence against Eren's soldiers," an official proclaims. "They will be punished by death."

The boys—they are *not* men—shuffle toward the scaffold. Their faces seem almost empty—whatever torture they've endured seems to have exhausted them beyond any fear of death. I want to embrace them, and then I wonder if it's simply to exonerate my own guilt. And yet I want to give them something good, something worth seeing, before they die. I find myself murmuring a prayer to Father Dagod—the Caerisian deity seems more appropriate than the Idaean ones I've mouthed reverence to most of my life. But the whispered words sound hollow, even to me. Father Dagod will not burn into life and sing away the boys' bonds, or cradle their souls in his hands. Or if he does, I won't see it.

And then, as they begin to climb the steps, their feet hampered by shackles, I realize I *do* know them.

They are the stableboys from Cerid Aven. The boys who started a fight with the Butcher's men. The one in the middle is the one I saved. The one who was concussed but lived.

I can't let them die.

The boys line up in front of the nooses.

The one in the middle looks down. I know his name. Domnall. He sees me.

A terrifying emotion splits through his empty face.

Hope.

"*Caveadear!*" he shouts.

Jahan's elbow jabs into mine, and I remember what he said earlier. Wood. The scaffold is *wood*.

I stretch out my hands. The earth pulses under me. My awareness of it is shaky, but it's there.

The other boys have seen me now, too. They're all shouting, the wonderful fools. "*Caveadear! Tire Caer-Ys! Caveadear!*"

The earth lives even in wood that has been cut and hammered into an instrument of death. It lives, and it grows when I touch it. Father Dagod can wait.

Denis looms in front of me, his face red and swollen with rage. He shoves me back into the guardsmen flanking me. "Get her out of here."

I dodge past him, lunging for the scaffold. When my hand touches it, it utters a great creak.

And it begins to grow.

"Lady Elanna, step away from the scaffold!" A soldier is pointing a musket at me, but the ground splits and shakes beneath him. The scaffold thrusts outward, into branches and leaves. A quick-growing branch strikes the soldier in the side. His musket explodes into the air.

The hangman's already leapt from the scaffold. The frame for the nooses is growing, towering into the sky, into a tree that's never existed.

The boys are chanting. *"Caveadear, Caveadear!"* They're jumping up and down.

It takes me a moment to realize they're free of their shackles. As if the chains exploded.

I glance for Jahan, but I don't see him.

Behind me, the crowd has erupted into chaos. The Butcher is pushing toward me. Shots are fired, and one of the boys on the scaffold flinches backward, blood turning his shoulder scarlet.

"Run!" I scream at them.

A soldier grabs me by the shoulders just before the Butcher reaches me. I struggle against him. I just manage to see that the boys have obeyed and that the crowd has pulled Lord Gilbert away, when something strikes my ribs, my back, my hea—

CHAPTER TWENTY-ONE

I wake, crying out.

The earth shudders under me. It is in pain. No, the pain is mine—or the earth's *and* mine—

"Drink this, lady."

A girl's plump hands arrive at my lips, pinching a glass dropper. A bitter liquid tear falls into my mouth.

I shove her away. "No."

"It's only for the pain. Until you heal."

I try to argue, but the bitter liquid carries me back under a thick not-quite sleep, and when I open my eyes again, the tall pink canopy on the bed lolls above me like a tongue. A high humming lingers in my ears.

"Keep your distance," a man says. I know that voice. "It's dangerous. A Valtai witch."

"*It* is a woman like any other, and she's hurt," a woman replies.

"Shall I send for the guards?"

"Please, Your Grace. I am a doctor. It appears you've given her such a high dosage of laudanum she can't fully wake. *That* is the problem—not that the bruises your thugs gave her are helping."

"They gave her the laudanum under my orders. What else are we to do with a Valtai witch? Lord Gilbert suggested we keep her sedated until the witch hunters reach Laon and send instruction. He said we mustn't, ah, have her 'disappear' until we know how to dispose of her properly."

"I see you also have a witch stone there."

"Lord Gilbert has some experience with witches. It's his."

"Mmm. Lord Gilbert seems very useful." The woman leans over me: tidy dark hair, clinical eyes in a pale face. I see a spread of anatomical drawings. It's Sorcha Kerr.

I try to speak her name, but it comes out in a grunt.

"Shh, Lady Elanna," she says, patting my arm. "Calm yourself. Duke Denis, really. I will do my work best if you leave us."

Denis's footsteps *thunk* over the carpet. "If you insist, Doctor Kerr. But send for me the moment she starts to speak. We need to question her while she's still under. She's done nothing but mumble for the last three days."

The door clicks shut behind him.

I move my fingers, which feel swollen and clumsy. I try to grasp the woman's sleeve. "Sor . . . ?"

"Yes, Lady Elanna. You need some salve for those wounds, and a lower dosage of laudanum. That'll fix you up." She leans over me, pressing an ear-horn to my heart. In rapid Caerisian, she whispers, "Keep silent. Pretend you don't know me. We're being watched."

I try to nod, though it makes my head seem too wide.

She moves the ear-horn to listen to my lungs. "Thank all the gods you're alive," she adds, her voice choking so much I hardly hear the whispered words. "We thought the duke had done you in."

This time, I manage to reach her hand. I squeeze it.

She wipes at her eyes as she moves briskly from the bed. To Annis, she says, "I'm going to modify that dosage of laudanum. I've brought some of my own—the gods alone know where you got the stuff you're using."

"Yes, ma'am," says Annis.

I roll my head to watch them. Sorcha clinks through glass bottles over on the table. "And I'll leave you this salve," she's saying. "Apply it to the lady's bruises—if you dare to touch her. She's been badly beaten, but nothing's broken. I didn't sense any internal bleeding."

Annis takes the jar of salve. "I'll put it on her. She doesn't seem very frightening to me."

"No. She'll do nothing to hurt you. She's just a badly injured young woman. She needs rest, and to move around as soon as the laudanum wears off."

"But the duke's going to—to—"

"Not just yet. It's your job to see she gets better, so she can tell you what you need to do to fight the Caerisians. Understand?"

"I just don't think it's right to have her executed," Annis says softly. "I don't think it's right to kill anybody."

"If only the rulers of kingdoms thought the way you do."

Sorcha bustles back over to me. "No more laudanum for you just yet, Lady Elanna. I want to examine your extremities a second time, now you're more awake. Just make a noise if anything hurts."

She runs her hands along my arms. I groan, and as I'm making noise, she drops her head beside mine and says in a whisper, "It's not laudanum—I put extract of cedar in the jar instead. Looks and smells the same, but it will have no effect provided you don't take it longer than a few days. Pretend you're still sleepy. We're going to get you out of here. But you need to heal first. You're going to have to run."

Then she moves on to my stomach and legs, talking over her shoulder to Annis. My sluggish thoughts linger over her words, unable to quite make sense of them. But I know I am no longer alone.

I SLEEP, AND wake sometime in the night to the witch stone's droning hum. My head is clearer, and my body no longer feels swollen and thick—it only aches all over.

Something woke me. A tapping.

I roll up onto my elbow, wincing, just in time to see Jahan step through the fabric of the wall itself.

"How do you do that?" I ask. "And with the witch stone here, too . . ."

He breaks into a grin, hurrying over to me, and seizes my hands in his. "You're awake. They gave you so much laudanum, I thought . . ."

I look at him. It is so good to see him. So good I seem to be softening, expanding, right through the middle of my body—a dangerous feeling if ever there is one. But just now, I don't care. I twine my fingers into the front of his shirt and pull him against me. Press my ear to his chest. His heartbeat pulses. I feel his warmth. I smell him.

And I start to cry.

"Oh, El. Shh." His hands cup the back of my head, smoothing down my hair.

I am crying in front of a man I hardly know. Me, who spent fourteen years trying not to cry before anyone. This is not what I would ever have imagined, just a few weeks ago.

But he just folds me against him. It hurts to cry, pulling on my bruised ribs. I let the tears fade and bury my face in his shirt. His warmth infuses the cloth. He starts to hum—a soft melody, foreign to me, in counterpoint to the persistent humming of the witch stone. The hiss of the stone in my head has become so steady, I forgot it was there.

"That's a Britemnosi song," he says after a while. "My mother used to sing it to me."

"Tell me about your mother," I whisper.

He settles back, carrying me with him, and I feel a tug in his chest muscles, as if he shook his head and then stopped himself. "My mother. She was sad, mostly."

Maybe he is used to crying women. "Sad how?" I ask, even though I sense he doesn't want to talk about it.

There's a long silence, and I worry I've made him angry, that he won't speak. I try to tip my head back, but this also hurts. Jahan stills me with a brush of his fingers along the back of my neck.

"My father raised us to be sorcerers, my brothers and I," he says. "Mother didn't approve—No, more than that. She hated it. It . . . It shamed her. But she had no power to stop the sorceress who persuaded my father to help with her experiments. She couldn't even tell her family, because they would have taken us away from her."

I draw back from him so that I can see the emotion in his face. I touch my hand to his chest, unsure what to say, and he reaches up and holds it there.

"One of the first things I learned how to do was walk through walls," he says with a faint smile. "It's a basic manipulation of matter. If you think of anything as being made up of tiny particles you can't see—of energy—then you realize anything can be changed."

"Is that why my ancestors could move the land?" I wonder.

"I have no idea why your ancestors could make forests and mountains move." He laughs softly. "Caeris has a different brand of magic than what I'm used to." Again, he brushes the skin behind his ear, then offers me a crooked grin. "That's why I came here to look for you. And when I found you . . ."

Impulsively, I follow his movement with my own hand. I feel the scar there on the bone, ridged and old.

I must look my question, because, though he drops his hand and leans away, he says in a reluctant voice, "The sorceress experimented with us. To see if she might make us more capable of magic. She made us resistant to witch stones, among other things—I scarcely even hear the noise they're supposed to make. That helped, at court, when the witch hunters were present. But the experiments . . ." He swallows so hard I hear the click of his throat. "My mother hated them. And the sorceress didn't only practice on my brothers and me."

"Jahan," I begin, but I realize I don't know what to say. I know what it is to be torn from your family. But to witness your parents' struggle, to be experimented upon in the name of science? It sounds unbearable.

Yet he bore it. He's here, pretending it is nothing.

"Your mother—is she . . . ?"

His fist digs into the coverlet. "She's dead."

Oh, gods. I'm ashamed of myself for asking, though I couldn't have known the answer. I glance at him and see the tendons standing out in his throat. He doesn't talk of her, I expect, and though I want to ask how she died and if the sorceress killed her, I can't bring myself to demand the explanation.

"We all have our pasts," he says at last.

"Alas. But then my present isn't looking so good, either."

Jahan gasps a soundless laugh. It is true and it is terrible, so I laugh, too, my head against his.

Then he traces the line of my cheek with a finger, and I catch my breath. I am aware of his touch like a point of hot light moving along my skin. "You are so brave," he murmurs. "If I had half your courage . . ."

"It's easy to be brave when you have nothing to lose," I say.

"No." His touch stops on my jaw. "It isn't."

I have nothing to lose. Only my aching, stubborn body. Beyond that I have not much left, but pride. And pride isn't enough to stop me.

I turn my head and let my lips brush his hand. It feels like an act of greater daring than lunging past Denis to the scaffold, and at the same time like the most natural thing in the world.

Jahan draws in a breath. Then he gently tilts my head up. He leans his head toward mine. "So you trust me now?" His breath touches my face; his fingertips linger on my neck.

"Maybe," I say with a laugh that catches in my throat. I close the distance between us. His lips are warm and moist and it seems like a miracle, though of course that's just what lips are like. We fumble against each other in the half dark, bumping foreheads, the stubble on his cheek burning my neck. I've forgotten my bruises. I just want him closer.

His touch is gentle, until both of us are breathing hard and his grip tightens on my waist and I gasp in pain. We break apart. Somehow—I've been so lost in a delirium of sensation I don't even know how—I clambered onto his lap and wrapped my legs around him. It seemed like a good idea at the time, but now my whole body screams in protest. Besides that, I'm only wearing a chemise. The indecency of it both shocks and delights me.

"Did I hurt you?" he's asking.

"No—" But I can't stifle a groan when his hand brushes my ribs.

"Shh." He disentangles my legs from him, and props up the pillows to help me lie back down. I twist my fingers into the coverlet, torn between physical pain and frustrated desire. The humming of the witch stone burns back into my ears. Jahan strokes the hair out of my face, then sits back. He takes one of my arms and unfolds it, running his fingers gently over my skin. He doesn't say anything, but I hear the click of his throat as he swallows. It must be bad.

He leans over and kisses his way down my arm, so lightly I just feel the brush of his lips. Then he kisses my aching stomach, my purpling thighs and knees. I dig my hands into his thick, soft hair; tears stand out in my eyes. No one has ever shown me this kind of tenderness. He leans back up, hovering over me, and brings his lips to mine. I wrap my arms around his neck, ignoring the pain.

At length, he pulls away, though I try to hold him down. "There's something I need to do." He paces across the room to a tapestry, pressing his hands flat against it, as if he's listening or feeling for something. "Ah. Here."

I get up and limp toward him, mainly by willpower. "What have you done?"

"There's a passage in the wall," he says, "but you can't reach it from this room. I've made a door."

I push back the tapestry, though its wool fabric is heavy and even this movement costs me strength. The wall behind looks just like a wall to me.

"If you need to use it, say *I pass through* in your mind, and push your arm in."

I stare at him. "Into the wall?"

"I'll show you." Jahan draws me to him for a last kiss, then turns to the wall. *"I pass through,"* he says. He grins at me and puts his arm into the wooden paneling. Another step, and it swallows his knees and head. And then he's gone.

CHAPTER TWENTY-TWO

They come to question me in the morning. No, not question. Threaten.

Demand.

"You're awake," Denis says. I notice he keeps his distance from me, as if afraid to touch my witch's skin. Good. That's one thing I can be thankful for. "About time."

The Butcher has followed him into the room and marches over to the foot of my bed, looking at me with a deep frown. In an undertone, he says to Denis, "Your Grace, I still don't believe this is the answer. We are not prepared for a war that will split our country in half. Lady Elanna is the figurehead of this rebellion, and to remove her without a trial will only bring us closer to the brink of violence—"

Denis flicks his fingers. "I've made up my mind."

The Butcher's jaw clenches, but he puts his hands behind his back and says nothing more.

I lie very still, pretending I didn't hear or understand. My head is clear, but I remember Sorcha's instructions to pretend the laudanum continues to affect me. It's not hard; the witch stone still hums in my ears, dulling my mind. I let my jaw sag toward my chest. I hope I look stupid.

"You have two choices." Denis holds up two fingers. "One, you will cooperate with us, answering our questions, and you will be moved to a comfortable cell in the Tower in Laon. Two, you do not cooperate, and we extract the information by any means possible."

Somewhere, he finds a smile and shines it at me. "You will not get a trial."

I look at the Butcher. His frown has deepened further, but he does not try to argue the terms.

"No . . . trial?" I let my voice slur.

"We're already aware that you're guilty."

I stare up into the canopy. The witch stone's buzzing makes it difficult to think clearly. Even if they did give me a trial, it would almost certainly reach the inevitable conclusion. Denis's bargain is simply a question of how much pain I want to endure.

But then there is Sorcha. There is Jahan, and the door hidden behind the tapestry. I am no longer alone.

Finn and Sophy are still free, out in the hills. Caeris still stands a chance.

"The first, you remain here before your removal," Denis says. "The second, you will be returned to the garrison, to your prison cell. No more doctors. No more laudanum."

The Butcher clears his throat. "It is really about whether or not one prefers a comfortable death." He raises an eyebrow, as if to underscore the irony of the choice, and Denis glares at him.

Tears flood my eyes, spill out over my cheeks. Maybe it is the lingering effect of the laudanum, or the ever-present sound of the witch stone, which makes me unable to control myself. Maybe it is simply a stroke of luck, because Denis lurches backward, his lip curling. The sight of my tears unsettles him.

I hiccup the words. "I can't make that kind of decision."

"Come, Lady Elanna." The Butcher pats my feet. "It is a clear and simple choice. And you always knew the punishment for sorcery." An ironic smile. "You may have your wish to go to Ida granted after all."

I stare at him. Tears slide down my nose. The knot in my stomach is cold and tight. "The witch hunters?"

He nods. "They will take you to Paladis for examination. Yours is an unusual kind of magic."

"But the justice is ours to dispense," Denis says. "Don't think Paladis is going to give you a reprieve on that."

*   *   *

THEY LEAVE, AND I lie with my tears in silence, or as much silence as I have with the witch stone's rumbling. The maid Annis tries to talk—"Do you think you could get on your feet this evening, my lady? The doctor wanted me to walk you around"—but I cannot muster an answer. We have to move fast. I could lie in answer to the questions, and buy more time at the castle in hope Sorcha attempts a rescue. Or I could get onto my own two feet and find a way out, with Jahan's help.

I will ask him tonight. I sense he'll be back.

There's a flurry at my door. I hear Annis saying, "Did they give you permission—?"

"They did, and if you will not let me in to see my own daughter, I will tell the duke of your insubordination."

The breath stops in my throat. My mother?

She sweeps in, trailing indignation. "Who closed those shutters? Open them straightaway. Yes. Push them all the way back." Annis, being meek, obeys without protest. Cold light floods the room.

Mother comes over to me, sinking down beside the bed with a soft *huff* of air from her gown. She collects my hands in hers, which are hot, faintly sweaty, the way mine get when I'm nervous. I look up at her profile, hawk-nosed and commanding. She does not appear uneasy.

If anything, I think she's furious. Though whether at Denis or me, I have no idea.

Annis clatters over by the table.

Mother rounds on her. "My daughter has precious *days* left in her life! Give us some peace."

"But my lady—"

"Do not *but* me! I have given Denis Falconier all his due respect. I am owed this as a mother!"

Cowed, Annis slinks out. I hear her answering the guards' questions in the hallway.

Mother watches her go, then looks down at me, her hands squeezing mine. "Can you walk yet?"

"I haven't tried." Getting out of bed to follow Jahan to the wall last night exhausted me.

"Well, try. Right now."

Before I even know what she's doing, she levers my legs over the side of the bed and pulls me into a sitting position. With a heave, she lifts me up, supporting me against her side. The floor presses cold through my thin bed stockings, but I move without trouble. Still, my ribs compress. If I tried to run, I'd have a hard time. But we pace to the window without too much difficulty. Even the wretched witch stone can't stop me from moving, only befuddle my thoughts.

Mother holds me there, in the window embrasure. I suppose I am meant to speak to her, but what is there to say? She betrayed us because she cared too much to lose me again. I understand that now.

She points. "Look at that. The hills beyond the hills. That's north. Wild country. The Ereni still haven't dared go into it—they can't read the maps."

"Can you?" I ask.

Her mouth quirks to the side. She doesn't deny it. "Your father didn't marry me only for my skill at the pianoforte."

"What do you—"

She points again. "There. Do you see it?"

A light flares over the hills. Cold runs up my spine. She's a spy. She knows the Caerisian signals, and she's going to tell.

"That," she whispers in my ear, "is Fionnlach Dromahair, coming to rescue you."

"I suppose you'll tell Denis. Or the Butcher."

Her arm goes slack around me, then tightens. She angles me around to look into my face. "Tonight. Jahan will come for you. Be dressed, as much as you can, by midnight. Finn and the Hounds will meet you above the castle." A faint, sad smile. "You should bind your ribs to keep pressure on them. It'll hurt less if you have to run."

"But—" I struggle to understand what she's saying, though it's perfectly clear. "But you betrayed us to the Butcher."

She gives me a long look, then glances at the door. We're still alone. She leans close to me, fierce. "I did not betray you. Not intentionally. Gilbert and I have known each other since I first came to Eren, though I hadn't seen him since he gave us up to Antoine Eyrlai when you were a child. Oh," she says, seeing my look, "I don't blame you, darling. I blame *him*."

"You *knew* him?" I'm still stunned by this revelation.

She ignores the question. "I know his servitude to Antoine Eyrlai ate at him. It's destroyed his humanity. Antoine demanded he do the most heinous things, to punish him for our old friendship. There was a time Gilbert believed in King Euan and our cause, you know. He was the one who first told me that many Caerisians and Ereni longed for another way. I admired his passion for the new nation he envisioned. But I was blind to his feelings for me; I should have known that strong feelings can quickly turn the other way. Because when I married your father, hatred ruined the friendship we'd all once had." She draws in a breath.

"The Butcher believed in our cause? But he *betrayed* us."

"He was young. And jealous. And stupid. And now . . ." She shakes her head. "He's in so deep he can't breathe the real air. But I thought there was a chance, so I wrote to him, prevailed upon him to gather Ereni supporters and come to Cerid Aven, to our side."

And instead, he let his men occupy Cerid Aven. He sent Hugh off to hang.

"Mother," I begin, my voice shaking. "Come with us."

She cups my face in her hands, silencing me, and kisses my brow. "There's still humanity left in Gilbert, I know it. And I'm staying here, my dearest daughter, until I find it."

With a clatter, the door opens and Annis returns. "Lady Teofila, the guards say *no one,* not even you, is to remain alone with the prisoner."

My mother and I look at each other for another moment, with all the words unsaid between us. The truth about the Butcher; the truth about her.

She puts her arm around me and leads me toward the bed. She sits me down and begins to brush out my hair, humming. "Our song," she whispers to me. "The land's song."

WHEN ANNIS LEAVES me for the night and the bolt shoots home on the other side of the door, I leap from the bed. I have to pace around in a small circle, biting my lip to keep from moaning at the pain in my ribs. Finally, it eases. At least my mind seems clearer; perhaps the laudanum affected me more than the witch stone. I limp over to the wardrobe with the single candle Annis left me, tugging open the drawers with breathless care in case they squeak or in any way alert my guards.

Not that the wardrobe contains a single shred of practical clothing. I discover three chemises and a massive fluff of petticoats, a gown, a skirt and caraco, but besides that, little indeed. I think of the glint of snow I saw on the high northern hills and the frost creeping the windows. It's going to be a cold night.

I drop my chemise in favor of one with longer sleeves. But then I stop with the fresh chemise in my hands.

My stomach is black and bruised. Long bruises run down my thighs. I have to be thankful for the candlelight, softening the sight of it. Even my arms are spotted with purpling marks. I sink to the floor, cradling my arms around my poor naked body.

I can't do this. What if they catch me again? How much worse will they beat me? How much more awful will my last days be?

If I have to die, I want it to be *for* something—for Caeris's greater good, for her freedom. But if I die here, I won't have done any good for anyone. The steward of the land is supposed to be fighting alongside her people. If I'm going to die for Caeris, I want to do it out in the open, on a high hill, trying to wake the land, trying to destroy Denis and the queen—not in secret, in an airless chamber behind closed doors.

I'm getting cold. And I'm being a fool. I don't want to die. *So get yourself up and get out of here, El.*

I swaddle myself in chemises and petticoats, stuff two pairs of stockings into thin slippers; there is no sensible footwear in the wardrobe, either. I tie a blanket over the caraco and spend some minutes bulking up pillows beneath the bedsheets, trying to make it look like someone is still sleeping under the covers. Anything to delay pursuit, even for a few short minutes.

I pace to the clock. Almost ten. My preparations took precisely half an hour.

I have a long time to wait.

Unable to sleep, I sit by the fire and stare at the clock. At my hands. The hands that can grow trees out of scaffolds.

And at the humming witch stone behind me, next to the bed.

I storm to my feet, seizing the witch stone from its place. It seems to fizz and spark in my hand, spitting angry electricity into my palms.

"You are a stone," I say to it. "You are just a stone."

I grip it in both hands, even though it protests and seems to struggle to get away from me. The humming rattles into my bones, up into my ears. Every instinct urges me to throw the thing away, cast it out the window. But it is a stone. I know stones. I understand them.

"Quiet," I say to it. It softens in my grip, turning malleable in my hands, but the buzzing persists. Still, it is talking to me now. I see how it was pulled from the ground, the dirt beaten off it. I see how hands cupped it, and someone wove magic into it—a kind of magic I don't understand and the stone doesn't, either—an unnatural magic woven out of fear and anger.

I remind the stone of its true nature. Of the mountain in which it grew, of the land once native to it.

It melts into my hands, its anger forgotten. The humming lingers, but softer now, more like a melody. As though the stone is speaking to me.

I slip it into my pocket.

MIDNIGHT ARRIVES, THEN passes. I sit with the witch stone, waiting. I pace to the window. To the door Jahan made.

Nothing.

Maybe my mother lied. Maybe Jahan lied.

Maybe someone else found out.

Maybe I have been left alone, after all.

Then I hear something. Footsteps coming closer out in the corridor. The sound of voices, guardsmen hailing one another.

My heartbeat starts hammering in my ears. It's the changing of the guard. It has to be.

They wouldn't come into my room in the middle of the night. Would they?

I've frozen in the center of the rug. I don't know what to do. Crawl back into bed? Hide? Pretend to sleep?

No. I can't go back into that bed. I can't just wait for them to come for me.

I dive into the corner, behind the tapestry where Jahan's door is hidden.

The door rattles as the lock opens. I flatten myself against the wall with a gasp. A blaze of light burns my eyes: guardsmen troop in, muskets strapped to their backs. They wear tricorn hats and heavy traveling coats.

I yank my head back behind the tapestry. I hardly dare to breathe. They'll see me here, and they'll know.

I'm not melting through the wooden paneling to the stone behind. *I pass through,* I think at the paneling. *I pass through!*

The wall seems to shift behind me.

"Lady Elanna, it's time to waken." It's the Butcher. Oh, all the gods. They *have* come for me in the middle of the night. They know about our plan. Or this is their way of torturing prisoners—startling them out of sleep, forcing them to answer questions and threats. No—the guards are dressed to travel.

At least my pillows must look reasonably lifelike. He hasn't caught on yet.

I need to move backward, but I seem to be frozen in place.

"We're taking you to a new location," he says to the bed. "A new place, where you'll be able to think more clearly. You will be more comfortable there, I promise you. The air will be fresh. Come along, wake up."

The wall has shifted behind me—it seems almost to be *melting*. I stretch back a hand to feel for the wall, but only a strange vibration hums through my skin and bones. *I pass through.* My hand touches cold, empty air.

I let one foot fall back. Another. The cold air bites up beneath my skirts. In the bedchamber, the Butcher is still talking to my empty bed, apparently reluctant to shake me awake. This may be the only time I'm glad for his absurd sense of propriety.

Another step. Thank the gods I'm wearing slippers; the soles are thin and soundless. One more step. Now I'm in the passageway, and when I stretch my hands out before me, they meet the hard, rough surface of the stone wall.

I bite down a desperate laugh. I just walked through a wall. Jahan's magic worked for me. And without the words to open it, no one else will come through.

I turn. I'm in a pitch-black corridor alone, with no idea how to get out or where Jahan is or how I'm supposed to meet our supporters. But this passage must go somewhere, and it must be safe enough, or Jahan wouldn't have made the door to it.

I feel my way along the wall. My slippers reveal every bump in the rough-hewn floor. I pass another door, an entrance to an unknown room, the latch's metal cold under my hand.

The ground falls out from under me.

I catch a scream mid-breath. I'm tumbling backward. My backside hits one step, then another. My feet knock a wall. My whole body jerks and jolts to a stop. I feel as if all my bones have been shaken; my bruises protest.

It's a spiral stair. The wall may have jarred my feet, but it stopped me from tumbling down into oblivion, breaking a leg—or worse. I pick myself up. Oh, all the gods, it hurts to move.

One leg after another. One step. I lean hard against the wall, feeling myself down each step. I have a reluctance to die, especially in the dark.

After an eternity, my foot skims level ground. By touch, I figure out that a corridor stretches out to either side of me, while the stairs continue to twist down.

I barely know this castle. Where will down take me? Do Denis's men know about the passages? Will I be able to get out?

Down seems to be the only way out, but still I can't make myself move. If I make the wrong choice, I'm dead.

A thump.

I freeze. My heart leaps.

But it's not in the passage—it's coming through one of the thin doors on my left. I know I should turn. I should go the opposite direction.

I feel my way toward the sound.

Raised voices echo on the other side of the door. I press my ear to the wood. All I can hear are snatches, guesses of words.

And then, "You *liar.*"

Jahan. I know the way he rolls his *r*'s.

I push open the door. A streak of light runs out into the black passageway. I can feel the wainscoting on the other side and glimpse a strip of carpet.

"Don't you dare threaten me," Jahan is saying. "I am the emperor's ambassador. If anything happens to me, it will cost you more than your life."

A forced laugh. "Accidents happen to anyone."

Denis.

I clutch the latch. We've been found out.

"I doubt even you can make an accident convincing enough to the imperial eye." Jahan sounds cold. "I have all the evidence I need. I've already written to the emperor."

"You *can't* have evidence—it doesn't exist. I was careful."

"So you admit it?"

"I—I—"

They must be in Jahan's room. Jahan wouldn't burst into Denis's room and then get threatened by him. It doesn't make sense. So Denis must have burst into his—threatening him, and now being threatened in turn by Jahan.

"Wouldn't you?" Denis says, suddenly coaxing, charming, confidential. "If you could do away with the emperor, marry one of the princesses, rule Paladis—wouldn't you? Or maybe you would just rule through Leontius; we all know what they say."

The rumors about the prince and the Korakos. I swallow hard. Maybe it is true that they're lovers. And would it matter if they are, or were?

It shouldn't, but it does. It changes how I see him, how I feel about him. It makes me wonder how he sees me. Where do I fit in his life?

But Jahan says nothing.

"We're quite alike, you and I. Nobody else understands what it's like, to come from little and always want more. To be constantly passed over by others with a more illustrious pedigree and lesser ability. If you could, wouldn't you make yourself a king?"

My ears are slow, my brain slower. Is he saying what I think he's saying?

"A king?" Jahan says. "But responsibility is so dreadfully boring."

"Oh, come. You can't tell me you're friends with Leontius because you enjoy his company? They say he's the dullest man alive! He likes *gardening*. No, Lord Jahan, I know you. You're clever. If you could see your way onto a throne, you would, too."

"A throne? Is that what you want, Lord Denis? Do you think the queen will divorce her husband and wed you instead?"

There's a moment of silence, then Denis says, "Don't I deserve it? I've bided my time. I've taken the steps to secure myself. I've endured *her*—all her moods and her demands and, dear gods, her bed. The stories I could tell you . . . !"

For a moment, I almost feel sorry for Loyce, being discussed in this manner.

"And the king?" Jahan says, so softly I almost miss it.

"It's the price of being in power. And Antoine Eyrlai ruled for too long."

I burst through the door. It's a green sitting room, and the two men stand by the fire, turning with astonishment to see me.

"I should have known from the beginning it was you who killed the king," I snarl at Denis. "I should have known you'd be low enough to do it, and pin the blame on me and Guerin. As if I would hurt the man who was like a father to me!"

Denis blinks rapidly. "Lady Elanna. You are supposed to be going to prison."

Jahan flashes a grin at me.

"You're the one who should be going to prison," I say, advancing into the room.

Denis stares between Jahan and me. His eyes widen. Then he begins to shout. "Guards! Guards!"

The sound echoes around us, bouncing back as if it hits a smooth wall. Jahan's magic.

"They cannot hear you, Lord Denis," Jahan says gently.

Denis bolts.

Jahan is on him in a moment, tackling him to the floor. I snatch a cord from the curtain beside me and use it to tie Denis's feet, while Jahan binds his hands and stuffs a cravat into his mouth. Denis glares at us over the bit of lace protruding from his lips, his cheeks blooming with scarlet. He's trying to shout, to no avail.

"Oh, come, Lord Denis," Jahan says in a fair approximation of Denis's own voice, standing back to survey our handiwork. "It's nothing more than you deserve."

Denis thrashes and glares.

I lunge forward and kick him in his thrashing legs. "This is for King Antoine. That is for letting me be beaten by your men. This is for accusing Guerin of murder. This is for Hensey. This is for my father. This is for—"

"El." Jahan grabs me by the wrist, pulling me off Denis—not that my thin slippers did any damage. Denis glowers. "We need to get out of here."

He's dressed to go outside; he lets go of me to shrug on an over-coat. I take the opportunity to aim a kick at Denis again—but then I stop myself. With his reddening face, fallen on the floor as he is and trussed like a pig, it's not really fair. He is pathetic, and I'm being no better than him. My hatred is turning me ugly.

Jahan throws an overcoat at me. He's got a lantern. I push my arms into the coat's sleeves, feeling a shock of relief at its warmth. I spare a final glance for Denis, who stares after us from the floor, before I plunge after Jahan into the passageway.

IN THE SPIRAL staircase, voices echo above us. We run, Jahan before me, down the sharp twisting stairs to a small door that drops us out into the night. The frost soaks through my slippers almost instantly. Jahan turns back to the door, working some magic over it, his palm pressed to the wood.

Shivering, I look around. We've emerged onto the palace's north side, facing the hills. A faint moon illuminates a vegetable garden. Jahan blows out the lantern and catches my hand in his. We both look around. Are any guards watching this side of the castle? I don't hear a sound.

"They're meeting us at the top of the hill," Jahan whispers.

I tighten my hand around his and we run, picking our way through the garden plots. The hill rises, steep and sudden, behind the garden. At the top of the ridge, the moonlight shines off the walls of some structure.

We climb, stopping every now and then to catch our breath. My legs are cramping from my still-aching bruises. No trees buffer the hill. When shouts sound below at the castle, I feel exposed, obvious. They will see us, and that will be the end of it. With my wounds, I can't run fast enough.

Jahan comes up beside me, his hand under my elbow. "Think yourself invisible," he whispers. "Think, *I am the wind. I am a fox moving in the night.* Convince yourself, and that's all they'll see and hear."

It's like what I did when Sophy, Alistar, and I were hiding from the Butcher—only I did that by instinct, and Jahan speaks with the certainty of knowledge. Not for the first time, I wish I'd been taught as he has been.

I grip his hand. *I am a fox.*

Our thoughts seem to work. Guards tramp below us, shining lanterns and calling for me to come out, but no one climbs the hill. No one shoots at us.

At last we emerge onto the top of the ridge—only to see another ridge beyond it. I groan. My ribs ache. If I stop moving, I don't think I'll be able to start again.

"El." Jahan nudges me, pointing to the right.

I can't believe I didn't see it.

A stone circle sits, moonlit, on the ridge above the castle. It is the structure I saw from below—not a building at all, but a mysterious piece of magic placed here by ancestors even the land struggles to recall.

The stones pull me toward them, a magnetic call. But when I place my hand against the entry stones, I feel nothing—except a soft hum in my pocket.

The witch stone. I pull it out, holding it in one hand while I touch the standing stone with the other.

Jahan has paced into the circle, looking up at the next ridge. I look after him just in time to see light flare for a single moment above us.

"They're waiting for us." He gestures up the hill.

I put the stone back in my pocket. Whatever secrets this circle contains will have to wait—until we've won Barrody back, probably.

I run to catch up with Jahan. He holds out his arms, and his warmth heats me even down to the soles of my thinly shod feet. He puts an arm around my waist, helping me climb the final stretch to the top.

A FIGURE WITH pale hair starts to run down toward us as we approach the height of the hill. The moment her braid flops loose, I know who it is, and I start to run, too, despite my protesting thighs. Sophy catches me in a hug that almost sends us both flying back down the hill.

"You stupid, stupid . . . El!" she exclaims, hooking her arm through mine. Then she sees Jahan and stiffens. "Who's this?"

"The Paladisan ambassador—"

"The one who betrayed us?"

I hiss in exasperation, and partly from a stabbing pain in my ribs. "Didn't Sorcha tell you? He didn't betray us. He's *helping*. We just tied Denis Falconier up with a curtain sash."

"The duke?" Though she's never even met Denis, Sophy utters a delighted giggle. "Really?"

Jahan, who's been looking back, comes up to us. "The queen's men must have found our tracks. They're heading up the hill now."

"Well, hurry, then," Sophy says.

We climb over a rock face to where a group of shadowed figures huddle under sparse pine trees. One of them lets out a whoop and is quickly hushed by the others.

I allow myself a grin for Alistar Connell.

He grabs me in a hug. "I don't know whether to kiss you or shake you, El."

"Don't kiss her," Sophy and Jahan both say at once.

Alistar laughs, and then I laugh, and it's all right—I'm back among my friends, back with the people I trust most in the world. I throw out my arms and breathe in the scent of the pines, feel their roots combing through the earth below me, saying, *Alive, alive, alive.*

"Fancy another night ride?" Alistar asks.

"Really," I say, "we must stop meeting this way, Master Connell."

Horses have been brought from behind the trees. We mount up. The night is clear and sharp, and our pursuit is far behind yet. Jahan nudges his mount up beside mine, and I reach out to squeeze his hand. Alistar calls the order out. We ride.

CHAPTER TWENTY-THREE

"Look what they've done to you." The doctor clucks her tongue, scooping salve by the handful onto my ribs and stomach. "Riding all night after you've been beaten by the Ereni! You're a sight stronger than I, Lady El."

"Just more desperate." I try not to wince as she applies the salve.

The rebels have made new headquarters here, at Taich-na-Ivaugh, in a crumbling old castle that's been partly turned into a country estate. It sits on a hill over a sleepy valley, which I can see from the window—along with the lines of tents and the smoke rising from campfires.

The people of Caeris are assembling. They've come from the sea and the hills, the moorlands near the border and the towns of Barrody and Threve. For the first time, looking out at the tents, I think maybe we stand a chance.

Though perhaps Jahan and I should have trussed the Butcher, too, while we were at it. I'm not sure I believe my mother's claims about him.

I tug up the front of my chemise and lower the back so the doctor can examine the damage there.

"You're like a hero of old," she says drily. "All your wounds are on the front."

A cough from the doorway. I look around and jump to my feet, heedless of my ribs and the chemise flapping around my back.

It's Hugh. He hugs me hard, pressing a cheek against my head. "You wonderful, foolish girl."

"You're alive!" I say.

He looks at me soberly. "And so are you. Better by far if it had been me on the executioner's block."

"We will never agree on that. But we're both here now. And you've raised an army."

The doctor goes out. While I lace myself up—my bruises are still too fresh for stays—Hugh paces to the window, his hands behind his back. The hair at his temples seems to have grayed even more since I last saw him, and a new scar cuts a line down his cheek, beside his nose.

"It's not enough," he says. "We need the mountain lords." A wry look at me. "Or a miracle. Both, probably."

"They still haven't agreed to help? Has Rhia gone back?"

"No, she's still here. Something about a bargain."

I'd almost forgotten. But surely, after all this, she can't expect me to go north with her. It's the first week of Artemenion—almost the Day of the Dying Year; almost winter—and I simply cannot abandon my friends again. I am the steward of the land; my responsibility lies here.

"Some bargains simply cannot be fulfilled," I say.

Hugh leans against the embrasure, looking at me, and he seems so easy there, so trustworthy, that I find myself saying, "Hugh, did the Butcher of Novarre ever support our cause?"

He startles; his hands clench the windowsill. "Your mother told you?"

"She said it was why she invited him to Cerid Aven—she thought he might help."

Hugh is shaking his head. "Teofila still believes in that bastard?" He looks at me and sighs. "Yes, Gilbert once supported King Euan. He was one of the most fervent among us—such people usually are. But he was also in love with your mother, even though it was plain to anyone that she loved your father and regarded Gilbert simply as a friend. Most men would have turned their affections elsewhere, but not him. When your parents married, he took against us."

"He betrayed you?" I ask.

"Not then—not until you were five years old." Hugh's disgust is evident. "He really seemed to think he might yet win your mother over. It was absurd! I remember, when we went to Laon for the Harvest Feast and coronation, a few days before you were taken hostage, he came to the house. I had to throw him out before Ruadan caught wind of him being there. He loitered in the garden for an hour, even so."

I stare at Hugh. Of course the Butcher loitered in the garden. He called himself Nobody, and he asked me questions. But Hugh didn't see us. Were we in a different part of the garden, hidden from the house's windows? I don't know.

But the Butcher came there for my mother. Not to steal information, not to betray us. Maybe he wished to make amends, for all I know. But Hugh threw him out. And when he got information instead of my mother's regard, from a child who didn't know any better, he made the choice to give us away.

Hugh folds his arms. "King Antoine knew Gilbert was a sympathizer. That's why he always asked him to be inhuman toward his enemies, so the king knew he could trust him." He snorts. "The Eyrlais have always had a twisted idea of trust."

I rub my palms over my eyes. My mother and the Butcher of Novarre. I try to imagine them as youthful friends, colluding to rebel against the Eyrlais, and fail.

"Mother still thinks he might come back to our side," I say. "That's why she stayed in Barrody."

"Hmm." Hugh seems noncommittal. "Well, if anyone could push him to it, it's the new duke. Still, I'll believe it when I see it, myself. But how far anyone will trust him is another issue entirely. Many Caerisians hate him for the crimes he's committed, and he knows it."

I know it, too. But I think of the Butcher's frustration with Denis; his strange, occasional almost-kindnesses toward me. And I wonder.

WE TALK ABOUT other things for a time—mostly the preparations for war being made here at Taich-na-Ivaugh. At last Hugh looks at me and says, "You haven't seen Finn yet."

"No."

"He's mentioned your betrothal."

Finn. Marriage. I realize I am frantically twisting my seal ring around and around on my finger. I force my hands into my pockets.

Hugh is watching me. "A wedding would be good for morale—the prince and the *Caveadear*. Give the message that we have hope for the future. Give us all a little joy."

I frown at the floor. "Surely someone else could get married. Sophy, for instance, and Alistar Connell."

Hugh flashes a smile, but his countenance remains serious. "You know it wouldn't have the same effect."

I swallow. I do know it. But I cannot marry Finn.

"I don't love him," I begin.

"You don't have to, El. It's a dynastic marriage. You both know that. But I don't think he would be entirely displeasing."

"No, but I . . ." But I kissed Jahan. "I could marry someone else."

Hugh raises his brows.

"Someone . . . politically important."

Hugh holds up his hands. "This is between you and Finn—but don't forget that your position makes you responsible for our kingdom's welfare. You must consider the needs of Caeris as well as your own. One might say, before your own."

I scowl over his shoulder. It's strange. When I was captured at Barrody, I felt willing to do anything for Caeris. I would have died for her, if I had to. But marrying someone I don't love? That I can't do.

At last I say, "You want me to sacrifice my happiness for Caeris's sake? I don't think it works that way, Hugh. Unhappiness in one place doesn't breed happiness elsewhere. It just breeds more unhappiness."

He shakes his head. "You are so young."

My irritation flares. "I'll think about it." I move past him to the door, out into the corridor—and stop short. "Finn."

How long has he been standing here, his head lowered, hands in his pockets?

"El." He straightens up to embrace me. He looks so tired. Did he overhear our conversation? But then he forces a smile, leaning his forehead toward mine so that we bump together. "You don't know how worried I've been."

"You . . . You look well, Finn. I'm sorry I left the way I did."
Tears spring into my eyes. I remember how I clung to the image of
him in Denis's study, in the castle where perhaps, one day, he will be
king. If the gods are kind. The sight of him now, in the flesh, gives
me a kind of terrible hope.

He looks past me. "You did what you thought was right." Then
he focuses on me again. "I wish I'd had the courage."

I reach out and squeeze his hand. "It was mostly stupidity." But
at least I saved Hugh.

His gaze drops to our joined hands. I shouldn't have touched him;
it was a foolish, sentimental instinct. But now he leans over to kiss
my cheek. "Maybe someday soon we will not be apart."

"Yes." I feel myself flush. "Perhaps." I start to move away from
him.

He stops my forward motion, holding up a hand. "I'm truly glad
you're back. I—I feared the worst, El." His eyes are moist.

"I know." I swallow. Our eyes meet, and I think he sees a little of
what I've endured.

"If you hadn't come back," he begins, "I don't know if I—" His
throat works.

I look at him. In Barrody Castle, I told myself that Finn was still
free, that Caeris still stood a chance against Denis and the Butcher.
But maybe I was deceiving myself. Maybe they need me more than I
knew. Maybe Finn needs me more than I knew.

They need their steward of the land. They need my magic.

"Well," I say, my own voice tight with the effort of holding in my
tears. "I won't be going anywhere now. I'm in this with you, you
know. For the duration."

Finn's eyes crinkle, though they're still too bright. "No matter
how many regiments Loyce Eyrlai sends against us?"

"No matter if the only ones left standing are you, me, and Rhia
Knoll," I say.

It's a terrible joke, but we both snicker. Finn manages a grin. He
says, his tone light, "You'll take part in the festivities tomorrow
night, I hope? The Day of the Dying Year. We need the steward of
the land to honor Caeris and the memory of her dead."

"Of course I will," I begin. I stop. Rhia was insistent that we arrive in the mountains before the Day of the Dying Year. Now it's tomorrow, and there is no possible way we will. She'll be angry—but it's too late to change things. I smile at Finn. "We'll dance together around the bonfires."

I FIND JAHAN outside, sparring in the yard with Alistar Connell. I have rarely seen gentlemen fight with anything but blunt-tipped foils, but they're using short wooden sticks to whack at each other. On the ride here from Barrody, Alistar was suspicious of Jahan until Jahan revealed that Denis had killed the king. Then they started joking about ways to punish Denis, each method more absurd than the last. It seemed to forge a tentative respect between them. But now, one of the Hounds informs me cheerfully, Alistar has invited Jahan to try to best him in a feat of strength. "It's traditional to use the sticks," he says.

I roll my eyes; only men would think this is a logical way to prove trust. They're both stripped down to their shirts. Alistar is grinning like a maniac and spitting out taunts, while Jahan remains focused and intent, moving with a silent grace. They seem well matched. I wonder if it will go better for Jahan to win or lose, or maybe the idea is to analyze his form and whether or not he cheats.

I'm about to leave them to it, but a woman in breeches and a waistcoat comes up beside me, sweat shining on her brow. Rhia has evidently been sparring, too.

"Our bargain still holds," she says. No greeting, no pleasantries.

"Tomorrow is the Day of the Dying Year," I say. "You wanted to arrive in the mountains before it. I'm sorry. And now . . ."

Rhia folds her arms. "Yes, you should have gotten yourself out of Barrody faster. But we can still go."

I remember Hugh's remark that we need the mountain lords' help if we hope to win our war. We need their numbers, and their ferocity. And their knowledge of the land. If I went to the mountains, perhaps I would finally learn how to use my magic as steward of the land—really use it, as Jahan does. Perhaps then I could do what I need to do, to save my people.

But how can I leave now, after everything that's just happened?

Denis and the Butcher have just proven to me, more than ever, the importance of our revolution. We have no choice except to fight against them and win Caeris's freedom. I can't risk leaving Finn and the others to fight without the power of my magic, even for a few weeks.

Rhia surveys me with that lowering scowl of hers. "If you want my father's help, you don't have a choice."

"Can't your father come here?"

"No."

She stares at me, and then she grins. It is vulpine and unexpected. I almost back away. She leans close—I smell her sweat—and whispers in my ear, "If you do, you won't have to marry the prince."

"Rhia Knoll!" I exclaim. "You—"

Damn it, she's right; it is tempting. And she knows it. "It's good you're back," she says. "I didn't want to have to break into that castle to free you."

I hold up my hands. "You know I can't go to the mountains with you. Not now. I'm needed here. I won't abandon everyone again."

Her grin fades, and then she's angry once more, her jaw bunched. "How do you expect to learn what you need to learn? You don't need to marry Finn Dromahair. And you can't win without my people and our knowledge."

"That may be so. But I can't go now."

"Then you've already lost!" she snaps. "And you don't deserve the title of *Caveadear.*"

Her words ring out so loudly that several people around us fall silent; Rhia's cheeks turn red, as if she's aware she's making a spectacle. We stare at each other for a long moment, accompanied only by the clatter of Jahan and Alistar's sticks against each other. I struggle to suppress the urge to reach for the power of the land, to make the ground tremble and show her I do deserve my title.

But before I can do something foolish, Rhia turns and strides away across the yard, her chin held high.

I turn the opposite way, walking briskly between the outbuildings that separate the castle yard from the forest and farmland surrounding it. I've done the right thing; I've given her the only responsible answer I can give. So it shouldn't feel so much like I might be wrong.

Rhia is right about one thing, though. Finn. I'll fight for him. I'll learn to wield my magic for him; I'll wake the land for him. But I don't see how I can marry him.

I DO MY best to lose myself in the forest. Needles crunch under my feet, and there are mushrooms growing here that I've never seen before. Plus new species of ferns, even different trees. I didn't bring a notebook, so I settle for breaking off leaves and fiddleheads and a single lavender mushroom cap.

The forest seems aware of my presence, but though I still can't do what Hugh's stories claimed Wildegarde could do—look through the eyes of trees, birds, brooks, stones—I wonder if it's possible. But maybe I'm glad to be separate. Maybe if I came to be one with the land, it would be too much.

And yet . . . what would it feel like, to be aware of so much, to feel the land living within my own skin?

I slide the witch stone from my pocket. The sound it makes still resonates in my bones, but if I were being fanciful, I would say it's making *my* song now.

Footsteps crunch in the woods behind me. I look around, expecting to find a deer or a hare, but instead I find Jahan, his collar loose and his hair sticking up in all directions. He hasn't seen me yet. I wait, watching him. I love the way he moves—swift and spry and almost wary. A faint sheen of perspiration lingers on his forehead.

"Did you win?" I call.

He sees me now and grins, threading through the undergrowth to me. "I disarmed Alistar, and then he punched me. But that disqualified him, because we were only supposed to use the sticks. So I suppose I won."

"Clever."

"Not really, it just happened." He seems satisfied, though, as he comes up beside me. "I knew I'd find you looking at bushes."

"These are *fungi,* you ignoramus," I say, "and this is a *fid*—"

He leans down and kisses me, and I forget about plants. When we pull apart, I'm breathless; I put my hand to his chest. He's watching me intently, and now he takes my hand and begins to kiss each finger.

I close my eyes. "You are so distracting."

He pretends to bite one of my fingertips. "It's one of my best qualities."

"Well, you're trying to eat one of mine."

He's examining my palm with his lips. I sigh, but finally I say, "Jahan. Do you intend to marry?" It comes out more bluntly than I'd intended. "That is, I've never heard you're engaged."

His lips stop moving. In the silence, I hear the land thumping beneath us—or maybe it's the racket of my own heartbeat. I open my eyes as Jahan straightens, dropping my hand. The line of his mouth has the weight of a sentence. What have I done?

I wet my lips. It strikes me how unknowable another person is, how you can think you understand them, and still you don't. We haven't even known each other that long. Jahan is staring at a tree, his arms folded and his head lowered.

I've said the wrong thing, though he doesn't seem *angry* exactly. Ashamed? Perhaps he *is* engaged.

Well, so am I. I knew it, and it didn't stop me from kissing him, or from wanting more.

Hugh told me I must put Caeris first. Perhaps even this—my body, my unborn children—must be sacrificed for the freedom of my kingdom.

I stoop to gather my plant samples; Jahan still hasn't spoken. I suppose I should ask him what's wrong, but it's hard to think outside the struggle in my own head.

He finally looks at me. He doesn't seem angry. Or even ashamed. There's a sort of grief in his eyes.

"Is that what all this is about, El?" he says. "Marriage?"

What does he mean, *all this*? I'm getting flustered. Several fiddleheads fall from my hands to the ground. "That's what I asked," I say. "It's a simple question."

Jahan stares at me. His lips tighten. Slowly, he says, "You want my position. You think I've got power. I don't. I exist at the whim of a prince who believes I'm his friend, that I saved his life by some sort of miracle. But as soon as someone tells him the truth—that I'm a *sorcerer*—then I'm dead. No one will save me. No one will speak up for me."

"I don't want your power." How can he even think such a thing? Except maybe I do—I want his sorcery, his charm and courage. If I must have a dynastic marriage, let it be with him. I say, "I want *you*."

He's already shaking his head. "I *can't* marry you." The words burst out of him. "I can't marry *anyone*."

"Well"—I'm getting angry now—"as it happens, I'm engaged to Finn."

His head jerks up.

"Oh, yes," I say to the astonishment in his face. "Since we were children. I suppose I gave my father consent. *I don't remember.* I was five years old." I wait for him to speak, but he's just staring at me. So I demand, "Why are you so surprised? It's the logical thing to do, uniting our houses."

"I don't know." He yanks his hands through his hair, leaving it sticking up in spikes. I want to tame it down with my fingers. "El, Finn is my friend. I can't—"

I bite my cheek hard against saying, *I'm not asking you to betray him. I don't even want this betrothal!*

But Jahan's not looking at me. He rubs a fist over his forehead. When he speaks, it's hardly more than a mutter. "I can't do to anyone what my father did to my mother. I can't put you in that kind of danger."

Then he swings around and walks away.

"That's not what I'm asking you to do!" I shout after him, but he doesn't answer.

I THROW MY plant samples at a tree trunk, but they only hit it softly and drop to the ground in the most unsatisfying manner. Finally I stalk after Jahan, though I know it's too late to catch him. Maybe I *should* marry Finn! I am the steward of the land; I have an obligation to Caeris. Maybe the only responsible thing is to put my country first. Maybe it's selfish of me to think otherwise.

Maybe I don't want to marry *anyone*! Let them say what they will about—

"El!"

I look up: Sophy leans out of a doorway, beckoning me. "Come quick."

I hurry over the churned ground of the yard. It's a relief to leave my thoughts.

"It's someone from the south," she says as I approach. "She claims to know you."

I frown. I don't know anyone from the south who would pursue me to Taich-na-Ivaugh—at least, not anyone who's free enough to come after me.

"She won't tell us a thing till she sees you." Sophy hurries me toward the great hall, which still retains the old grandeur of a former castle. Under the vaulted ceiling, the people gathered before the fireplace appear shrunken. I glimpse Finn, Hugh, Alistar, and his sister Oonagh. No telling where Jahan is.

Before them, her back to me, stands a woman in a mud-splattered riding habit, her black hair falling loose from under her hat. She plants her hands on her hips and declares in haughty, precise Ereni, "The last we heard, Lady Elanna was a captive of Denis Falconier. We will not treat with you if you continue to be so careless with her person."

I stop short. My mouth falls open. *"Victoire?"*

She whirls. It's her. Her face is less round than I remember, the dimple sharper in her chin. She looks fierce and stern. But then, when she sees me, she loses her composure entirely.

"Elanna!" she cries.

We collide in the middle of the room in a bruise of elbows and relief.

"What are you *doing* here?" I say, and at the same time she says, "I thought that wretched Denis Falconier was going to have you *killed*. Do you know your people here have been *interrogating* me for the last half an hour in case I'm one of his minions? As if I haven't spent weeks galloping all over the country trying to incite rebellion on your behalf!"

So it *was* her Denis mentioned in Barrody. I feel myself break into a grin. "Interrogating you? But Hugh knows you."

"My opinion was overruled," Hugh says drily. He has approached, along with the others. "The Connells are taking no risks."

I spare a glance for Alistar and Oonagh, who both look unrepentant. I look back at Victoire, who, I'm astonished to see, is on the verge of tears.

"I thought I might not—I thought I might never—" She chokes, swallows. "I thought I might never see you again!"

I squeeze her hand. My own throat is tight. "I thought the same about you."

We look at each other, the weight of the last few weeks heavy between us.

"What are you doing here, anyway?" I say.

She straightens. Her chin lifts; the ferocity returns to her expression. She glances around at all of us with a commanding stare. "I've come from Eren to treat with the prince and yourself. People are rising across the south—rising in revolution against the Eyrlais. We want to aid your cause, if you will help ours."

WE SIT TOGETHER in Oonagh's green study, and Victoire tells me everything that's happened in the last few weeks.

"It's all down to Count Hilarion, really," she says. "Who would have thought?"

His people saved her the night we abandoned her in his house— I still struggle to release the guilt I feel for leaving her there. They woke her from sleep and ran her through the dark rooms to a hidden chamber behind Hilarion's study. She remained there, in the small windowless room, listening to the tramp of the royal guard outside her hidden door, praying the Butcher did not discover the latch disguised in the bookshelf.

When the Butcher finally left, declaring he must have made a mistake to accuse Count Hilarion of conspiring, the count sat Victoire down and told her that she could not go home. Nor could she follow us north.

"Both are too dangerous," he said.

He made her an offer. She could remain at Ganz, as his guest, troubled for nothing and wanting for nothing.

"But I don't want to do nothing," Victoire told him. "I can't bear sitting around." She thought of running away from Ganz, taking a horse and riding for Cerid Aven—but even in her desperation, she realized it was a foolish idea. At best, she'd get lost; at worst, captured or even killed.

Then Jahan returned without us, sick with his own anger at having to abandon us on our way north, at having to return to Laon and the court. He stayed for only a couple of hours, but those hours—Victoire says with a toss of her hair—changed her life forever.

Because Jahan Korakides told Count Hilarion that the emperor of Paladis would help him to revolt against Loyce Eyrlai.

"They got out maps, started making plans," she says. "And I listened to them until I couldn't bear it anymore. I stood up from my chair and I said, 'I want to help. Let me help you.'" She smiles. "That was it. I've been going around the country with the count for the last four weeks, telling the people how my father falsified the country's revenue, how the queen intends to lie and steal from them instead of letting them have a voice in her government. Then Duke Ruadan got captured, and Denis took you, and I knew I had to come here so the people who remained could consolidate our efforts—work together."

Tightness seals my throat again. Ereni and Caerisians could cooperate. It's my father's plan, which I forgot in the shock of losing him, my mother, and Hugh in the same day.

Hugh is smiling at Victoire. "It was well done. Hilarion must be proud."

"But your father," I manage. "Your parents support the crown. You've told people how he lied."

Victoire's gaze drops. She picks at a loose thread on her riding habit. "That's a consequence my father must live with, for submitting to the king's will. I sent him and Mama word. I told them to leave the city because the riots are going to get worse. Besides which, the queen's people aren't stupid. They'll have sorted out that I joined your side, and they'll go after my parents." She takes a breath. "I only hope Mama and Papa listened."

Finn stands up. We all look to him. "You did well coming here, Demoiselle Madoc," he says. "We will most certainly lend our aid to your cause."

Victoire lets loose a sudden, brilliant smile. The way she's looking at Finn worries me, as if there's a shine about him. "I thought you might have been the prince, when we met at Ganz. It's a pleasure to make your acquaintance again, Your Highness."

I twist my ring. I know what it means when she wrinkles her nose like that. I don't want her to get hurt.

A noise from Oonagh disrupts Victoire's meaningful stare. "Your Highness, far be it from me to remind you, but the decision is not yours to make. It must be put to council."

Finn bows his head, though I catch the tightening of the skin around his eyes. "Of course," he says. "Let us put it to council. And delay further."

Oonagh looks at him. Finn stares back, his eyebrows slightly lifted in challenge.

"We need five to make a council," Oonagh says in her most lady-of-the-castle manner. "There are you, me, the *Caveadear,* and Chief Poet Hugh. We don't have a fifth, unless Rhia Knoll consents to sit, which I do not wish to ask of her. We'll have to wait until tomorrow. Falaon the Black is due to arrive. He will make a fifth."

"We can't tomorrow," Alistar says. "It's the Day of the Dying Year. We can't make any binding contracts. It's unlucky to look to the future on the day when the dead walk. And then the *Caveadear* must lead the ceremony, along with the king. It's the custom."

Oonagh nods. "It's important to keep the traditions when we're at war—to give the people some comfort."

Finn bares his teeth in an expression that is more grimace than smile. "I see custom, as ever, is not on our side. The day after, then. Surely Caeris doesn't have a law against council meetings on the Souls' Day. Especially when the matter is urgent."

Oonagh and Alistar exchange a glance. "It's not a *law,*" Oonagh begins.

"The revolution will wait another day," Victoire adds, sitting up very straight and addressing Finn. "I'll just have to stay here a bit longer."

Finn spreads his hands in a polite gesture.

"Yes," I say pointedly to Victoire. "We have much to catch up on."

* * *

AFTER HER BATH, I drag her off to my bedchamber—the only place we have any hope of privacy. Victoire sits by the fireplace, brushing out her wet hair, which drips on the shoulders of a quilted dressing gown she borrowed from Oonagh. "I've grown quite accustomed to mud," she says with a sigh, "but it does feel so delightful to be clean."

My chest tightens as I watch her slip the comb through her long black hair. It is such a familiar gesture, such a comfortable, ordinary thing to do. It's strange to think, while we've been fighting for our lives, we can still return to moments like this: chatting beside a fire, the pleasure of being clean, the simple act of brushing one's hair.

How familiar it is, and how different. Victoire's face is thinner, sharper. The last few weeks have turned her from the girl I've known for so long into a fierce, fearless woman. A woman who's willing to tell the people her own father lied to them, for the sake of justice.

"You look sad," she says.

I shake my head. "I was just thinking about—peace, I suppose. Before all this, I wanted to go to Ida because I thought everything would be so much simpler there. And now . . . I never will. And I wonder if we'll ever have in Caeris what I imagined having in Ida— peace, and comfort, and no more fear." I clear my throat. "It's strange, that's all."

Victoire's brow wrinkles with sympathy. She starts to speak, but just then there's a knock at the door.

It's probably one of the Connell girls, bringing us supper. I asked if we could have a tray in my room. I call for her to enter.

Jahan steps in, his head bowed. My heartbeat lurches into my throat. What is he doing here? He doesn't seem to notice Victoire: he's too set on what he's about to say. "I've been thinking. If you are betrothed to—"

I cough loudly.

He looks up. He's frowning—but then he sees Victoire, and his expression transforms into politeness. "Pardon me. I didn't know you had company."

"Lord Jahan?" Victoire is on her feet, performing a curtsy. "I didn't know you were here. It's such a pleasure to see you again."

He doesn't seem to hear her. He looks at me. "You should do as your duty demands." He adds, "We both should."

I feel my nostrils flare. "I did not choose this. I won't be bound by a contract my father signed when I was a child. I just want a *choice*, Jahan."

"Then you may *choose* to tell Finn no. But I won't be party to it, either way."

He backs toward the door—the coward. "It's too late!" I shout as it slams behind him. "You already are!"

Victoire is grinning at me. "I knew it. When he came back to Ganz, I *knew* it. He likes you."

I smack the bedspread. "I'm going to kill him."

She giggles, perching beside me on the bed, as if it's all wonderfully romantic. "You're betrothed?"

I stare at the fireplace. "To Finn. Since we were children. I didn't know. I'm supposed to marry him for the sake of Caeris." I hear her intake of breath, and I wince at her. "I'm sorry. I saw how you looked at him today."

"I did not!"

We sit in silence.

Then Victoire says, "He's the prince. He wouldn't marry someone like me anyway." Another pause. Out of the corner of my eye, I see her twist her fingers together and apart. "Are you in love with the Korakos?"

"His name is Jahan." I flop onto my back and stare up into the bed canopy. "And he claims he won't marry anyone. *I* don't know if I want to marry anyone. I've only played at love before."

Victoire spreads out next to me, propping her cheek on her fist. "Even with Martin Bonnaire?"

She's trying to make a joke, and I smile instinctively. We used to invite the boys we liked to our Soledia salons. Martin Bonnaire was a fixture for almost a year—intelligent, handsome, quick to laugh and quicker still to make a joke. Though we talked for hours together, he never professed any feelings to me, which I found an agonizing torture. "Today he'll say something," I would say every Soledia, and Victoire would agree.

Then, six months ago, he announced he was going to the university in Tinan to study rhetoric. In the first letter he wrote back to us, he told us about the most marvelous girl student, one of the few girls admitted to the university, whom he hoped to marry. I cried for about a week.

"Even if Martin Bonnaire liked me that way, and I'm not sure he did," I say, realizing the truth for the first time as I say it, "he couldn't have acted on it. Marrying me would have been suicide. He'd have spent the rest of his life under suspicion as a Caerisian conspirator."

Victoire swallows. "You're right." She rustles her hand over the coverlet. "We all knew it. But I could never bear to say it to you."

I nod up at the canopy, though my eyes have filled with frustrated tears. Not for Martin Bonnaire, but for the girl I was, and for the guilt clawing at me. Why is Finn willing to give up his body, his bed, his future children for Caeris, and I'm not?

"You don't have to marry anyone, either, you know," Victoire says. "We're in the middle of a revolution. You're the steward of the land! There's no *time* to marry. When it's all over, you and the prince can decide what will benefit the kingdom most. It will be easier then."

I blink the tears away. "Yes." There might not be time for marriage—but there will be time to speak to Jahan again.

CHAPTER TWENTY-FOUR

"I'm going to be a hare," Sophy says. She snatches up the mask and holds it over her face. It looks almost real. The soft fur ears seem ready to twitch; the black nose looks damp.

I laugh despite myself. Sophy does not seem like a rabbit. "You'd do better as a nightingale."

Victoire rifles through the armful of masks that Oonagh deposited on the bed. "There aren't any birds. Oooh! A fox." She lifts it over her eyes. The pointed snout seems to grin at us.

"Clever as a fox." Sophy takes off her mask with a smile. "The Day of the Dying Year is my favorite holy day. The bonfires, the masks, the songs! You don't wear masks in the south, do you?"

"Costumes," I say. "Not masks."

"Not *animals*." Victoire selects a cow and hides her face behind it. "So barbaric—so *beastly*."

We all laugh at the bad joke.

"I don't think the cow suits you." I pick up a wolf's face. The masks are works of art—fur and felt sewn onto molded paper. They've belonged to the Connell family for generations—the collection added to and restitched and improved each year. I trace a finger along the markings on the wolf's muzzle, then slip it over my face. The mask is hot, weighty. "What do you think?"

Sophy wears a strange look. "You're the *Caveadear*. You don't have a mask."

I lower the wolf's head with a stab of disappointment. "But what if I want to?"

"It would be silly to wear a mask. You're the steward of the land. You are all the animals—you see through all their eyes."

Victoire catches my eye and rolls her gaze skyward. She still thinks being the steward of the land is a quaint Caerisian custom. She hasn't yet accepted that I, her friend of a decade, have always been able to do magic. She still believes some of the lies told in the south, that sorcerers are untrustworthy and Caerisians a bit mad. Of course, I believed many of the same things myself, until quite recently, and I still don't know how many of the legends about Wildegarde are true. But maybe more is possible than I once thought.

Sophy picks up the wooden box that Oonagh also brought in. She removes its lid. "You don't get a mask. You wear a crown."

My question dies on my lips as she lifts it out. Woven from cut branches, softened with pieces of moss, it springs to full height in Sophy's hands, more than a foot tall. I reach for the branches, feeling the buds under my fingertips. They've woven the crown from willow, and life lingers in the wood, the memory of being a tree.

Sophy lifts it onto my head. It sways, then settles. It seems to weigh nothing.

Victoire and Sophy both stare at me. I've raised my hands, and I turn them over with a start. The pads of my fingers are turning green-brown, a streak like bark running up the insides of my arms, changing the very color of my skin. As if I am becoming a tree.

I hope it doesn't stay this way.

There's a noise at the door: Oonagh, coming in with gowns. She slows to regard me with a curious expression—not quite a smile, not quite reverence.

"*Caveadear,*" she says simply, inclining her head.

Sophy also bows.

I feel strange already—off balance, powerful without knowing what power I am touching. The land pulses within me. The willow branches seem to whisper to themselves, and the moss knows secrets far older.

"We have a story about the Day of the Dying Year," Oonagh says. "They say it is one of the days when the *Caveadear* could wed the land."

"Wed the land?" I repeat. Sap seems to pulse through my veins. I am disconnected, inhuman—more than human. I blink myself back into reality. I don't have sap in my veins, but somehow the willow's memories are twining with my own. I force myself to think clearly; I read about Wildegarde wedding the land back in Cerid Aven, before my father was captured. "What does that mean?"

Oonagh shrugs. "No one knows anymore."

"It's just an old story," Sophy says, as if she senses my fear. "It's nothing, El."

But it's not nothing. The Day of the Dying Year is not an ordinary day, and the crown on my head is no simple creation of wood. The stories I've read were written for more than simple amusement. I feel the truth of it, now, in my body. The hair is standing up on my arms, and heat flushes through me.

Victoire lunges for the gowns in Oonagh's arms. "How marvelous! Green silk. That will look wonderful on Elanna. This lovely yellow will do for me, and for you, Sophy, I think blue."

That quickly, we lose ourselves in selecting gowns. But I cannot forget what Oonagh said. It's the day the *Caveadear* can wed the land, which must mean it's the day Hugh wanted me to wed Finn. Except I am not going to wed Finn.

I wish I understood my power better, and the customs around the *Caveadear*. Maybe they would tell me I don't have to marry anyone, either, just like Jahan. Like Wildegarde.

Maybe this is why Rhia wanted to get me to the mountains before this day. Maybe I shouldn't have told her no, even if it would mean leaving the others temporarily.

And maybe I am reading too much into an old story. Maybe nothing will happen at all. Maybe we will just dance around the bonfires and laugh, and that will be it.

WHEN WE WALK down to the great hall, I know I'm wrong. Everyone in the room turns to me: to the streaks of green blending into the skin on my bared arms, to the crown weaving itself higher and higher upon my head. I hear it hiss and creak as it grows taller. It has sprouted roots, tucking around my ears, forming a tracery of lines over my forehead. It's as if touching me makes it grow, faster than should be possible, into a tree.

They have not finished donning their masks yet. I glimpse Alistar Connell swiftly hiding his face behind a dog mask. Rhia Knoll glowers from behind a bear's face. She hasn't spoken to me since I told her no yesterday, just glared from a distance.

Far in the corner, I glimpse a lean, olive-skinned man tying a raven's face over his. Jahan. Sophy was wrong—there are birds.

Finn approaches me. Like me, his face is uncovered. Antlers sprout above his ears, worked with cunning into his hair, so that they appear to be part of his head. He looks golden, as if the antlers are a crown and he the future king.

"You look," he leans down to whisper, *"extraordinary."* I smile. The antlers swing a bit with his movement. They're not part of his skull, then. That's somewhat reassuring. I don't know what I would do if Finn turned into a stag. It's strange enough—extraordinary, indeed—that a tree seems to have rooted itself on top of my head.

He takes my hand in his warm one. We exchange glances. I give him a small nod.

Alistar Connell walks up to us. "We begin with the *cuach*."

Hooking our arms through each other's, Finn and I each take a sip of the whiskey, which burns and burns down into my stomach. Into my legs. Is this liquor, or is there something else in it? I am burning into life, glowing into a brighter existence. Across the room, the raven looks up and meets my eyes.

Finn gestures me toward the door. "Light the fires!" he calls out. "The *Caveadear* is come."

THE BONFIRES ROAR around me, burning hearts of fire, orange flecked with blue. My eyes sting when the smoke blows into them, but I've begun laughing when it happens. Somewhere I lost my propriety and my dress, but I don't care that I'm almost naked in my chemise. The tree's roots have crawled down my back, and its branches have begun to grow out from my head like a bush.

It shouldn't be possible, but it is. It's the night of the Dying Year, the night when the horned god Kernone rides with his hounds, pulling the moon backward in its path across the sky to reveal the bridge to the world beyond this one. It's the night when anything is possible.

I'm running between bonfires, the moonlight streaming through the branches of my tree-crown, the wind cooling the sweat between my breasts. From every direction, a beast's face lurches toward me— deer, wolf, cow, fox. They dance and leap and laugh. I throw open my arms and stamp my feet. My shoes are gone, too. Is it the whiskey or the ritual, sending the wildness coursing through me, the full moon on the night when the dead walk?

A group of dancers explodes toward me, swinging a black bear from their midst. The bear nearly collides with me before rocking back on her heels. The mask quivers and falls, and I glimpse Rhia's pale gaze. I offer a smile—we must be reconciled!—but she glares and says, "This isn't how it's done in the mountains. You lowlanders don't understand anything."

I glare back at her. We swing around each other, back into the dancing crowd.

A man comes toward me, clad only in a length of cloth twisted around his hips. Finn has lost *all* his clothes. The stag's antlers loom like wings on either side of his head.

I laugh and hold my hands out to him. His grip is hot and damp, and when he comes closer, I smell the earth on him, the scent of the fires. His eyes appear black and almost hungry.

We're moving back out now, toward the topiary that borders the woods. His hands are rough on my arms, my stomach, the curve of my hips. He leans in to kiss me and I twist away, one arm knocking into an antler so that it begins to tumble backward. Finn lifts his face, swollen with ecstasy and lust. "El—"

"No." I feel strange, disoriented, almost betrayed. He's not the one who should be holding me like this.

My raven. Where is my raven?

Finn is trying to say with his hands and lips that we belong together. I press my palms to his chest and shove him back. He staggers. A woman swoops from the crowd—a fox. Victoire.

The woods call to me, to the tree. Finn and Victoire have already swung away into the crowd. I crawl through a gap in the hedge, digging the dirt up under my fingernails. I inhale the heady scent of loam. My feet meet the coolness of new-fallen leaves. I follow the call of an owl into the forest.

The sounds from the fires fade quickly among the old pines, mingled with oak. The trees stand black against the pearly sky, silent as any sentries. I walk from one to another, trailing my fingertips over their cool bark, though it does little to cool the burning in my body.

I seem to be in a kind of grove. The trees make a circle around me, and the land pulses under my feet, up along my legs and into my body. I am burning hot. The simple weight of the tree is becoming too much for me.

I lift it from my head, scooping the growing roots into the duff beneath an oak. My nostrils flare at the smell of dirt. My body sparks with awareness.

Water is running over my foot. I shuffle backward in surprise, crouch to look closer. From the freshly planted roots of the willow, a spring has burst into life. The water pools between my feet, wanders away into the forest.

Overhead, the tree branches sway and dance. The night has been still until now, windless. The moon appears between the tossing limbs, round and brilliant. I feel as swollen as she is with possibility.

Bracken crunches. I startle, bracing myself to run.

But it's a raven who glides into the grove, a blacker shadow in the night. My breathing is loud in my ears.

He sweeps back the mask. It falls to the ground. The moonlight is silver on his face.

We meet in the middle. He's wearing a cloak and a pair of breeches but his chest is cold to the touch. "My poor southern raven," I murmur. I wrap my arms around him. His cloak falls over my back, so I am wrapped in the embrace of its warmth—and his.

His hands press along my spine, drawing me closer. His breath is hot and soft in my ear. "I thought I'd lost you."

I look at him. His face is full of shadows. "You can't lose me."

Both our bodies are hot now. I remind myself that yesterday he accused me of wanting to marry him because he's the Korakos. But right now we stand in the silence of the grove, and my body is heavy with yearning. The land is waking beneath my feet. I don't care about my confusion or Jahan's secrets. I don't care about Finn. I don't care about responsibility or my people.

I pull his head down—he's talking, of course. "Be quiet." I cover his lips with mine.

He doesn't seem to mind.

Our mouths work together. His lips trail toward my ear. He's tucked one hand between us, rubbing his thumb over my nipple. I gasp. My own exploration grows bolder, and he arches against me.

Around us, the trees shift on their roots. The willow is growing up into the embrace of the oak. The trickling spring turns into a stream. The pulse of the land matches the throbbing in my body.

I reach for Jahan's hips. He pulls back, breathless: "Are you sure?"

I can't for the life of me imagine why he's hesitating—he's as ready for this as I am. I pull down his breeches; he unties my shift so it falls to pool around my ankles. Somehow we're on the ground. Wet leaves push against my back. Jahan heaves me up and throws his cloak down to protect us. I'm kissing him—his jaw, the dimple beside his mouth. He pushes me back gently so I land on the cloak. His hands are hot on my thighs. I dig my fingers into his shoulders, his hair. He's kissing between my breasts, working his hand between my thighs. I'm whispering his name; I wrap my legs around his hips. He pushes into me. I throw back my head.

And I'm unraveling from within. Our bodies are moving together and suddenly the land roars around me—into me. It floods into my body, shuddering through flesh and bone. My breasts arch into hills. My belly is the bowl of lakes, my ribs the striations of rocks, and my face is the moon. Jahan is the wind, the heat of the sun, moving urgent against me. I'm crying out. The sound is not human—it is wild, feral, earthy, redolent. All of Caeris must hear it. And I do not care.

Then I am shrinking—squeezing back into trembling, sweat-slick human flesh, shuddering with pleasure. Jahan's lifted me up against him. He's saying in my ear, "What was that? What's happened?"

I open my eyes. Wet leaves are stuck to my naked back. Jahan pants against me, his heartbeat slowing.

The trees have stilled now, but they are . . . different. I hear the water surging from the spring. I don't want to let go of Jahan, but I force myself to peel my arms off him. On trembling legs, I stand and look around the altered grove.

All the trees have moved. And the energy of it, the bolt that shook up through the earth into me, makes me feel as if my skin shines with stars. My naked body is not cold.

"They wanted you to do this with Finn. That's why they wanted you to marry him." Jahan's standing, shivering already, pulling the cloak around himself. "I'm not Caerisian. They won't like that I—"

I stop his protests with my lips. I put my arms around him, kissing him until his mouth softens and relaxes. I refuse to argue with him about Finn right now. "I'm the steward of the land," I say against his mouth. "I get to choose who I do this with."

At least, I hope so.

"I was not the one to choose." He's still shivering.

"Yes. You were. You are." And I realize I am more certain of this than of anything else in my life. "You *are*, Jahan Korakides."

"El . . ." he says.

"It's done. It can't be undone." As I say it, I begin to shiver, too. Not exactly with cold. With a kind of terrified realization.

I have wed the land.

But what does that mean?

What have I done?

CHAPTER TWENTY-FIVE

I wake up with my face plastered in a pile of damp leaves. Beneath me the earth is pulsing and I seem to hear everything—the trees drinking water from the soil, a squirrel chittering above me, the press of a deer's hooves in the forest, the cool movement of a stream. The slight breathing of someone standing over me, the rustle of leaves as they nudge me again with their foot.

I have wed the land.

I lift my head, expecting Jahan. I stretch out my arm to him. The green streaks linger on my skin, bright against the tawny-brown color of my wrists.

But it's Rhia Knoll. She looks disgusted. And annoyed. She's also dressed for travel—buckskin breeches, a heavy woolen coat. It boggles the mind that someone so short can look so tyrannical.

"Get up." She throws a pile of clothing on top of me.

I sit, clutching it over my bared breasts. My ears are ringing, and my stomach aches. "Where's Jahan?"

Rhia shrugs. "I brought you some cider and a butter pastry."

I eye her. There's something she's not telling me, but my mind is too scattered to quite make sense of it. The lack of sleep and the noise of the land distract me.

The cloak—Jahan's—slips off my shoulders, and Rhia smirks. I may as well get dressed—I'm wearing almost nothing and a chill's starting to creep over my skin. I wriggle into the shirt and trousers she's provided, while Rhia paces to the perimeter of the trees, looking back in the direction of the castle.

"Where did Jahan go?" I ask again. It seems impossible that he would have left, unless he was angry with me. I don't want another argument, especially not over Finn and marriage and whatever happened last night. I just want us to be.

Rhia's shoulders hitch. "I sent him back." A glare in my direction. "Hurry up."

I don't like the look on her face. It makes all the hair on my body stand up. I quickly lace the boots and button up the coat, wrapping Jahan's cloak over the top. It smells of him, the lingering scent of the spiced tea he drinks. Rhia throws me a hat and gloves.

A bell begins to ring, back at the castle. We both still.

It's the warning bell. *Clang-clang, clang-clang-clang.* They code patterns into the rhythm, and this one is saying—

Rhia grabs my arm. "This way."

Everyone to the castle. Danger. Everyone to the castle. Danger.

The ringing sets off an echo in my ears, leaving me wildly disoriented, so I follow Rhia up the shoulder of a hill, where a break in the trees gives us a view of the castle, smoke rising from its chimneys and the bell still clanging.

I start toward the castle.

"No," Rhia barks. "This way." She points up the hill.

I swing back to face her. The pleasant lassitude I felt when I woke up is all but gone, and I am in no mood for Rhia Knoll's dictatorial manner.

"Do you want to walk right into whatever danger we're in?" She puts her hands on her hips. Her tone has softened, but not by much. "We go up higher. We'll have a vantage point. We can see what's happening."

She points at a rock outcropping some distance beyond us. It will take us a long while to get there, and thus longer still to get back to the castle, but I hesitate all the same. I feel rather wary of putting my life in danger yet again.

Rhia sees my hesitation. Without waiting for me to agree, she turns and begins to march over the hill.

I sigh and go after her.

We hike down into a hollow between the hills, a benign mossy place that nevertheless sets my teeth on edge. The land seems to mutter around us, and I grip my witch stone, which I knotted yesterday in a cord about my neck. The faint humming I hear can't be coming from witch hunters—can it? We clamber up the ridge. I cast a glance over my shoulder, anxious for the sight of the castle or the river, any familiar landmarks to tell me we're circling around.

We climb higher—strange, this ridge didn't look so high from the other hill. When we reach a rock outcropping, Rhia turns to look back at last. I clamber up beside her, panting, and turn to see.

It's not there. The castle is not there.

Come to think of it, I haven't heard the bell since we went down into that mossy hollow.

The river's gone, too.

But the mountains are there. When I look to the other side of the ridge, they rise behind us, snow-peaked and sudden.

We weren't this close to them before.

I think I'm going to be sick.

"Rhia," I say slowly.

She's pulled out a map—to avoid looking at me. "The land shifted. It does that, this far north. It still remembers the old ways."

"It shifted in that hollow, didn't it?" I am pleased at how calm I keep my voice.

She nods, still avoiding my gaze, busying herself with the map. I remember the maps in Denis's study, the ones that made no sense because the landmarks shifted in each of them, because no hill or valley was ever quite the same. You have to be Caerisian to understand it—not just Caerisian, I realize. You have to be from the mountains.

I pace away from her, and then I start back down the hill.

Rocks clatter as she hurries after me. "Stop! That's not the way it works. You can't just go back and arrive in the same place—"

"I don't believe you." I jump over a fallen log, and my feet skid on the steep slope. I force myself to slow down. It's not worth a broken leg.

Rhia says nothing more, but I hear her coming along behind me. We reach the hollow faster than we left it, and I am dismayed to see the hill on the other side is only a low rise, made up of birch and hardwoods, not the pine and fir I remember walking through.

I grind my teeth together. I am the steward of the land. The land should obey me, but I have no idea how to make the land shift. When we crest the low hill, we encounter a flock of sheep huddled in a pasture, and beyond, the smoke and stone walls of a town. A hamlet, really. I see no more than six buildings.

I stop at the wooden stile separating us from the sheep and take a breath before turning back to Rhia.

She folds her arms, raising an eyebrow, uncompromising.

"Where are we?" I demand.

"I think it's called Altan." She shrugs.

I have never heard of it. I fight to stay in control—to keep myself from screaming at her. "We're a long way from Taich-na-Ivaugh, aren't we?"

She nods.

"How far?" My voice is rising despite my effort to control it.

"Sixty miles. Seventy." Another deliberately casual shrug. "I don't know exactly."

"How did we *get* here?"

"The land shifted us."

"Well, then, make it shift us back!" I'm almost shouting.

"You made a bargain."

I jab a finger at her. "And you tricked me."

Her nostrils flare. "And *you* wed the land last night without so much as a second thought! Why do you think you feel ill? Because you attempted something you should never have done, you ignorant southerner. You were supposed to come with me to Dalriada before the Day of the Dying Year so this didn't happen."

I splutter, but it only magnifies the ringing in my ears. "I am the steward of the land. It's my right! It's my choice to wed the land with whomever I wish."

She stares at me, then loosens a sharp, high-pitched laugh. "You think I care who you made love with? Fionnlach Dromahair or your Idaean sorcerer; it doesn't make a difference to me. It doesn't make a difference to the land. No." Her nostrils pinch again. "But now you've bound yourself to the land. You've made a bargain you can't even begin to understand."

My hands fist—because, of course, she's right. I don't understand.

"Oonagh said no one even remembered what it meant," I begin.

"Oonagh!" Rhia rolls her eyes. "As if the Connells have ever been keepers of the ancient knowledge. *We,* the wardens of the mountains, are the ones who have guarded the old ways since the invasion. *We* are the ones who know what it means to wed the land. You think you can just come here and put on a stupid animal mask and let your lovemaking wake the earth and lead your revolution with glory? It's not that simple. You're the *Caveadear* now—you never were before, no matter what your ignorant lowlanders believe—and *the land lives in you.*"

I feel it as she speaks, a deep thrumming that pulses in my bones, far more present than the small whispers I used to sense. My teeth clench together. I feel a fool, which only makes this worse. I hate admitting ignorance, especially to Rhia Knoll. "The land lives in me?"

"It means you have a responsibility. The land is part of you now, and you can't deny awareness of it." She takes a breath, squares her shoulders. "You must come north, to where your true people live in the mountains."

I look toward the mountains. I do want to go there. I want to learn what Rhia's people know, I want to see the singing golden pines, I want to understand the land whose awareness crawls under my skin. But how can I, when the warning bell rang just before we left?

"Rhia," I say, "the Butcher could be laying siege to Taich-na-Ivaugh *right now.*"

She folds her arms. "And how do you expect to stop him, if you don't know what you're capable of?"

We stare at each other for a moment. Rhia's eyes are fierce with determination.

"If we go back now," she says, "you'll never come to the mountains. You'll never learn the secrets we've guarded for so long, and without them, you'll never succeed. Our revolution will fail, and that will be the end of it."

"*Our* revolution?"

"We want Caer-Ys to be free as much as you do. If Loyce Eyrlai finds a way into our mountains, she'll cut our golden pines the way her ancestors cut them in the lowlands." Rhia's voice is rising. "She doesn't care that they're the symbol of my people—she doesn't know the stories about how they sing, and she doesn't care that the wood must be worked a certain way to preserve its song. She doesn't care for my people or our customs."

I should have understood that the revolution matters to Rhia— almost as much as it does to me. I see it in her eyes.

But the bell . . .

"I'm sorry." My voice is small and strained. "We need to go back."

A vein ticks in Rhia's temple. I thought maybe, in the face of my fear and worry, she'd back down. But more than anything, she seems betrayed. Her mouth is a dark, curved line. "My people have been under attack for two hundred years. Your people made friends with the Ereni. You adopted their customs. Their language. You let them cut the golden pines, our sacred tree. The pines never grew back, but you still wear their symbol on your finger." She points at my signet ring: the tree encased in knot work. "You still wear the symbol of united Caer-Ys, but Caer-Ys is hardly whole and you know almost nothing of our true customs and history. But we, who know, have always been hounded, mocked, derided, because we live in the mountains and keep the old ways. Now you want our knowledge— you *need* our knowledge—but you refuse to pay the price of getting it. I almost believed in you. I almost thought you had what it takes to be a real *Caveadear.*"

My mouth opens, but no words come out.

She stares at me for another moment. Then she swings herself over the stile and marches off toward the flock of sheep.

She almost believed in me? Rhia Knoll almost believed in *me*?

"Hey!" I pull myself onto the first step of the stile. "You're going the wrong way. The mountains are behind us."

"It doesn't matter which direction I go," she shouts back at me. "The whole damned thing is over."

I start walking in the direction I assume to be south, but my footsteps slow. I seem to be moving uphill, though I have gone hardly any distance at all, and, if anything, the pasture slopes down.

I take another step forward. Treacle. My stomach is churning, and the echo dins in my ears. The land pulses and groans. Ahead of me, where Rhia and the sheep should be, the clear air dissolves into mist. Figures push through it toward me. Their silhouettes look strange, peaked at the head and shoulders, and as they come closer, I realize it's because they're wearing armor. Their peaked helmets were used more than two centuries ago.

Cold trickles up my spine.

I have to run, but I am fixed to the spot. The Ereni advance, their gaits wary. I am only peering into the past, I remind myself. It is only a glimpse; it's the Souls' Day and the veil is thin. The land is doing this to me. They don't really see me.

And then they do.

One man holds up his arm. He points. The man behind him draws his broadsword. He starts to run toward me.

I have no weapons. I have nothing. I hold up my empty hands. "Don't!"

He jerks to a stop. Not out of compassion. His eyes roll up in his head and he falls, slamming into the ground.

I stare at his slumped body, at the dagger impaled in the chink in the back of his armor. On the other side of him, Rhia Knoll strides toward me through the mist, which is dissipating around her. The shouting Ereni soldiers tear into scraps of figures, then into clouds of memory, and at last into nothing.

The dead man has also disappeared from the ground before me. But the dagger remains.

Rhia crouches to pick it up, cleaning the blade on the grass.

I'm shaking all over, and the land booms in my ears. "What—?" I can't speak any other words. There are no words.

"Time is thin here." Rhia stuffs her dagger back into her boot. Her tone is short. "It's part of the land shifting."

"But," I stammer, "you never shift into the past, do you?"

She looks at me. "Not usually."

I swallow. Then I drop to my knees in the sheep dung and am sick all over the damp grass.

When I look up, wiping my mouth, Rhia stands over me. Without a word, she offers me the flask of cider. I drink, then drop back on the grass, rubbing my forehead. My legs are shaking.

I close my eyes. "Explain this to me."

Rhia shifts from foot to foot. I hear the squeak of her leather boots. "My aunt Granya could tell you better than I can. She's the memory-keeper of Dalriada." A pause. "And if you came to the mountains, you could hear it from her lips."

"Just try."

"During the invasion, there was a sorceress," Rhia begins. "A very powerful sorceress. Back in those days, magicians were itinerant, you know. They lived everywhere. During the invasion, King Ossian employed a sorceress to help Caeris, and when Barrody fell, the sorceress wove a spell of protection around the mountains. That's what keeps the land awake here, why we're able to shift the land. But somehow pieces of the past are caught up in it."

I squeeze my eyes tight and then open them. I force myself onto my feet. My stomach writhes with nausea. I turn in a half circle until I'm facing north. Facing the mountains, the land of the golden pines, the place where Caeris's deepest secrets are kept.

The nausea eases. Looking north makes the pounding in my head grow less.

I sigh. "All right. We're going north."

"We are?" Rhia sounds astonished.

I squint at her. "That's what you want, isn't it? North. We're going to see your father." The land's not going to let me rest until it gets its way, I can tell that much. I totter back to the stile. The nausea is easing, but I still feel dizzy. I grab on to the stone wall, the stones cold and gritty under my hands. A terrible thought occurs to me. "Rhia. This 'wedding the land.' It doesn't mean—Does it—I'm not pregnant, am I?"

Rhia Knoll comes up beside me. She looks down into my face. Then she throws back her head and roars with laughter.

"Somehow I don't find this quite as amusing as you do." A damp sweat lingers on my upper lip. What a fool I was last night, not even to think of using any herbs or moss to prevent pregnancy—I just came together with Jahan in blind, dumb lust.

Rhia clambers up onto the stile. The mountains are grim and white behind her. "You aren't pregnant. *Caveadears* can't have children once they're wedded to the land. Come on."

I crawl over the stile, though each step north makes me feel slightly clearer-headed. I can't have children? How does she know?

I swallow, and follow Rhia toward the mountains.

THE LAND WHISPERS to me as we walk. It tells me of things that happened long ago, and just yesterday.

Around noon, as we wind out of a village, a hare shoots out from the undergrowth and across the road before us. I smell the feral odor of the mountain cat pursuing it. Then I feel my heart pumping, my legs scrabbling not quite fast enough, smell the damp ferns flying past my nose as I leap deeper into the woods.

A touch on my arm brings me shooting back into my human body, which seems large and clumsy and breathless.

Rhia frowns at me. "The hare?"

I manage a wordless nod. My lungs still ache with the urgency of flight.

"They say the *Caveadears* can see through the eyes of the animals," she says. "Now you've wedded the land, I suppose it's stronger."

I shake my head, but my skin still feels too large, shining with uncomfortable awareness. I am the steward of the land. It's the land I'm supposed to feel, not every animal on it. If I can see the world through a hare's eyes, how will I ever eat rabbit stew again?

We tramp on, up into the hills. The trees hide the mountains from sight. It smells different up here, and the forest composition has changed again. I wish for my field notebook and hand lens—both lost for good by now. A lump swells in my throat. Everything has changed—so much, so fast. I want to learn the magic of the land, but I still want to study botany. Why do the laws of the Paladisan emperors prevent me from doing both? It isn't right. It just isn't.

"How do you know I can never have children?" I demand of Rhia.

The subject seems to startle her. She gives her typical shrug. "It's in the lore. You're wedded to the land now, and you can only make things of the land. You'll select and train the next *Caveadear* instead of having a child. What?" she says, when I bite my lip. "You can make a tree grow from your hands, but you'd rather have a bawling infant?"

"No. I—That is—I don't know." I stare up at the trees, which seem to shift in order to better look at me. For the first time in my life, I feel uncomfortable beneath their eyes. "It's not that I dreamed of having children, the way some girls do. Some girls can't wait to be mothers. I never felt that way. I just thought—you know, when I got married, if Antoine let me live that long, I imagined I would have children. With my husband."

"Well," says Rhia.

I glance at her. "Oh, no. Now you're going to tell me the *Caveadear* can't get married after she weds the land."

"I don't know that it's strictly forbidden," Rhia says. "Or, like having a child, physically impossible."

"But it's a good thing I didn't marry Finn."

"Since he probably would have wanted an heir . . . yes."

I run a hand through my hair. I don't have a ribbon to tie it, and it's gone wild, a tangle of knots. The worst part of it is the feeling of relief. Relief that I don't have to marry Finn; relief that I don't have to reduce my life to making heirs for the future of Caeris.

But if I'm not to be a wife or a mother, then what am I to be?

The answer whispers through the earth under my feet. I am the steward of the land, and now I'm wedded to it. I *am* Caeris. All the magic I loved as a child belongs to me again—more powerfully than I ever knew. I find myself starting to smile.

Rhia has pulled out the map. "There's another line just up the hill. We'll shift there. We should be able to make Dalriada tomorrow."

Dalriada: the home of the wardens of the mountains. The gateway to the high peaks.

WE SET OFF early the next morning, having spent the night in a village called Noch-Ysal. Yesterday was the Souls' Day, and by custom, all the villagers gathered around a fire to speak the names of their ancestors aloud. I stiffened when I realized I didn't know the names beyond my father's and grandfather's on the Valtai side, and on my mother's, just her. Even the shepherds know their lineage better than I do.

Rhia takes us to another shift. With a show of great reluctance, she lets me look at her map. Like the ones Denis and the Butcher had, it is a mess of jumbled towns and landmarks—but unlike theirs, hers is traced over with long lines stretching the length of Caeris. They seem to amble, but, like the veins on a leaf, they all stretch forth from a single point: Barrody.

The principal artery stretches from Barrody north, straight to Dalriada.

"This is what the sorceress did?" I ask. "She made the lines?"

"No." Rhia shakes her head. "The lines have always been there. They put the stone circles on them, back in the time before Wildegarde, before Caer-Ys existed as Caer-Ys. Maybe it was the gods who built the circles, before the Children of Anu came. I don't know; no one does. But the sorceress kept the lines alive, though they were only used by memory-keepers and others trained in the art. Instead she made it so they would shift constantly, so that no one who is not of the mountains would know where they are."

But if Denis and the Butcher learn how to read them, they will know. Does my mother know how to read them? She might; she certainly knows about their existence. If Denis finds a way to pull the truth from her . . .

Neither of us says it, but the urgency of knowing the danger drives us forward.

We access the point of shift simply by walking through it. The line, Rhia shows me, goes straight through Dalriada, so the shift will bring us closer to the city and her father.

This time, as we walk into the line, I pay attention to how it feels in my body. It hums in my bones, as if my blood and marrow are reshaping themselves along with the earth.

We walk for hours. Snow trickles from a gray sky.

And at last, through a gap in the trees, I see it: the sharp edges of the mountain above Dalriada, sudden and close.

The wood murmurs with the memory of the past.

Rhia is actually smiling. I look at her, and she shrugs and says, "Home."

As if home is such a simple thing. I have never envied Rhia Knoll before, but my jealousy springs to life now, bitter and unexpected. I wish I had known all my life what it is like to know where you belong. To have a home, to have a people, who claim you without question or qualm.

But I do have a home. I've wedded the land, and all of Caeris is my home. The realization makes my heart soften. Awareness of the earth pulses through me with renewed intensity, as if the land is affirming my choice.

The road grows steeper. We pass an orchard clinging to the rocky soil, and sheep spread out at pasture. A river rushes into sight, roaring between the narrow walls of a high canyon. We trudge on into the lowering sun, and eventually the canyon opens into a green valley: the gateway to the Tail Ridge, the *Bal an-Dracan*. The white mountain peak gleams behind a palace growing precipitously from a cliff face. With its high, pitched roofs and rambling gables, it does not look like any noble residence I have ever seen. I try to remember what I read about Dalriada at my father's house. There used to be a school here centuries ago, for sorcerers, and their library contains many books that have been banned. But that is all I know.

We approach through the town flanking the palace, its half-timber, half-stone houses painted in bright yellows and blues and greens. People sing as they work, and stop to look after us.

As we switchback up the road to the palace, a boy comes running out from the open courtyard, skidding over rocks to fling himself into Rhia's arms. "You're *back*," he bellows, his voice ringing against the stone.

Rhia Knoll, whom I always thought as tough as these mountains, breaks into a grin and grabs the boy into a hug. They are talking, quickly, in mountain dialect, so fast and heavily accented that I can only make out one word in ten. I stand back, watching as Rhia ruffles the boy's hair. He's about twelve, and submits to the hair-ruffling with a mock scowl.

He glances at me, then back at his sister. They must be related: they have the same black hair and pale eyes, the same sharp, uncompromising chins.

"Make a bow, Aengus," Rhia says. "This is the *Caveadear Caer-Ys*."

Aengus Knoll bows, wide-eyed, and I nod back at him.

"Are you here for the gathering?" he asks. I have a sense that, unlike his sister, Aengus does not often guard his words.

"The gathering?" I look at Rhia, whose cheeks actually flush pink. "Yes," I say to Aengus. "I believe I am."

AENGUS LEADS THE way into the palace's open courtyard. It is wide and airy, with low walls, and seems more designed to defend against the elements than enemies. People crowd it—mountain lords in bright cloaks, jostling and shouting their conversations, and in another corner, musicians playing a lively tune. But my eyes are drawn, not to any of the people, but to the courtyard's center, where a tree grows.

It must be a golden pine. It towers overhead, the fisted needles on its high branches burnished by the lowering sun. It does look as if it is made of gold.

And its sap sings to me.

I swallow. Even Markarades has never seen a golden pine, for they grow only in the *Bal an-Dracan*—or they do now. And as Rhia told me, I wear the symbol of these trees on my ring.

"You see?" Rhia says, at my elbow. "They all came for the gathering. Everyone, on the verge of winter. Because they knew you would come. My aunt reads the auguries. She knew."

I blink at her. So this is why she wanted me to come so urgently. She knew the mountain lords were gathering here in Dalriada—gathering now, for me, because her aunt had predicted it. But how much of the prediction, I wonder, is coming true due to necessity, and how much due to Rhia's dogged determination to bring me here?

A staircase dominates the courtyard beyond the golden pine, and as Rhia and Aengus guide me forward, a man emerges at the top of the stairs. A bell rings. Everyone goes quiet.

This must be Ingram Knoll. In his weathered face, his eyes are the flinty gray of the mountains themselves, and he wears the most magnificent cloak of all, its back woven with the shape of a golden firebird.

He crosses down the steps. "*Caveadear.* Be welcome in Dalriada. You are the first of your family to set foot inside her walls since Eren conquered Caer-Ys. For the last two hundred years, we wardens have kept the old knowledge alive; we have held the secret of shifting the land and lived side by side with fragments of the past. We have kept the peace among the mountain people in the hope that someday all of Caer-Ys could reunite. We have upheld the old laws. And now, at last, I have heard the voices of my ancestors speaking in my dreams. The land is waking."

"Thank you." I bow to Ingram Knoll. "I feel it in my body—the land. I've wed the earth."

He smiles, and the weathered skin around his eyes folds up into creases. "We heard it, lady. We heard the land sing when you wed her."

Someone in the crowd around us claps. Others take it up, and Ingram Knoll gestures to me to turn and face them. I hold out my hands; the green stains from the tree-crown still color my palms and wrists. I feel bright, visible, seen.

I turn back to Ingram Knoll. "I hope this means you'll help us against Loyce Eyrlai and Denis Falconier?"

A murmur passes through the crowd; their accents are too thick, too difficult, for me to understand quickly what they're saying, but I know the simple joy of a moment ago has vanished. The rumble of their voices tightens the skin of my back. I feel how much I am a stranger here. I was raised in the south. I do not belong in this place, among these people whose accents I can't even understand.

I look for Rhia, expecting her to scowl at me. But she gives me a nod.

"If the king wishes our support against the Ereni, he must come here himself and be subject to our election," Ingram Knoll says. "Just as every other true king of Caer-Ys has since the laws were made."

"The king lives in Ida." Their outmoded logic makes me impatient. "He's not well. He won't come until we've won Caeris for him."

"Then he's not a true king," says a man in the crowd.

"Hebar Manahan, my father's war consul," Rhia murmurs to me.

"A true king must be sound of mind and body." Ingram Knoll nods at the speaker. "Euan Dromahair does not appear to be either."

"If you won't support him, then support his son," I say. "Fionnlach Dromahair has the capacity to be a true king. My father said so." I hope it's actually true. It has to be; we have no choice. And he *will* grow into his crown, if he gets the opportunity to wear it. I'll make him grow, after I give him a piece of my mind about his lecherous behavior at the festival the other night. "Go and meet him if you insist, and decide for yourselves. But if you won't help, you won't even have him. You won't even have a *possible* king."

Silence meets my words. I twist the ring on my finger, force myself to stop. I am a botanist, not a diplomat. A job like this should be left to—my father, rotting in the Tower in Laon?

I can't think about him. *Father, if you could see me now.* I am the steward of the land—this is what I must do. It's where I belong.

A woman steps forward from beside Ingram Knoll's elbow. She wears her hair in two long braids bound with blue ribbons—this was probably a fashion two hundred years ago, during the invasion—and streaks of blue spirals linger on her cheeks and forehead. She speaks quietly, but everyone listens.

"Fionnlach Dromahair will not be our king."

Exclamations erupt around us. "You see?" Hebar Manahan says loudly. "We will have no foreigner claim the soil of Caer-Ys for his own—"

I stare at the woman. Her black hair is veined with silver, and she looks much like Rhia—small, slim—but her eyes are gentler. She must be the augury-reading aunt. She looks back at me, and almost at once I want to go closer to her, despite what she just said. I want her to look at me, to really see me.

"Enough," Ingram Knoll calls out. "Or shall I send for the speaking stone?"

They subside into quiet. Hebar looks sullen.

I open my mouth, but Rhia gets there first.

"Father, may I speak?" When he nods, she goes on, turning to face the crowd: "It is my belief that this fight is a just one. Even if Fionnlach Dromahair will not be our king, his intentions are better than those of Denis Falconier and the Butcher of Novarre. And we may not have an elected king, but we have a steward of the land. The first steward in generations to be awake to the land."

She doesn't look at me. I realize I'm gaping. Rhia Knoll has just spoken for me? For Finn? Against the inclinations of her own people?

"I have brought the *Caveadear* here, that you may all see her and recognize a true steward of the land," she says. "She has more sense of honor than any of her countrymen, and she is willing to give her life for another. I do not know if any of you are so courageous."

"Thank you, Rhia," I whisper.

"At the least, come meet Fionnlach for yourself," Rhia says to her father. "We do no good to Caer-Ys hiding in the mountains."

"We are safe here," someone protests from the crowd.

"The land protects us!" another calls.

Rhia faces them. "The land does not protect our countrymen. It's time to recognize both mountains and lowlands belong to one country—Caer-Ys. Our ancestors knew this. The golden pines once covered all our lands. The *trees* knew it."

"But *her* ancestors sold out!" Hebar Manahan points at me. "Her ancestors let the Ereni conquer them. They gave up their traditions. They let the Ereni cut the golden pines. They gave up their right to be called people of Caer-Ys."

"I am not my ancestors," I flare back at him. "I may have grown up in Laon—against my will—I may speak Caerisian with an accent, but I still belong to Caeris. I have wed the land; I feel her in my blood. Yes, the land protects you. But how do you think it protects the rest of us? It doesn't protect *me*. Do you know what would happen to me, as a 'witch,' if I were ever caught by the Ereni?"

Hebar Manahan glowers at me.

"I would be sent insane," I say slowly and clearly. "I would be tortured, probably. Interrogated, certainly. And then I would be executed."

Silence around the courtyard.

I lower my voice. "I have had to hide my magic since I was a child, because to be caught would mean death and worse than death. Now it's time for us to claim our power. To stop being cowed by Ereni and Paladisan oppressors, with their intolerance and fear." I close my eyes, thinking of my father's vision of Caeris as a haven for magic. At the time, I didn't believe in it, but now—after being captured by Denis, after being threatened with execution—I wonder if it isn't what we need, even if it means fighting against the empire of Paladis itself. Practicing magic openly is Jahan's dream, but it can be mine as well. "Let us create a place where people can practice their magic freely. That is the vision my father had for Caeris—a haven not only for us, but for all the so-called witches who live in hiding throughout the world."

They are watching me in silence. I steel myself—*think of all those years at Eren's court*—and continue. "You imagine your mountains are a refuge, but you have no idea of the danger you're in. Denis Falconier and the Butcher of Novarre have the maps showing the shift lines. If they find a way to read them—and there is always a traitor willing to sell that information for the right price, isn't there?—then your mountains will no longer be safe." I think of my mother, trapped in Barrody Castle, and have to drag my mind away. She's strong; she won't sell our secrets. Unless they force her . . . "They will come to Dalriada, and they will cut the golden pines so that you no longer have their songs or their knowledge or their magic. The Ereni will drive you from your homes. This fight is yours as much as everyone else's in Caeris—more, because you possess knowledge that we don't in the lowlands. If that knowledge is lost, if Caerisian customs are lost, then there truly will be no more Caeris."

The silence lingers. Ingram Knoll is frowning. For a moment, I think I have them. I told the truth. My words rang with conviction.

But then Hebar Manahan says, "Denis Falconier and the Butcher will never learn to read our maps. No mountain folk would ever sell their knowledge, no matter the price."

I stare at him. "Are you insane? We're at war. Everyone—*everything*—is for sale. And if knowledge isn't bought, it can be forced out, even from those on our side! Don't you understand how the Ereni work?"

He scoffs. "We have lasted more than two centuries, hidden here, and they have not learned our ways. And as for your vision of unity, *Caveadear,* you're dreaming. The lowlanders have never done a

thing for us, nor have the Ereni. They call us barbarians and luna-
tics. I'll not have my country exploited to be a 'haven' for those who
despise us."

A grumble of agreement passes around the circle. I glance in desperation at Rhia, who grimaces and shrugs.

"Besides, Granya says Fionnlach Dromahair will never be king—
and praise the gods for it!" Hebar adds.

How does Granya know? I turn to stare at Rhia's aunt, who is
looking off over everyone's heads, her hands clasped together.

"There is another," she says at last, apparently aware that we're
all staring at her. "Another will come."

I grind my teeth together until I can say in an almost-calm voice,
"Another *what*?"

"Another ruler," she says, as if it's obvious.

Rhia puts a hand on my arm—a good thing, since I don't think I'd
be able to stop myself from shouting at the woman otherwise.

Ingram Knoll intervenes. "Even my sister Granya does not see all
that may happen in the future. The *Caveadear* has come a great
distance to plead for our help," he says to Hebar Manahan. "We
might do her the honor of not dismissing her words the moment
they leave her mouth."

Hebar folds his arms with a scowl. "I know a losing argument
when I hear it."

"It is not a 'losing' argument!" I flare. "It's the only way you're
going to *win*."

We stare each other down. After a long moment, Hebar lifts one
shoulder. I look away. I don't feel as if I've won, exactly, more that
the battle lines have been drawn.

Ingram Knoll says, "We will put the matter to council. You will
be given time to speak again, *Caveadear,* just like everyone else." A
pointed look at Hebar.

Rhia nudges me. "I'll have a turn to speak as well. They *will* listen."

I have my doubts. The circle seems to be fragmenting. My words
were not enough to convince them to change their ways. I turn back
to Ingram Knoll, who looks thoughtfully after the receding lords,
and to Granya, who frowns.

"Let us go in," Ingram Knoll begins. "We will make you welcome, *Caveadear*."

But I don't move. I say to Granya, "Why do you claim that Fionnlach Dromahair will not be king?"

She looks at me, then at Ingram Knoll and Rhia. They do not rescue her: We are all waiting. She presses her hands together. At last she says, "Because he is going to die."

CHAPTER TWENTY-SIX

I don't understand it. I don't understand how anyone can consign another human being to death merely because they saw it in a vision.

We're in a pleasant, old-fashioned room covered in wood panels and tapestries. We're supposed to be listening to a harpist pluck strings and sing Wildegarde's poem, while smiling maids bring us tea and palm-sized cherry cakes. But I am not in the mood. I stare across the table at Granya, who calmly cradles a teacup to her chest, as if she hasn't just pronounced the end of the entire revolution. "What else did you see in your vision?" I demand. "The destruction of Barrody? Fire and smoke?"

"*Caveadear,*" Rhia mutters. "My aunt is the memory-keeper of Dalriada. She's held in great esteem. Don't interrogate her."

"I wouldn't," I retort, "if she didn't make pronouncements that my friends are going to die."

Granya glances between us, then at Ingram Knoll. She seems faintly accusatory. "I didn't realize you'd told Hebar Manahan, brother."

"I didn't. Word spread."

"What else did you see?" I ask Granya again. "Please tell me. Are we all going to die?"

Her mouth twists down. "I didn't see it, *Caveadear.* I heard it."

Oh, yes—because hearing voices is so much more reliable than seeing visions. I stab my knife into the butter that's supposed to go on my cherry cake. I tell myself Granya's wrong, but it doesn't help, because part of me is all too afraid she might be right. What if Finn *is* going to die? What if he's already dead now?

Rhia maintains her equilibrium much better than I do. She's probably used to Granya's visions. "What about the revolution, Auntie? Does it mean we lose everything?"

Granya chews her cake. It seems an eternity before she says, "Another will come—come here, I think, unlike Fionnlach Dromahair. But I don't know more than that, chickie."

Chickie? Granya calls Rhia Knoll *chickie?* I almost burst out laughing.

Rhia narrows her eyes at me. "Then we'll have a different king—not Finn. It's not the end of our hope. If," she adds to her father and aunt, "you'll agree to help."

I'm glad for Rhia, even if she does dismiss Finn too fast. He deserves better than that.

Ingram and Granya exchange a glance. The harpist reaches toward some low strings, and under the cover of the sound Ingram Knoll says softly, "You know we are agreed, my girl. But it's a matter of persuading the lords."

"What do they want?" I ask. "Can't they see that they're putting themselves at risk? That we would all benefit if Caeris acted as one united country?"

"They want respect." He spreads his hands. "It's an understandable thing. They feel our customs—our laws—have been ignored too long."

"Then they should want revolution," I say. "We'll restore the old laws." I think of the pamphlet I read on the way north, of the poverty in Eren, of Hugh's passionate declarations about the superiority of the old laws, and I know it's what we must do.

"You might," he says. "But will Prince Finn? Will King Euan, who has never set foot in Caeris but knows only the ways of the empire?"

I study the woven runner on the table. It's ironic that the question makes me angry, because it's the same question I asked my father, just before they took him captive. The memory presses a lump into my throat.

At length, I look up at Ingram Knoll and Granya. "I can't speak for King Euan, or even for Finn, but I am the *Caveadear*. If that gives me any power at all, it must give me say over the laws of our country. Over what's right and what's wrong. So I promise you, if we win, I will see the mountain lords gain the respect they deserve. And everyone will know you deserve it, because we can't win without you."

Ingram Knoll smiles and holds out his hand. I clasp it. His grip is warm and strong.

"Tell this to the council, *Caveadear*," he says. "We convene in three days, when the lords should arrive from the Western Isles. Bring your fire, and you'll convince them."

I smile back, but his warm grip can't erase my lingering doubt. What if I can't? What if Finn's already dead?

When the song ends and we gather ourselves to leave, Granya approaches me. Like her brother, she stretches out both hands to grasp mine. "Lady. *Caveadear*. You heard my niece call me the memory-keeper of Dalriada."

"I did." It's hard to look her in the eyes; my anger that she predicted Finn's death won't let me go. But maybe she's wrong. Voices in your head don't necessarily speak the truth. And I remind myself that I've come here to learn, as well as persuade the mountain lords to fight with us. "What is a memory-keeper?"

"Ah, you wouldn't know." She pats my hand. I suppose it's her nature to be motherly. "We are the ones who keep the memories of the old ways alive. Not only the stories and rituals of the gods, but the histories and traditions of Caer-Ys. Each clan has their own memory-keeper—not in the lowlands, though, not since the conquest."

"So you know the stories about the stewards of the land?"

Her eyes crinkle. "More than that. The Dalriada memory-keepers have always had the honor of teaching others; this place used to be a school of great learning. Students came here from the world over to learn magic—many of the books still remain—and we trained many sorcerers." She leans closer. "By tradition, the stewards of the land came here to learn some of their craft from us, too, except for those secrets only the other *Caveadears* knew. It would be my honor to teach you what has been preserved."

"Hugh—the *Ollam*—told me you still possess much of the ancient knowledge."

"We do—though we haven't trained a *Caveadear* in two centuries! And you've already wed the land. But there are other traditions that have been passed down, and we can explore them together." She pauses. "And there are secrets you must learn—King Ossian's secrets."

I take a deep breath. "I'm ready to learn."

GRANYA AND I agree to meet in the morning, since, she says, Rhia and I must both be tired from our journey. But, despite my weariness, I hardly sleep. I keep thinking about Finn, about the bell ringing *danger*. Does Jahan think I abandoned him? Do they think I'm dead?

I get up early. There's no point in trying to sleep longer. Part of me wants to pack my things and run—back to Taich-na-Ivaugh, back to keep Finn alive, back to take my part as steward of the land.

But I have to stay here. I've got to convince the mountain lords to help, or what's the point in me abandoning everyone again?

My room is lovely, hung with tapestries of unicorns and commanding a view over the mountains and the rushing stream, but my nerves are still too tight-strung to relax. I'll go out instead.

The long hallways sit quiet. I let myself out into the main courtyard, shivering at the shock of the cold near-winter air. The golden pine rises in magnificent silhouette against the pale sky.

Somewhere nearby, someone is singing. I pause, staring about. No singer appears. I listen again, more closely, and I realize it's coming from the tree.

I look again at the golden pine, old and ridged and tough as any of the mountain lords. It's difficult to imagine these trees growing across all of Caeris. Why would my ancestors let them be cut? The song drifts from it, not quite humming, not quite words, but a melody nevertheless, pooling around the tree's great roots. As I stand there, I feel the tree *moving*—the lines of sap running up through it, the inching growth of its wood. The movement mimics the song. The song is its movement.

It is not quite a melody, yet it reminds me of the song my mother wrote for me. The land's song.

A flash of white catches the corner of my eye. A woman walks past me around the tree, her stride purposeful, her white hood billowing around her head, though there is no wind. She glances over her shoulder at me, and I glimpse the markings on her face—spirals of green and yellow.

It must be Granya. She tilts her head toward me—an invitation to follow.

My feet begin to move even before my mind has decided on it. I have to jog to catch sight of Granya, out at the edge of the courtyard. She must be running herself: she is already winding halfway up a hill above the city. She pauses on a rock to look back. The just-woken sun makes wings of her white garment. Fog clings to the hillside, not yet burned away.

She resumes her climb.

I hurry after her. She must be tougher than me: the steep hill puts me out of breath fast, even after days of walking, and she's already disappeared over the top.

My legs and lungs are burning by the time I stumble onto level ground. The fog is dying into scraps of cloud, and through it, shining under the new sun, rises a circle of standing stones.

I stop short, panting. I ought to have expected this. It is just like Barrody—just like Cerid Aven and Laon—a hill rising over the city, crowned with a stone circle. The histories said that most towns in Eren and Caeris were built beneath the monuments, but they never explained why.

The stones jut toward the sky, slender and sculpted only by weather. Even from a short distance I can see veins of white quartz shining in them. They seem to hover, though moored in the earth, at once in the land and outside of it, part of time and beyond time.

A figure moves in the circle.

Granya. I walk forward. The stones appear delicate, almost ethereal, though they tower over my head, almost twice my height, like unearthly giants. Heat pulses off them. A radiance of light seems to shine through their cores. This is not like any other stone circle I have seen. All the others have a certain heaviness. This is pure light.

I step to the edge of the circle and gasp.

Two figures occupy the center of the stones. One, a man, kneels on the ground before the altar stone. With his thick red-gold hair, for a moment I think he is Finn.

But he's not. He's older, for one thing—lines feather from his eyes—and for another, he wears a beard. Its color is bright against his pale, drawn skin. His hands rest, palms up, on his thighs, and he holds himself canted forward, as if he's in pain. Beneath his cloak, I glimpse bandages wrapping his stomach, stained dark with blood. But he has Finn's eyes, blue and clear. He looks beyond me, as if I'm not even there, toward the place where the tops of the stones meet the sky.

A woman stands at his side, a silver dagger in her hand. Even from here, I can tell she's been crying; her eyes are swollen, red, her lips ready to crumple. Though her hair is black as the Knolls', knotted in an untidy braid over her shoulder, this is not the woman I saw in the palace just now; it is not the woman I followed up the hill. Her garment is blue—a deep indigo, woven with a border of orange—and her face clear of the lines and spirals I saw on the other woman's forehead and cheeks.

"I'm ready," the man says.

I startle at the sound of his voice, deep and resonant. It seems to echo off the stones. He's speaking Caerisian, but with an Ereni accent. Like me.

The woman turns the dagger over in her hands. "This is wrong." I can't place her accent at all.

"I've made my peace." His voice hitches; it must hurt to speak. A dark trickle of blood has soaked down the length of his thigh. "I'm ready. *Mo cri, mo tire, mo fiel.*"

She starts to cry again, and moves back behind him so he can't see it. As she wipes her eyes with her sleeve, I think she notices me. Her gaze flickers toward where I stand, then away.

"We cannot undo this," she says.

He closes his eyes. "You tell me the soul does not die. And a part of me will continue to live on, here, in these stones."

"You, and every other *Caveadear.* Every other king, every other warden." Her voice gentles. "But it will not be *you.* You will travel on."

"I am not afraid. And I am going to die from this wound anyway." But the veins stand out in his neck. "Let me have the drink."

She hands him a cup from the ground. He drinks quickly, then resumes his position, open-handed before the altar stone. We all wait. I want to move forward, I want to question them, but some powerful instinct holds me where I am. I watch his eyelids droop shut. "I can't feel my feet," he mumbles. The woman drops down beside him, wrapping an arm around his waist, supporting him against her chest. She kisses his forehead. As he sags against her, she lifts her hand, holding the dagger. Just as he falls, she makes a quick gesture.

The man tumbles onto the altar stone. Blood pools, crimson, beneath him. The woman stands, holding the dagger with its bloody blade.

"No," I exclaim.

The earth cries out at the same time, echoing through me—a deep, inhuman bellow. It aches with grief.

The woman hears it. She flinches and cowers.

I run toward her, across the open ground between the stones, but I can already feel the circle changing, closing in. The light has gone out of the stones. They are heavy now and their grief tastes thick as blood.

This time, she sees me. Her eyes are huge and green, her lips red with grief.

"You," she says. "Set him free."

The earth quakes. I stumble backward. The stones turn from light to thick blackness. The shaking knocks me to the ground; I give up fighting it and lie there till, at last, it ceases.

I crawl upright. The man and woman are gone. The circle lies empty.

Except for the slight silver shape of the dagger, fallen beside the altar stone. Its blade is clean.

I pick up the dagger, study the hilt: bone, with a pattern of running deer. It is identical to the one I still have from the Hill of the Imperishable. Old-fashioned, needle-sharp, and untarnished. What will happen if I let my blood fall?

I lower the dagger, drawing a thin line down my palm. The blade is wicked. It cuts without any pressure from my hand. I make a fist and squeeze.

Two drops of blood fall to the altar stone.

I take one step back. Two. I am ready to run.

Because the stone has turned black—black as old blood, where my blood fell, running in cracking lines. As I stare, a bitter taste in my mouth, a man unfolds from the stone. Or maybe he was always there, just out of sight.

He looks like Finn, with a beard. His eyes are heavy and tired. Heavy as the weight of the stones on this hill.

"*Mo cri, mo tire, mo fiel,*" he says.

I RUN OUT of the circle.

Is this what I must do, then—sacrifice myself, my life, my soul, for Caeris? How can I do that? How can I become like that man, tied to the stones forever, even in death?

"*Caveadear?*"

At the sound of someone calling out my title, I freeze.

Granya puffs to the top of the ridge, her cheeks pink with exertion. She smiles to see me. "Aengus saw you come up here. I thought I'd come after and show you—"

"No!" I blurt out. I won't go back to those stones. Not to any stones, now that I'm beginning to have a glimmer of what they mean.

Sacrifice. Blood. Death.

Granya looks at me, surprised, her brows drawing together. "You're pale as snow. Let's sit for a moment. Sometimes the past peeks through up here, and it can be unsettling, especially for those who are sensitive to it."

I shake my head and push past her, breaking again into a run. The path down the hill is rocky, treacherous, but I'm more afraid of what's behind me than I am of falling. I run until I reach level ground. The land pulses within me. Is this what it's wanted all along—my life, my blood?

Mo cri, mo tire, mo fiel. My heart, my land, my blood.

It must be.

I'm on a high bank over the river. For a moment I actually consider throwing myself in, just to drown the terror beating through me.

"What are you doing, *Caveadear*?"

I startle. It's Aengus, bouncing over a rock. I must look strange, because he halts and stands there, his face solemn, as Granya approaches from the hillside.

She puts an arm around my shoulders. "Aengus, go tell the maids to make up a pot of tea and a hot-water flask. Lady Elanna's just a bit shaken. It can happen to anyone, up at those old stones."

The breath shudders through my open mouth. I feel as though everything certain has shattered. The stones that seemed to shelter me all my life don't mean safety, but sacrifice. I want to run. Only there's nowhere left to run to.

I let Granya guide me back to the palace.

SHE TAKES ME to her library, a vast, high-ceilinged room with a view onto the mountains, and sits me down in front of the fireplace. Soon, with the fire roaring, the hot-water flask wrapped in cloth by my feet, and a cup of tea between my hands, I feel more human. The earth's angry pulse has died to a dull throb.

I'm afraid to tell Granya what happened in the stones, but I find myself babbling the whole story to her anyway—partly because she asks no questions, and partly because I don't want to keep silent. Sometimes horror is lessened if it is shared.

She listens closely, her head cocked down, and sighs when I finish.

"Rhia says time is thin here," I say.

Granya gives a slow nod. "It can be. Though not often quite as thin as you found it to be today." She looks at me. "How well do you know the history of the invasion? Do you know who it is you saw today?"

"It must have been the last king of Caeris," I say. "Ossian."

Ossian, who fled mortally wounded to the mountains. Who began the blood rituals to protect Caeris once he died.

By giving his own life. My father didn't tell me that. Did he even know?

"Ossian was both king and *Caveadear,* as you know," Granya says. "He wedded the earth, and he ruled it." She pauses and then, with a practical gesture, refills my teacup.

I drink.

Granya sighs. "You've stumbled on the truth of Ossian's death. He sacrificed himself for Caer-Ys. His blood created the magic that protects us, that has bound our ancestors to the stone circles. It's one of the great secrets we've kept, along with the traditions surrounding the *Caveadear.* That is one reason why we needed you to come here, so that you can learn the truth of it."

So Rhia knew the secret—at least in part. I think of the woman's grief, her certainty when she said, *This is wrong.*

"She was the sorceress, wasn't she?" I ask. "The one Rhia told me about."

"Tuah," says Granya. "They say she still lives, somewhere beyond the mountains—but that is a story more far-fetched than the ones we tell."

"But . . ." I think of the scene I just witnessed in the circle. "How did she do it? And how do you even *know*? They looked alone, up there, just the two of them."

Granya looks grim. "Tuah was never one for explaining her methods. Most sorcerers of her caliber left records, treatises, or journals at the very least. She left nothing. The story goes that they went up to the circle at dawn, just the two of them, slipping away under cover of her sorcery, and by the time others discovered what had happened, the king was already dead. The people confronted her—some of them wanted to accuse her of murder. But she insisted that she and Ossian had done the only thing that could possibly preserve the *Caveadear*'s magic and protect Caer-Ys against the Ereni conquerors."

"It doesn't seem to me she did *anything*," I burst out, "except kill Ossian and bind our ancestors to the stones for no good reason."

"Ah, but there must be a reason. You understand that she only bound ancestral *Caveadears,* wardens, and monarchs, do you not?"

I blink. This has never occurred to me.

"More than that," Granya goes on, "she bound *the land* to the stones. Why do you think the circle above Cerid Aven weeps and keens its grief? Somehow, Tuah harnessed the power of the earth, too, because it is as if we feel the full force of the land's sorrow."

"So she bound the land and *some* of our ancestors . . . but not all of our ancestors?"

Granya shakes her head. "The old ways tell us that the souls living in the otherworld will be reborn in this one, and die here to be reborn there—an endless cycle of rejoicing on one side and grief on the other. Yet somehow she cut these ancestors off from their natural path."

"But why?" I say. "How does that protect Caeris?" I pause. "And Eren, too? At the Hill of the Imperishable, above Laon, I've also woken ancestors in those stones."

"Have you indeed?" She looks surprised, then thoughtful. "It must have to do with the partition of lands—before Rionach and Tierne established Eren and Caeris as separate nations. The stones don't know political boundaries. The binding must have affected the whole land."

I nod slowly; that, at least, makes a kind of sense. "I still don't see what good the binding does."

"Don't you?" She looks keenly at me. "The power of all those ancestors—the power of the land itself—is gathered into those stones. And it can be *used* . . . by the right person."

The right person. Me. The first *Caveadear* to wed the land in two centuries.

"Must I," I begin, but my voice trembles so much I have to start again. "Must I be sacrificed, then, like Ossian?"

Granya meets my eyes, and then she looks away. The line of her mouth is long and troubled. "What Tuah did, sacrificing Ossian," she says slowly, "that's not a custom of Caer-Ys. It was an aberration—an act of desperation in the face of the Ereni invasion. You know how brutally the Ereni had slaughtered Ossian's family, and so many others; they would never have allowed a *Caveadear* to survive, much less the man who was both *Caveadear* and king. But I think"—she looks at me—"his sacrifice was not what the land wanted. Maybe it has kept us safe this long, and kept the border spell working. But it has also kept the past alive in ways it should not be. It has made the power of our earth a thin trickle instead of a flowing river. I think the land grieves for his death."

I nod, wordless, recalling how the earth bellowed after he died, and how Tuah looked at me.

She looked at me, and she said, *Set him free.*

"Dropping my blood to the stones has never done anything but summon the ancestors," I say quietly, "or wake the land's grief. Even if I bled out—"

"Hush!" Granya exclaims, throwing up a hand with surprising violence. "Do not speak of such things. You will not die like Ossian. That's not what the land wants. Nor is it, if I read the history correctly, what *Tuah* wanted." She stands abruptly. "Come and look. There are books we must read, and things you must learn."

GRANYA AND I spend the next days cloistered in the library, struggling with the old texts written in difficult, archaic Caerisian. Most of the time, she has to help me make sense of them. She explains that once I wake the land, setting the ancestors free of their bonds, I will be more deeply aware of the earth in my being. Not only that, but my increased awareness means that I will be able to control it better. Wildegarde could bring trees alive in her hands and make springs spontaneously shoot from the ground; she could transform into a mountain or a wave in the sea. Now that I have wed the land, now that I have integrated my body and the land, these phenomena seem almost within my own reach, though surely I will never possess all her power. It sounds utterly overwhelming.

Rhia occasionally joins us; she has a surprising amount of patience for digging through books, though her father inevitably calls her away. Once when she leaves, I say to Granya, "Is Rhia training to be a memory-keeper, like you?"

She chuckles. "Oh, this is a debate Ingram and I have almost every day, whether it's Rhia who should be the next warden or the next memory-keeper of Dalriada."

"I suppose her father wants her to be the warden."

Granya snorts. "Not at all. Half the warden's duties involve settling disputes and maintaining the old laws—Ingram is a lawyer as much as anything." She sees my puzzled look, and sets down the scroll she was reading to explain. "Before the conquest, the *Caveadear* kept the magic of the land alive, while the king or queen carried out affairs of state and went to war, and the wardens wrote the laws and kept the traditions. Now, of course, the warden mostly settles disputes within the mountains, but once their jurisdiction extended over all of Caer-Ys." She tries not to smile. "Ingram doesn't think Rhia has enough diplomacy in her to manage such a thing."

I bite my lip against a laugh. "It's a bit hard to imagine."

"But the warden had other abilities," Granya adds, more seriously. "You've seen Rhia walk the folds of the land. The folds, and the maps showing them, are part of the ancient knowledge, so it is something wardens do. And also, according to this writer"—she shakes the scroll she's holding—"the *Caveadear* and the warden worked together in times of war or strife. They could shift armies through the folds of the land."

"Armies?" I reach out my hand. "Let me see that scroll!"

We resume working in quiet. The scroll describes an ancient battle against the Tinani—a border dispute alarmingly similar to the one ten years ago—in which the *Caveadear* and the warden won a victory for Caer-Ys by shifting an army through the land to outflank the Tinani.

I drum my fingers on the table. We could use this knowledge; Rhia and I could work together.

I have to tell Finn and the others that we have another way to fight. Something that could give us an advantage, especially with our smaller forces.

But I can't go back until we hold the council meeting and the mountain lords agree to offer their help. No wonder the wardens are in charge of the ancient laws; the mountain lords are querulous enough that keeping them in order must require someone's full attention.

Granya looks up from the book she's reading, an account of Ossian's last days. She looks rather pleased, but seems to be trying not to show it. "Listen to this. After Ossian's death, the bindings went into effect, and we've often believed that Tuah told the people to start the blood rituals. But perhaps that's not right. According to this writer, who was there, she said, *Blood has bound your ancestors and your land, and blood can unbind them. But you will need more than blood to wake the land again and use the power in the circles.*"

"What more?" I ask.

"That, she doesn't say." Granya is smiling. "But this is good, Elanna! Don't you see? Spilling blood became ritual because it does unbind the land—to a degree. *Your* blood brings the ancestors and the land's power to you. But that's only half the secret."

"The other half is how I free them," I say, thinking of their grief.

She looks at me sternly. "Not only that, but how to use the power they've given. How to wake the land."

She's right, although I'm not sure how she knows our ancestors have been bound to help me, not to mention the land itself. But however it happened, I must make use of their sacrifice. There must be a way to not only wake the land and loosen the bindings, but also use that power to win our rebellion. Jahan seems to have known this all along; I think of his talk of winning through using our magic openly.

Is he safe? Alive? What of Finn and the others?

I can't let myself think of them, or I start snapping at Granya and retaining nothing from the books.

"The stones have intelligence, it seems," Granya says. "The oldest stories, the ones that predate Ossian, tell of the *Caveadears* weaving their magic in cooperation with the power in the circles. Perhaps that's why our ancestors built their settlements near the monuments—because they knew they could use the energy. If you loose the bonds, you can direct the stones to help you."

I drag my hands through my hair. "But to do what? Shall I make a forest walk, like Wildegarde, or streams switch their courses? Shall I summon herds of deer for my army and flights of crows to swoop on the Ereni? We don't live a thousand years ago in Wildegarde's time, Granya. Even if I *could* make those things happen, what good would it do us?"

She looks at me sidelong, as if the answer is obvious.

And perhaps it is. Magic has been held as an anathema for more than two centuries now. But there's power in anathema: terror. No matter how good the Butcher's training, the Ereni armies would turn tail and run at the sight of marching forests.

Besides which, how on earth would they fight moving hills or swelling streams? It's not as if a musket shot would stop the earth itself.

Perhaps we can win—and without bloodshed. We could stop the cycle of violence by reclaiming Caeris and Eren without battles and costly deaths. The land itself could claim what's hers.

And if Rhia and I can work together . . .

"Would I have to go from circle to circle, then?" I ask Granya. "Freeing the ancestors from one place, then the next?"

"It seems likely," she says. "You could begin here in Dalriada."

"Or in Barrody or Cerid Aven. Wherever the Ereni are gathered— wherever we might win a tactical advantage." I wish I had paid more attention during my lessons on military history in Laon now; I was always thinking of the greenhouse instead. But, of course, this is why I have colleagues who know strategy better than I do. Ingram Knoll, Hugh Rathsay, and Alistar Connell can guide us.

I twist my ring. "But we still don't know how to free the ancestors and actually summon their power—how to actually wake the land."

"No," Granya says, with the first hint of real anger I've seen from her. "Tuah left no instructions."

If we can't wake the land by freeing the ancestors, my power will be confined to small, local things—fogs, swollen streams, the aware-ness of the earth and the creatures on it. It is something—it is a great deal—but it's not enough. Not enough to win with less violence; certainly not enough to terrify Eren and maybe even Paladis into recognizing Caeris as its own nation.

But the answer to this question doesn't exist in any of the library records or the memory of the people, because Tuah never told it to anyone.

I know what I need to do.

CHAPTER TWENTY-SEVEN

I wake from an uneasy dream the next morning. Granya tells me that the dreams are part of my wedding the land, for my night-images are filled with stones and streams, the fleeting movements of animals, the ever-present weight of Ossian's blood.

This morning I dreamed of Taich-na-Ivaugh as a ruin: a destruction of ash spread over the peaceful valley.

Was it now, or will it be in the future? Has it happened in the past, and they have since rebuilt the castle I know? All I know is that I heard the bell crying *danger* before we left. I have abandoned my friends—again—to try to bring the mountain lords to our aid.

But the lords still haven't arrived from the Western Isles. We still haven't held the council meeting.

I dress and let myself out of the palace. I think of telling Granya what I intend to do—but no, she might stop me. And what if it doesn't work?

In the half dark, I climb the hill. It doesn't wind me so much this time. The words of the old poem spring to mind. I speak them, letting their cadence fall on the not-quite-dawn air.

"*From the cold mountains behind the moon, Wildegarde came . . .*"

Wildegarde lived long before Tuah and Ossian. She lived in the days when the stones were radiant with light, not heavy with the memory of Ossian's blood. Granya tells me that almost nothing is known of her, except what is preserved in the poem, in which she sounds more like a goddess than a human *Caveadear*. She is not quite a goddess, for she lived after the old gods departed our lands; yet she's not quite human, either. But, I am told, she often appears to those who see her—which is rare—in a white garment. Like the woman I saw on my first morning here.

She doesn't guide me up the hill this morning, but I have the feeling that she observes me from someplace beyond time.

When I reach them, the stones sit deep within the earth, heavy with unforgotten grief.

I walk through to the altar stone. Instinctively, I reach for the dagger in my pocket, but I stop short of scoring my palm. I shouldn't need blood for this, and I already know what Ossian will say.

Mo cri, mo tire, mo fiel.

My heart, my land, my blood. *My* land—not Tuah's. What brought her here? Why did she bind our ancestors? Why did she care?

I shake out my shoulders. My heart is beating fast. There is no reflective surface for me to use, but maybe I don't need one. Jahan said that speaking a sorcerer's name can act as a summons, if you have power enough. The right kind of power. I'm betting that Tuah's ties to this place are strong; that when I speak her name, the mix of her own grief and magic will spur her to respond.

Time is thin here, and it's her specter I anticipate, pulled from some other time.

"Tuah." I don't know her full name. I don't know if the simple two syllables are enough.

Nothing happens.

I try again. Still nothing. Anger pulses up from my stomach. This woman bound my ancestors to these stones, and she doesn't even respond when I call her?

Maybe I do need something stronger.

I score the dagger down my palm, wincing at the sting of it, and drop blood onto the earth. "Tuah," I order, "come to me now. Tell me how to loosen your binding and wake the land."

The air hums around me, static and alive. The witch stone in my pocket is vibrating. The earth seems to shake. A fog is gathering, pooling between the great tall stones. I brace my legs wider and hold my ground.

There's a movement through the fog: a silver fox darts into the circle. Its gait is wary, and its keen orange eyes look straight at me. It comes toward me, one step, another.

Then it dashes off, back into the fog, with a sweep of its white-tipped tail.

I glance around. Even though I spilled my blood, Ossian hasn't appeared. None of the ancestors are here to whisper *Mo cri, mo tire, mo fiel;* the ridge seems deserted except for me. And the fox.

There's a warmth behind me. The faint sound of a breath.

I whirl.

It's a woman—no, a silver fox. My vision blurs between the two. The woman is small, her black hair in a messy braid, her arms folded. The fox pins back its black velvety ears and stares me down.

"I don't like blood magic," the woman hisses in archaic Caerisian.

My head aches from the double vision. "You began it. They say you didn't have a choice."

Her eyes—the fox's eyes—soften a little. She shakes her head. "There is always a choice. Not always a good one."

"How do I break your bindings?" I ask. "How do I wake the land?"

The fox cocks its head. "Your ancestors agreed to be bound and serve Cacris with one great act after they are freed." With a sudden movement, the creature dashes forward: Then the woman, Tuah, is in front of me. She leans down so our faces are inches apart. I feel the puff of her breath as she whispers, "Sing them free, Elanna. You know the song."

Before I have time to blink, to question her and ask how she knows my name, the fox spins away and flashes on its swift feet into the fog.

"*CAVEADEAR!*"

The shout rings up from below the hill.

I'm on my feet. The fog has dissipated, as if it never was. And the silver fox, I know, is long gone. Though whether she came out of the past or present, I can't guess.

"Caveadear!" The shout comes again. It's Aengus.

I hurry to the edge of the circle. He's at the base of the hill, waving his arms and grinning.

I walk down the path. *Sing them free,* she said.

Songs. The golden pines make a song; their sap sings. But how am I to use that?

Aengus has run off already, and I wonder if the last mountain lords have arrived from the distant islands. If it is time, at last, for the gathering to begin, for Ingram Knoll and his lords to decide whether or not they will travel into the lowlands, to help us.

Thanks to my conversations with Granya, I have a better idea what to say when the mountain lords call on me, how to convince them. This time, when I speak to them, they will listen. They *must.* We have no more time. No choice. The vision of Taich-na-Ivaugh, destroyed, passes through my mind.

But it's not the remaining lords from the Western Isles who have arrived.

It's a woman in the courtyard: a woman with blond hair bound up on her head. And behind her, a man, whose olive skin and short, disheveled hair do not belong here.

It can't be.

"El!" Sophy runs to me, clasping me against her in an embrace.

"What are you doing here?" I stammer.

Then I'm looking up at Jahan, reaching for his hands, pushing myself into his arms. I inhale the smell of him, the cinnamon and cloves, the smell of horse and sweat. He squeezes me, then sets me back. The corners of his uncanny light eyes are crinkled with a smile. "We found you, *Caveadear.*"

The way he pronounces the word warms me. I reach up to touch his cheek, but he captures my hand, kisses it, and pulls my arm around his so that we're side by side, facing the courtyard.

"Why did you do that?" I say, exasperated. "I was going to kiss you."

"Do you want everyone to know we're lovers?" he retorts.

"Is there some reason to hide it?"

Sophy clears her throat. "We're not alone, you two."

Other people are crowding out into the courtyard—Ingram Knoll and Rhia, Hebar Manahan and his supporters, other mountain lords. A hand touches my shoulder, and I look over to see Granya, who has arrived somewhat breathless. She stares between Jahan and Sophy.

"Lady," she says to Sophy.

Sophy flushes. "I'm not a lady. Just plain Sophy Dunbarron."

Granya nods, but I see the thoughts forming behind her eyes. *There will be another,* she said—and Sophy is Finn's sister.

"I had a vision," I say. "Taich-na-Ivaugh—is it still standing?"

Sophy and Jahan exchange a glance.

"The Ereni attacked us there," Jahan says, while Sophy looks down, her throat working. "They drove us out the morning you disappeared." He keeps his own voice even, but I sense the reproach under his words. "We thought you'd been captured—or killed."

I glance at Rhia, who has the grace to appear somewhat embarrassed. "How did you know I'd come here?"

"She was missing, too." Sophy nods at Rhia. "We knew she wanted you to come up here."

"And why have you come now?" Ingram Knoll asks.

Sophy turns to him. "Because our band of rebels is being driven back to the mountains. We need your help. You need to give us shelter—or aid."

"Is it an order?" Ingram Knoll says with some irony.

But Sophy doesn't back down. "We're all Caerisians—perhaps not Caerisians *alike,* but Caerisians together. We're fighting for your freedom as much as ours. Don't you get tired of hiding in the mountains? Of not having a say in council, of having your traditions disrespected? I know I'm tired of it, and I do not even know all the old ways."

"And does the new king promise that he will not follow the ways of the Ereni?" Ingram Knoll asks, the same question he asked the other day. "Can you make that promise for him?"

Sophy bows her head. Then she looks at me. I give her a nod. She turns back to Ingram Knoll. "I can't. But the *Caveadear* is with us, and she gives her word to support the mountain lords and the old ways."

"A king in the Paladisan style may not listen to a woman with such ancient power," says Granya.

"I know," Sophy says. "But he may listen to both of us. Because I am his daughter, though unacknowledged and born out of wedlock. And I give you my word that I will make every effort to put your case before the king—because it is my belief that you are right to follow the old ways."

There is silence, and then a murmur spreads through the courtyard. Jahan winks at me.

"We must hold council and deliberate upon this," Ingram Knoll says at last. "You are fortunate, daughter of the king. This is the time of year when all the clan chiefs assemble. The lords have not yet arrived from the Western Isles, but we will meet without them—now."

PAGES RUN OUT to summon all the lords to council. Those who have already assembled gather in small groups in their brilliant woven cloaks, talking earnestly, sending sidelong glances at Sophy. If she's self-conscious, it's hard to see it. She moves into the corner, her spine straight, and talks in a low, serious voice to Ingram Knoll.

I look at Jahan. We've retreated toward an alcove, together, out of the crowd but not quite out of sight. I want to curl up against him and wrap my arms around his ribs. I want to be tucked up, content, at ease.

"You're not upset?" I ask him softly. "Are you? That I left, or—or about—"

"Your betrothal?" He raises an eyebrow. There's an odd look on his face, as if he can't decide whether or not to smile. "Do you know what Finn said to me? He said that a betrothal is just a slip of paper."

I catch my breath.

"He said," Jahan adds, "that his father wouldn't want him to marry you anyway. You're too alarming. King Euan doesn't trust magic." He snorts. "Even though he claims to be the rightful king of Caeris."

"Finn isn't in love with me, then?" I flush as I say the words.

Jahan actually laughs. "Did you think he *was*?"

I punch him in the shoulder, and he just laughs more. "He wanted to marry me, so I don't think it's exactly *unreasonable*."

"You were betrothed as children. There's a difference between desire and obligation."

"Well," I huff, "I don't think I'm such a poor catch as all that . . ."

Jahan is grinning. "Besides, he was mooning about with your friend Victoire before she went back to fomenting rebellion in Eren. Like two puppies about to be separated."

I glower at him. "You really know the key to a woman's heart, don't you?"

He shakes his head. "Elanna Valtai," he says, "you are an utter neophyte at love. If Finn Dromahair loved you, he'd be here. He'd put you before his kingdom and his responsibility. And the moment he saw you again, he'd know you are the best thing he's ever seen. The person who matters more to him than anyone he knows, and for no reason he can understand except for the opening of his heart."

I stare at him; he's not quite meeting my eyes, but then he does. He looks almost resentful, as if he didn't mean to say what he did. "Jahan Korakides," I say, pretending tears haven't clotted under my eyelashes, "you are a rogue, and if you don't say things like that more often, I'll—I'll—"

He leans closer, so that our lips are a hand's breadth apart. "You'll what?"

I slide my hands around the nape of his neck, where errant hair curls, feeling the smoothness of his skin there. I bring my lips to his ear. "I'll turn you into a tree. Or a toad."

"You can't do that," he whispers back, his mouth catching at mine. "But if you do, just so you know, I'll turn you into a toad, too. We can have warts togeth—"

I cut him off with my lips. He only resists for a moment; then his arms come around me, gathering me up against him.

And I am home.

WE SIT TOGETHER in the alcove, his arm around my waist. I lean against his shoulder. The question comes spilling out of me. "Why can't you marry anyone?"

He's quiet for a moment. Then he says into my hair, "I made a vow not to."

I push back to look at him. "Why?"

His free hand reaches for the scar behind his ear. I watch him force the hand down. He looks away from me, and his mouth twitches as if in memory of some grief I can't share with him. "My parents. What my father did to my mother . . . And then," he adds, "there's the fact of what I am."

"But you aren't your father. I know," I add to stop his unvoiced protest. "Besides, there's the fact of what *I* am."

He draws in a breath. "El . . ."

I wait for him to continue, but he doesn't. So I say, "Listen. I've never been interested in marriage. It's always been a sort of obligation to me, something I knew I would have to do. But I don't mind not doing it."

His eyes open wide. For once, I've startled him. He starts to speak, but I tap his lips, shushing him. It's time to be bold.

"I just want to love you," I say. "And like a betrothal, marriage is just a slip of paper. I don't want it. I only want you."

He pulls me back against him, cradling me against his chest so that I feel the beat of his heart in my ear, a counterpoint to the pulsing of the earth, which I seem always to be aware of now, even when I'm not searching for it.

So softly I almost can't hear it, he says, "Then I am yours, in all the ways that don't require that slip of paper."

CHAPTER TWENTY-EIGHT

Ash blows on the wind, curling amid the falling snow. It does not smell of the comforting odor of peat fires.

It smells as if something has died.

My horse shifts under me, and my knees squeeze together. Everyone else hangs back: Rhia, Sophy, Jahan, Ingram Knoll. The message boy who came to us, running up the path to Dalriada, crying, "They've broken through! They're in the mountains!" stumbles off his horse and onto his knees. He's weeping, silent tears.

"How did they get here?" Rhia is saying to her father, a furious whisper. "How did they get past the shifts in the land?"

Someone betrayed us. Was it my mother; did they force it from her? Or did someone else sell or sacrifice this information? The anger that burned within me when we first got the news has dimmed into a hard, cold grief. I have to go back to Barrody; I have to find my mother.

But not yet. And that hurts as much as anything else.

I swing down from my horse, passing the reins back to Jahan. He looks down at me, his lips a tight line, then he, too, dismounts. He comes to stand beside me, fitting one hand into mine.

It gives me the courage to go to the weeping messenger boy. To put a hand on his head. He doesn't look up.

A whistle pierces the snow-and-ash-filled sky: one of the scouts from the village. All's clear. I start forward, Jahan behind me. There's a flurry and the sound of running feet, and Sophy bursts up to the other side of us.

We walk together toward the destroyed town. Altan. The village Rhia and I shifted to, when we left Taich-na-Ivaugh. The place we didn't set foot in, because we turned north instead.

Its windows gape, soot-smeared and black.

A scout meets us on the edge of town. "There's no one left. Not one Ereni or Caerisian. Must have been a raiding party."

Jahan tethers the horses, while Sophy and I continue into the village.

The first body lies ahead of us, alongside the street. Blood stains the trace of early-winter snow crimson, though it is mid-Artemenion, surely too early for snow. The body belongs to a girl; she lies curled on her side with one arm flung out. Her glassy eyes stare at nothing. Ash pours over us, awhirl on the cold wind.

The land aches its grief.

Sophy makes a choking sound. I swallow my own revulsion—not so much at the corpse as at the soldiers who did this—and put out a hand to grasp hers. She tightens her fingers around mine.

This must have happened under the Butcher's orders. Who else? The mountain lords finally decide to lend their help, and the first thing that happens is this atrocity: an entire village, slaughtered and burned.

I lean down and gingerly tug at the girl's hood. It pulls up, crackling with dried blood. I let it drop to cover her face. *"Mo cri, mo tire, mo fiel,"* I whisper. Let Father Dagod come and take her soul in his hands, if he hasn't already. Let him carry her beyond the veil, into the light of the otherworld.

Sophy is weeping and Jahan has come to my other side, putting his hand on my arm. But though I'm grateful for his presence, I don't feel like crying. I don't need comfort. It's rage that burns through me, scalding away any tears I could think of weeping.

It's rage that sends me striding into the rest of the village, the land pulsing in counterpoint to my stride, so that I can see the rubble of burned-out roofs, the twisted horror of bodies. Finn's flag, the Dragon, is trampled into the cobblestones in the village square, covered in dung and burn marks, but still intact.

The scouts move around me, gathering the bodies for burial.

I stare at the half-destroyed flag. Patriotic rage rises in me, and then I'm on the ground, tugging the fabric from the stones with my fingernails. The land pounds in my head. Jahan drops down across from me without a word and starts working at the other side.

Sophy arrives at my shoulder, her eyes wide with anger above the tears silvering her cheeks. "We don't have time."

I stand up, ripping the flag from the ground. Pebbles bounce off it. Jahan grabs the other side, and between us, we hold up the tattered flag. Sophy stares at it, wordless.

I look at her. "They have to pay for this."

BY MIDAFTERNOON, THE scouts have gathered the word: The Ereni and Caerisians have met for battle some miles south of Altan.

So that is why the earth aches and keens with grief—not only for this village, but also for the battle. The sound makes me feel hollowed out.

We don't have a choice. We have to fight.

Jahan comes up beside me. "We might still get there in time." We both glance at our assembled forces: a few hundred mountain lords. Certainly nothing like a full army. They didn't bring enough forces from the distant cantons. I wish Finn hadn't gone into battle so quickly, but of course he didn't have another option.

"Rhia," Jahan calls.

She comes over to us, brisk and impatient. "We're trying to make a plan."

"And while you plan, people are dying," I snap. "Listen. I have an idea. In the books, Granya and I discovered that the *Caveadear* and the warden used to work together in battle. But what if all *three* of us work together? You know how to shift the land; you're better at it than your father. I can listen to it—I'll know where the battle is taking place. We can pull our entire force through with us."

I should be able to raise an army of trees. I should be able to make streams flood. But I'm not Wildegarde. I have wedded the land, but I don't have her power. Not yet.

Rhia folds her arms and raises a brow at Jahan. "And what can he do?"

Jahan looks between us. "I've been in battle before. I can destroy the enemy guns—when we get there."

Rhia nods. They both look at me.

332 ~5 CALLIE BATES

"That's perfect," I say. I knew Jahan would be better than any of us on a battlefield. The burning desire for revenge is making my heart pound faster. And the terror that Finn and Hugh and Alistar, their forces already reduced, cannot possibly hope to win this battle. "Now."

Rhia gestures to her father, who nods for her to take his place, for the moment, as warden. The mountain lords assemble around us in their colorful cloaks, with Sophy pushed toward the center, her eyes large in her pale face.

The three of us make a circle. It's Rhia who grasps both our hands, and Jahan and I reach out for each other's. As we are joined, a shock of heat passes between us, one hand to the other, leaving a ringing in my ears. Awareness of the land explodes within me. Trees rustle in my ears, and water runs through my veins. I see through a wolf's eye, breathe with a fish's gills.

And, some distance away, I feel the echo of gunfire rock up through the soles of my feet.

Rhia gasps. "I see the line—it's like a light, running through the land."

Her voice is so small in the vast, living world.

"Can you tell us where, El?" Jahan says.

I concentrate. It is a matter of altering my perception, of listening *for* something rather than *to* everything. I sink through the earth, toward the south, past fields and forests, to a place where the stone walls fall away and the earth is bare except for grass and the desperate bodies of fighting men. A crack of musket fire startles me back into my slight human body. Jahan and Rhia hold me tight.

Rhia nods to the mountain lords assembled around us, then the three of us form a line, with me at the center. Heat from their hands radiates into my body. The mountain lords gather themselves to follow us. We walk, more than a hundred of us, through the shifting earth.

WE ARE TOO late. Even with our speed, even knowing just where to go, our small force is too late.

We've come to the edge of a forest. Beyond it spreads a wide field, and the field is a mass of carnage, with the bodies of the dead slowly freezing into the wintry ground. Far off, an Ereni soldier looks up from scavenging the corpses, letting loose a single shot into the gray air. It comes nowhere near us. He's no better than the crows who circle overhead.

Other Ereni, discernible by their blue sashes, move among the dead.

But the only Caerisians are on the ground.

I've fallen to my knees. Behind me somewhere, Sophy is stuttering. "But how—Where—" Jahan grasps my shoulders, turns me to face him. I can't feel anything, not even the warmth of his touch.

So many bodies.

"Scouts!" Ingram Knoll calls, and, as if from a great distance, I hear the rattle of the scouts riding out to see what's become of our Caerisians.

Sophy says in the smallest voice, "Are they all dead?"

"Some will have escaped." Ingram Knoll's voice floats, grim but pragmatic, over my head. "Maybe more than some, if we're lucky. But the Ereni will pursue them. We have to act fast—go after them, harry the Ereni off."

On my shoulder, Jahan's hand closes into a fist. He forces it back open.

I stagger onto my feet, moving forward among the bodies, alone. Bodies trampled by horses, ripped pinkly apart by bayonets and cannons. I pass among the dead, looking into what remains of their faces.

One man—a boy, really—is still alive. His lips part as I approach him, like a fish gasping for air. There's a wound in his stomach. I look away from the glistening organs that show through his flesh, up into his bloodshot eyes. His lips form the word *Caveadear*.

I crouch beside him. His fingers are sticky with gore, but I hold them tight. A distance away, another Ereni soldier fires another shot at us. Sparks flare. A distant crack explodes; I hear cursing.

The boy's throat works. I hold his fingers tighter. He's breathing shallowly now, quick gasps for air. The space between breaths grows farther and farther apart, until that is all there is: space, and silence.

I set his hand back on his chest and stand up. The boy's open eyes reflect the clouds overhead. I didn't feel Father Dagod take his soul in his hands, but I felt the quiet as the life left him. Perhaps it is the same thing.

I squelch through the churned mud. The Ereni soldiers shout at me, but I ignore them. I'm aware of Jahan somewhere behind me, picking his way toward me over the dead. Still a distance away, though.

Another body moves just ahead. I quickly step closer, and stop. It's another young soldier with an identical wound in his stomach. His cheeks flash as he tries to breathe, his legs pushing at the mud.

But he wears an Ereni sash.

I drop down beside him. The soldiers are shouting, "Hey, you! Bugger off!"

The boy's huge eyes widen at the sight of me. He didn't expect a woman on the battlefield. He certainly didn't expect me.

His legs keep thrashing. I take his hand in both of mine, and I find myself humming a song—an old Ereni song, one Hensey used to sing to me.

I start to sing. *"Hush little baby in the shroud of the high moon . . ."*

Tears leak out of the boy's eyes. He tries to stretch his other hand up to touch my face, but his chest convulses. He falls back. The soul flies out of his eyes. I don't see which god catches it.

I fold both his hands over his chest, just as I did with the other boy. I press a hand to his brow. *"Mo cri, mo tire, mo fiel,"* I whisper, because the words belong to him as much as to any Caerisians. The earth rumbles.

I stand up. The carrion thieves fire again at me. "Stop!" I scream at them. "Leave the dead in peace!"

"Witch!" they yell at me. "Caerisian witch!"

With a racket, their guns *explode*—I see the burst of smoke, the startled exclamations of pain. I glance over my shoulder to see Jahan some distance behind me, grinning a savage grin. It's his magic, then.

My foot catches against something. I startle and look down, and for a horrible moment, seeing the spiked hair, I think it's Alistar Connell who's lying there dead. I kneel, heaving the body over.

It's not Alistar. It's Declan. Declan, who was with us when my father was captured, who climbed the walls of Portmason with Alistar. Whom I last saw full of life.

Rage pulses into my temples. I lunge toward the Ereni scavengers. A long twisting rope seems to be growing from my hair. Leaves and water and rocks shoot from my hands, scatter before my feet. The earth shakes.

The scavengers turn and run.

I watch until I'm sure they're gone, their figures lost to distance. Then I face back to the battlefield, my throat tight with grief. Horses come running from the edge of the forest—the scouts coming back to Ingram Knoll.

Jahan is just behind me. He must have comforted others of the dying; blood splatters his hands. He hurries to me.

"The dead need to be buried," I say.

He looks at me in confusion and some distaste; in the Paladisan tradition, corpses are burned, not buried. "What do you—?"

I gather the words Alistar spoke over the two Hounds, the night my father was captured. To think it seemed so much to lose two of them.

Two is such a small number, amid all this.

"Mo cri, mo tire, mo fiel."

I speak the words with intent, pitching my voice as loud as it will go. *Come,* I whisper with all the grief tight within me. The earth rumbles again. Now, just as it did when the Hounds died, it swallows the bodies of all the dead—Ereni and Caerisian alike—within it.

Jahan and I stand alone on an unmoving patch of ground amid the tumbled remains of the battlefield. Dust lingers in the air. It is all that remains of everyone we lost. If we lose many more Caerisians, there won't be a Caeris left to claim its freedom.

This cannot be the answer. It cannot be the only way.

Jahan catches my hand in his, and I feel a tremor running through him. There are tears in his eyes, but I feel too hollowed out to weep.

"Come on, El," he says. "Let's see what they've found."

CHAPTER TWENTY-NINE

Gunfire reports as we approach the forest. We break into a run just as Rhia and Sophy burst from the trees with a few others.

"They're behind us," Rhia shouts, throwing me my horse's reins.

We swing into our saddles and gallop off a moment behind the others. Shots echo after us. Jahan swivels in his saddle and makes a gesture, nearly falling off his horse.

"What did you do?" I demand.

He grins. "I broke their guns."

Sophy and Rhia curve around, leading us off the field and up a hillside into another patch of forest. We slow in the woods, the horses snorting, branches whacking riders in their faces. I ask the trees to make us a clear path. The branches draw aside.

We can ride a bit faster now. Most of the mountain lords remained at the battlefield, along with Ingram Knoll. It's just us and a handful of others riding this way. As we reach the hilltop and plunge down the ridge on the other side, I realize we're tracking someone.

"A party of cavalry went this way," Rhia pants at us, "followed by Ereni. We don't know who, but—" She stops, reining in. "Shift! Halt! There's a line in the land—"

But it's too late. We're already plunging through—I *feel* the line crawling over me, prickles and sparks of light—blind as any southerners, the land pulling us where it will.

We stumble through to a patch of green outside a village. Buildings lean close to one another before us, timber roofs colliding. Somewhere beyond them, muskets fire. I hear the sheer sound of glass shattering. A woman screams.

Rhia and Sophy rein in, exchanging a glance. Maybe the land shifted to send us after the people we're pursuing. The horses are sweating.

Jahan's head comes up. "What do you—" I begin, but he's already bolting through the riders, bursting away from us down the street, toward the fighting.

We plunge after him, all together.

They're in the town square. A brigade of Ereni are lined up on this side of the fountain, shooting into a building on the other side of the square. A pale face shows through the jagged remains of a window, and I see exhausted horses let loose down a side street. These are our people, then, hiding in the houses.

The Ereni are reloading as Jahan rides up behind them, Rhia close on his heels. At a shouted order, some of the Ereni start to fire across the square, while others turn to gape at us.

The guns don't fire. I hear the clatter as they begin to explode, one by one, then all at once. Men scream, clutching faces and throwing up their hands.

Jahan throws himself off his horse, hitting an Ereni man—the captain?—in the chin. Then the others close in and I can't see Jahan anymore. I'm thrown off my horse, onto the ground. A soldier thrusts his bayonet at Sophy. I duck under his unprotected left arm and thrust my dagger into his sternum. It catches on a rib, but I twist it up and it digs between his ribs, deep into his flesh. He chokes, trying to hit me, but his hands are clumsy with the bayonet. I get my knee between us and thrust him back with all my might. He falls, convulsing, to the ground, my dagger embedded in his chest.

My hand is soaked with cooling blood.

I start to shake. I just killed a man.

A shout rises from the building across the square. A man with spiked hair—Alistar—runs toward us, crying his ululation. Then more Hounds pour from the building—a small band, but enough. I glimpse a shock of pale hair among them.

Finn.

He's alive.

We're locked in now. I kick a man in the groin. Sophy rushes up to me; she has pulled my dagger from the man's chest. As we put our backs together, she presses the dagger into my hand—and I slice at an Ereni soldier, who falls under a blow from one of the mountain warriors.

I wipe the sweat from my eyes, glancing around. We're *winning*. We're win—

Lights shine from the street we just rode down. An explosion of shots deafens my ears. More lights flood in from the other side of the square. Blue-and-gold sashes catch my eye. Ereni. I swivel around, but I can't see Finn anymore. It's chaos.

An Ereni soldier hits my arm. My dagger goes flying. The man wears a savage grin, swinging his bayonet into the air.

A blow strikes the soldier from behind—an ax between his shoulders. He falls, and I see Finn, standing there with the bloody ax in his hand, his blond hair uncovered, his face white with terror and battle-joy.

"Finn!" I'm crying out his name, dazed with relief. He's alive, alive!

"El—"

Something explodes behind us.

Finn stops. The ax falls from his hand. Slowly, he brings his hands to his chest. Blood blossoms over his jacket. His heart is running out.

No. No no *no*—

"Finn!" I scream, lunging for him as he staggers onto his knees. His eyes are glassy. I catch him against my stomach. He's speaking, saying something, even as he slides toward the ground. I scrabble my fingers in his jacket. It does no good.

Hooves. A horse pulls up beside me, a dappled gray. I stare up at the Butcher, blood on his lace cuff, at the gun he's pointing into my face.

It seems my mother has failed in her mission to reform him.

And all at once, something in me shatters. I scream at him. "Murderer! Criminal! Shoot me, if you're going to! I know what you are!"

His eyes have widened, just a fraction; the barrel of the gun lowers. And then his horse jostles backward—Sophy has rammed into him. His pistol fires, exploding wildly over our heads. Finn has fallen to the ground. Sophy strikes the horse's hindquarters with all her might, and it bolts away across the square, carrying the Butcher with it.

Finn. I drop to my knees, my own ragged breathing harsh in my ears.

An enormous *crack* sounds around the square. Jahan has broken all the guns at last.

It's chaos. I have no idea who's winning, but Finn is the most important thing. Between us, Sophy and I heave him up and carry him toward the quiet side of the square, into the shelter of a building. It's a bakery—racks half filled with pastries and bread, a still-warm oven. We lay Finn on the floor. His eyes are shut, and it's so dim I can't make out whether or not his chest is moving. I lower my ear and feel the cold weight of blood against it.

Cold. The blood on Finn's jacket is cold. Congealing.

Beneath the blood-soaked fabric, I feel nothing.

No.

No, no.

I tear his jacket open, scattering buttons everywhere. Sophy's face is chalk white. I feel the smooth skin of Finn's chest, and then the terrible hole—the deep, inset wound.

I drop my ear against the place where his heart should beat, but there's only blood.

Only a body. No Finn.

I sag back on my heels. My chest burns with pressure, but I can't cry. I want to take a pistol, I want to kill the Butcher. After all this, he kills *Finn* and not me?

A strangled sound pulls me from my shock. Sophy crouches above Finn's head, her hands fluttering around his face, as if she doesn't quite dare touch him, even though he can hardly stop her. I remember Granya's augury—Finn's death, another will come—and I feel cold, so cold.

Sophy is weeping—ragged, undignified tears. "He was my brother. He was my brother, and I never told him. He never knew."

I reach for her grasping hands, trying to hold her steady, but she fights me off. She turns her face up to mine and whispers, "What good is waking the land if you can't bring him back?"

My lips part. We stare at each other. She's panting. "Soph," I begin, my voice shaking.

The door bursts open behind us. I whirl, snatching a bread knife from the counter, but it's Jahan and Alistar. They're both covered in blood.

"It's getting bad out there," Alistar says. "We have to get out."

Jahan sees Finn first. His mouth opens. Then he makes a terrible noise—a gut-wrenching sound that tears upward into a shout. He falls to his knees at Finn's side.

"He's dead," Sophy spits. "Can any of *your* magic bring him back?"

"Sophy." I kneel beside her, reaching for her arms, but again she pushes me away.

Jahan is breathing hard. He's stopped making the horrible sound, but his lips remain parted.

"Can we bring him back?" Sophy screams at him, at me.

"Be *quiet*." I shake her. "You're giving us away."

She stares at me. I grip her hand. A breath pours out of her; her forehead bumps against mine. I feel her whole body shaking. Cold tears bunch behind my eyes, but I can't cry now.

The door bangs again: Rhia, blood crusting her nose. "We have to get out now. They're setting fire to the town."

"The men?" Alistar asks, his voice high and tight. "My Hounds?"

"They . . ." she begins, but falters, meeting Alistar's eyes. I have never seen Rhia Knoll be gentle before, but her voice is soft when she says, "A few have escaped into the woods."

Only a few. I swallow hard; Alistar is fisting his hands. We can't afford to lose anyone else. There has to be another way.

"We need to go," Rhia says. "Now."

WE RUN OUT the back, into an alley where the baker and the butcher must empty their slop. Just behind us, I hear the roar of the flame, the sound of breaking glass.

We leave Finn. We have to leave his body there, to be consumed by the fire.

Jahan grabs my hand. We're running, pelting down the alley, onto another street. There are no Ereni, but the town behind us blazes. We run and run, out into the farm fields, where we stumble through another fold in the land, emerging into deep woods, running again until we come upon an empty, abandoned croft. There we throw ourselves onto the floor like animals, all pressing together. It's dark outside, but for the first time in my life, the woods seem full of danger.

THE OTHERS SLEEP, I think—or something close enough to it. But I lie, staring into the darkness, my hand balled up in a twist of Jahan's coat. Again, again, I feel Finn's body slide to the ground even as I try to hold him. The slick, dead weight of him. How his limbs flopped when Sophy and I carried him across the square. How Sophy screamed at me and Jahan.

The Butcher lowering the pistol. The rawness of my throat when I shouted at him.

The man I killed, the dagger silver in his chest. How his mouth opened. The weight of his terror between us. How I kicked him and he fell. How the blood was sticky on my hand.

Around and around the memories churn. My stomach is sick and tight but I don't feel like vomiting. My eyes hurt but I can't close them.

Finally I get up in the timeless dark. Jahan shifts as I move, but I don't turn back for him. He will be blaming me for Finn's death—and if he isn't, he should.

The croft lacks a door. I step out into the night. A mist is falling. I let the delicate drops wet my face; I pull off my hat so they can spangle my hair. Maybe the earth can cleanse me. Maybe the land can absolve my guilt.

The mist lessens. I look around. There's not much to see—the bulk of trees in shadow upon shadow, an ill-repaired wall. We don't even know where we are. The Butcher's presence in the town could mean we're close to Barrody, or it could mean he got there through the shift. How far did the land take us?

And does it even matter? We've lost so many of the Hounds, and so many more Caerisians in the battle. We're cut off, for the moment, from Ingram Knoll and the mountain lords. Are they still alive? Free?

Finn is dead. My father, too, for all I know. My mother is a prisoner, perhaps being forced to reveal the secrets of the land's shifts. Denis Falconier rules Caeris, the man who killed a king so he could make himself one.

He'll probably succeed.

As many times as I've been captured, threatened with death, I never really knew what it meant until I lost Finn today.

A sliver of moonlight cuts through the clouds. It shines on a cedar tree growing beside the stone wall. I walk to the tree and curl into its roots. Somewhere beneath my numb body, the land pulses its awareness. But not even the land can save us now.

From the croft's gaping doorway, a shadow emerges, sees me, and comes over to the tree. Jahan settles down on the other side of the roots, our hands near but not touching.

There is nothing to say. We sit for a long time in silence.

"I failed him," Jahan says out of nowhere, as if we've been having a conversation the whole while. Maybe we have, in a way. "He asked me to make this revolution a success, and I said I would. He—"

I am shocked to hear his voice thicken with tears. Alistar Connell cried when his Hounds died, but not after. I remember that horrible bellow Jahan uttered when he saw Finn's body. I can't bear to hear that again. I can't bear him to feel the same grief I feel, the grief that should be mine.

"It's not your fault."

"I didn't bring the black ships. I didn't even try to persuade the emperor to send them. I thought starting a revolution would be simple if we used our magic. I never thought we might lose." He turns to me. "I never thought it would kill him."

My throat clenches. Why do people die so easily?

"It should've been me," I mutter.

"What? No!"

"I was there. Right there. The Butcher was going to shoot me, too, but then Sophy—" I stop. The Butcher should have shot me right there, a fast death. But he didn't. Did he even recognize me until the moment I shouted at him? Did he *mean* to shoot? And I realize I didn't see him fire at Finn. He came up beside me immediately after.

Immediately. With no time to reload his gun. It fired into the empty air.

He didn't kill Finn.

But it doesn't matter, does it? Because whether or not he killed Finn, the Butcher has committed enough other damning crimes. He's still leading this war against us, despite my mother's hope. And how can we possibly win against him?

If he were on our side, he could bring the military over to us. It would be an easy victory then.

Jahan is cursing in Idaean, oblivious to my internal strife. "All the gods damn it. I hate battle, El. I *hate* it—I hate what it makes me into. It makes people's lives seem not to matter. But they do. No one should have to die like that, not even for freedom."

No. No one should; and no more of us will, if I can stop it.

I reach for his hand, and Jahan grabs onto me, his grip so tight it seems about to crush my bones. But I welcome this small pain, as if it can make me share, somehow, in Finn's greater pain. I whisper, "Did he even want to rule? He never . . . he might have . . ." I stop. I can't say it aloud, not now. I can't say that Finn was a good man, but he might not have been the king Caeris needs.

Jahan doesn't say anything. I suppose he knows what I was trying to say; even Finn knew he wasn't cut out to be a king. He tried to take on the duty. He gave his heart to our cause. And it killed him.

"He believed in Caeris's freedom." Jahan's voice rasps. "He would have tried to rule well, when the time came."

I hold Jahan's hand tighter and the terrible truth comes to me. He could die, too. Just as easily. And my mother, my father. Sophy. Alistar. Rhia. They could all be taken from me so quickly, by a single explosion of gunpowder and shot.

It's wrong. It's so wrong.

I crawl over the roots, directly into Jahan's lap. He stiffens, startled, but then his arms come around me. I tuck my face between his shoulder and his neck, closing my eyes. He rests his chin on the crown of my head. His breath stirs my hair.

The cedar's roots shift under us, coming up and around to clasp us, to hold us there, tight in an embrace with the tree.

"I won't lose you," Jahan whispers in my ear.

I swallow hard. "I love you, Jahan Korakides."

There's a breath, a pause, before he answers me. For a moment I think he isn't going to say it.

But then he does. "And I love you, Elanna Valtai."

DAWN ARRIVES: a lightening of the gray sky. I stir against Jahan. I don't think either of us slept, but though we've been outside for hours, we're not cold. The earth warms us.

There's a murmur of conversation from the house. Rhia emerges, squinting for us in the shadows under the tree. She comes over and perches on the roots. Her face is drawn, as if she hasn't slept, either.

"We need to find my father and the mountain lords," she says abruptly. "And figure out where we are." She doesn't quite meet my eyes.

I don't like the way she's acting. "What's the matter?"

"Sophy and Alistar have been talking. All three of us have." Rhia looks off at the sagging roof of the croft. "We have no leader. No king. We all know Euan Dromahair will never come back from across the sea." Her eyes meet Jahan's, fierce with challenge. "Will he?"

Jahan's lips press together. He shakes his head.

Rhia lets out a sigh. "So we have no king, except in name. Our army is scattered. We need my father and the others; we have to make sure they're safe. Then we should retreat to the safety of the mountains. We'll keep there for the winter, in Dalriada; my father can hide your presence. When the thaw comes, you can—"

I'm on my feet, rage spitting from me. "*That* is your plan? You're going to give *up*? You're going to *retreat*?"

Rhia backs up. "We don't have a choice, El."

El. This is the first time Rhia Knoll has ever called me by my name, not my title.

"We have no leader," she's saying. "We have no organization, just a mess of scattered rebels. All we have is the safety of the land."

"I think it's rich that you talk of safety, Rhia Knoll," I burst out. "And a lack of leaders? What about you, the future warden? What about me, the *Caveadear*? What about Jahan—he's the Korakos!" I fling a hand toward the croft. "What about *Sophy*? She's the king's bastard. Why shouldn't she be queen?"

Rhia opens her mouth, but I don't let her speak.

"And the land hardly gives us real safety. Denis and the Butcher won't give up till we're locked in prison with our orders for execution. I don't know why you talk of giving up when we have hardly even *begun*."

There's a noise from the croft's open door. Sophy and Alistar stand there, staring. I don't know how much they've overheard. I'm panting, shaking with fury and exhaustion.

Sophy shakes her head. She takes one step forward. Another. Her eyes are bruised, but the terrible, flailing rage seems to have gone out of her. "What would you have us do, El?"

I close my eyes. I think of the king, Ossian, kneeling in the stones above Dalriada, in the memory of the past come alive. His hands open on his thighs. How he claimed not to be afraid.

I must be like him. I must not be afraid, no matter what sacrifice the land asks of me.

"We need to find another way to win," I say.

CHAPTER THIRTY

"Did you hear that?" Jahan says. He's stopped short, pulling on my arm, so that I swing back to face him. The moon is lowering behind the trees that buffer our narrow track, and it's hard to make out his face. I'm not sure how much time we have before dawn—an hour? It's taken us at least an hour already to get here from the Knolls' camp on the north side of Lake Harbor, where our small force is hidden deep in a valley, protected by the land as much as I can manage. We had to walk through the hills, rocks and roots parting to let us pass safely in the dark, so there was no chance of us being seen by the guards on Barrody's ramparts. We're both dressed in shepherds' clothes, and we blend into the shadows, but I'm still afraid that any movement out here, in the wee hours of the morning, will make them suspicious.

I listen through my feet. Nothing comes to me but a strange quiet—strange because we are close to Barrody now, and I should feel the tremor of the city even so early in the day. I concentrate. It does not feel like a threatening quiet. It feels like nothing at all.

Perhaps it's because Denis and the Butcher think they've defeated us in battle; they killed our prince, after all. The bulk of the Ereni army is camped just north of the city, while the Butcher reportedly returned in triumph to the castle. Perhaps they think they can rest on their victory.

But they don't know that Jahan, Sophy, Alistar, Rhia, and I re-united with Ingram Knoll and the mountain lords after the battle in the town, traveling back through the folds in the land to find them.

They don't know that Ingram Knoll had gotten word to Hugh, who arrived soon after, bringing with him additional supporters from the lowlands, including the soldiers who fled the disastrous battle. They don't know that we walked the folds of the land and pitched camp directly between Barrody and the Ereni army.

They can't even imagine that my plan is to break the bindings of the earth at the stone circle in Barrody, to ring the city in impossible mists and forests and water, cutting it off from the army to the north—and from its supply lines and roads to the south.

It will be harder still for them to imagine that I'll rejoin Rhia and Hugh and walk the folds to the place where the army is camped, where Ingram Knoll waits with a force of lowland soldiers. They're near a town, and of course there's a stone circle above it. I'll wake the land there, as well.

Then our small army will march on Barrody, our ranks swelled by the specters of the past, the ghosts I will summon from the land. We will scare the Ereni out of their wits, and remind the Caerisians of the power of our land. We will win.

Circle by circle, I will break the bindings and reclaim Caeris. Then we will move into Eren and do the same.

And then we will be free.

If waking the land and the ancestors goes in the way Granya and I expect. If I can control my power and act quickly enough. If the Ereni surrender.

Jahan stops, then grabs my arm and slows us both. The moonlit path curves ahead of us. "Someone spoke my name."

A shiver runs over my skin. "Who?"

"It's nothing," he says. "It could be anyone." But then he pauses, and I hear him take a breath. "El. Whoever it is, they're not far from us."

I feel a burning heat against my hip. It takes me a moment to realize it's the witch stone in my pocket. I pull it free. It lies in my hand, vibrating with energy.

A distant *boom* breaks the quiet. As explosions go, it seems small, shrunken.

"The garrison," Jahan says, half to himself.

After our meeting with the army, Sophy and Alistar went straight to Barrody to alert the underground and to claim the ammunitions our supporters have been stealing from the deposit in the nearby port town. They're in the city now, coordinating an attack on the garrison to coincide with our arrival at the stone circle. In the dark, it will send the garrison into complete chaos, diverting attention from what we're doing—and keep the Ereni busy so they don't think of sending for help until it's too late and they're surrounded.

If all goes well, after the attack on the garrison, Sophy will bring the Barrody underground to meet us at the north gate. We will flood through the city and claim it.

But we could not get word to my mother. We don't know what, if anything, she's accomplished inside the castle—or even if she's been forced to betray us. Somehow, I have to reach her.

Another small explosion shakes the air. It still does not seem loud enough—and I realize it's because I am hearing the noise with my ears, not through my feet. Not through my whole body.

I shake my head. My heart is pounding. It's nerves. I don't feel the land because I am afraid.

I must not be afraid.

We continue, Jahan's arm tight through mine. On this deer path, winding down the hill toward Barrody, no one can possibly see us in the darkness.

All the same, I whisper to the trees to draw closer.

Nothing happens.

"Jahan," I whisper. My voice is catching in my throat. It should be easy. We have avoided Ereni regiments thus far. No one, not even Denis—not even the Butcher—would think we're fearless enough to walk right into Barrody—right into the stone circle above the castle, where the whole city could see us, even if it is still night. But do they know that I can wake the ancestors in their midst, that I can bring the land alive? If they have Caerisian maps, they have more than that; they have Caerisian help, coerced from either my mother or someone I don't know. They saw what I did to the scaffold. They know the stories about the *Caveadear* are true.

An enormous *boom* shakes the air. In the distance, orange sparks shatter the darkness.

I don't know if it's Jahan or me who starts running first. But we're both racing through the black forest, skidding around the tightly nested trees. His hand is hot in mine. Then we hurtle out into the open, onto the ridge overlooking the shadowy bulk of the city. On a ridge below us, limned by moonlight, sits the stone circle. And beyond that, Lake Harbor, the castle, the city.

The hair on the back of my neck prickles. Even in the dark, we are too much in the open here, too exposed. But we had to come to Barrody, to cut the Ereni army's head from its body. We have to chance this bold maneuver in order to force Denis and the Butcher to surrender, thinking their forces lost.

It's too late to retreat now. The circle sits empty on the ridge below us. The lingering moonlight shows that the ridge is barren except for a cluster of darkness off to the left of the circle—trees.

"Remember what we did?" Jahan pants. *"You don't see me. I am a—a—"*

"A fox."

But even I can feel that it's not working—for either of us. We haven't shrunk into invisibility against the bare shoulder of the ridge. We are definite points—shadowed, yes, but still exposed to any eye that's looking.

Yet we don't have a choice. We have to trust the night to protect us. I plunge over the edge, down to the stone circle.

More *booms* echo across the city. Smoke hangs over the garrison, lit by the stars. Distant sparks shine and vanish.

For Finn. I am doing this for Finn. For my father. For my mother. For all of Caeris. For the land.

For Jahan. For me.

The dagger makes a snug weight against my waist, where I strapped it in under a belt.

The ground levels out beneath me. The stone circle waits ahead.

"El!"

Jahan bellows my name. I skid to a stop, falling hard against one of the stones.

The dark wood on the other side of the stones has begun to move. I peer around the stone. I still don't feel the land shifting under my feet. How can the trees move and I don't feel it?

That's because they aren't trees. It's not a wood.

It's a blind of some sort, stuffed with stubby shapes that I now realize are brush. Someone's hiding in there; someone's seen us. They've been waiting. They *knew.*

Someone told them—or they intercepted some of our intelligence. I can't imagine who would betray us now; I don't want to.

Unless Mother guessed this, too.

Sparks flare. Musket fire reports toward us.

I duck behind the stone. Jahan calls out. I glance around; the moon and the flaring muskets light him up. He's holding up his hand, trying to break their guns.

But the guns don't break.

He does.

I see the musket shot catch him—a spreading darkness in the shoulder, in the chest. He twists to the side. A soft, shocked sound puffs from his mouth. He falls.

I'm on my feet. I can't even scream.

The soldiers pound between the stones behind me. "Halt in the name of the queen!"

Jahan is hit. Jahan could be dead.

I scrabble for my dagger. There's not much I can do—stab one person. That's all I'll have time for. And there are many of them.

Or I can try to slip past them in the dark, while they're distracted by Jahan. Paint my blood onto the stones.

But Jahan—

Then a man walks past me.

Not a soldier. The moonlight illuminates a bandolier, but it's not stuffed with ammunition. It's covered in stones.

Witch stones.

Their hum deadens the air. The nothingness I felt before concentrates around him: this tall man who holds a bell in both hands.

A witch hunter. Denis said he would send for one. It seems he arrived.

I can't feel the land. If I try to break the bindings with him here, I won't succeed.

"Stand back," he calls to the soldiers. "A sorcerer is dangerous, even a wounded one."

Wounded. Not dead. I bite my lip against gasping in relief.

"Where's the other one?" the witch hunter barks.

I am right here. Behind him. But there's another man between me and him. That man turns, and sees me. In the dark, it takes him a moment to register the fact that I'm not a soldier. The bulky, unfitted shape of my clothes gives me away.

I dive to the other side of the stone just as he swears. "There!" They haven't reloaded their muskets.

Not yet. And it's dark.

I run, darting through the center of the stones, my heartbeat scattering in my ears.

Musket fire explodes. Just two. They must not have fired before.

I dodge behind another stone. Safe.

Except for the burning along my lower back. It rubs, raw and tender, against the rough stone. I hiss.

I've been hit.

I reach behind me, feel for the wound. Wetness touches my hand. I curse.

They're reloading their muskets—I hear the *clink* of powder flasks. I grind my teeth together. I have to act now. Where is the witch hunter?

I peer around the stone. They're all just shadows in the dark.

My witch stone is burning a hole in my pocket. I pull it out. It fizzes and hums. It's not as strong as the stones the hunter has, but as I hold it, it begins to burn. Its hum vibrates with me—a deeper, stronger vibration than the witch hunter's stones. Heat flashes up my arms, deep into the pit of my stomach. I look down. Light is vibrating out from the stone's clear quartz surface, radiating up my arms—a brilliant white light that seems to be dissolving my body. I am no longer quite there, no longer quite substantial. It's as if I'm becoming one with the stone, as if my body is turning into a clear surface that reflects light.

All their eyes are adjusted to the dark. If I step out . . .

I run into the space between two stones, burning, shining. The soldiers fling up their hands with groans, cursing me. Someone's musket goes off in the wrong direction. I run through them, right up the slope until I see the witch hunter.

He turns toward me, his eyes squinted shut. Blinded. And unarmed.

I stab my dagger into his throat. He falls.

My witch stone hums, deeper and brighter than the stones lining his bandolier, as if in triumph.

Jahan is still on the ground behind him, but I can't go to him. I have to run.

Muskets bellow again as I dash back down the ridge and behind another stone, my jaw tight with rage. The burning light from the witch stone subsides, shrinking back down into the stone itself, no longer radiating through my body. I run to another stone, invisible again in the dark. I have to do this—for my country, for Jahan's sacrifice. Now.

My hands are wet with blood. The witch hunter's—and my own. I touch the wound on my lower back, hissing at the pain of my own dirty fingers touching it, then press my fingertips to the stone in front of me.

It begins to hum.

And from the other side of the circle, I hear a familiar, hoarse voice call out. "Take him to the castle! Where's the girl?"

When did the Butcher get here?

Oh gods, *gods*! I have to act fast. I race to the next stone, smearing it with my blood. The soldiers are shouting; the Butcher is shouting. I'm practically invisible in the dark, and—I glance behind me—the ancestors are appearing from the stones in flashes of brilliant light. A man screams.

Far off, the explosions continue at the garrison.

"I'm surrounded by imbeciles!" the Butcher bellows as I reach the next stone and slather it with more of my blood. My legs are shaking; the wound gapes open on my back, spurting a fresh, hot wash of blood into my shirt.

I don't have time to spare for pain or even rage. I have to complete this. I have to wake this circle, even if it kills me.

I run, staggering, to the next stone. I'm halfway around the circle now. The light of the ancestors jars my night vision; I can't tell how many of the soldiers have gone, only that there seem to be fewer voices.

Of course, as I'm going from stone to stone, the ancestors flaring bright, it won't be hard for them to track me. I should turn around, double back, try to confuse them.

It's hard to stop, but I do. I turn.

The Butcher is stepping between the stones directly behind me.

I reach automatically for my dagger, but I left it in the witch hunter's throat. The Butcher doesn't know that, though. His eyes are still squinted against the light.

His hands are empty. There's a pistol strapped at his hip. He hasn't seen me yet.

It's time to take the risk. We're as alone as we're going to get; I don't see or hear any soldiers. Right now, despite the Butcher's crimes, despite everything, I have to trust my mother. And I know that winning will be easier with him on our side.

"Lord Gilbert," I call. He squints in my direction. "I could do away with you now, but I'm not going to. I know the truth about you, and I believe you can help us. I *want* you to help us."

His gaze focuses on me, but he doesn't call my bluff even though he must guess I couldn't really kill him. "Is that so?"

I persevere, despite the blood trickling from my wound, despite the time running out. "Under the new order, no one would force you to lead a war you don't believe in, against people who used to be your friends. It's a chance for all of us to make amends. To redeem ourselves. To start again."

He's frowning deeply, but he only says, "Lady Elanna, are you wounded?"

"When I come to the city gate," I persist, "you'll have your chance. One chance, to prove your loyalty to me. Do you choose me, or Loyce? It's your decision. But I hope you choose me."

Down the hill, someone shouts. We both startle, staring toward the source of the noise. Then the Butcher turns back and meets my eyes.

"Would you have a nation of living magic, Lady Elanna, when it means you risk the black ships and the emperor's wrath? You aren't saving yourself or Caeris or Eren; you're putting all our people in greater danger than ever."

"It's better to stand for a cause than die in obscurity."

"Is it?" he says, and scratches his chin.

More shouts echo from down the hill, resolving into one voice crying his name. *"Lord Gilbert! Insurgents! The garrison—the city!"* The Butcher half turns, but stops himself. He looks at me.

"Those are my people," I say. "Or—ours."

He reaches for his pistol. I tense all over, but then there's another shout from down the hill. *Lord Gilbert! They're storming the streets!*

I'm shaking all over with pain and the fear of the gun and the urgency of completing my work here. After all this, he's not going to kill me now. Is he? He should. "This is your opportunity," I say. "You could help us. You could be better than this."

"Why would I do that, Lady Elanna?" But he doesn't fire the gun. And as he glances over his shoulder at the latest shout from below—*Lord Gilbert! To the castle!*—I dash between the stones, back into the circle, rushing to the next stone. It flares with light, and when I peer around it to where the Butcher stood moments before, he's gone. I see his silhouette running down the hill; shots are being fired in the streets below the castle.

He could have come after me; he could have shot me from behind. Still, I know better than to assume my words made any difference.

I have to wake the circle. I rush on to the next stone, and the next, until the whole circle is humming. Until the light coalesces into a blinding ring. I sag in the center, against the altar stone; its rough gray skin scrapes my hands. So it has been anointed, too, by my blood. Around me the circle of ancestors, men and women in ancient garments, grasping spears and scepters, flares white. And then they begin to cry out.

"Mo cri, mo tire, mo fiel. Mo cri, mo tire, mo fiel!"

I shove myself upright. I've woken them. This is the moment. "My heart, my land, my blood!" I shout back to them.

It's time to set them free.

Sing them free, Tuah said. *You know the song.*

The only melody in my head is the one I've known all my life— the one my mother wrote for me when I was a child. Except she didn't invent it; she heard a melody beneath the grief of the stones at Cerid Aven. Her musician's ears made sense of the chaos of noise, where mine couldn't—where no one else's could. She must have spent hours listening, teasing it out and crafting it into a true melody. She couldn't have known it was the key to waking the land.

THE WAKING LAND   355

It's the song the golden pines make. The keening of the stones above Cerid Aven. The song only my mother could hear. The true song, beneath the story of their grief; all of it, the same song, uniting all of Caeris.

My voice is thin and scratchy. I have no range. Nor can I recall the words my mother set to the music, the ones that Sophy sang. *"In dreams and silence,"* I venture. At last I give up on the words and simply hum.

The earth pulses into life beneath me and I match my voice to the sound of it until we're humming in unison, trading notes, splitting apart and coming back together.

The land unfolds. It opens. It *wakes.*

And it pulls me in.

I close my eyes, which are leaves. I swallow, and a stream moves down a mountainside. I taste an early-winter acorn from the ground. I am aware of the layers of soil under me, the thoughts of each rock and tree, the anxious movements of the animals.

My arms drop to my sides. Then I fall to my knees. But I'm like Ossian. I don't collapse.

A great *crack* deafens me. My eyes fly open; I'm on my feet. It's the altar stone beside me. It seems to be exploding from within— radiating with light. Light runs in shining lines from it to the other stones around the circle. I've stopped humming, but the melody continues. My ancestors have taken it up. It echoes around me, waves of sound, as the light from the altar bursts into each of the stones around the circle.

I sang to the land, and it woke. And its waking has broken the bindings at last.

The light seems to implode inside me—in my head, my chest, my gut—as well as through the earth. I'm thrown back down, to my knees, to my side. The wound in my back is screaming with pain. I have to get up. I have to command the earth and the ancestors.

But my mind is being pulled away—north, high up, to a woman in a stone circle on a mountainside. Granya. She looks down the hills that form my body. My brother and sister stones open their eyes. The golden pines dip their branches; they tear their roots from the ground. Stones and trees begin to sing.

This cannot be. I dig my fingers into the turf, trying to bring myself back to reality. The circle at Dalriada can't have broken its binding—I wasn't there, I didn't do it—

But again I'm drawn away, to a different ring of stones. The Sentry Rock over Cerid Aven. These stones are singing now, too. My song; their song. The song that echoes in my bones.

Then my mind is spread wide as circles all over Caeris begin to sing.

Is it *all* of them? All at once? The whole land, waking?

I am wrenched south, farther and farther, to a ridge overlooking a city, where a warrior leaps from the stone and shouts, *"Mo cri, mo tire, mo fiel!"*

The whole city rings with it. All of Laon. All of *Eren.*

The circles in both Eren and Caeris have thrown off their bonds. The entire land has woken. This is more than I ever expected—more power, more awareness. By freeing one circle, I've freed them all. All of my ancestors. Every piece of Tuah's spell is shattering.

I am swelling, overflowing, too large for my skin. I have no skin. I have the covering of forests, the girdle of rivers, the crown of mountains. I have two bodies: the human, and the land. The human is frail, but the land is awake. And she has been chained too long, bound along with my ancestors.

But now she begins to move.

I OPEN MY eyes.

The world rushes in my ears as I sit up. Figures burn around me in the circle—men and women, my ancestors, set free from the stones. Standing at attention surrounding me, waiting for me to tell them my bidding.

The *land* is waiting for me to tell it my bidding. All of Eren and Caeris.

My witch stone twitches in my hand and I clamber to my feet. The blood still seeps from my wound, but no longer as thick. It sags in the waist of my pants.

I don't have a lot of time.

How does one communicate with the land? With *ghosts*? A map of the earth seems to run through my muscles and bones: I feel the weight of the mountains above Dalriada, the flowing rivers, the denseness of trees, the press of the sea against the shore. I can touch the minds of the creatures that live in the land. It's all there, part of me.

And it's moving. It's *awake*.

"Come," I say simply, and the trees around Barrody leap into life, dragging their hoary roots from the ground. I feel the weight of them thrumming through the earth, walking to surround the city's walls. The river that flows out of Lake Harbor turns into a different channel, rerouting itself so that it floods over the road leading south. A flock of crows rushes to my summons, crying out over the city and the burning garrison. Fog gathers, woolly and dense, along the shores of Lake Harbor.

I whisper to the land, and a hill shoves sideways to block the road between Barrody and the Ereni army. The whole earth seems to tremble. I stagger, but remain standing.

I send more trees to surround the Ereni army and, for good measure, reroute two more streams and whisper to the clouds to deluge the soldiers with rain. I don't know if the clouds will obey, but they do. It won't be a pleasant day to be an Ereni soldier.

The walking trees are clearing a path for my army, for the mountain people, down to Barrody. It won't take my people long to get here now.

I open my eyes. The ancestors still surround me, waiting. Shining.

"Go outside the city walls," I order them. "Let the soldiers see you among the trees. And when my army arrives, call your brothers and sisters from the other circles. Call your armies from the memory of the past. On my order, show yourselves!"

I look around for confirmation that my orders have been heard, but the ancestors simply disappear, as if swallowed by thin air. I'm suddenly alone, surrounded by an empty circle of stones that are only stones now, not vessels for my ancestors' spirits. Yet, even so, they hum. They still have a power of their own, as Granya said. But light, shining, no longer bound in death and sorrow.

Dawn lights pink on the eastern horizon.

I have to go. I take a step forward and stumble, almost falling.

My trousers are soaked with blood. A gasp escapes me. Pain grinds through my back. I'm losing too much blood, and I can feel the flesh gaping open at my wound site, the pockmark effects of the shot peppering my skin.

I'm not going to make it back to the army. I could take off my neckcloth and wrap it around my hips, but that won't be enough. The wound is too open, the blood still flowing too freely.

Yet I refuse to sit here, waiting for help, and miss my own victory.

The humming of the stones around me shifts in frequency. They once had an intelligence of their own, Granya told me, a kind of magic that could be harnessed by a sorcerer with enough power— which is what Tuah did. But the *Caveadears* used this energy, too.

I drop back down to the altar stone. It's a relief to sit. I spread my hand over the stone's gritty surface. I can see the white speckles of quartz; the daylight is growing.

"Will you help me?" I ask the stone.

As if in answer, the humming deepens, aching up into my body, pulsing through my veins. I hear myself groan. Then I feel, low on my back, my skin begin to crawl. It *sews* itself together, sealing out the dirt from my hands and the ground.

I'm shuddering, shaking all over. My body pulses cold, then hot. A sudden, unbearable thirst dries out my throat.

The humming recedes. I touch the wound, just to be sure, but indeed the skin is healed over. Only the blood remains, sticky and cold.

"Thank you," I say to the stones.

I push myself to my feet. My head swims a little, then steadies. I walk to the edge of the circle. Smoke puffs into the air from the castle chimneys. The Butcher has Jahan there, prisoner. Or does he? If my plea made any difference—if my mother and the weight of his own conscience made any difference—maybe the Butcher is willing to help us. We'll see if he takes the opportunity to prove his loyalty once we arrive at the gates.

Either way, I have to believe that Jahan is safe and can fend for himself. I have to wait to find him, for the sake of my country.

The trees have begun to move down from the top of the ridge. A storm of birds bursts into the air above the stone circle. From here,

I can glimpse the city walls and the notched stone of the north gate. Beyond the ramparts, it's dark with trees. The sun muddles through the fog rising from Lake Harbor.

I allow myself a smile. Then, one foot in front of the other, I make my way toward the army that will soon be amassing on the other side of the gate.

CHAPTER THIRTY-ONE

A battalion of trees meets me en route to the city gates. They crawl like massive spiders on their roots, flinging dirt into the air; the wind hisses through their branches. I have a sudden, irrational fear that they'll trample me if I get too close—but instead they part so that I'm walking amid them, like a general surrounded by her regiments.

Birds circle overhead. It's hard to see much else through the dense, moving trunks and branches except for patches of lightening sky.

"Surround the walls," I command the trees, and a great line of them peels off to obey me. Twenty or so remain, their roots skritching through the soil, an honor guard escorting me to the road.

We descend an embankment and arrive on the northern road at the same moment as my army's outriders come into view around the curve. Behind me, near the city walls, I hear men shouting.

I hail the outriders. They greet me and my tree guard with a mixture of reverence and terror.

In a few minutes, Hugh, Rhia, and the others catch up and surround me; even on horseback, they seem small among the shifting trees. Hugh gives me a smile and a small nod, and the pride in his eyes makes me stand even taller. This is what he brought me back to Caeris for.

Rhia pulls up right in front of me. Her eyes are enormous. I look back at her. Then she breaks into a laugh and points at me. "I was right about you, Elanna Valtai!" She punches her fist into the air. "Caveadear Caer-Ys!"

All the others take up the shout. *"Caveadear Caer-Ys!"*

I hold up my hands for a moment to accept their adulation, trying not to smile too broadly. We haven't won yet.

Hugh's second in command has a spare horse for me, but I decline to mount. I need to feel the earth under my feet. "Keep in formation," I order Rhia, Hugh, and their commanders, who relay it to those beyond them. "And stay back. Let the ancestors take the brunt of any attack the Ereni might attempt. It's my hope we'll terrify them into surrendering without bloodshed, but I don't want to lose any of our people."

While they assemble behind me, I focus myself, digging my roots into the land. I feel for the ancestors; I still have some doubt that they'll come, or that I'll even sense them. But I do: They shift like unseen fire, waiting.

"Ancestors," I call, and they appear in ranks surrounding us, their light blinding in the dimness of the trees. There are hundreds—thousands—of them. The nearest have come from the circle above Barrody, for I recognize their faces, but they must indeed have summoned their brothers and sisters and the armies of the past. The armies are not only human: I see a ghostly cavalcade of deer and the lumbering forms of bears among people carrying pikes and claymores. Not all the humans hold weapons. Some are armed with glowing stones and carved staffs, and one grasps nothing but a candle.

And among them are the ghosts of trees: golden pines shining brighter than the rest.

Rhia's horse startles, but she keeps her seat. Around us other horses are shying, and the warriors are shouting at one another. "It's the past!" I hear someone say. "No," someone else answers, "it's the *Caveadear!*"

Alone among them all, Hugh is gazing around in wonder, as if marking each ancient face.

At last everyone settles. I glance at Rhia. My mouth is dry, but I'm damned if I'll let her sense my nerves. She raises her eyebrows at me. A challenge.

I nod. "Let's go."

I march forward, and they follow. The ancestors lead the way, glowing through the tree trunks. I have to trust that Sophy, Alistar, and the Barrody underground have finished with the garrison and reached the north gate—but even if they haven't, I have another plan.

The bricks of the gate become visible through the trees. My ancestors surround them, a silent, near-translucent force, all the more terrifying for the light that emanates from them. I pause on the edge of the trees. The gates are closed; neither the underground nor, more unlikely yet, the Butcher has opened them. Spots of blue and gold reveal soldiers up on the ramparts, but among the shining ancestors, the mist seeping in from Lake Harbor, and the shifting trees, I doubt they've seen me.

I touch the ancestor nearest me. Her substance fills my hand with a hot buzz. She looks like one of the older ones, a mountain woman with spirals decorating her face, a horned helmet on her head, and a broadsword in her hand. "Ask the Ereni to surrender," I tell her.

She makes a fist at her heart and strides away, impossibly fast, to the ground below the gate. *"Barrody!"* she bellows. "Do you surrender?"

No one answers from the ramparts.

The gates are wood, reinforced with iron. The wood is old, rotten in places; these gates haven't been used to keep assailants out in decades or more, so confident have the Ereni governors been in their hold on Caeris. I reach into the wood for the lingering warmth of life, a green streak in my mind, and I murmur to it to grow. To open.

Branches burst out of the planks, warping the gate. Someone screams on the other side. The ground shudders as the gates take root in the earth and the roots crawl through the ground, like my army of trees, until the gates swing open.

More people are shouting inside the walls. A musket blasts off, spraying shot into the trees. A man bellows, "Hold your fire!"

The Butcher. But I don't wait to see if he intends to help.

Again, the ancestor by the gates shouts, "Barrody, your gates are breached! Do you surrender?"

No answer.

I reach for the cobblestones that pave the road. They shake. The ground beneath them shakes. The soldiers on the ramparts are moving in a blur of blue and gold—running, I think, most of them.

One last time, my ancestor shouts, "Barrody! Surrender!"

But their running is good enough for me. The ancestors surge through the gate—and several trees follow, without my permission. I order the rest to stay back. Hugh, Rhia, and our force come behind me.

As we approach the gate, a group of Ereni soldiers plunges out of the gatehouse. I swear, reaching again for the dagger I don't have, as they swarm among the ancestors and the trees. But then I realize they're holding their bayonets over their heads, and on someone's order, they all drop to their knees.

The Butcher steps out from among them. He has another man by the collar. "Lady Elanna," he calls, "this is Master Villeneuve, captain of the city guard. Tell the *Caveadear* you surrender."

"I surrender," the man gasps. "Barrody surrenders."

"Barrody is ours!" I cry out for the benefit of my troops. Then I look at the Butcher, who meets my eyes with a cool nod. "And you, Lord Gilbert?"

He drops to one knee. "I pledge myself to the *Caveadear* of Caeris."

Beside me, Hugh swears and mutters, "How did you manage this one, El?"

I allow myself a smile.

The Butcher leaves the soldiers with orders to stand down and comes to join us, though Hugh pins him with an openly hostile stare. I pretend not to notice; we'll confront the Butcher's history and crimes later. "Where's Denis Falconier?" I ask him.

"Still at the castle."

"And Jahan?"

The Butcher raises an eyebrow and points at the gate. "Right there."

I stare. It *is* Jahan, standing on the other side of the gate, as whole and hale as if he never fell beneath musket fire not two hours ago. He's watching us approach, hands on his hips. Grinning.

"He broke all our guns," the Butcher grumbles. "I don't know what we'll do to repair them."

But I can't hold myself back any longer. I'm walking fast, and then I'm running, and then I've grabbed Jahan Korakides by his hair and pulled his face down to mine, kissing him in front of everyone. Let him just try to stop me. "You're *alive*," I say against his mouth.

He pulls away, still grinning. "It's very hard to kill me."

"But they shot you! I thought you were dead!"

"This"—he touches his chest—"is just skin and bone. It's easy enough to knit back together, if you know how to do it."

I'll have to get a real explanation later because, through the gate, I see a great mob of people coming down the street toward us. They're brandishing a flag: a red creature on white. The Dragon. It's the Barrody underground, and Alistar Connell is running ahead with the flag in his hands, giving the Hounds of Urseach's ululating cry. Others join him.

Jahan grabs my hand and we both stride forward, through the gate. Almost immediately, we're overtaken by Alistar and the crowd of Caerisians chanting, *"Caveadear! Tire Caer-Ys!"*

Sophy comes barreling toward me, too, her face flushed, also shouting.

They're nearly out of control. I bellow to Hugh to have the trumpets blown. Then Alistar and Jahan offer to hold me up so I can address the crowd; I step into their cupped hands and am lifted. The mob shouts louder yet when they see me. I wave at them until, finally, they quiet. The men's arms, holding me, are rock-solid.

"Caerisians!" I shout. "The city has surrendered, but the duke has not! We must take the castle!"

They cheer, and they're moving almost before the words are out of my mouth, surging in a river of bodies toward the boulevard to the palace. I scramble down. Sophy grabs my arm. "Where do you want me?"

"Beside me, until we take the castle. Then you address the people, and I'll take care of Denis."

We're already being propelled along, and Alistar and the others shout for the crowd to make way so that Sophy, Rhia, Jahan, and I can shove our way toward the front. We're still well back, and by the time we arrive in the castle courtyard a man is at the front door on his knees, surrendering. "The castellan," the Butcher tells me. A Caerisian man drives a fist into the castellan's face.

Before I have time to think, I'm racing forward, shoving people aside. Another man has joined the first, and another; they're going to beat the castellan to death.

"Stop!" I shout. No one hears me.

So I point at the earth. A shrub struggles out of the ground between the men and the castellan, surging upward into a sapling, to a tree.

I stare at my own hand. I didn't know I could make a tree grow *that* fast.

Maybe waking the land has made my own magic even greater.

It's shocked the men out of their bloodlust, though the castellan is lying on the ground, his hands covering the mess of his face. The men are all staring at me. Rhia cries out, "This is the *Caveadear Caer-Ys!*"

The men look suddenly frightened. The others around them have caught the words and raise a cheer.

I point at the wounded Ereni official and stare the men down. "There will be no fighting," I say to them, and to the crowd beyond. The earth roars under my feet. "This is not about Caeris and Eren anymore. Our countries are *one*—and they always have been. We are fighting for the freedom of *all* our land, not just one half of it."

A cheer runs through the crowd. I manage a smile. Perhaps if I can show them that one does not have to be Caerisian or Ereni—that one can be *both*—they will begin to believe it.

But it's going to take a lot of work.

Hugh is helping the injured castellan to stand, and just as I turn to Sophy, the Butcher taps my arm and jerks his chin toward the castle. "The duke's waiting."

"Get this man to safety," I call to Hugh. "I don't want this to get any more violent."

Then I look for Jahan. He nods at me. Together, we push through the crowd after the Butcher and into the castle, to find Denis.

* * *

THE BUTCHER STOPS in a side room on the second floor and comes back out with a pistol in his hand. It's loaded. He looks at Jahan with raised eyebrows. "I gather you didn't break the guns here in the castle?"

Jahan eyes the pistol. "Not yet."

The Butcher frowns, then shrugs and leads us on. At least, for once, he's not aiming it at me. Unless he's planning on taking me into the study and shooting me; unless this is an elaborate ruse.

Denis is in his study, throwing papers into a chest. He doesn't even seem to notice us walk in until the Butcher clears his throat.

That makes Denis straighten. He looks pale and angry; his suit is rumpled. He sees the Butcher first. "What's the word, Lord Gilbert? I want to get out of here before those savages—"

I step past the Butcher, and Denis stops. He stares from me to the Butcher to Jahan and back again.

Since he looks poleaxed, I decide to explain the situation to him. "The land is awake. The city is mine. Lord Gilbert is mine. *Caeris* is mine. And you, Denis Falconier, are under arrest for high treason for the murder of Antoine Eyrlai, king of Eren."

Denis's face turns red, almost purple. He snatches something off the desk—a paper knife. He's flying toward me. I fling up my hands—

Jahan and the Butcher move between us at the same time. There's a deafening explosion; a shot reverberates in the confines of the room.

Denis Falconier falls to the floor. I stare at the bloody mess of his face, unable to look away. My ears are ringing. Jahan is holding my elbow, saying my name.

The Butcher turns to us, lowering his pistol. "I hope you didn't want him alive, Lady Elanna. He really is the most appallingly tiresome man. *Was,* I should say."

I squeeze Jahan's fingers to let him know I'm all right, and face the Butcher. "Why did you kill him?"

"Execution is the proper punishment for regicides," the Butcher says. "Maybe you would have preferred the noose, or a trial, but really—after the events of today, no one will question it."

I stare at him. "How do you know he killed King Antoine?"

The Butcher nods at Jahan. "Lord Jahan told me his suspicions. And after we brought him down from the circle this morning, he had a confession from Lord Denis. It's close enough to proof for my purposes."

"He believed you?" I stare at Jahan, who shrugs.

"I already suspected it for the truth," Lord Gilbert says. "Denis Falconier was always much too smug to be a decent liar."

He seems about to add more, but running footsteps scuff into the study. A woman cries out, "Elanna!"

It's my mother, wearing a riding habit over her dressing gown, her hair wild around her head. She runs to me; I grasp her hands. She looks haggard, the circles dark beneath her eyes. Have they hurt her? Forced information from her? I don't think she's noticed Denis's corpse yet—but she must, because she says, "You did it. Caeris is ours!"

"Yes," I say, but then she sways a little, as if she's going to fall over. The Butcher comes up behind her, guiding her by the elbows, and between us we settle her down on a divan.

"Who let you out?" the Butcher is asking.

Mother shakes her head. "That servant girl, Annis. She picked the lock once the guards ran. It took her ages."

The lock? I drop down beside her. "What happened to you, Mother?"

"Denis," she says, and looks at his corpse with loathing.

"He discovered your mother . . ." the Butcher begins.

Mother gives him a look. "He discovered *us*—but he didn't have the wits to understand Lord Gilbert and I were collaborating in our discussion of troop movements and the land shifting, thank the gods. He thought Gilbert was extracting information from me. I had to buy him off with some stories about the old stone circles." She shakes her head. "Denis locked me up, of course."

So that's why the soldiers were there, waiting for us. The Butcher must comprehend the look on my face, because he says, "Lady Teofila did not give away anything Denis Falconier and the witch hunter didn't already suspect. They had read the accounts."

I look at my mother's wan face, and the fear that's dogged me clutches my throat again. "Did Denis harm you?"

"No. Only tried to starve more information out of me."

I study her careworn face, her body slight under the riding habit, and I throw my arms around her. "You are so brave, Mother. Thank you." She must know I mean more than her bravery; I mean for collaborating with the Butcher and showing me it was possible to bring him to our side. She leans back and cups my cheek with a smile.

I glance from her to the Butcher. "I'm so glad Denis didn't harm you. I thought—when the Ereni discovered the truth about the land shifting, I thought he must have forced it out of you."

Mother pales. "Gilbert?"

I stare at my mother and the Butcher, as they look at each other. The truth passes between them, painfully obvious.

She told him about the shifting in the land, hoping he would use it to help us, and instead he used it against us.

He says quietly, "In war, I must use all the knowledge at my disposal."

"You could have used anything but that," my mother whispers.

I stand up beside her. "You should have kept that silent."

To his credit, he meets my gaze. "I had not decided to help you then, Lady Elanna."

As if it's just that simple. Maybe it is, and maybe there's no use in being angry with him now. But how many people would still live, if he'd kept silent?

The Butcher has dropped his gaze, now, wiping and holstering his gun. He and Jahan stand on either side of Denis's body.

"I think the carpet's ruined," Jahan remarks.

I look at Lord Gilbert. His face is almost as worn as my mother's, and his shoulders seem bowed. But he came to our side. He cost us lives and towns and grief, but in the end he helped us to take Barrody.

He meets my eyes. "I trust," he says, gesturing at Denis's body, "that this at least proves my loyalty?"

If I stay angry, it makes me little better than Antoine Eyrlai, who did his best to render the Butcher inhuman. I want to say that I will never make him do the kinds of things Antoine Eyrlai forced him to do; I want to say that, with enough effort, he might even be able to redeem himself, at least in some eyes. I want to say that I am trying to forgive him.

But he also didn't need to kill Denis. He'd already pledged me his loyalty.

And he certainly didn't need to give away the secret about the shifts.

So I say, "You have. But you must be aware that many Caerisians—and not a few Ereni—still consider you their enemy. It will take a long time to change their minds. Once we've finished our work here, it might be best if you remained in the south."

He lifts an eyebrow, but then makes a short bow. "As you say."

"And," I add, "ultimately your appointment will rest with our council, not my sole choice. Consider yourself in a trial period, Lord Gilbert. But you've done well so far."

He takes this in stride. "I understand, Lady Elanna, and I will also support Sophy Dromahair, once she is elected queen. I shall do my best to ensure Eren's cooperation. The army, at least, I can guarantee."

I nod. "Then you will help me again. We have one more thing to do."

I can feel the land moving; we must take advantage before it stops, before the ancestors vanish into the spirit world.

And just opening my awareness to the land makes my mind fragment into pieces—or perhaps swell, huge, into a glorious whole. The moving forests seem to be shifting across my own body, and when the mountains rumble, scraping their plates together, it seems as if my own bones are rubbing. I can feel that Ingram Knoll, the mountain lords, and another army of trees and ancestors have surrounded the Ereni army just to the north of Barrody. And if I listen hard, I can even hear someone shouting, *We surrender!*

I try to focus back on my surroundings, on my mother, on Jahan, but I'm being drawn away again. The rivers are rising—a swelling I feel in my own blood, and the forests and the animals are still moving. The ancestors shine like brilliant stars on the earth.

There's a hand on my cheek. Jahan.

"El," he's saying, and I focus on his frown, the line by his mouth, the stubble on his jaw. He actually looks frightened. "You were gone."

I'm still being pulled from within, but if I look at him, if I flex my hands, I'm more in my body. I remember that I have a voice beyond the cries of animals and the sound of falling rain. I remember what I have to do, before the ancestors at last take their rest in the spirit realm, before the waking land escapes my control.

"We have to go to Laon," I say. "Now."

CHAPTER THIRTY-TWO

Laon smells of gunpowder. I'm standing outside the city, in the shelter of a moving forest, again; Rhia brought us here by the folds in the land, and the weeklong journey took less than a day, for the sun is just now lowering. The queen's men have been shooting at the army of trees and the specters of the ancestors that surround the walls, but now the Butcher has made his way inside to suborn the guard. The guns have stopped firing—either he succeeded in ordering the men to stand down, or Jahan managed to break the muskets. I've made all the city gates grow into misshapen trees and fling themselves open. Walls have fallen when I've spoken to the rocks. Sophy, beside me, is tense and breathless. On my other side, Alistar and Rhia are arguing about whether to approach the gates now.

Within me, the pulse of the land has risen to a roar. I'm not sure how much longer I can control it, the entire kingdom being awake. My chest and limbs have begun to feel heavy. Soon I need to let the land go, or I'll collapse.

But I can't lose control yet.

Just as I think I can't hold on any longer, the Eyrlai standard falls from the gate, and the Dragon rises in its place.

We advance into the city.

Jahan and the Butcher meet us inside the walls, flanked by a line of military men. Jahan's face is smeared with powder; he squeezes my elbow. "The guns are broken."

The Butcher nods. "Laon is yours, *Caveadear*." A nod at Sophy. "Your Majesty."

Sophy starts to protest that she hasn't yet been elected, but I shake her wrist to silence her. We'll see her elected once the dust has settled. For now, we need no one to question us.

Fewer people occupy the streets than I expected—I see them watching, instead, from windows and doorways as we pass. But as we draw nearer to the Queen's Square, more folk emerge from their homes, swelling up from the side streets, and soon there's a mob behind us bigger than the small force we brought here.

In the square, a crowd has already gathered, and Victoire is standing up on the speaker's platform. She shouts when she sees us. "The *Caveadear*! The queen!"

And the people roar their approval.

I grab the Butcher's arm. "Where's Loyce? The palace?"

He nods. "Give me half an hour to remove her guards, then you can march in and claim it."

I agree, and he slips away through the crowd, jerking his chin for several lieutenants to follow him.

Victoire is pulling Sophy up onto the speaker's platform now. Sophy has a speech prepared, shouting over my head, "People of Laon! I will give you what Loyce Eyrlai could not—a queen who serves her people first! Eren and Caeris may for generations have considered themselves different, but today they are united—under Elanna Valtai and myself!"

A woman is pushing toward me. Her face is marked with gunpowder, her hair is uncovered and her dress filthy, but she's smiling and I know her.

"*Hensey?*" I just barely manage not to scream, but I can't stop myself from running forward. Then I'm in her arms, holding her tight as Sophy's voice rings out above us.

"The Butcher told me you escaped," I whisper, because I can't speak any louder through the tightness in my throat.

Somehow she hears me. "I did, El. And we're both here. Still standing."

It almost seems like we really have won.

BUT WE STILL have to confront Loyce.

Just before I gather everyone to march on the palace, Victoire hops down from the speaker's platform and takes both my hands. Her gaze is intent, her voice pitched low. "There's news about your father, El."

Tears start in my eyes, as if my body knows what she's going to say before she says it.

"He was executed two days ago, in this very square." Her voice lowers still further. "On this very platform."

I think I'm going to be sick. I can't even speak. The tears won't even fall.

It's Sophy who cries out and crushes her fists to her mouth. I think she's going to fall to her knees; I reach for her at the same time as Jahan does. We hold her between us. She's sobbing silently, her whole body heaving, as if she's trying to hold the grief in but she can't. My eyes burn. She knew my father better than I ever did; he practically raised her. For her, this is an utter loss. For me, it is regret mixed with fury. Once again, the Eyrlais have stripped my father from me.

When her breathing calms, I embrace her. "You can stay here with Victoire," I whisper. "You don't need to come to the palace."

She yanks back from me. Her eyes are red. "That woman murdered him, El. I'm coming with you. I'm going to see her kicked out of that palace if it's the last thing I do!"

"Soph . . ." I begin, but then I don't say it. She pushes away, calling to the people around us. Jahan grasps my hand as we begin to move forward, shoved by the press of the crowd and Sophy's rage.

"You're not going to let them execute the queen, are you?" he says in my ear. "That is, I am sorry for your loss, but we've already gotten through this so bloodlessly . . ."

"I know. And if we let her die, it's just an excuse for someone else to come along and use vengeance to claim the throne."

"You could imprison her."

I shake my head a little, though not exactly in denial. Depending on what happens when Loyce comes out of the palace, all these options must be faced.

When we arrive at the palace gate, it's standing open. Loyce's flag has been flung to the ground, trampled on. The former queen's guard stand on either side, their colors flung off and the uniforms cast onto the cobblestones, which means most of them are down to their shirtsleeves and waistcoats. A trickle of snow dusts our heads. The sun sinks; it's growing colder. The people press around the square, some of them pushing up into the palace compound itself, shoving aside the guards. "The new queen!" they shout, and, "The steward of the land!"

The Butcher is coming down the drive. Several soldiers walk behind him, and as they come closer I see they're pushing someone: a woman in an elaborate gown. Loyce.

Beside me, Sophy breathes hard through her nose.

I put a hand on her arm. They're almost to us. The Butcher steps to the side and grasps Loyce by the wrist, pulling her forward and then shoving her to the ground, so that her knees slam into the filthy cobblestones. She utters a shriek, fury mixed with pain. Half her hair is falling down; it looks as if someone grabbed her by it, ripping out the pins.

"Tell the *Caveadear* you surrender," the Butcher orders. He speaks quietly, but they're near enough I can hear him. The crowd around us has fallen silent at this new spectacle: their former queen on her knees.

I step toward them. I want Loyce to see me. I want her to surrender to *me*. Not Sophy, not Rhia, not even the Butcher. Me.

But she's glaring at Lord Gilbert. "I should have known you'd betray us. You have no principles. You didn't want this war, and now you're taking revenge on me for your family—"

His family? I stop short.

"This is not vengeance," the Butcher answers, "though the gods know you and your father have wronged me time and again. This is supporting a true queen—a queen who doesn't murder her own father to gain the throne."

Other people heard that; there are gasps around us. Loyce has gone white.

"Lord Gilbert," I call, "step back from Madame Eyrlai."

For a moment, I think he's going to ignore me. But then he nods and moves to the side.

Loyce makes no move to rise. She's looking at me now, at last. The word *madame* wasn't lost on her. She knows what it means: She's no longer the queen of Eren.

Before I can speak, she flings herself around, frantic. "Where's Denis? Have you thrown him in prison?"

I don't let the Butcher answer. "Your lover Denis Falconier is dead," I say, letting my voice ring out so that everyone nearby can hear. "He was found guilty of regicide, and executed for his crime."

Around us, people exclaim. "Murderer!" "Did she—?" "Patricide!"

It hits Loyce more slowly. Her face turns even whiter, and a strange, high-pitched noise rips from her throat. She doubles over, keening, her fingernails scrabbling at the cobblestones.

I take one step closer. Another. She must glimpse my boots through her falling hair; she rears up.

"Elanna Valtai!" she spits. "I might have known. You look as if you've walked out of a Caerisian pigsty."

I almost laugh. Instead I raise a hand. "You still don't understand, do you, Loyce? I'm not the hostage you mocked and derided for years. I'm the steward of the land now."

The power swells through me—a sweet, earthy warmth—and the cobblestones shake. Roots burst out of the ground, crawling over Loyce's ankles, tethering her down. She screams.

I lean closer to her. "Tell us you surrender."

She glares at me. "You *witch*!" But the Butcher kicks her slippered foot with his booted one, and she yelps.

"Father-killer!" someone shouts from the crowd.

Her head whips toward them.

"You will surrender," I say, and she looks back at me. "You will renounce all claims to the throne of Eren."

Her voice is almost too low to hear. "I surrender."

"Say it louder."

"I surrender!" There's a sneer under her words, but she says it.

"Good." I snap my fingers, and a cluster of ancestors spring, glowing, into being around us. This time, Loyce flinches but doesn't shriek. I look down at her. In the pallor of her face, her small eyes seem more pinched than ever; she's afraid, but she still stares up at me.

She's been abandoned by everyone—her ministers, her courtiers, her servants and retainers. Denis is dead. I wonder if the ministers called for her abdication as soon as the trees surrounded the city, as soon as our force appeared. I wonder how it must feel to be crushed like this, flung onto your knees in front of a person you've despised, surrounded by people who want you dead.

And I know what I must do.

I say at the top of my voice, "Loyce Eyrlai, by my authority as steward of the land, you are herewith banished from the lands of Eren and Caeris. You will lay aside all pretensions to queenship, and neither you nor your children nor their children shall make any claim to the throne of Eren. A party of my people will escort you and your husband to the border of Tinan. King Alfred will grant you sanctuary, since he is your husband's cousin. You will remain there, in exile, for the rest of your life. Neither you nor your heirs will ever again cross the border into Eren, or I will have the land tear you apart."

The roots tighten around Loyce's ankles. She gasps.

The square is completely silent. Even the Butcher looks astonished. Loyce herself is openmouthed. I realize they all expected me to take her captive, to put her in the Tower, to give her a trial and execute her just like she did my father.

But I am not like her.

I nod to the Butcher. "Arrange a carriage for Madame Eyrlai and her husband, along with an escort, as befits a former queen." I glance again at Loyce; she swallows. I want to say something, a final dismissal, to make sure she understands what I've done. But in the end, I simply step past her and gesture toward the palace. "Queen Sophy, this place is now yours."

I STRIDE UP to the grand, gilt doors, with Sophy at my shoulder. She's furious, her hands clenched at her sides, but she won't vent her anger publicly. I pretend not to notice, and I also pretend I don't feel the tremor running through my body, a sudden cold. Awareness of the earth is pulling at me again, trying to draw me wide open. I have to hold it off, just a little longer.

Inside the palace, it's chaos. Some people are trying to get out past us; others fling themselves in our path with protestations of loyalty.

Guards are yelling after one man who's carrying out a king's ransom of trinkets stacked in a basket. We pass several footmen in a corner, throwing their wigs on the tiles and trying to light them on fire. Out of the corner of my eye, I see Jahan put the fire out and sweep up behind the footmen, his hands on their shoulders. Whatever he says makes them snap to attention.

Then we're up the stairs, into the grand audience chamber, where several people are trying to saw the gilt legs off the furniture.

"Stop that at once!" I shout, clapping my hands. "This palace belongs to Queen Sophy now!"

They flee, making obsequious noises, as our people flood the room. Sophy orders the doors closed.

The land is tearing at the edges of my mind, but I turn to her. "You'll need to make a speech—"

"You let Loyce go, El. She should have had a trial. She should be in a *cell*."

I focus on Sophy's face; greenness is blurring my vision. "You understand why I had to do it, don't you? If we executed her, we'd be reviled as regicides, the same as she is, and the violence would never end. Someone else could claim the throne in her name, avenging the wrong done her. It's better this way. Her fear will keep her in check."

Sophy puts her hands on my arms, bringing her face close to mine. "She killed Ruadan. I don't understand—I don't understand how you can be *merciful*." She's weeping.

"We have to be merciful, Soph." I'm so tired. "If we're not, then what are we? What have we changed?"

The door opens; we both look around. It's Victoire, followed by the Butcher. Victoire rushes toward us. "The people are still at the gates! They want to see you again, Your Majesty. Just a few words, to assure them things are over for the night."

Sophy rubs her eyes on her sleeve. She squeezes my hand, then turns to Victoire. "Very well."

They go, and I start to follow, but stumble. Jahan is at my elbow in a moment, hugging me against him. "Let Sophy do this on her own. You don't need to be there."

"But I'm the *Caveadear*—"

"Exactly. You've woken the land, and you're exhausted."

I let him hold me back. The door closes, but the Butcher is still waiting. I smother a groan. "Lord Gilbert?"

"Loyce Eyrlai and her husband are on their way to Tinan," he says. "I thought it best that they leave at once."

I look at him. "What has she done to your daughters?"

He winces. "They are alive yet, Lady Elanna, to my knowledge. The former queen and I had a . . . disagreement over this war against Caeris. When I tried to resign from my post, she had my girls locked up."

I stare. So this was what pushed him over to our side in the end, I realize—not only my mother and belief in our cause, but a hatred of the Eyrlais so deep he could no longer abide it. I find myself saying, "Then you must send for word of them at once."

"If you'll excuse me, I will do that." He bows and goes out.

Jahan frowns after him. "I know we need his support, but he isn't exactly a *comforting* presence, is he?"

I snort and open my mouth to answer, but a wave of cold guts me. Now that everyone else has gone, I'm aware of the land again, like a second skin pulling mine wide open. When I look up, my ancestors crowd the room, so many of them, so bright their light hurts my eyes.

They've completed their work. I feel their struggle to remain rooted in this world like a pain in my own body.

"Thank you," I say to them. "You may go. *Mo cri, mo tire, mo fiel.*"

The light grows even more blinding—and then they leave in a great gasp, carrying with them their armies and the lingering pieces of the past. The whole binding unravels in one final blow, and I seem to be falling with it. I feel the vastness of the land moving, shifting underfoot, the rivers and forests flung off their natural courses.

I woke the land. Now I have to stop it from turning into chaos. Granya's stories don't say anything about that.

I reach again for the land, feeling it course through my own body, and an answer comes to me. The land is always moving. Even the great plates of rock under the surface of the earth are shifting—a movement I feel in my bones. So it's not that I must stop it; it's that I must quiet it.

I let my inner senses swell, vast enough to hold all of Eren and Caeris, and I whisper, "Hush."

A great ripple runs through the earth, as if it sighs. And though forests and rivers are still moving more than they ought to, their agitation has lessened. It may take time before the land quiets back to its natural rhythm, but it's begun.

Yet I am still so vast. As if I contain all of Eren and Caeris within me.

Somewhere in the smallness of the audience chamber, in my confined, human body, an arm comes around my waist. Jahan murmurs in my ear, "I've got you."

He settles me onto a divan and finds a soft knitted blanket to cover me. I'm so tired my eyes have fallen shut, but there's one thing I need to know before I succumb to exhaustion. I grab for Jahan's arm and catch his wrist; he's crouched beside me. "Tell me how *you* knit skin and bone back together."

A soft laugh escapes him. He smooths back the hair from my forehead. "You talk to it, softly, like this. You form an image in your mind and tell it what you want it to do. You say something like, *Come together, nice and snug, perfectly shaped, well grown.*"

It sounds almost like a nursery rhyme, and I slide even closer toward sleep. I force the other question out. "And how do you get strong again?"

"I call to any power around me—anything that lives or grows. The earth, a fire."

Like the stones above Barrody. I'm smiling. "I knew it. I knew you were a little like me."

He laughs again. "I am very little like you, Elanna Valtai, and that is what makes me love you."

There must be a clever response to this, but I'll leave it for morning. I let myself fall into sleep, my hand still clasping his wrist.

EPILOGUE

The council acclaims Sophy queen in a unanimous vote.

Representatives from all the clans of Caeris stream into Barrody in the two weeks following our victory—mountain people and lowlanders alike mingling in the town and castle. Yesterday, Sophy took up the key and scepter—the symbols of Caeris's monarchs—in the castle's great hall, while anyone who wished came to pay her homage. It was a long ceremony and I left early; my feet hurt from standing for hours, and my mouth ached from smiling. I don't know how Sophy managed it. She's strong, but it will be a long time before she loses the weight of grief from Father's and Finn's deaths. It will be a long time before any of us will.

Jahan and I came down to Cerid Aven afterward. Next week there will be another vote, this time in Laon, with the same results expected; after all, no other candidates have come forward to challenge Sophy. And after that, there will be more meetings as we decide how this country with two capitals is to function. Sophy has already said she will deputize two first ministers to maintain order from both Barrody and Laon, while she herself travels between. Beneath the ministers will be a parliament of representatives from the clans in Caeris and from the towns in Eren.

It's a start.

And for a few days, we have the peace of Cerid Aven. The house feels strangely empty with just Jahan and myself here; even the staff has been reduced to a handful after the Butcher claimed Sophy and my mother. Mother is in Barrody now, overseeing the reorganiza-

tion of the city government and writing music for Sophy's coronation. Hugh is there, too; he'll almost certainly be elected first minister
of Caeris, and he and Ingram Knoll are busy rewriting our legal
codes. Rhia has attached herself to Sophy as a kind of bodyguard,
along with Alistar, and for the time being they are busy arguing
politics and the use of magic in government.

Sophy transferred the Butcher to Eren, once he oversaw the initial
withdrawal of military forces from Caeris; he's now reposting the
men to the borders by land and sea. It's wise, I think, to keep him
out of Caeris now, for his crimes have not been forgotten.

A few days ago, Victoire sent a letter from Laon, telling me that
Guerin had returned to the city. Loyce had dispatched him to a
prison south of Laon; now he and any others wrongfully incarcer-
ated have been freed.

And we have no more to fear from Loyce. Following our victory
at Laon, Sophy appointed a new ambassador to King Alfred in
Tinan—Count Hilarion of Ganz. He both smoothed the way for
negotiations between our nations and reported back to us that the
deposed queen and king of Eren arrived safely at the foreign court.

The latest news, come this morning over breakfast, suggests that
the Paladisan emperor may be looking less favorably upon our bid
for freedom. Rumors claim he's ordered the black ships to set sail
for our shores, to punish us for the use of magic to achieve our freedom.

"You don't think the emperor will send them, do you?" I ask
Jahan. "Knowing what I can do, would he really declare war against
us?"

Jahan frowns. His eyes are distant as he touches the scar behind
his ear. He's thinking of his brothers, I know. One of them is a student at a military academy near Ida. If we go to war with Paladis,
will it put this boy in danger?

"Maybe I ought to go back to Ida," he says, looking at me. "If I
could speak with Leontius—if I could prevent repercussions . . ."

"Can you stop the witch hunters?" I say gently, leaning forward
to put my hand on his arm. "Can you change two centuries of suspicion and persecution?"

"No. Not alone. But maybe I could stop the worst from happening . . ."

I study his face. "Do you want to go back?"

He winces a little, then shakes his head. "I don't know, El. It is home. I don't want to leave you, though—not yet, not now. But if it would help . . ."

"We don't know that. We don't know what the empire will do. So stay."

He looks at me, and a sudden grin transforms him. "Stay? With the *Caveadear* of Eren and Caeris?"

I roll my eyes. "Is that such a dreadful prospect?"

"On the contrary." He comes around the table and pulls me up into his arms so quickly the breath is swept from my lungs. "Nothing makes me happier."

I smile as I lean up to kiss him, then duck out of his arms to collect our coats. "Come."

Winter has fallen. We make our way through a woods softened by snow and up the ridge to the Sentry Rock. The stones *thrum* with energy as we approach and, when I put my hands on them, they begin to sing.

I hum in harmony with them.

The day after our victory, the forests and hills and water stopped moving. Some things went back to the way they were before the land woke, but some others rooted themselves in new places. Barrody has a vanguard of trees surrounding its northern wall, while Laon's main road is blocked by the river it once crossed. But bridges can be rebuilt, and the dense forest around Barrody seems almost comforting. And now I know, if I wish the land to move for me again, I need only call.

I let myself sink into the land, feeling it unspool around me: the sea cradling the mountains and rivers, the high hills and soft glens, the farmland and forest of Caeris and Eren. My land, free.

And I realize I've done more than free the land—I've freed myself. I am the *Caveadear,* and I have woken the land before the whole world. I don't know what the future will bring, if the empire of Paladis will declare war on us or worse, or what other battles we will have to fight. But I have given my heart to this land and these people, and together we will withstand anything.

There's a touch on my arm, and I look up to find Jahan standing next to me. He's looking out over the black-and-white winter landscape. Almost to himself, he says, "There's something about this land. It's in my blood, now."

I wrap my arm around his and grin up at him. "Maybe you wedded the land, too. Maybe it wasn't just me."

He looks at me, and meets my grin with his own. "Whatever the case, Elanna Valtai, I have you now."

"Maybe," I say, "we should make sure." I pull his head down so his mouth fits against mine. The hum of the stones around us grows deeper.

I tuck my hand into his and, together, we start down the ridge through the softly falling snow. Behind us, the stones continue to sing.

ACKNOWLEDGMENTS

A book is like an ecosystem: It needs nourishment from so many sources. I couldn't have made this on my own.

Thank you to my phenomenal editor, Anne Groell, not only for her humor and insight but for continuing to teach me so much about this craft. I can't overstate my gratitude to my wonderful agent, Hannah Bowman, whose enthusiasm for this book still amazes me; without her encouragement to revise, this book would never have made its way into the world. My gratitude goes to the team who created the cover and interior design—Ben Perini, Kathleen Lynch, Diane Hobbing, and David Stevenson—for making this story's wrappings look more beautiful than I could have imagined. Thank you also to the teams at Del Rey Books and Liza Dawson Associates, as well as my UK publisher, Hodder & Stoughton.

My beta readers are superstars. Heaps of gratitude to Emily, whose belief in this book propelled me through to the end and gave me the confidence to send it back out into the world. Martha not only jumped on a plane for a writing conference with me and gave crucial feedback on a tight deadline, but has been a dear friend and wonderful writing buddy for fifteen years. Here's to many more.

Thank you to Vanessa and Jean-Marie for support and generous feedback through various drafts—but more than that, for being great friends. Additional thanks to Elizabeth, Michael, Andrea, and Sean for helping with the opening chapters.

I'm lucky to have an amazing support group in my family, friends, and the local community. Thank you to everyone who has kept the faith, often unconditionally. In particular, enormous gratitude to my aunt Nancy and sister Eowyn. And a shout-out to my aunties Jean and Ann—look, now you're in the book!

Finally, I am so grateful to my parents for their unwavering belief and support, and for reading many drafts over many years. Also, for the record, this is what happens when you read your daughter The Lord of the Rings at age nine, then drag her into old-growth forests and nurture her desire to be a writer. Thank you both for everything.

About the Author

Callie Bates is a writer, harpist and certified harp therapist, sometimes artist, and nature nerd. When she's not creating, she's hitting the trails or streets and exploring new places. She lives in the Upper Midwest. Her debut fantasy novel, *The Waking Land*, was released in 2017 and its sequel *The Memory of Fire* is forthcoming in 2018. She occasionally writes non-fiction. Her essays have appeared in *Shambhala Sun*, *The Best Buddhist Writing 2012*, *All Things Girl* and online journals.

WANT MORE?

If you enjoyed this and would like to find out about similar books we publish, we'd love you to join our online SF, Fantasy and Horror community, Hodderscape.

Visit our blog site
www.hodderscape.co.uk

Follow us on Twitter
🐦 **@hodderscape**

Like our Facebook page
f **Hodderscape**

You'll find exclusive content from our authors, news, competitions and general musings, so feel free to comment, contribute or just keep an eye on what we are up to. See you there!